Praise for the Kittredge Ranch series
Secret Nights with a Cowboy

"The romance is red-hot. Fans will rejoice that Crews has two more rowdy Kittredge brothers to pair off in future installments."   —*Publishers Weekly*

Praise for the Cold River Ranch series
The Last Real Cowboy

"Romance fans will eagerly devour this high-heat love story."   —*Publishers Weekly* (starred review)

"A thoroughly entertaining and deftly crafted romance novel by an expert in the genre."
                                          —*Midwest Book Review*

Cold Heart, Warm Cowboy

"*Cold Heart, Warm Cowboy* is definitely a feel-good cowboy romance. . . .Will warm your heart through and through. An excellent read."   —*Affaire de Coeur*

"A fascinating read . . . If you love rodeo-riding, stubborn cowboys, heroines who don't give up even when the odds are against them, an adorable little boy and a love that won't die, then you have to read *Cold Heart, Warm Cowboy*!"   —*Fresh Fiction*

A True Cowboy Christmas

"Readers willing to brave the emotional turmoil like a frigid winter day wi̶ ̶ ̶ ̶ ̶ ̶ ̶ ̶ th Christmas warmth a̶ ̶ ̶ ̶ ̶ ̶ ̶ ̶ ̶ *st*

Also by
Caitlin Crews

The Cold River Ranch series

A TRUE COWBOY CHRISTMAS

COLD HEART, WARM COWBOY

THE LAST REAL COWBOY

The Kittredge Ranch series

SECRET NIGHTS WITH A COWBOY

All Night Long with a Cowboy

CAITLIN CREWS

St. Martin's Paperbacks

This is a work of fiction. All of the characters, organizations, and events portrayed in this novel are either products of the author's imagination or are used fictitiously.

First published in the United States by St. Martin's Paperbacks, an imprint of St. Martin's Publishing Group

ALL NIGHT LONG WITH A COWBOY

Copyright © 2021 by Caitlin Crews.

All rights reserved.

For information, address St. Martin's Publishing Group, 120 Broadway, New York, NY 10271.

www.stmartins.com

ISBN: 978-1-250-75000-6

Our books may be purchased in bulk for promotional, educational, or business use. Please contact your local bookseller or the Macmillan Corporate and Premium Sales Department at 1-800-221-7945, ext. 5442, or by email at MacmillanSpecialMarkets@macmillan.com.

Printed in the United States of America

St. Martin's Paperbacks edition / September 2021

10 9 8 7 6 5 4 3 2 1

1

Jensen Kittredge was kicked back in his favorite booth in the most disreputable bar in town, enjoying the usual spoils of a fine Saturday night.

The blonde was named Candace, the redhead was calling herself Tammy, and the two brunettes were too busy taking pictures of themselves to offer any biographical information. But the night was young and really, who needed a biography? This was the kind of bar that prided itself on its commitment to anonymity—even when a person was a regular, like he was.

He had eased into the bright, long summer evening with a few beers over a burger at what had once been the only family-friendly bar here in Cold River, Colorado. The Broken Wheel Saloon with its truffle fries and live bands had been the local watering hole since Jensen was a kid. These days—this very day, in fact, if the GRAND OPENING signs festooned over one of the old barns down by the river were any indication—there was a brand-new microbrewery in the mix that Jensen had been reliably informed planned to serve excellent beer and good food too, but he hadn't gotten around to finding out for himself. Not tonight.

Because it was a Saturday and after a burger and a beer

or two, when the summer sun finally made its lazy way toward the horizon, Jensen had headed over to the reliably gritty Coyote on the other side of the river, where the booths were too dark, the music was too loud, and trouble was always brewing.

Jensen liked himself a good helping of trouble.

But the apparition that suddenly appeared at the end of his booth, looming over the brunettes with a frown on her face, was not the kind of trouble he liked.

He was a big fan of the no-last-name, don't-call-me, but-let's-get-sweaty variety.

The woman standing there like she had a ruler running down her back—like maybe she'd appeared in a puff of prim-and-proper smoke and was feeling crabby about it—made him remember other kinds of trouble. The far less entertaining kinds. The kinds that had involved humorless authority figures, detention, and the parts of high school he hadn't enjoyed as much as he had the stuff he was really good at. That being girls, football, and more girls.

And Jensen might have been a native of Cold River, surrounded at any given time by folks who knew his mama better than him and could recite every last stunt he'd pulled in middle school from memory—not to mention an alarming number of statistics from the high school football career *he* had gotten over a long time ago—but that was the point of the Coyote. He might know perfectly well that the lovely, blonde Candace was a nurse over at the hospital with two kids from her no-account ex, but *tonight* she was no more and no less than a pretty woman in a low-cut top who was tossing back shots and giggling while she did it.

You could be anyone you wanted at the Coyote.

Jensen couldn't figure out for the life of him why the

pinched-face woman in her buttoned-up cardigan and ugly glasses that hid half her face wanted to be . . . that.

"Jensen Kittredge?" she asked.

She didn't really ask. She said it the same way they'd said his name in all those detentions back at Cold River High. With all that persnickety *intent* that always led to discussions about the ways in which he was a big ole disappointment to all and sundry.

Jensen took his time knocking back his whiskey, not sure why he couldn't get high school out of his head when normally he wasn't the type to sit around waxing nostalgic about his teenage years. He'd had a fine time in high school, insofar as a person could be *fine* when forced by law to attend a series of boring classes every day, but he greatly preferred being a grown-ass man. Coming as it did with his own money, his own space, and all the women and whiskey he could handle.

Turned out he could handle a whole lot.

"Are you Jensen Kittredge?" the woman asked, her voice a little sharper, like she wasn't used to being kept waiting. And certainly not by the likes of *him*.

Something in Jensen kicked into gear at that tone. He knew that tone.

Because it turned out that another thing he was real good at was being ornery—especially when folks seemed to think he was a little too simple, a little too brawny, or a little too *much*. Which was most of the time, but Jensen didn't care. He smiled wide, laughed too loud, and they never saw him coming.

He did all of the above and watched the woman stand even straighter as if his laughter was an affront. He sure hoped it was.

"Darlin'," Jensen drawled, his own tone much too knowing, "I think you know who I am."

He expected her to deflate at that, so that she was no longer holding her giant purse shoved half under one arm like it was a weapon. Or a security blanket. He thought she might flush, shuffle her feet, and do any number of the flustered, silly things that women usually did in his presence. Whether they were twenty-two or eighty-five.

Instead, this woman's eyes sharpened. He noticed they were a pale blue, and he had no idea why the noticing made him almost . . . tense. She did not get silly. It had to be said, she didn't look like she was capable of silliness. Instead, she held his gaze with an uncomfortable directness that might have made him sit up and take notice if he hadn't been so deeply committed to the lazy way he was currently lounging there.

Then she surprised him even more by shifting the force of her attention to the other women in the booth.

"Ladies," she said in a brisk, matter-of-fact voice that managed to cut through the haze of jukebox music, bad decisions, and questionable behavior that were the Coyote's main selling points, in Jensen's opinion. "If you'll excuse us, please."

To Jensen's astonishment, all four women looked up and seemed to freeze where they sat for a moment. And then actually slid out of the booth, one after the next, as commanded.

Huh.

When they'd all staggered away, Ms. Prissy Cardigan perched herself in the booth across from him without touching anything but the banquette. And somehow managed to wrinkle her forehead in such a way that he was fully aware of her thoughts on the relative hygiene of the tabletop, the Coyote itself, and not to put too fine a point on it, him.

Again, not the reaction he usually got from women. Especially not women who sought him out in places like this after dark.

"No need for all the theatrics," Jensen said mildly, amping up his drawl a little because it felt right. "There's enough of me to go around."

The woman opposite him, sitting there so primly and looking at him as if he were some kind of unappealing specimen beneath a microscope, smiled.

A wintry, crisp sort of smile.

Not the kind of smile Jensen normally had aimed his way. Especially not here, in this rowdy bar, on a Saturday night.

"I'm sure that kind of boastful statement goes over beautifully with a great many of your usual . . ." And she actually pursed her lips like some kind of Old West schoolmarm. If he recalled correctly, Cold River High still had a few. "*Friends.*"

"I'm a friendly guy."

"How charming." She did not look charmed. "I'm not here to become a member of that . . . brigade."

Jensen laughed. "That breaks my heart, darlin'. I have it on good authority that I have the best brigade in town. Ask anyone."

"I'll take your word for it." She made as if to fold her hands before her on the table, thought better of it, and dropped them to her lap. Still folded neatly, he was sure. "I'm here on a different matter altogether."

"You do know it's Saturday night, right?" He shook his head at her sadly as if she really were breaking his heart. "And you're sitting in a bar. Not just any bar. The Coyote used to be a good old-fashioned, authentic Western house of ill repute. People don't come here for *different matters.* They're here to get their sin on."

"That's as may be. I've left you a number of messages. None have been returned."

"I appreciate that, darlin'. I do. But I'm pretty sure I'd remember if I'd given you my number." He didn't give out his number to women as a rule. He'd need a new number. But he didn't see the need to tell her that.

Another wintry smile. "That seems unlikely, given your . . ."

He didn't lean forward. He sprawled, grinning. "My . . . ?"

It was possible he was goading her.

She adjusted her glasses on her nose. And sniffed. "Your enthusiasm for your friends."

His grin widened. "I'm known for my enthusiasm, that's for sure."

She blinked, a lot like she was collecting herself, and there was no reason he should be paying such close attention, surely. No matter how much he might enjoy suffering a fool when one appeared, even if it was here.

"The outgoing message claims that it is the official voice mail of the Bar K ranch. You are an employee of the Bar K, are you not?"

Jensen laughed again, louder, and only partly because that was a little bit of a sore subject. Like all family things tended to be in one way or another. "Do you know what the *K* in Bar K stands for?" But he didn't wait for her to answer that. "It's for *Kittredge*. I'm not so much an employee of the Bar K as a member of the Kittredge family. It's a messy line, I grant you, but it's a line all the same."

"I take that to mean that you are, in fact, employed by the ranch."

Jensen could have broken it down for her. The Bar K had been in his family since way back when his ancestors decided to hightail it out of the stuffy east and over some mountains—but not all of them—to settle down here in the Longhorn Valley. Where they'd been fighting with the Colorado weather, sometimes with their neighbors, always with the Rocky Mountains, and pretty much daily with the horses they'd been training and breeding since an enterprising ancestor had decided he didn't much care to run a large-scale cattle operation. He could have told her his thoughts on the stewardship of the ranch and his family's longtime commitment to the land, bred into him so it felt like a part of his bones. He could have talked awhile about the tension between his grandfather and his father growing up and how that had trickled right on down to the way he, his brothers, and his sister interacted with and second-guessed his parents even now.

But there was no getting into that without further discussions about the current management of the ranch, which shouldn't have concerned him at all. And wouldn't have, normally. Because normally, Jensen spent his summers fighting the wildfires that chewed up the western United States year after year. Particularly his beloved Colorado. Jensen hadn't been around Cold River in the summertime since that first, brutal summer after high school.

And that was where the Bar K was less an employer and more a family concern, like it or not. Because if Jensen had been merely an employee, he might have offered some thoughts and prayers when his father had experienced what everyone was calling *a cardiac event,* but he would have carried on as normal.

Instead of what he was doing, which was his part of the necessary all-hands-on-deck now that Donovan Kittredge was laid up and driving everyone crazy. Even crazier than he drove them when he was being his usual remote, inaccessible, angrily silent self.

Too bad, his younger brother Riley had said when it was clear how things were going to go this year. *No vacation for you.*

Jensen had wanted to take Riley's head off, but only partly because of his comment. Mostly because he just wanted to take Riley's head off as part of his personal policy as second oldest.

And also because what he did with those fires had nothing to do with a vacation.

His penance was his own business.

But none of his business was up for discussion with this strange woman who was still observing him like he was in a zoo. And on the wrong side of the bars.

"Sure," Jensen said, slow and easy, her snippy tone still echoing in his ears. *I take that to mean that you are, in fact, employed by the ranch.* That *in fact* about killed him. "I work there."

And he knew something about the woman sitting across from him, then.

Because she didn't laugh at that, or point out that she knew perfectly well that he was a functioning member of the Kittredge family, which anyone from the Longhorn Valley—or anyone interested in the Bar K for business purposes—would have done. Clearly, she didn't know what it meant to be a Kittredge. And that could only mean that she wasn't from here.

Jensen looked at her more closely, but he still didn't recognize her. Not even in the *saw her across a potluck buffet table somewhere* way that comprised most of the folks who lived in this hard-to-reach part of his favorite state. And while he was no stranger to women seeking him out, especially on a weekend night at the Coyote, they usually didn't come dressed like this one was.

As if she'd gotten lost on her way to church.

There was the cardigan that looked as if it doubled as a blanket in cold weather. It was buttoned up over a fussy sort of shirt that was also done up, all the way up her neck, as if she wanted to teach her breasts a lesson by keeping them caged up good and tight. Then again, nothing about that frumpy cardigan or that bizarrely ruffled shirt indicated that she thought even that much about her breasts in the first place.

Which was a pity. Jensen was pretty sure he'd spent his entire fifteenth year thinking about nothing *but* breasts.

She was blond, though she had her hair coiled around and pinned up in a manner he could only describe as distinctly old-fashioned. She had those clunky glasses perched on her nose, and not in a come-hither kind of a way, like she was trying out a sexy librarian thing. Sadly. And if he recalled correctly, she was also wearing what he'd heard his little sister refer to, and not in a complimentary fashion, as *slacks*.

Women who tended to spend a lot of time in the Coyote preferred bare skin as a fashion statement.

The only thing this one was flashing was irritation. She was positively vibrating with it.

"You're not from around here, are you?" he asked.

He watched as the woman across from him bristled. "I fail to see what that has to do with anything."

"I'll take that as a yes, and I don't know what it has to do with anything, because I don't know why you're here. I don't even know your name."

She smiled, but it was pure impatience. "My name is Harriet Barnett."

And she announced that in the same crisp way, like she expected him to sit up straighter at the sound. He would have to decline. Jensen preferred to live down to low expectations wherever possible.

"I can't say I recognize you, Harriet."

Of course that was her name. She looked like she could be anywhere from thirty to sixty, and the name matched. Although, as he gazed at her, he kind of doubted she was much past thirty. It was something about her mouth, far plumper than it had any right to be when he doubted he'd be getting a taste.

"I prefer to be called Miss Barnett," she informed him, her gaze serious. "And I don't expect you to recognize me. We've never met."

And to his astonishment, something happened as Jensen gazed back at her, waiting for her to tell him what she wanted from him—which he suspected wasn't going to be the usual thing women wanted from him. Almost against his will, he found himself . . . intrigued.

Jensen wasn't a hard man to please most of the time. He liked to work hard and relax harder. He liked sex with no strings, because he already had too much family and that was more relationship nonsense than any man needed. And more than he deserved, because he'd made his vows a long time ago. Most years, he liked his life well enough. But this was already a strange summer. It made him feel edgy that he wasn't out there fighting fires the way he was supposed to be doing—because that had also been a part of the promises he'd made when he was eighteen. Turned out, even his favorite, no-strings forms of entertainment seemed a lot less fun because of that. Something he previously would have declared impossible.

Yet here was Miss Harriet Barnett. And she was completely different, for good or ill.

"What exactly is it you think I can do for you?" he asked. Mildly enough that it set her to frowning again, so mission accomplished on that. "Here in Cold River's favorite den of iniquity?"

Her frown did not go away. "A date."

Jensen really laughed at that. "I'll admit it. I did not see that one coming."

Harriet looked even more annoyed, and Jensen accepted the strange and somehow glorious fact that he was enjoying himself.

"I take it neither you, nor anyone else, listens to the voice mailbox at the Bar K," she said.

With great censure.

Jensen couldn't stop grinning. Maybe he also wasn't trying too hard. "I can promise you that you have already given more thought to the voice mail situation at the ranch than I ever have in all my days on this earth."

"The existence of a voice mailbox suggests that messages can be left there, Mr. Kittredge. And there would be no purpose in that if no one ever listened to them, would there? That's the bare minimum. At the very least, I'm sure we can agree that a *business* should do the bare minimum, shouldn't it?"

"I'll be sure to take that up with the secretarial staff," Jensen assured her. Meaning he would take time out of his busy day tomorrow to give his youngest brother, Connor, a hard time about not listening to those messages, simply because he could, because he was older. Although it was less fun to needle his baby brother these days, now that Connor had gone ahead and shacked up with his woman. He was far too revoltingly satisfied to take the bait, most days. "But you should probably know that women don't usually use the ranch voice mail to ask me out."

"To ask you out?" She looked as if he'd lapsed into a different language.

"And to tell you the truth, Miss Harriet, I don't date." He smiled, letting it get hot and edgy, just for fun. "But I might be convinced to make an exception for you."

Harriet Barnett blinked. The glasses perched on her nose seemed to call more attention to her eyes, which meant that he couldn't help but notice she happened to have just about the longest eyelashes he'd ever seen. They made her blue gaze even prettier.

It almost outweighed the way she was still frowning at him.

"You misunderstand me," she informed him. A bit severely, in his opinion. "I'm not attempting to *ask you out,* heaven forbid."

Jensen wasn't sure if he was entertained or insulted at that point. Or both.

One of her hands rose to her throat, and he thought that if she'd been wearing pearls, she would have been clutching at them just then. "I *won* a date with you, Mr. Kittredge."

"It's much more likely that I knocked you up," he said idly, with a grin that made her fingers tighten around those imaginary pearls. "I don't make a habit of raffling off dates."

Jensen would never call his social life *dating*. It was usually a little too naked, intense, and happily temporary for that. Besides, he had his hands full without throwing any formal *dates* into the mix.

"The Harvest Gala takes place every year the night before Thanksgiving," Harriet told him. Sternly.

"It sure does." He eyed her lazily as they headed down this tangent. Still game, apparently, though he couldn't have said why. "My little sister organized it last year."

"One of the things that were raffled off were nights with various men in the community, and not in a romantic sense. It was all in good fun, for charity."

That did ring a bell. Jensen recalled sitting in his best

suit with his cowboy hat on, laughing uproariously as some of his friends—the ones who hadn't figured out how to say no to his remarkably tenacious little sister—paraded themselves around onstage so that the rapacious women of the Longhorn Valley could throw money at them.

Luckily, Jensen was generally immune to his younger siblings, to their usual dismay.

"I considered bidding myself," he told Harriet now, smirking a little. "Just so I could make my brother Zack take me out to a nice meal and call me pretty, but my grandmother did not approve of me wasting the good sheriff's time like that."

And besides, it had been even more fun to watch Sheriff Zack get bought by the president of the Ladies Auxiliary, who had been after him to sit down and defend his recent decisions for months.

"Three firefighters were raffled off that evening," Harriet continued in that same prissy voice of hers. A lot like Jensen was having no effect on her whatsoever. Which was so unusual that once again, he found himself more intrigued than he should have been. "I personally bid on Buddy Spears."

"Buddy Spears moved out of the county this winter." Jensen knew Buddy. He was pretty sure Buddy had coached him in Little League approximately a million years ago. The Spears family had lived in town instead of out in the fields like the Kittredges, and Buddy and Elaine had moved away so they could live closer to their grandchildren. Who were presumably being raised somewhere with less intense winters.

Information Jensen possessed because people told him things without him asking or had conversations he couldn't help overhearing. That was Cold River. There was no such thing as private business. There was only the town and the valley, and everyone in it was part of the same old story.

"As I was duly informed when I called the fire station," Harriet told him.

"I don't know why Buddy was auctioning himself off, anyway. Unless he expected Elaine to bid on him. Though to my recollection, Miz Spears did not exactly have the kind of personality that would find a bidding war on her own husband all that amusing. No matter if it was for charity."

"He was standing in as a proxy, it turns out," Harriet Barnett informed him. She did not speculate on the Spears marriage or Elaine's potential thoughts on her husband taking bids, once again proving that she was not a local. "The fire chief said he had always planned to nominate someone to take his place. But I don't mind telling you, as I told him, I found that false advertising."

Jensen settled back against his seat. "I just want to make sure we're on the same page here, Miss Harriet. We're sitting in the Coyote, without a drink between us, discussing your hurt feelings that you didn't get to go on a date with Buddy Spears. Who, decent guy though he was, was also what my mama would call no oil painting. And old enough to be your grandfather. *And,* not to put too fine a point on it, married."

"I'm not talking about a romantic date, Mr. Kittredge," Harriet said, a little snap in her voice as if he were being ridiculous. As if *he* were the problem here. "I'm the librarian at Cold River High. I intended to give money to charity, which is the entire purpose of the Harvest Gala and the Heritage Society that throws it, but not only that."

"You do know that a large part of the heritage celebrated by the Heritage Society has to do with my family, right?" Jensen grinned widely as if he were doing her a favor. "If you're that excited by the history around here."

Harriet ignored that—also novel. "I think it's incredibly useful for the children to understand primary sources. I wanted to use the date I bought with Buddy as a learning opportunity for the students."

"It's summer. Shouldn't your students be off on summer vacation?"

"Some of them, yes. Others find themselves compelled to take summer classes."

"Summer school. Ouch."

Over by the bar, he saw the brunettes again. And this time, without their phones in hand. They both pouted in his direction.

It occurred to him to wonder what he was doing. As entertaining as this woman was, he did not intend to spend his Saturday night talking to the high school librarian. Not because she was a high school librarian, but because he doubted she was here to get her sin on.

And because another benefit of being a grown-ass man was that Jensen didn't waste his time trying to convince people who didn't like him that they should. He figured it was their loss.

Even if she did have pretty blue eyes.

Which suggested to him that she wasn't exactly the dried-up old spinster she clearly wanted to be mistaken for. Not like the long-term high school secretary, the terrifying Miss Martina Patrick, whose very name was enough to make any teenage boy's blood run cold. Harriet dressed like his memories of that famous local dragon lady, but a closer examination made it clear that though Harriet dressed like an old woman, she really wasn't one.

Jensen couldn't help but find that interesting. Interesting, sure. But certainly not as compelling as two young women of deliciously loose morals sending him *come-hither* glances from across the bar.

"I appreciate you seeking me out to discuss your Heritage Gala bid from last Thanksgiving," he said, uncurling himself as he pushed his way out of the booth and stood. "I'll give you this, Miss Harriet. It's not the usual conversation we get around here. Good luck with your primary sources."

He wasn't surprised that she stood with him, once again clutching the bag on her shoulder as if she were either protecting her worldly goods or was fully prepared to *take measures* should any ruffians attack her.

In fairness, this being the Coyote, there were ruffians aplenty.

"You're not understanding me, Mr. Kittredge. The proxy that the fire chief selected was you."

"Me?" Jensen laughed at that. "I'm afraid old Howie's putting you on, ma'am. I'm a smoke jumper, not a local."

"I don't know what that has to do with the date I won."

"Howie Duncan isn't the boss of me." Though Jensen had always liked him well enough. But proxy dates and the feelings of the librarian involved weren't his problem. He shrugged. "You're going to have to find a different date."

Harriet lifted her chin. "He said you might say that."

Jensen was a big man. He was used to looking down at women—and other men, for that matter. But there was something about this faintly agitated little hen before him that got to him, and not only because she was so tiny even as she stood there before him, looking defiant. Something about her made him want to . . . mess her up.

Just a little. Just for fun.

And it was disconcerting. He knew what to do with a regular old urge to get naked. This was something else.

He concentrated on that surprisingly belligerent chin.

"He told me to remind you that you owe him a favor," Harriet said.

Jensen considered. "I do owe him a favor. But I don't date."

He watched, definitely growing more entertained by the moment despite the brunette duo waiting at the bar, as Miss Harriet Barnett in her layers of church clothes looked at him in pure exasperation.

Jensen was used to bringing out the worst in folks. He was big. He was loud. He'd played football in high school, and whether men slapped him on the back as they counted his triumphs on the field or women clucked over the same, it was usually couched in words they expected a dumb jock to understand. He was good at geniality. It served him well on the ranch where he was in charge of business affairs, though he liked to pretend that he was a little too simple to fully understand what he was doing—right before he went in for the kill.

He was well acquainted with the way Harriet Barnett was looking at him.

As if she greatly resented that she was being forced to contend with a man who was as dim as he was.

Normally he found moments like this hilarious.

"Don't consider it a date, then," she was saying, looking like she resented having to explain herself to the likes of him. Also a common theme in people's reactions to him that he usually thought was fun. "Here's the situation. For whatever reason, you are held up to be a role model in this town. I'd like to give you the opportunity to use your position as said role model for good. That's all. If you had answered even one of the seven messages I left, I wouldn't have had to come find you in this . . . place."

"I'm not a role model." Jensen wasn't amused any

longer. He held her gaze until she blinked, and he didn't smile while he did it. "I'm not your date. And if you'll excuse me, there's a whole lot of sin calling my name, and I don't intend to ignore it."

He walked away from her and her big blue eyes then, not sure if he was focused on the girls at the bar or the bottles behind it, because they were the same thing, really.

Oblivion.

Because the other option was remembering, and he didn't do that. Not if he could help it.

When he got to the bar, he found his smile again and found the pair of brunettes far more receptive.

But for some reason, as the night wore on and sweet oblivion beckoned, it was Harriet Barnett's direct blue gaze that he couldn't seem to shake.

2

Harriet Barnett woke the following morning to discover her hair smelled like cigarettes, thanks to the clouds of smoke she'd been forced to cough her way through on her way to the neon-framed door of the Coyote. And if she wasn't mistaken, there was also the faintest odor of sticky alcoholic substances on her skin, even though she'd gone out of her way to touch as little as possible and to drink nothing at all.

Because she, for one, had learned significant life lessons from *Alice in Wonderland*. Or, to be precise and not merely colloquial—as Harriet liked to be about her books—*Alice's Adventures in Wonderland*.

Yet it was as if merely stepping inside that place had stained her, just as her friend and colleague Martina had warned it would. In suitably dire tones, as if she'd proposed a day trip to the underworld to see the devil himself.

How galling that Martina had been right. She felt, distinctly, that Jensen Kittredge himself had *tainted* her with all his . . . extreme and unapologetic maleness.

But Harriet did not intend to remain tainted, stained, or appallingly fragrant a moment longer. It was a beautiful summer weekend morning. The early light outside

was making her bedroom glow happily. And she was a
woman of purpose who chose her path and her mood instead of letting them be inflicted upon her from without.

She was most assuredly *not* the sort of woman who
woke up on a Sunday morning reeking of the night before, thank you very much.

Harriet threw back her covers and got up, then made
her bed more briskly than usual. She normally preferred
to take her time getting her many pillows *just so*—
because making a bed made the whole day, as her mother
liked to say—but this wasn't a typical morning. Then she
marched downstairs to her laundry room, where she ran
last night's clothes through the wash once again. And
took the cardigan she'd soaked when she'd gotten home
last night out to the small clothesline behind her little
house and hung it carefully so it wouldn't lose its shape.

Once the sweater was catching the breeze that swept
right down from the mountains, which Harriet felt was far
better than any disinfectant, she marched right back inside and took herself straight to her shower. Where she
carefully, thoroughly, washed her hair. Twice.

Only when she felt that she'd truly banished any linger-
ing remnants of the Coyote did she climb out, dry herself
off and dress, then commence her usual morning routine.
That included feeding all five of her cats, murmuring to
each of them in turn as she set out their dishes. Eleanor,
her dignified elder tabby, only gazed at her in disappointment for the late start while Milton, Eleanor's deeply lazy
brother, complained lustily. Her other male cat, the enormous Chaucer, was shouting about his imminent death-
by-starving in the guest bathroom, even after she put his
dish down. Brontë, her moody black cat, was silent—but
judgy, Harriet felt.

And then she had to go looking for little calico Maisey,

the smallest of her cats, who was half-feral, liked to bur-row deep into improbable places, and had to be coaxed out to eat her breakfast.

Only after she'd crooned Maisey out from the depths of the hall closet, deep in a bin of winter scarves, did she head to the kitchen to put her kettle on at last.

And only then, once she'd brewed up a proper pot of tea, did she permit herself to think about Jensen Kit-tredge in all his glory.

"And his glory is considerable," she told Eleanor when the cat jumped onto the kitchen counter to monitor the tea making.

Harriet sighed, because he had been . . . entirely too much, really. Her brain, always her favorite part of her-self, shorted out as she recalled it.

Him.

Eleanor did not look impressed, but she did present her belly to be dutifully rubbed.

As a rule, Harriet preferred cats to men, glorious or not. And to most other people as a whole. It wasn't that she was a recluse or actively disliked anyone in particu-lar. But she wasn't like them. She never had been, and she counted herself lucky to both know and accept it. On the few occasions she'd attempted to pretend otherwise, other people had been quick to point out her differences to her.

Cats, by contrast, never cared if she was odd.

Harriet had come by her oddness honestly. She had been a late-in-life surprise to her parents, who'd been contentedly childless until her arrival. Harriet had been raised with books, cats, and two distant academics who had always behaved as if they were vaguely shocked to discover there was an actual child roaming about the place—especially one they'd made.

When she described her childhood to her friends, they always seemed sad. And Harriet didn't know how to tell them that she hadn't been sad at all. Ever. She'd been treated like an adult from the time she could talk, which had made her remarkably ill-suited for both social interactions with other children her age and the typical classroom instruction offered to small humans. When called in to discuss Harriet's isolation from her peers and many behaviors incompatible with the classroom, her parents had usually taken the meeting as an opportunity to debate her teachers about their methodology and governing philosophies.

This had not made Harriet popular with either other kids or her teachers, but as Harriet had not been raised to care about other opinions unless they were presented to her in a well-reasoned argument, she hadn't much minded. Outside of school, she'd always had a remarkable measure of independence. And her parents had been wildly indulgent in their own way. If Harriet could make a decent case for it, she could do it. Whatever it was.

That was how she'd argued herself out of the unquestionable torture of seventh grade and had merrily turned to homeschooling for the remainder of her basic education. This meant that she'd completed her schoolwork in record time and had spent the rest of her days reading whatever books took her fancy, educating herself as she went. With the guidance of the local librarians, she'd read almost every book in the school and town library by graduation.

By the time she'd gone to college, Harriet was so far out of step with her peers that there was no way back. She didn't understand the things that consumed them—like the uncomfortable clothes the girls in her dorm were so obsessed with, not to mention the dimwitted boys they all found so swoon-worthy—and after a few, brief, and unhappy attempts to blend in, she'd given up entirely.

Harriet was too impatient and intense to *blend*. There were far more interesting things to worry about. Such as . . . anything, really. Yes, she knew she dressed like an old woman and was no fun, according to the other freshmen on her hall. But it was a relief all around when she stopped pretending otherwise, because dressing to conform with others she didn't much like or keeping her opinions to herself wasn't going to change who she was inside.

She liked quiet. She liked cats. She enjoyed research, reading, and studying. She preferred comfortable clothes that she could move in and hairpins to keep her heavy hair from annoying her while moving. Most of all, she liked her own company.

She wasn't sad when she was left alone. She was happy.

And as time went on, she became serenely unconcerned that these things set her apart from most of her fellow students. If people were put off by her oddness, good. She knew then that they wouldn't be friends. Her actual friends didn't care what she wore, how early she went to bed on a Friday night, or that she'd adopted a pair of tabby kittens—Eleanor and Milton—while still living on campus her senior year and liked them better than most of her peers.

After college, she'd decided to get an MLS degree, because she'd spent so much time in libraries—she would even say they'd saved her more than once—that it seemed a natural fit. And after a pleasant-enough stint in a much larger and busier high school library a few hours from her parents' home in Missouri, she'd ended up in Cold River, Colorado, three years ago.

Harriet carried her tea tray out onto her front porch,

where she could sit there looking out on the tidy little street that was home now and soak in the summer morning.

A front porch is a gift, her mother always said. *Just because the rest of the world is locked inside, watching yet another pointless television program, that doesn't mean you should neglect the simple pleasure of breathing in your world in its particulars.*

Harriet made a point to sit out on her front porch whenever the weather was fine, which was no hardship in her cute little house. Especially when Chaucer thundered out after her and heaved himself into her lap. Harriet sighed happily as she accommodated him. Having lived through three brutal Rocky Mountain winters now, she took her good weather seriously.

This morning it was cool, and she was happy to have the considerable weight of a purring cat to keep her cozy. From her porch, she could see the mountains rising up behind the town, keeping watch over the perfect little Old West jewel that was Cold River, straddling the pretty, sparkling river that gave it its name. She could still vividly remember driving into this valley when she'd moved here, aiming her rattly old Mazda around and around the twisting, winding mountain roads, climbing up one side of a dizzying height and then dropping down the other. The views from the hills had astonished her—and still did. The Longhorn Valley had been stunning there beneath the big, blue Colorado sky, the province of farmers and ranchers with real live cowboys wandering the streets of town, and all of it filled with a kind of quiet charm that Harriet found nothing short of delightful.

Soul-restoring, even.

Harriet had grown up in a leafy, historic river town outside of Kansas City, Missouri, thick with families and students and the typical rush of semesters and seasons and the busy nearby city many residents commuted to daily.

Cold River felt like a step back. A deep breath.

For Harriet, who had always felt out of step with the world—and never more so than when she'd been at college in Minnesota—Cold River felt like a blessing.

Though she knew that wasn't the case for everyone.

And that was why she found herself firing up her trusty old hatchback that afternoon. She headed out from town, driving along Cold River's pretty main street with its Old West façades, clever little shops, and the Grand Hotel that rose up a few stories and whispered of long-gone copper barons and storied Western outlaws to anyone who passed. She drove over the hill, smiling as the view stole into her the way it always did while she navigated down into fields drenched in summer, gleaming bright beneath the crystal blue skies.

Harriet loved where she'd come from, but she couldn't deny that there was something about the Rocky Mountains that took her breath away. The soaring peaks and that Colorado sky, so big it made her heart beat faster.

She didn't spend much time on this side of the hill since her pleasant little life was located in town. The first thing she noticed today was that she didn't pass a single other car on the county road, not even one of the ubiquitous pickup trucks that were usually everywhere. She was glad that she'd printed out the directions, like the Luddite she was, because she wasn't sure that there would be any cell phone service way out here. There didn't appear to be enough people to warrant it.

She drove and drove, listening to Lori McKenna sing into the summer sweetness outside her windows. Eventually, she found her way to some proper Old West fencing and a big, attractive wooden archway with *Bar K* written in iron at the top.

You do know that a large part of the heritage cele-brated by the Heritage Society has to do with my family, right? Jensen had asked her last night.

Harriet had to blow out a shaky sort of breath at the memory of that rumbly voice of his. So . . . *male.* She couldn't get past it.

"At least I'm in the right place," she said out loud and maybe a little overbrightly as she turned in.

The driveway—or maybe it was just called a road, not a driveway, this far out from civilization—was dirt. She slowed down, because her little Mazda might be trusty in most ways, but she suspected it wasn't up to a confronta-tion with this much pure country.

And also because, as she drove, she could see the horses.

Some stood in one place, watching as she bumped along. Others placidly ignored her.

And still others ran along the fences as if challenging her to a race. Or simply for the sheer joy of running.

By the time she came around the last little curve, through the trees, and saw the ranch house waiting, Har-riet was as exhilarated as if she was out there running like that, so liquid and beautiful beneath the sky. And had half forgotten what she was doing here in the first place.

She tried to regain her composure as she drew closer to the house, a proper Western affair with rustic dark wood and big windows that looked exactly the way Har-riet imagined a ranch house should. It wasn't the only building in the clearing, but it was the prettiest. The rest were a collection of other structures that she was sure served some or other functional purpose.

Because this wasn't simply a home. This was a business.

The Kittredge family bred quarter horses. In researching what that meant while she let her hair dry, Harriet had lost the better part of her morning following the history of the quarter horse through the American West. And was somehow unsurprised to discover that the Kittredge family was widely held to have produced some of the finest over the last hundred and fifty odd years.

Like many of the ranching families in this area, their roots ran straight on back to the founding of the town. Just as Jensen had told her.

She learned that Jensen was one of four brothers, with a younger sister, parents, and grandparents, all of whom were something like legends around town. The grandparents still held sway over local decisions, even though they'd retired from actively running the Bar K. The parents were prominent in their own right, involved in all the charities and on all the governing boards. She already knew that the eldest brother, Zack, was the county sheriff and the sister, Amanda, had not only run the Heritage Gala last fall but had opened her own shop in town— where Harriet had bought most of her Christmas gifts last year. That left Jensen and his two other brothers to handle the horses.

All those marvelous horses.

And Harriet could admit, as she parked her car in a yard that was bristling with all the pickup trucks she hadn't seen on the road, that the thought of Jensen Kittredge *handling things* made her . . . silly, really.

When she had somehow bypassed all the silliness she'd seen displayed both in seventh grade before she'd abandoned the public schools and then again in college.

How curious, she thought.

But she wasn't here for silliness. She was here for her students.

Thinking of those students made her stand a little straighter when she got out of the car, jerking her newly dried cardigan into place. She was aware that it was Sunday and that most people in this area stuck to the same Sunday routine—or so her colleagues at Cold River High had informed her. Chores, church, then a big old family dinner. Wanting to be respectful, she'd worn a dress instead of her usual no-nonsense trousers.

But one thing she'd learned in Colorado was that even in summer, the wind coming down from the mountaintops could very well be cold. That was why she never left home without her sweater.

Harriet told herself that's what it was. *Cold.* That was why—when she rounded the back of her car and headed for the ranch house's front door, only to find Jensen himself standing there, gleaming in the sunlight outside what she thought was a barn—she broke out in goose bumps.

Everywhere.

"You're a persistent little thing, aren't you?" he drawled.

Not exactly in a complimentary fashion.

She was definitely cold, she assured herself, and that was all. "Persistence is the difference between surrender and success," she said. Because she couldn't stop quoting her mother, especially when she was stressed. Not that she was stressed. Why should she be *stressed*? "I'll tell you right now, Mr. Kittredge. I prefer to be successful."

Last night in the bar, she'd been agitated. Harriet could admit that. It wasn't the Coyote itself. She was perfectly well aware of its history as the local bordello, and if she'd had her wits about her, she could have given Jensen a small dissertation on the topic of the women who'd resided there and how the way they'd made their living wasn't necessarily shameful, but in many ways a revolutionary act out on the frontier of a new nation. Instead, she'd been too taken aback by the whole . . . *thing*. It had been darker than she'd expected. Much, much louder. There had been a lot of flesh on display and not, she quickly surmised, only because it was summer. There were men she was pretty certain were the real version of the bikers she'd watched on TV—purely for research purposes, of course—and if she wasn't mistaken, the parents of some of her students.

Not that there was anything wrong with that, she had told herself sternly, assuming no children were being neglected. It had simply been surprising to see them in such a different context.

But the most surprising thing had been Jensen Kittredge himself.

Harriet had known who he was before she'd walked through the door of that bar, of course. Everyone knew who he was. It was impossible to be alive, female, and a resident of the Longhorn Valley without knowing who Jensen Kittredge was.

She could still remember, so distinctly, the first time she'd ever seen him. She had only just moved into the little house she rented on Spruce Street. One of its many benefits was that it was a few minutes' walk to Main Street in one direction and to the high school in the other. In a part of the world where most people had to drive for a half hour or more to get anywhere, Harriet could stretch her legs and not worry about whether or not her car would start on cold mornings.

That day, she'd spent hours unpacking and setting up her new home and had wandered over to the town's coffeehouse before she faced more of the same. Cold River Coffee was a charming little brick-and-wood affair, with a big black chalkboard always crowded with drinks and food, a seating area that sported a comfortable couch, happy-looking chairs to disappear in before a glorious fireplace, and a bookcase stuffed with books. She'd been waiting for her drink when she'd heard that laugh of his.

Big. Booming. Infectious.

Oh yeah, said the woman behind the counter that she'd learned later was the manager, Abby. *That's Jensen Kittredge.*

He seems very happy, Harriet had said primly.

He seems a lot of things, Abby had replied with a smile. *Mostly, they're true.*

Harriet had taken her coffee, found a seat, and told herself she was observing her new habitat. She had not been *staring.* She'd known that there would be cowboys here. It was a rural area. Cowboys in Minneapolis might have been surprising, depending, but here in the mountains, they were just part of the scenery.

On the other hand, the scenery in Cold River was pretty spectacular. That day, Jensen had been outfitted in the local cowboy uniform. A T-shirt, Wranglers, and cowboy boots. A Stetson on his head. He had been talking to—and laughing with—two other men dressed more or less identically. But neither of them had possessed his muscles.

She couldn't actually remember who they were. But she remembered him.

Today, standing uninvited in the summer sun at the Bar K, Harriet noticed he still had all those same muscles.

He was a beautiful man, built huge and packed hard into those T-shirts of his. She was short, so everyone was tall to her, but Jensen made other men look small too. Up close, last night, Harriet had expected to see all the flaws that surely lurked out of sight when looking at a stranger across a coffeehouse or a gala, but there hadn't been any. His hair was dark and short, yet somehow managed to look unruly. His gaze was arresting. A surprising amber—*hazel,* she corrected herself crossly—ringed in a deep black. *Wolf's eyes,* something in her whispered, even as she cringed, if only internally, at her own histrionics. His shoulders were wide. *Very* wide. His torso was long, lean, and rippled in all the most fascinating places. He looked tough, hard, and male.

Male. She kept thinking that word, as if it were a surprise that Jensen Kittredge was a man.

But it felt like a surprise every time she saw him. A very intense, personal surprise.

Especially because he'd ambled closer to her without her fully taking that on board. Meaning he was no longer over by the barn. He was *here.* Harriet had to crane her head back to look all the way up at him—not that it was a hardship.

She pulled her sweater closer, because she was very, very cold.

It didn't surprise her in the least that he leaped out of planes to put out fires. For fun, by all accounts.

"I admire hardheadedness," Jensen told her in that same low drawl. "I do. But I told you last night that I'm not interested. I'm no role model."

Harriet crossed her arms and frowned, which had no discernible effect on him. Alas. Last night he'd been so languid and lazy she'd been amazed he hadn't slid off the booth into a boneless heap on the sticky barroom floor, but today he looked different. The look in those astonishing *not-wolfish* eyes of his was serious.

She figured she had one last shot to sell this. "Summer school is not the kids' favorite, as you can imagine.

They're usually there because they need to make up a class or two. I'm not a teacher, but I do offer a small, supplemental course to help certain students get up to speed with things like research methods that can help lead them toward success in their future academic pursuits. They don't like it, but then, if I'm honest, they don't tend to like much about their situations." Harriet looked for the hint of something soft on his hard face, but there was nothing. Just hard lines and that serious gaze. "And in fairness, there are often other factors. Troubled families, for example."

It was disconcerting that he didn't have to grin or laugh to make her feel as if he had. He could look as grave as he did then.

"I appreciate the tug of heartstrings, but I can't help you."

"There's a ringleader of the supplemental course this summer," Harriet continued as if she weren't disconcerted in the least. "When I said I planned to bring in members of different professions, like a firefighter to discuss the realities of being first responders, they were not impressed. The ringleader seemed to feel it was like kindergarten, not high school. And he said the only firefighter worth listening to around here was you, but he figured that I'd probably bring in someone lame. He didn't actually call you a role model, I will admit. And in the spirit of total honesty, Chief Duncan didn't pull your name out of a hat. I asked for you."

Jensen studied her like he was looking for something. Then he shook his head slightly. "Who is this kid?"

"His name is Aidan Hall."

And she watched as Jensen's expression changed. Belatedly, she allowed herself to really take in the picture he presented, blocking out the Colorado sky with those shoulders. In another T-shirt that looked as if it might lose its fight against his biceps at any moment.

Once again, the silliness threatened to take her legs out from under her.

She doubted, somehow, that her collapsing at his feet would inspire him to help her. He probably couldn't walk the length of Main Street without having to step over heaps of collapsed, lovelorn women.

Of which she was not one, Harriet reminded herself tartly. She was merely *observing* the effect he had. Not suffering from it.

"I know Aidan." Jensen shook his head. "He's a little punk."

"He is a sixteen-year-old boy who has no idea how to be a man," Harriet retorted. "His father spends more time in that bar you like than he does at home. His mother, meanwhile—"

"I don't need a biography of the Hall family, Miss Harriet. I know them."

She didn't like the way he said that. *Miss Harriet*. It made something hot roll over her. Deep into her. It did not feel much like an observation.

Harriet tried to ignore the heat. "He could have named any grown adult, or none at all. He named you. Would it really be the end of the world to come in and talk to him? To all of them? To show them that there's more to life than drunk fathers, checked-out mothers, and a whole, long history of grown-ups who don't care what happens to them?"

"Why are you so determined to jump into the middle of this?" Jensen asked. "I could probably name all the kids in your class if I tried, based on gossip alone. There are such things as lost causes, you know."

"I don't believe in lost causes." She scowled at him.

"And the fact that there are adults in this town who engage in gossip about teenagers but fail to help them is an indictment of the entire Longhorn Valley. You should be ashamed."

Jensen did not look ashamed.

"But why are *you* leading this effort to stamp out gossip on the mean streets of Cold River? You're new in town. You don't know all the players."

"I've been here for three years."

"You're new until three generations have been born and died here, at least." Jensen was grinning again, but that only made it all worse. Or something that she chose to call *worse,* anyway.

Harriet refused to allow him to sidetrack her. "Do you have something against a sixteen-year-old boy who might actually learn something from you?"

"Aidan Hall has no interest in learning anything from anyone. That's likely why he's in summer school. And he doesn't look up to me. Or anyone else. He probably thinks you can't get me to come in."

"Since you have such strong opinions about a high schooler, surely you should come prove him wrong."

"I know Aidan about as much as I know all the other members of the Hall family. Mean old Lucinda Early likes to say they have bad blood."

"Lucinda Early is a lovely old woman and a respected elder in the community."

"She's mean as a snake." Jensen grinned. "Personally, I like her. And I'm not saying she's right. What I will say is that every time there's a burglary or a car chase or any other bit of lawbreaking around here, there's usually a Hall involved."

"Aidan is *sixteen.*"

"Great. Two more years before he gets tried as an adult and joins his brethren in jail."

"Or maybe not," Harriet countered. "If you showed him he could imagine something better."

She couldn't have defined the look she saw on his face.

Then it didn't matter, because the door to the ranch house swung open, and another man stepped out.

Harriet recognized Zack Kittredge, the Longhorn Valley sheriff, and smiled politely in greeting. Even though inside, she was all . . . jumbled up.

Jensen looked over at Zack too. And somehow, immediately, managed to look as if he were still faintly intoxicated, when moments before he'd been as close to stern as she imagined laughing, happy-go-lucky Jensen Kittredge ever got.

"Harriet." Zack thumbed his hat. He looked from her to his brother, and his gaze got sharp. "What are you doing here?"

"She's here to talk to me," Jensen said, his voice big and loud again. Harriet was already folding her arms, so she hugged herself a little, not sure why the switch bothered her. "She's looking for a role model, and apparently, I'm the only Kittredge brother that fits the bill."

"I hate to be the one to disabuse you of this notion," Zack said, supposedly to her. But he was grinning at his brother. "He's no role model."

"I'm sorry to interrupt your Sunday," Harriet said, struggling to keep her runaway *feelings* out of her voice. She was sure it was simply that she was *that passionate* about her students' welfare. It had nothing to do with Jensen Kittredge in a T-shirt, looking lazy and a little bit disgruntled behind his usual wide grin. "But I really do need your brother to help me out."

"I'm sure he would be happy to help you out," Zack told her, with another look Jensen's way.

Jensen laughed. "Would he?"

"He would," Zack retorted. "And Harriet, you drove all this way to find a role model and found Jensen instead. That's bound to leave a person hungry. Why don't you join us? We're about to sit down for a good, old-fashioned Sunday dinner."

Harriet opened her mouth to politely decline but saw the dark look Jensen was aiming her way. With his wolf eyes that made her feel no less histrionic the more she looked at them. *He* would not have invited her to Sunday dinner, she felt sure. What he would like was for her to go away and take her talk of role models with her.

But Harriet was not a quitter, and she intended to make this man show up in her library and act like a role model whether he liked it or not.

"I'd love to," she told Zack.

And assured herself it was *for the kids.*

No matter how silly Jensen made her feel.

3

Jensen followed Miss Harriet Barnett and Zack, who was not doing a great job of hiding his smirk, into the house with a sense of something a lot like dread.

Because this was a bad idea.

He should have ordered Harriet off the property the moment he'd seen her, but he'd needed a moment to get his bearings. Because she'd haunted him a little more than she should have after he'd walked away from her last night, but he'd comforted himself with the sure knowledge that he would never lay eyes on her again.

Yet there she was.

Right out there in the yard.

Tiny and determined-looking, like an officious duck.

He eyed Harriet's back as she walked behind his brother, finding that same shapeless cardigan no more appealing in the light of day than it had seemed in the depths of the Coyote. And somehow—between that and a dress he would have expected to see on an Amish woman, should the Amish unexpectedly turn up in the Longhorn Valley—he wanted to do something crazy. Like shake her a little bit and ask her why on earth she dressed like a woman fifty years her senior.

Or maybe not shake *her,* a voice inside suggested.

Because despite himself, Jensen found he was a little too close to mesmerized as he watched the movement of her hips beneath all those yards and yards of floral fabric.

Meanwhile, Zack was clearly enjoying himself far too much as he led Harriet inside and through the house. He was asking Harriet questions in his public sheriff's voice, that, to Jensen's mind, had a lot in common with a regular old bossy voice that he'd assumed at birth.

Or so Jensen assumed, since he was two years younger than Zack and couldn't recall ever *not* hearing it.

Jensen didn't believe for one moment that Zack had been moved to this level of hospitality at the mere sight of Harriet in the yard. He had seen an opportunity to annoy Jensen and was taking it. And he knew he would have happily done the same if the situation were reversed, but that didn't lessen his current irritation any.

Though Jensen would happily die on the spot before he gave Zack the satisfaction of seeing that he was bothered in any way.

"Look, guys," Zack said brightly as he delivered Harriet into the living room where most of the rest of the family was sitting and waiting for dinner to start. "Jensen has a guest."

Behind him, Jensen smiled blandly, because that was all the reaction he planned to deliver. Especially when every other member of his family currently in the living room stared straight past Zack, and the improbable sight of Harriet beside him, to get a load of Jensen's response.

He had no intention of giving them one.

As the member of the Kittredge family most likely to dish it out on any and all occasions, a title Jensen wore with pride, he knew full well it was his turn to take it. And therefore, take it he would. Because when things went his way again, as they usually did, he would remember this moment. And give no mercy to any of them.

That was what kept his smile bland and his body language downright lazy no matter what kind of speculation he saw heading his way.

And there was a whole lot of it.

"This is Harriet Barnett," Zack was saying with overdone joviality, in Jensen's opinion, given his older brother's usual seriousness in all things. "She's the new librarian down at the high school."

"I've actually been here for three years," Harriet corrected him immediately.

And Jensen did not have to see her face to know that she was frowning in that way of hers. It turned out he could *hear* her frown in her voice. Prissy and ferocious and adorable—

Adorable?

"Three years is still brand-new," Zack was assuring her in his hearty public servant tone. "In Longhorn Valley terms, anyway."

That was another way of saying she was considered brand-new according to the laws of this land laid down by one Janet Lowe Kittredge. Otherwise known as their grandmother, who took the history of Colorado in general and the Longhorn Valley in particular very, very seriously. And personally.

Jensen continued to prop up the wall beside him, looking around the overcrowded family room. It was just his luck that this week's Sunday dinner was a full house when often there were only a few people around. But not today. His grandparents had walked across the meadow that separated the little house they'd built from the ranch house and were already sitting in their usual chairs. Jensen's father was looking gloomy in the recliner he'd had to treat as a second home since the cardiac situation he still refused to knowledge directly had laid him low.

The baby of the family, Amanda, was there with her husband, Brady Everett, who'd been underfoot as long as Jensen could remember. The Everetts were another old-time Longhorn Valley family who'd been here so long that they'd once had a blood feud with the Kittredges, according to local lore. A feud Jensen had been inclined to renew when he'd found out Brady was dating the much-younger Amanda. But he was over that now. Mostly.

Connor, the next youngest, was there with his Missy, the two of them sitting next to each other on the couch without even a hint of any PDA. This was a surprise indeed given that their decision to move in with each other, without benefit of marriage, had by their grandmother's reckoning scandalized the country from one end of the Rocky Mountains to the other.

Opposite them were Riley and Rae, who had gotten married right out of high school, then broken up—or pretended they were broken up—for years. They'd worked it out last fall, and now Rae was so hugely pregnant Jensen was half-afraid she might go into labor at any moment. Something he knew better than to say to a hormonal woman.

From the kitchen down the hall, he could hear the usual sounds of his mother clattering around with her pots and pans, something she always did without accepting any help, no matter how much help was offered. And unlike his siblings, Jensen did not feel the need to perform. Ellie Kittredge knew how to ask for help, or so he assumed, even if he couldn't recall her ever actually making use of that knowledge. She certainly knew her entire family could be summoned easily enough, but she didn't do it. He supposed she liked to be a martyr. Jensen, on the other hand, liked to refrain from continually offering help he knew would be refused.

Though he had never wanted to disappear off into the kitchen more than he did just then.

He resisted the urge.

"How exciting," Rae said, smiling with entirely too much satisfaction. She had her hands on the sides of her belly and her gaze on Harriet. "Maybe I missed something over the years, but has Jensen ever brought a woman home before?"

"He has not," Amanda replied at once as if she and Rae were joined at the hip. The way they'd been a long time ago, and only again recently. Because Kittredges could hold a grudge. "Not once."

The pair of them looked entirely too delighted.

"I think I liked it better when you hated her," Jensen said to Amanda.

Amanda rolled her eyes. "I never *hated* her."

"You wanted to hate me," Rae amended, grinning. "I can't say I blame you."

Riley, always the grumpiest of the Kittredges, took a lot longer these days to work himself up into a full scowl. But when he got there, he aimed it at his sister. "Yeah, but I do."

Next to him, Harriet looked from Rae to Amanda to Riley, then back again. As if she were cataloging them. Then she turned a bit so she could look at him, too, with a flash of all that direct, bright blue.

"Amanda is very protective of her older brothers," Jensen told her, deadpan. "A word to the wise."

Harriet shoved her glasses back up her nose, frowning slightly while she did it, then turned back to the room. "I don't want to give anyone the wrong impression," she said, seemingly unconcerned with the scrutiny she was receiving. It was almost like she didn't notice it. "Jensen didn't ask me here today. I'm certainly not *with* him. I was hoping that I might convince him—"

"Where are my manners?" Jensen interjected before she could say anything further, while Zack's shoulders shook from laughter. "Let's get you a drink."

He didn't wait for her to obey, somehow sensing that obedience was likely not high on Miss Harriet Barnett's list of priorities. He slid an arm around her shoulders and steered her away from the living room, heading for the kitchen, after all. Sure, his mother might be in the kitchen, but that was the good thing about Ellie's frosty reticence in pretty much all things. She was unlikely to ask obnoxious questions like the rest of them.

Harriet stiffened under his arm, which only called more attention to how nicely shaped her shoulders were beneath the mound of her sweater and all that floral fabric.

He let go. And was taken aback by how little he wanted to.

"I don't drink," Harriet told him, glaring up at him, which was a welcome distraction from whatever was happening inside him. "And I don't like being interrupted, Mr. Kittredge."

"You can keep calling me Mr. Kittredge, here in a house with five other Mr. Kittredges, but that might be a little bit confusing. And my family might end up thinking you have a weird fetish."

She gave the distinct impression of sputtering even though she didn't make a sound. "A weird fetish?"

He shrugged. "I don't make the rules, darlin'."

"Why would calling someone *Mr. Kittredge* have anything to do with—" Harriet stopped abruptly. "Oh."

Despite himself, Jensen found himself grinning. Not

for show this time. And despite the fact he'd been pretty set on staying just as good and ornery as he'd been when he'd woken up that morning. Alone, despite the many opportunities he could have indulged in the night before, and he was a little too aware that was thanks to the blue eyes currently gazing up at him.

"What do you mean you don't drink?" he asked, when he probably should have run in the other direction.

But he wasn't a run-in-the-other-direction kind of guy. When he saw a fire, he moved toward it, not away.

Harriet didn't have her giant purse to wield before her the way she had last night, and he watched, unduly fascinated, as she shoved the bulky arm of her cardigan up. To display her wrist. Her *wrist*.

There was not one single reason Jensen could think of that his heart should be pounding at him the way it did then. It was a wrist.

Her frown was a relief, distracting him from her freaking *wrist*. "You do know that's actually a remarkably rude thing to ask another person, don't you?"

"If you say so." He could not for the life of him understand why the huffy way she spoke to him entertained him so much. "I thought it was more along the lines of exhibiting hospitality, but what do I know?"

"Maybe I'm an alcoholic and do not wish to explain such a personal thing to a perfect stranger."

"Are you?"

"I am not. I drink upon occasion." She sniffed. "But not this early in the day. And no one wants to be interrogated about their personal choices."

"You could have asked for water, Harriet." He sounded indulgent. He even *felt* indulgent, which was worse. There was whatever his heart was doing, but more, they were standing in the hallway. She was so little, wrapped up in yards upon yards of that strange, frumpy dress that made no sense, and yet again sporting a totally unnecessary sweater in the middle of summer. She was *ridiculous*. But he didn't look away. "Tea. Coffee. I don't recall offering to whip up a few car bombs to get you drunk and sloppy."

"I wanted to be clear. For all I know, your idea of an innocuous Sunday afternoon drink includes a vat of whiskey."

"Miss Harriet." His voice was low and laced with mock astonishment. "Have you been stalking me?"

"Everybody knows you have a thing about whiskey," she said tartly. She considered him solemnly, then gave a little nod as if coming to a decision. "Jensen."

That rolled through him the way the sight of her wrist had. Like a slow, improbable, confounding little earthquake when it was just his name. People had been yelling it at him as long as he could remember, on football fields and across paddocks. Girls had liked to giggle it when they were younger. And when they were not so much younger too.

Harriet Barnett pronounced his name as if it were, in and of itself, a declaration.

Of some or other kind of genteel war.

And it turned out, to his enduring astonishment, that Jensen was apparently prepared to be all in for the fight. Because he was still here, wasn't he? He hadn't laughed and walked away. He hadn't left her to Zack, who had invited her in. He hadn't done any of the approximately ten thousand things he knew how to do to redirect female attention when he didn't want it.

Because of . . . her *wrist*? Her *eyes*? He was losing it.

But he still didn't walk away.

"I shouldn't have accepted your brother's invitation," she said then, surprising him. She laced her fingers together in front of her, and he found himself wondering what it would be like if she were the kind of person who reached out and touched. Because it turned out, he was something like desperate for the feel of those soft little hands on him.

Get it together, he growled at himself. If this was what happened because he'd gone home alone, that was clearly a lesson he needed to heed in the future. And avoid the issue. He'd gone home alone by choice, sure, but that almost made it worse. Because why on earth had he made that choice?

"Feel free to leave any time," he encouraged her. "Though at this point, obviously, that will only make it worse."

Harriet blinked. "Make what worse? You already said no."

"You really are new in town." He leaned back against the wall behind him and made a little show out of lounging there, crossing his arms as he gazed down at her. She, for her part, looked at him directly and made no attempt to flutter or deflect while she did it. He suspected she was equal parts officious and fearless. Jensen wasn't generally fond of the first, but he was fascinated by the second.

Even—maybe especially—because it was fearlessness all done up in that sweater and that dress and her hair wrapped up in a bun that made him think of the old women at church, and he didn't understand why he couldn't look away.

"You're right, I didn't grow up here, or happen to have found myself born to a family that settled here in the 1800s." She shoved her glasses higher on her nose. "Yet I still would not describe three years as new."

"My grandmother considers herself new, Harriet. She

came here from Fort Collins when she was sixteen. Three years hardly counts."

"According to the State of Colorado, I'm considered a resident. Like it or not."

"That's the state. This is a small town. Different rules, darlin'."

"But what I was trying to say," she said then, loftily, as if it was difficult to carry on in the face of such provocation, "is that, of course, your family doesn't have to feed me."

"And what I was trying to say is that you've already piqued their curiosity." He nodded back to the living room, where he could hear Riley and Brady talking, which probably meant that their troublesome wives were whispering. Cooking up trouble, one way or another. "They'll never believe you showed up here on a Sunday to try to talk me into showing up for your class."

"That's exactly why I showed up here. I shouldn't have, I know, and I wouldn't have if it wasn't so critically important, in my opinion, that these kids have someone to look up to." She lifted a hand as if she expected him to object. "I'm not asking you to think of yourself as a role model if you don't want to. These are kids. Some of them act tough, others are withdrawn, but all they really want is someone to talk to them like they're real. Like they matter. And I may not know you from a can of paint, but you don't seem incapable of talking. To anyone. After all, you seem to have no trouble talking to me."

Her generous mouth shifted into something rueful, and he was glad, for a minute, that he had that wall to hold him up. "How could anyone have trouble talking to you? You do most of the talking yourself."

Her wry smile deepened. "You might be surprised how few people appreciate the pleasure of my conversation."

His heart thumped in a different way then. "Talking is something I'm pretty good at, I guess. Maybe it's my superpower."

Harriet's eyes were too blue. And he had the wild notion that he ought to reach over and push her glasses up her nose this time. But he didn't.

"Then why not use your superpower for good?" she asked. "Simply because you can?"

Jensen was still caught up in that moment later, when they were all sitting around the dinner table, passing around his mother's typically over-the-top roast, potatoes, and a variety of different vegetables grown out in the garden. Roasted and raw alike, because this was a family that took its vegetables seriously.

"I grew up in town," he heard Missy telling Harriet. "But I feel like I'm new because I only moved back here last fall. After being away for a long, long time. Mostly in Santa Fe."

"Where did you come here from?" Jensen asked Harriet from her other side. "Lancaster, Pennsylvania?"

Harriet blinked at him from behind her glasses. "Lancaster, Pennsylvania, seems oddly specific. And no."

"Have you ever been to Lancaster, Pennsylvania?" Jensen asked.

"Not to my knowledge." Harriet frowned at him, then turned back to Missy. "I grew up near Kansas City, Missouri. Went to college in Minnesota, then got my master's in Illinois. When I had the opportunity to come to Cold River, I couldn't refuse. I'm a born-and-bred midwesterner, but I knew it was the place for me."

"So what brought you here today?" Rae asked from across the table, sounding perfectly innocent. So innocent, in fact, that her own husband snorted from beside her. "To the Bar K, specifically?"

"Not *with* Jensen," Amanda murmured, her eyes piously lowered to her plate. "But to see him, all the same."

"Killing it on the narration there, monkey," Connor said from his seat across the table.

Amanda made a face at him, and Jensen prepared to wade in and knock some heads together. Metaphorically. Or maybe not so metaphorically, given the way Zack and Riley were smirking at him.

"I'm looking for role models," Harriet said in her brisk, matter-of-fact way. And clearly misread the stunned silence it took over the table. Jensen sat back in his chair, prepared to look lazy and unbothered no matter what, because that was the best way to handle what was coming. Harriet plowed on ahead. "I'm trying to teach some students I have in summer school about things like primary sources, and I find it's more helpful to have guests. It keeps them interested. And everyone seems to know who Jensen is."

"I'm sorry," Connor said with a big laugh. "Did you say *role model*? Jensen?"

Jensen sat there, a big grin on his own face, while his entire family burst out laughing.

Funny thing was, on any other Sunday, he might have laughed with them. He knew he was no role model. He'd never wanted to be anything of the kind. He'd known a real role model once, and he knew he was to blame for what had happened there.

But this wasn't the time to think about Daniel.

Because there was something about how much his family laughed, and how long, that settled in him in a way he didn't much like. And there was something else all wrapped up in the Miss Harriet Barnett–ness of it all. About how still she was, sitting with her perfect posture in the chair next to him with all that blond hair piled so strangely on her head.

And he was close enough now to see that it wasn't simply *blond,* because nothing about her was simple. It was too many shades of gold to count, and how annoying was *that*?

Amanda wiped at her face. That was the level of her hilarity. "What exactly are you going to teach those poor, impressionable children, Jensen?"

"I did a pretty good job with you," Jensen drawled, not really taking the edges off it.

Amanda rolled her eyes at him, but it was Riley who spoke. "I don't think *barfly* is the kind of role you're supposed to model for young folks. Their parents tend to object."

This from a man who was not yet a parent, but clearly spoke for them all.

"You make *barfly* sound like a bad thing," Jensen replied lightly, and figured he deserved a halo for not pointing out that Riley had propped up his share of barstools in the years when he wasn't a happy, expectant father, and Rae had been a forbidden topic of discussion around this very same table.

No halo appeared, but he knew he'd earned it all the same.

"Zack is the sheriff and a role model for us all," Connor said, sounding far too amused. "As he will be the first to tell you, at length. But all that law and order should set those kids on the straight and narrow. You should get him to do it."

"Maybe they've seen enough badges already," Jensen found himself saying. And not entirely because of that obnoxious Aidan Hall and his criminal family. "You ever consider that?"

"I do consider it," Zack said. "Usually an aversion to the badge is a good sign that there's some delinquency that needs addressing."

"I think it's lovely you want to help out, Jensen," his grandmother said as if she hadn't heard all that laughter. "Which is more than the rest of them can say, I think."

That didn't stop the laughing, which was probably good-natured. Probably. Even his father looked like he almost smiled, which, for the remote Donovan Kittredge, was as good as falling on the floor in hysterics.

It didn't really feel all that good-natured, though.

Jensen was a pretty laid-back guy. He prided himself on it. He was surrounded on all sides by family members who got wound up at the slightest provocation, so maybe he'd developed his particular brand of easygoing charm in opposition to that.

He could psychoanalyze himself all day. Just like all of his ex–temporary flings liked to do. And usually he ended up laughing it off, whatever the analysis was. Because he'd learned too young the difference between an honest-to-god tragedy and . . . everything else.

Any second now, he'd join in the uproarious laughter at the very notion that he might be a role model to some kids stuck in summer school.

But Harriet Barnett was sitting next to him, perched on a chair shoved in tight with the rest of them around his parents' dining room table. Her glasses were falling down her nose. He could smell whatever she'd used on her skin because she was sitting so close, and he didn't know what he was supposed to do with that knowledge. A hint of cinnamon and a touch of vanilla that made him think not only of dessert but how much he, personally, liked himself an extra helping of dessert. Her hair was too many shades of gold, that ridiculous cardigan was falling off one shoulder, and he had never seen that much floral anywhere except maybe the wallpaper in his grandmother's guest room.

She was not laughing.

Instead, she cast that steely-blue gaze of hers all around the lot of them, her mouth in that unsmiling line that, in his opinion, only called more attention to the fact that it was a fine mouth to begin with.

Then she turned that gaze on him.

Jensen had never felt the sensation that swelled inside him then. He had made it his life's work to laugh at the joke first, last, and loudest, but he felt his grin fade as Harriet just *looked* at him.

With a gaze that held enough weight to shove his ribs around.

Like she knew—like she just *knew*—all the things he kept locked up tight, far beneath all that laughter. Far away from the light of day.

Harriet Barnett seemed to look straight through him while his own flesh and blood laughed and laughed and laughed.

He would have preferred it if she'd hit him.

"Yes, Grandma," Jensen drawled, before he thought better of it. Before he asked himself what he thought he was doing. "I can't wait to help. As you all know, there's nothing I love more than giving back. Especially to Cold River High, the alma mater that I love so much."

"I think that's laying it on a bit thick," Harriet said with all that reckless determination from beside him. How could she not know how dangerous it was to walk around the way she did, so intense, where everyone could see?

But then she smiled, and Jensen stopped worrying about anything else. "But thank you, Jensen. I won't forget it."

And he had the sudden and distinct sensation that he was lost, right there in his childhood home.

4

"Where do you want me, Miss Harriet?"

Harriet had known that Jensen was coming into the library that day. Bright and early on a Wednesday morning, as planned. She had given him a selection of dates after Sunday dinner, when he'd walked her out to her little car and had scowled at it as if the inoffensive hatchback were a personal insult to him.

I wouldn't want to get caught in any real weather in that thing, he had said.

Happily, she had replied, *it is July, not January.*

He hadn't smiled, which had felt . . . portentous.

But he'd chosen a day to come speak to her students, portents be damned. He had even called her to confirm the night before, and she'd heard her own, tinny voice in the background, suggesting he had just then gotten around to listening to the messages she'd left for him on the ranch's answering machine.

She had woken up far too early this morning after not sleeping well last night. At first she blamed her restlessness on Chaucer, who often tried to smother her in her sleep with his weighty love, when she knew she could have locked him out of the bedroom if she'd wanted.

Harriet had accepted, sometime around three o'clock,

that it was not the cat's fault that sleep was eluding her. An hour or so later, she'd given up and had grumpily gotten out of bed. She'd folded all her laundry. She'd rearranged her cupboards. Then she'd gone out and re-potted some plants in the predawn half-light, hoping it might settle her.

It was hours later now, and she felt a great many things, none of them *settled*.

And she still wasn't prepared.

That voice of his, so unrepentantly *male,* curled into her and knotted itself up until she thought she might drop the books she was reorganizing on her little display behind the main library counter.

She took a moment to *not* drop her books. And to slap some sense into herself. Metaphorically. Maybe she didn't really understand why it was that Jensen Kittredge, of all people, was getting to her in this way. But she didn't need to understand.

What she needed to do was get through the upcoming class period without acting more like a silly teen than the actual teenagers who'd be shuffling in soon.

She could beat herself up about her outsize reactions to this man later.

When she turned around, Harriet was sure she was ready to deal with him the way she dealt with everyone else, or at least pretend she could. But she was not pre-pared to see Jensen Kittredge *lounging there,* once again outfitted in full cowboy regalia. The jeans and boots. A Stetson on his head, and another T-shirt. A T-shirt that did truly astonishing things to his absurdly well-carved torso, certainly, but also to her.

It was just her luck that the first time she had such an overwhelming physical response to someone, it was him. The sort of man Harriet would never, ever touch because, well. Because she knew better than to let her head get turned by the captain-of-the-football-team type.

"Jensen," she said, and instantly felt like the silly, excitable girl she'd never been. "Good morning."

Then had to stand there, in her place of work—her *sanctuary*—while he treated her to one of those lazy, too-knowing grins of his.

Harriet was deeply dismayed that she was susceptible to such a blatant display of masculinity, calculated to disarm and disconcert. She had always been immune to such things before.

She did not feel even remotely immune today.

Then again, as her mother had always said, it was actions that mattered. Not thoughts. Not wishes.

Not intense physical reactions to men she found otherwise vaguely distasteful.

You do not find him distasteful *at all,* an inner voice challenged her. *That's the problem.*

Except Harriet thought that, actually, he was the problem.

"Good morning," Jensen said. Eventually.

After *looking at her* in a way that made all those heated, knotted things inside her seem to hum, tuneless but too loud. She felt certain that whatever he was doing, it was deliberate. And more, that he knew precisely what effect it had.

Harriet felt scandalized, though she was perfectly well aware no scandalous behavior had occurred. And would not occur.

And maybe, just maybe, it should have occurred to her before now that a man she had to track down in a place like the Coyote was not exactly the kind of upstanding adult role model she should be presenting to children who were already halfway lost.

But it was too late for that now.

"Thank you for coming," she managed to say in what she hoped were quelling tones. And she thanked all that was holy that she was not prone to blushing. "Did you check in at the front desk?"

"The legendary Miss Martina Patrick knew me by sight," he said, and she couldn't tell if he sounded as if he was about to laugh, or if he always sounded like that and she was just *feeling* it inside her now, the horror. "I thought she was about to send me to detention, if you want to know the truth. Between you and me, I think she wanted to, like it was my sophomore year all over again."

"Why am I not at all surprised to discover that you spent a lot of time in detention?"

"I can't help it if people talk to me," Jensen protested. "I'm a friendly guy."

"I'm sure that argument swayed your teachers."

"They were staunch enemies of socialization, it turns out. And it would have been a whole lot more time in detention, but folks got testy if random punishments kept me from football practice. During football season, at least, I seemed to end up there a lot less than I would have otherwise."

Harriet stopped what she was doing—which was fluttering, she was all too aware, though she'd been trying to mask it by frantically stacking things that did not require stacking on the desk between them—and frowned at him. "It's deeply objectionable that high school athletes are held to a different standard. It's not fair to the athletes themselves, who never learn that there are consequences for their behavior, and it's certainly not fair to any of the other students."

"Miss Patrick shared your views, as I recall." Jensen's

grin widened as if his apparently disreputable adolescence was making him nostalgic. "I never much minded detention. I'm not afraid of consequences. But I was a good running back, and Cold River loves some high school football, so there we are. The world is unfair, Harriet. Sad but true."

She had not invited him to call her Harriet, despite his bizarre comments about *fetishes* at his parents' house. And yet she found she didn't have it in her to correct him.

Harriet assured herself that she was being polite to a guest in her space and nothing more.

And she had more important things to focus on than names or fetishes or his abdominal excellence. Like the list she'd typed out of questions to ask him should he flounder, or if her students did not engage with him enough to ask their own. "Well, none of the kids you're about to meet are athletes. I'm sure they would all benefit greatly from a bit of moderate exercise, teamwork, and fresh air—as would we all, of course. I wanted to take them on a hiking trip, but the principal wouldn't allow it." Harriet sighed in remembered frustration. "He felt it had too much potential to go badly."

"You hike?"

The tone of the question was utter amazement. When she looked over at him again, all he was doing was leaning in that boneless way of his, as if he needed to prop himself up on the library desk to make it through his next breath.

"Why wouldn't I hike?"

"This isn't wherever you're from—"

"Missouri."

He looked almost pained. "We have actual mountains here. And real trails."

"As it happens, Missouri is a part of no less than three

mountain ranges. The Ozarks, the St. Francois Mountains, and the U.S. Interior Highlands."

Jensen looked at her. For a while.

Harriet did not look away, though her ears began to feel singed.

"You hike a lot?" he asked.

"I hike enough." Meaning, she had researched the proper shoes, tested out several different pairs, and now made a brisk trip into the foothills behind town a part of her weekly routine. She liked routines. "You are aware that hiking is just walking, but at elevation, aren't you?"

"This is Colorado, Harriet. Nothing here is *just* anything."

"In any case, I'm not allowed to take my class on the hiking trip that would likely do them the most good. You will have to be the next-best thing."

"I'll try to live up to the Rocky Mountains," he drawled.

And inside Harriet, a thousand little fires kindled and burned.

She didn't have the slightest idea what to do with that. How was she supposed to extinguish them while he was standing there, looking at her? "Hiking aside, all the kids in this class have at least one failing grade from the previous year. Unlike some of our summer school students, who were ill during the school year or are trying to place into AP classes or get college credit, these kids have received formal academic warnings. Some are on the verge of expulsion. As you might imagine, there are a variety of teenage reactions to the situation they find themselves in. None of them are what I would describe as charming."

"I wouldn't be all that charmed by having to give up my summer, either."

"Yes." Harriet nodded sagely, hoping her incendiary

state wasn't visible. She told herself it was heartburn. "You're usually out of town, aren't you?"

"You make it sound like a summer vacation," Jensen said lightly, but when she snuck a look at him, his arresting gaze was anything but *light*. "That's not quite how I would describe wildfire season."

"You should talk about that," she advised him. "They may sneer at you, because they're teenagers and they're required to, but that kind of bravery matters."

He was quiet. And regarding her the same way he had at his family's dinner table. Which did not help her personal, internal wildfire season at all, even if he was looking at her as if he were trying to figure her out. She supposed it was because, as usual, she'd done something odd when anyone else would know the right thing to do or say.

If she let herself get sidetracked every time it happened, she would never get anything done. So she smiled at him instead, as professionally as possible. "Do you have any questions?"

"I thought you were the librarian."

"I am. Behold the library in which we stand."

"Why are you teaching a class?"

This was a topic Harriet could talk about forever. And she never felt odd while she was doing it. "A lot of these kids who end up in summer school against their will seem to have a set of overlapping challenges. I'm not sure taking a remedial math class here and a makeup chemistry class there can really address those challenges, so I suggested we create a resources module that focuses on things like literacy rates, reading retention, and how to write an actual essay for that English class. If all they get out of summer school is punishment, we've lost them."

"Does it work?"

It should have been impossible. She told herself she was imagining things. Because it seemed to her that when he wanted to, Jensen Kittredge could focus his attention in such an intense way that she would've sworn he was hanging on her every word. And more, as if those words mattered to him, deeply.

In case she wondered if she was still being silly.

"I think it does." Harriet knew it did, but that was her gut feeling, not facts. And she always preferred facts. "I only started last summer. Obviously, you can never be sure about competing factors, but of the five students I worked with last year, none were expelled, all either graduated with their class or are still enrolled, and two improved so notably in the fall semester that they were off academic probation this last semester. Maybe it has nothing to do with my course. But between you and me, I like to think that it does."

"I believe you, Harriet," he said in that rumbly way of his that made her, uncharacteristically, want to turn a few cartwheels.

That would be undignified. Appallingly unprofessional. And worst of all, profoundly silly.

So instead, Harriet smoothed her hands on the front of her serviceable dress in a practical ponte fabric that did not require smoothing and rounded the desk, breezing past Jensen as she marched toward the big table she'd set up for her class in the center of the library.

And Jensen Kittredge might have been lounging about behind her, huge and smoldering and impossible, but she still took a moment to look around her with pride.

Harriet had always loved libraries, of course. She particularly loved school libraries. When she'd still attended public school, it had been the elementary school library that had made indignities like forced PE class bearable.

The librarians there hadn't treated her like an oddball or judged her for being forever out of step with her peers or being unable to climb a rope in full view of the whole of the fifth grade. They'd asked her what she wanted to read, suggested books, and helped her escape.

Now this one was hers, housed in this lovely old brick building with Old West flair and wooden accents everywhere. She was in charge. She was the one who got to suggest books and make lost kids feel found. She was the one who got to teach young minds how to be limited only by the spines of the books they held.

It turned out Harriet quite liked having charge of her own domain. Jensen here in the middle of it made her simultaneously aware of how much she liked her space while also being keenly focused on how very much of that space he took up.

In her head, she'd envisioned a very tidy, well-thought-out presentation to her class. Possibly involving her whiteboard. She'd imagined Jensen would sit at the head of the library resource table, make some sort of rousing speech about manly, heroic things, and jot down some notes with a dry-erase marker.

But she should have known that this man had no intention of doing a single thing unless he felt like it. And now that she thought about it, who could imagine Jensen Kittredge at a whiteboard? Even now, with him standing in proximity to hers, she couldn't make the image come together in her head.

Instead of sitting at the head of the table, despite her clear indication that he should do so, Jensen kept on lounging about. He stood back against one of the low shelves that surrounded the table on three sides, reminding her a little too intensely of the way he'd leaned against the wall in the hallway of his parents' house. Looking boneless and lazy from head to toe, as long as she didn't look too closely at that gleam in his eyes.

"I really did think of this as more of a classroom situation," she told him when he showed no signs of doing anything but *leaning*. "Less lounging and more learning."

"I didn't realize they were mutually exclusive."

"Maybe that's why you spent most of your high school days in detention halls," she replied tartly, and then remembered herself. She wasn't here today to match wits with Jensen Kittredge. Even assuming that he possessed the kind of wits that a person could match in the first place.

Her secret shame was that she wished he did when so far, she thought that what he'd exhibited was a fascinating ability to project *potential*. Because surely the truth about him was right there in all the stories she knew about him already—and everyone else knew too, because they'd told her those stories, unbidden, as soon as she'd arrived in Cold River. But high school heroes tarnished with age. That was exactly the sort of truism Harriet had clung to in high school herself. Or in her case, happily not confined to any actual high school building but still perfectly aware that she was no one's version of teenage royalty.

Not so Jensen. She was ashamed to say that she had made a point of looking for him in the trophy case downstairs outside the front office, cluttered with sports regalia that she'd never paid any attention to before. She hadn't been surprised to find his name.

Repeatedly.

"You have a pretty ferocious glare," he said, sounding even lazier than he looked, which should not have been possible. "But if you really think you're going to stare me down, you should probably remember that I spend most of my days face-to-face with horses far more ornery than you could ever dream of being. And my brothers, who are worse."

"Are you suggesting that I could be stared down by a horse?"

"I couldn't rightly speculate, Miss Harriet. But I'm still not sitting at your table."

"Because you have a bone-deep need to do exactly the opposite of anything that's asked of you, presumably."

He didn't laugh that big, booming laugh of his. He didn't even smile. But still, the light in his gaze changed, and she felt as if he had.

"That, and more practically speaking, I'm way too big for those chairs."

"Oh." Harriet blinked, looking down at the standard, school-issue chairs. Now that she was thinking about it, they obviously wouldn't fit a man of his size. Comfortably, anyway. "I'm embarrassed that didn't occur to me."

"They didn't fit me all that well when I was a teenager. I'd be just as happy not to repeat that experience."

"I can go down the hall and see if they have an extra—"

"Also," he drawled, "it's not going to hurt a bunch of juvenile delinquents to literally look up at someone. Reinforce a little authority. No offense, but even when you're standing, I don't think anyone has to crane their neck."

She gave him the severe look that made up for whatever she lacked in height. "This isn't supposed to be an opportunity for you to get all domineering."

"Darlin', that's not how I roll." This time, his mouth really did curve. "Except for certain circumstances, and those are usually invitation-only."

Harriet understood that he was being provocative. And more, that being provocative was probably a simple knee-jerk response to being alive when you were a man like Jensen Kittredge. No more meaningful than the adolescent attempts at wit from any high school boy she dealt with.

Her reaction should have been the same blank stare she employed here at work in the face of trying teenage witticisms. And while she aimed that stare at Jensen, because it was a habit, inside she felt . . . shivery.

And she maintained a consistent temperature here in her library, regardless of the season, so she knew perfectly well that she was not cold.

Besides, it was a shivery heat.

Worse, she liked it.

The bell rang above them, and her students began shuffling in shortly after, making their usual noise in defiance of the library's posted rules demanding quiet. Harriet threw herself into shushing them and directing them to their seats, while absolutely, 100 percent not thinking about the implications of *shivery heat*.

Shivery heat and Jensen Kittredge and—

But no. She couldn't allow herself to go down that road. For any number of reasons, but chief among them, because Jensen Kittredge had *dead end* written all over him. And Harriet did not get mired in anything, much less in dead ends, no matter what color their eyes were.

All this, of course, in the unlikely event that he ever invited her to take part in another crowded booth at the Coyote with him and his female friends.

That image was so outlandish she almost cracked herself up right there. Thankfully, she caught herself before the students noticed. Because she wasn't a big blusher, thank goodness, but she really did not want to explain to them why she was laughing.

The second bell rang, announcing Aidan Hall as he made his always-almost-late entrance. Today, he let out a low, clearly mocking whistle as he slouched into the library, looking the way he always did. Tough and guarded, Harriet supposed, in black and the expected band T-shirt and leather things wrapped around his wrist. But all she saw was a lonely kid. His eyes glittered in Jensen's direction, and his chin was up high as he made a show of taking his sweet time to find a seat.

"Jensen Kittredge," he said as he sat in what Harriet could not pretend were tones of awe, no matter how she wanted to. "Imagine that."

"Aidan," Jensen replied. Sounding, for his part, no less mocking.

It did occur to Harriet—as it should have done before she braved a sticky, crowded bar on a Saturday night—that, perhaps, Aidan had not requested this particular local luminary with the purest of intentions.

But that didn't change the facts. Whatever else Jensen was or wasn't, he also happened to be a living, breathing hero who'd sat in the same chairs these kids did, however uncomfortably, and was now grown up and successful. Whether that success could be laid at his feet or simply because he was a part of his family's enterprise, she couldn't say. But the fact that he was standing upright, looking clean and in control of himself and not under the influence of anything—well, that was already a step up from the parents of most of these kids.

Not to mention, he'd shown up for them.

"Mr. Shroy, please remove your gum before I'm forced to notice you're chewing it, against school policy," Harriet said briskly as the students settled around the table. "Mr. Beck, that much candy will rot your teeth, and if it's still visible in thirty seconds, it will be confiscated. Mr. Hall, if you must be late, please do so without calling attention to yourself when you turn up. And you all know better than to talk that loudly while you enter the library."

There was the usual muttering, shuffling of feet, and redistribution of teenage bodies that didn't always obey even their owners' commands, and then her six charges were about as presentable as they could be. They were sitting, if not up straight. They'd all opened up their notebooks, though whether or not they would actually turn studious remained to be seen. And they were all either staring at Jensen or pretending not to, while he simply stayed where he was, leaning there against the bookcase as if he planned to prop it up for the rest of the summer.

"As you can see, we have a guest with us today. Some of you may already know him."

"Everybody knows Jensen Kittredge," Aidan said with an edge in his voice that made Harriet frown. "The way I hear it, he dated pretty much every single one of our mothers. Even yours, Shroy."

Harriet masterfully chose to ignore the hand gesture Liam Shroy didn't do a good job of hiding. "You're the one who requested Mr. Kittredge's presence, Mr. Hall. And he graciously accepted your invitation. For those of you not as conversant on Mr. Kittredge's biography as Aidan, he is a local business owner and regional smoke jumper. A photograph taken of Mr. Kittredge fighting wildfires last summer in California appeared on the front pages of newspapers from coast to coast and in many end-of-year photo roundups nationally as well as internationally."

And currently hung in shops and other businesses—and no doubt many a private home—all over Cold River. Because not only was it Jensen, but the photo itself was beautiful, if heartrending. A firefighter bracketed by intense flames making unholy candles out of trees, calling attention to how fragile a single man must be in the face of all that natural fury. Yet on he fought.

That the very same man was standing here in her library today, looking faintly amused and entirely too healthy for her peace of mind, just seemed to knock around inside her. A little too hard.

"Yeah, congrats," Aidan muttered. "Must be nice to be famous."

"If you want to ask me about my personal life, Aidan," Jensen drawled, "you're welcome to it. But I expect you to answer my questions in return. It's only fair."

Harriet braced herself, expecting Aidan to lash out. But to her surprise, he only muttered something under his breath and subsided.

She looked back at Jensen. He smiled as if he'd expected no other possible response, and then he began to talk.

Harriet braced herself for that too.

"I don't envy you," Jensen told her kids. "I never had to go to summer school, but I spent my fair share of time in detention while I was an inmate here. Can't say it took." He moved his gaze from one student to the next, intensely enough that even angry, silent Marcy Coates actually looked up from her fierce sketches of skeletons and bloody hearts. "The things it turned out I needed in life they sure weren't teaching in my classes here. If you don't like high school, you're in good company. You don't have to go off and get a fancy college degree afterward if you don't want. But you do have to do this, and you should. What high school really teaches you is how to get along doing things you don't feel like doing, because in the end, they serve a greater good that might mystify you at the time. Sad to say, that's adult life in a nutshell. And who knows? If you stop expecting high school to be anything but what it is, you might actually learn something."

There was a small silence. Six pairs of widened teenage eyes found Harriet.

She smiled calmly. "That is certainly an out-of-the-box approach to an educational pep talk, Mr. Kittredge."

Jensen grinned but kept his attention on the kids. "I didn't take to school and grades and exams. What I had to ask myself, eventually, was what was going to allow me to do more of what I wanted. For example, if you're mouthy and getting Ds, people dismiss you. They toss you in detention, ignore what you have to say, and treat you like you're dumb. If, on the other hand, you're just as mouthy but you're getting As? Things look a whole lot different. I was actually more of a handful when I was getting better grades, and I got in less trouble." He shrugged. "Teachers focus on the grades first and judge you accordingly. If you can control that, why wouldn't you?"

Harriet supposed she should not have been surprised to see at least three of the students writing that down.

"And I get it," Jensen continued in that conversational way of his that made it seem like he was just hanging out here, ruminating. "School seems pretty low on the list of priorities. And if it's not so great at home, if it's chaotic or even worse than that, when are you supposed to do all that schoolwork? I'm not saying it's easy." His gaze seemed to sharpen then, fixing on each of the six kids before him in turn. "But something else I learned is that if I let what was happening at home affect me so much that I was getting Ds and therefore putting myself in a position where even more adults could exercise their power over me, I was letting them all win. Fun fact about me: I prefer to win."

Harriet had expected something more along the lines

of, How I Became a Smoke Jumper and Ended Up on the Cover of *The New York Times*. But she couldn't deny that however unorthodox this might be, Jensen seemed to know these kids better than most people did. Including most of her colleagues.

"Your family has a ranch," Aidan said, and he sounded . . . not exactly subdued. But different. "Kind of easy to mess around in high school when you don't have to worry about what you're doing after."

"True," Jensen agreed. "I'm not going to tell you that you don't have things in your life that suck, Aidan. Maybe some more than others. But it's up to you to decide if that defines you. As you're already sitting here in summer school, I'm thinking it does. Your call. Let all the things you can't control tell you who you are, or be your own man in spite of them."

Aidan looked as close to shaken as Harriet had ever seen him. Someone else coughed.

"I'm not saying it's easy," Jensen told them. "I know it's not. But I'm afraid it really is that simple."

And Harriet stood there, useless by her whiteboard with her heart doing alarming things in her chest, while Jensen carried on like that for the rest of the class period. He answered questions. He dispensed his own form of wisdom wrapped up in some tough love. He was as funny as he was serious. He made her too-cool kids smile, when that was rare.

He was perfect.

There was no getting around the fact that he was *perfect*.

And finally, she couldn't hide anymore from that shivery heat that wound around and around inside of her. She couldn't pretend she wasn't feeling exactly what she was feeling.

Oh, how the mighty fall, she told herself, not quite despairingly.

Because it stood to reason that Harriet, who never did anything by half when a full bore intensity could be brought to bear, would do this to herself. She'd managed to avoid horrifying teenage crushes and more of the same in college. It had helped that the kind of boys, then men, who felt comfortable not quite asking her out, or prolonging encounters so that she might do the asking, were all the same. Each and every one of them had been possessed of two fatal flaws, in her opinion. No matter how many times her friends lectured her about lowering her high standards and giving people a chance, she couldn't get past those flaws. First of all, they all seemed certain that they were doing her a favor when she disagreed. Second, and more pertinently to her mind, they were never hot.

Never even *remotely* hot.

Harriet had concluded that it was entirely possible that her charms, or lack thereof, destined her for the questionable attentions of the weak-chinned, the pasty-handed, and the crushingly boring. But rather than settle for a toad of a man who thought *he* was lowering himself to *her,* she could also, she had realized eventually, not settle at all.

The truth was, Harriet didn't want to settle.

And apparently, she hadn't ever been all that interested in anyone because she was made wrong. Or different, anyway, as many of said toads had speculated when she had declined their half-hearted, passive-aggressive invitations. Apparently, her unwillingness to settle wasn't part of her oddness.

Apparently, Harriet had been aspirational all along.

Because one look at Jensen Kittredge in his T-shirt

and those jeans, and she felt as basic as basic could be. Because he was beautiful, and he made her shiver and burn, and that was something she was going to have to learn how to live with. No matter how horrified she was with herself.

Because maybe he wasn't quite the dumb jock she'd anticipated. She could admit that. But he was still *Jensen Kittredge*. He was still the man she'd found sitting in a booth with four women, looking like maybe those women were nothing more than an appetizer. And if the stories she'd heard were even half-true, that was just a regular old night out for Jensen.

She'd had a good idea who he was before she'd sought him out. But more to the point, Harriet knew who she was too.

There wasn't going to be a sexy librarian makeover, complete with a triumphant movie soundtrack. She wasn't going to let down her hair, put on a tight dress, and turn into some kind of siren.

Even if she did, all that would do was make her one of a very large crowd.

And Harriet had never done well in crowds.

So she stood there in her library, her refuge, and allowed herself the fantasy. Even though she knew that when Jensen finished his talk and left, that was going to be the last she saw of him. There would be no more lazy-eyed lounging against her bookshelves. There would be no more accidental Sunday dinners with his family.

But she couldn't complain. Because she supposed that it was easy enough to get a certain kind of attention from a man like him in a bar one evening. It had looked easy, anyway, if a person dressed the part. And giggled a lot.

She'd already had more than that.

And she was a practical woman, so she knew she wouldn't *yearn*. Or anything quite so embarrassing. Not for long.

Soon enough, that shivery heat would pass. Soon enough, if she heard his laughter across a public room, she might not even notice.

Soon enough, she thought, as that dark amber gaze of his found hers and held. As the fires in her danced, banishing any stray memories of underwhelming toads from long ago.

Soon enough.

But not just yet.

5

A week or so after his command appearance in Harriet's library, Jensen found himself heading into town on another school day morning. Twice in the space of about ten days was enough to make a man start having unpleasant flashbacks of all the dreary early-morning drives into town he'd been forced to suffer as a kid. Not having to make that drive unless he truly felt like it still felt like a perk.

Even if this time, he was headed to the sheriff's office.

Zack had been annoyingly unforthcoming when he'd called very, very early that morning. Jensen's daily *welcome to your life as a rancher* alarm had gone off mere moments before, as hideously piercing as ever at such an ungodly hour. He hadn't even made it out to his small kitchen to start mainlining his usual coffee.

"Got a kid in lockup," Zack had said. The words had barely made sense. "Vandalism."

Jensen had rubbed his hand over his face and shuffled toward the kitchen. "You do know that I don't have a kid, right?"

"He's asking for you."

Coffee hadn't made that exchange any clearer. And Jensen had not exactly rushed into town for clarification on early-morning foolishness from his older brother. He'd handled his share of the morning chores, had dealt with a few calls that couldn't wait, and only then had he aimed his pickup toward whatever nonsense awaited him in Cold River proper. He had half a mind to stop and help himself to a workingman's breakfast at Mary Jo's diner, where the pancakes were the size of a man's head, the coffee was like rocket fuel, and no one ever left hungry. Most years, he treated his body like a temple, because that was the best way to make sure that when he faced fires like the one that had ended up in that cursed photograph, he was ready.

But nothing was the way it was supposed to be this year, starting with him being here in Cold River instead of following wildfires across the West. Continuing with the fact that he'd actually done a little civic duty and had talked to some surly kids. And maybe most shocking, that he hadn't been back to the Coyote since Harriet had found him there.

He chose not to ask himself why that was.

Jensen took the turn down toward city hall and the rest of the municipal buildings, including the sheriff's office, instead of carrying on down Main Street. Or taking the turn that led to Cold River High and certain librarians he didn't need to be thinking about any longer, now that his proxy raffle date was done and dusted.

He parked out front and found his way inside, tipping his hat to Adaline Sykes at the front desk. Adaline served as Zack's secretary in addition to running dispatch. She wore handknitted sweaters that often featured her beloved corgis, like the short-sleeved lavender one she sported today. And she had been the hub of gossip in the Longhorn Valley for as long as anyone could remember.

Jensen expected that by the time he made it back to his truck, half the county would have been informed that Zack had hauled in his own brother for some or other nefarious deed.

"I got a summons from the big man himself," he told her.

Adaline nodded, indicating the private door that led directly into Zack's office. "He's expecting you."

Was he now.

Jensen left Adaline with a smile, then pushed open the door to find Zack at his desk with mounds of paperwork before him and coffee so hot it steamed at his elbow.

"I sure hope you're not arresting me," Jensen drawled as he sauntered in. "I'll feel awfully foolish that I walked right into it without even a decent car chase for my trouble."

His older brother didn't laugh, because Zack was far too stern and serious to lighten up long enough to let a single laugh escape him on the job, but he pushed himself back in his chair. His gaze was weary, but sharp. He ran a hand over his face, which Jensen supposed was a tell that his brother had enjoyed a long night out there fighting the bad guys.

Which in the Longhorn Valley tended to be garrulous drunks, fractious teens, and the odd tourist who didn't get that those pretty fields and pastures belonged to someone and that someone likely took trespassing seriously.

"Why would I arrest you?" Zack's dark eyes gleamed. "That's an actual question. I'd sure like to arrest you, Jensen. Confess something."

"If you didn't call me here to issue scurrilous accusations, I'm not going to give you any ammunition."

Jensen got a smirk for that and took it as leave to throw

himself down in one of the chairs before Zack's desk. And then waited, because Zack's phone rang. The sheriff lifted a finger to indicate he needed to take it, and did. Jensen could have tried to interpret his brother's monosyllabic responses to whoever was talking in his ear, but instead, he studied the locally famous oldest Kittredge son, who had confounded everybody by walking away from his birthright.

Not that it was quite that dramatic in reality, but who didn't like a good story? Zack spent a significant amount of his free time helping out at the ranch. But he was the first Kittredge son in generations to actually go out and get another job. Their grandfather had been the oldest son in his generation, and his two younger brothers had stayed on the ranch and worked while they could. One had died fighting overseas. The other had worked until his heart gave out. Their own father had sisters, but neither of them had been particularly interested in spending their life on the ranch. Aunt Carolyn lived up in Laramie. Aunt Jeannie had gone slightly farther afield to Wichita. Yet when the ranch needed extra hands, they turned up with their husbands and the cousins to pitch in.

No one ever really escaped the ranch. Jensen had no interest in escaping the ranch.

But Zack sure was doing his best to try.

"The suspense is killing me," Jensen drawled when Zack finished his call, as lazily as he could. "Am I a father? Did you call me down here to introduce me to some long-lost child I didn't know I had?"

Zack glared at him. "I hope you're not that careless."

"I think we know, big brother, that if I were careless at all, I could fill the bunkhouse with little Jensens. That hasn't happened."

"Not sure I'd brag about that."

Jensen smiled broadly. "Those who can, do. Isn't that the saying?"

Zack definitely smirked again then. Maybe it was even a smile. But that was Zack, always so persecuted by his own sense of responsibility that it inhibited his facial expressions.

Jensen was not similarly encumbered.

Zack got up and walked toward the other door that led out of his office and into the actual meat-and-potatoes part of the station. It was where his deputies had their desks and where they kept the county lockup. Which was only a couple of cells, as Jensen recalled. He had happily never seen the inside of them, despite the carousing he'd done in his time.

"We got a call in the middle of the night," Zack told him as he crossed the floor. "A report of vandalism in process down by the river."

"Amanda's shop okay?" Jensen asked. Because he'd helped renovate that old barn Brady Everett had given Jensen's baby sister before he'd gotten around to marrying her. It was currently a shop that housed a selection of fine goods from all over the valley, people seemed to love it, and he would take it pretty personally if someone had messed it up.

"Down a ways from Amanda's in the youth center Pastor Jim's congregation is fixing up," Zack said with a similarly forbidding look on his face. He had also helped renovate that barn. "By the time we got there, we figured the vandal would be long gone. But he was still there, almost like he wanted to get caught. So we obliged. We brought him in and told him he could make a call, thinking he'd call home, but he asked for you."

"You got me." Jensen laughed. "I'm the leader of a pack of vandals. To be honest, it feels good to confess at last."

"I wanted to call his father," Zack continued, ignoring Jensen and his booming laugh entirely. He'd had a lot of practice. "But I figure if he really wants to talk to you, he can do that first."

Jensen followed his brother out into the main room of the station, smiling a greeting at his brother's deputies as they passed. Then he directed his attention to the cells that lined the back wall.

Where Aidan Hall was standing behind bars. Watching his approach with arms crossed and his face defiantly blank.

Jensen hadn't spent a lot of time thinking about Miss Harriet or her library class. Okay, maybe that wasn't entirely true. He'd thought some about Harriet Barnett. More than some, and he found the whole thing unsettling.

As for the delinquents he'd spoken to on that day, he figured he'd done his duty. And yet it still wasn't a huge surprise that it would be Aidan who tried to rope him into . . . whatever this was.

"Really?" He drawled out the word as he neared the cell. "Did you take me for a father figure, Aidan? Because if you did, I must not have been as clear in my talk as I thought I was."

"What talk?" Zack asked from beside him. "You give talks?"

"Aidan is one of Harriet Barnett's students," Jensen said, pretending he was talking to Aidan when he knew he was filling in the whole room. "About a week and a half ago, or thereabouts, out of the goodness of my heart, I dropped into summer school at the high school to give the kids an inspirational pep talk."

He'd expected that to land hard and leave them all quiet, which was a version of the hilarity his own family had succumbed to at the very notion of Jensen doing such a thing. But he didn't really love it when that was exactly what happened.

"*You?*" asked one of Zack's newer deputies, who was, as of that moment, dead to Jensen.

"Yeah, I'm not actually looking for a heartwarming adoption tale here," Aidan said from behind bars. "I already have a father."

"Not much of one," Jensen retorted.

The kid smirked, unfazed. "Like yours is a prize."

Zack and Jensen exchanged a look and both said, "Fair enough."

Because Donovan Kittredge was a whole thing, it was true.

Jensen crossed his arms and stared down at this teenager in front of him. It didn't take any particular skill with kids to know that Aidan was a whole lot of talk when anyone could tell that really, he was afraid. Jensen could see the fear in his eyes. The tough way he lifted his chin, and yet all those skinny, hungry angles, because the kid was all limbs and attitude.

"Don't I get to talk to him alone?" Aidan demanded of Zack.

"You know my brother isn't a lawyer, don't you?" Zack asked the kid in that words-like-bullets manner of his that seemed to go along with his badge.

"I'm his spiritual advisor." Jensen grinned at Zack's expression. "What? Are you questioning my spirituality?"

"Not your spirituality. Maybe your sanity."

But with a hard look at Aidan, Zack walked away from

the cell. Jensen moved closer and propped himself up by a shoulder against the bars, like this was a social call.

"Okay, kid," he said. "You got me here. What do you want?"

"Nothing from you," Aidan belted right back at him, his eyes flashing.

"Great. Then I'll leave you to your downward spiral."

"No. Wait."

Aidan's hands curled into fists at his sides. He looked young and lost, and despite himself, Jensen felt a pang of sympathy.

Because he knew too much about Aidan's family. The Halls had seemed to decide, several generations back, that every good Western town needed its share of home-grown outlaws. They, by God, had been prepared to provide.

Jensen had gone to school with Aidan's father, and Andy Hall had been a loser even then. As far as Jensen knew, he'd then launched himself into an adulthood that built on those unfortunate beginnings and expanded them exponentially. Jensen had been pretending not to see Andy Hall pretty much since high school graduation, because there was no point getting caught up in that mess. He'd have been happy enough if that mutual unseeing kept right on going. But Jensen personally knew Aidan because, one fine evening a few years back, he'd caught the kid puncturing tires outside the Coyote. Including his.

That he had not called the sheriff's office to handle the situation had only seemed to piss the kid off more. Jensen had secured Aidan in his pickup and then changed his tire. He'd let the bartender know that there were some punctured tires before closing time, so maybe folks could handle it then and there. Then he'd taken Aidan home.

Because everybody knew where the Halls lived. They

had a compound a few miles out of town, in a heavily wooded bend of the river where there was always room for another trailer, or shack, or rusted-out old car next to the rattly old houses that seemed to always be falling down on one side and sporting new construction on the other. Halls seemed to multiply like rabbits, and everybody knew that the good ones left. The ones that stayed mostly liked to consider themselves noble outlaws of one degree or another.

When the truth was, they were mostly just punks.

Aidan swallowed a few times. Jensen waited, because really, it was the least he could do. At the end of the day, he knew perfectly well that being born a Hall was a whole lot harder than being born a Kittredge. It didn't cost him anything to take a minute. And who knew? Maybe he could take a bad Hall and turn him into a good one.

Besides, he was already here.

"I wanted to call Miss Barnett," Aidan told him, no longer meeting Jensen's gaze. "But I didn't want . . . Maybe it would be better if it came from you."

"Me? Kid. Listen. I don't know what kind of trouble you're in. But—"

"Miss Barnett always said that she would help us if she could," Aidan said, his voice fierce even though that look in his eyes was more scared than anything else. "You said you would too."

He had said that, hadn't he? Jensen didn't know what he'd thought that might entail, but it wasn't a jail cell. Or Aidan, if he was honest.

"I already helped you," he pointed out. He decided not to mention the time he hadn't dropped Aidan off at the police station. "I gave you the benefit of my wisdom. I think we can both agree it hasn't served you well."

"I just want you to ask her. For me."

"To help you?" Jensen shook his head. "She's your teacher. If she told you she wanted to help you, then you already know what her answer is going to be. Why not call her directly instead of playing these games?"

When Aidan met his gaze then, there was something bleak there. The kind of bleakness that shouldn't have been anywhere near a sixteen-year-old kid, no matter what his last name was.

"I want Miss Barnett to help me get emancipated," Aidan said, quietly enough that something in Jensen tightened. Quietly enough that there was no way anyone heard but him. "But you've seen her. She's so little. And smart, but smart can be real stupid sometimes. And you know my father."

Jensen ordered himself to unclench his jaw. "I do."

Aidan nodded, a jerky sort of motion. "I figure you must like her if you showed up at our class because she asked you to. When everybody knows classrooms aren't where Jensen Kittredge tends to spend his time."

Jensen lifted a brow. "Are we talking about the Coyote? I was refraining out of respect for your current predicament, but I can stop."

"And if you like her," Aidan said more hurriedly, "then you can help her while she helps me. Because you're the only one around who's bigger than my father. And he already hates you, so really, what's there to lose?"

Jensen took that in. "I don't have the fondest feelings about your dad, I grant you, but mostly I don't think about him at all. Why does he hate me?"

Aidan looked at him with an expression only teenagers could wear. It was that scornful. "Um. Hello. You dated my mom."

Jensen laughed at that. "What? Kid. Get a grip. I don't date."

"Yeah, well, take that up with my dad. Growing up was an endless fight about how she settled for him after things ended with you."

"I never—"

But Jensen stopped. Because it was a little bit of a blur, but now that he thought about it, there had been that one summer where he might have found himself getting cozy with Alana Gaines, back before she'd married Andy Hall. Back when she'd been a whole lot of fun at a party and he'd been twenty and too drunk on hormones and beer to understand where that kind of desperate fun tended to lead.

"Way I figure it," the kid said, clearly seeing Jensen's recollection all over his face, "you owe me."

"Do I now. How does that work, exactly?"

Aidan shrugged, another sharp motion of his bony limbs. "Because you didn't mess around with my mom and get her knocked up. Which means my dad did."

Ouch.

Jensen was not prepared for this.

He told himself a teenage boy couldn't be any worse than a forest fire. And therefore to sack up. "I haven't seen your mom in a long time. But I liked her. She was a good woman." He didn't actually know if that was true, but the things he remembered about Alana probably weren't things her son wanted to hear. Not that they were particularly racy, but still. "I'm sorry she hasn't been happier."

"Join the club," Aidan tossed back at him. "No one's seen her in, like, years. And if she were that good of a woman, she probably would have stayed home. But none of that matters. I need Miss Barnett to do her thing. Will you help me make that happen?"

Jensen wanted, badly, to shrug it off and walk away.

All those alarms in him, installed to keep him from getting tangled up with people and all their needs because he already knew how that ended, were going wild. He wanted to tell the kid that he was sympathetic but that none of this was his problem. All of that was true.

But for some reason, Jensen didn't do any of that.

"I'll talk to her," he heard himself say.

And he was trying to come up with a single good reason why he would say such a thing as he turned and headed back to his brother's office.

"What's all that about?" Zack asked, eyeing Jensen in that flinty way of his, back behind his desk and looking harassed. "Since when do you have some relationship with Aidan Hall? Or any Hall, for that matter?"

"I thought we covered this," Jensen said with a grin. "It's a spiritual thing."

"Jensen."

He shrugged. "I don't know what to tell you, Zack. The poor kid was born a Hall. If he wants some help with that problem, who am I to deny him? We were blessed in comparison."

But his brother knew him. "That's very noble, Jensen. I'm touched. But let me remind you who you are. You're not Pastor Jim, you're Jensen Kittredge. I've never known you to help anyone."

"Just the other day, I carried all of Marisol Dewitt's groceries to her car," Jensen protested. "Sure, she may have confused me for a bag boy, but I didn't correct her. I'm basically a one-man charity."

"You're a lot of things. But not that."

Jensen sighed. Theatrically. "I'm forced to point out that I literally jump out of planes to help put out fires, thereby saving a whole lot of lives. More lives than you, big brother. I know that's hard to swallow. Is it a competition?"

"I'm not talking about the firefighting. Everyone knows you can take off and be heroic out there." Zack shook his head. "I'm talking about our community. *This* town. Where you don't play the hero because you're too busy pretending you're not very bright."

"Maybe, Zack, this really is living up to my potential, after all." Jensen's smile had a little bit of an edge now. "Just like I told Mom in the sixth grade."

"Then, and now, you like to hide the fact that you're brilliant with numbers, magic when it comes to business, and not nearly as happy-go-lucky as you pretend." Zack let out a sound that he would probably claim was a laugh, though it was harsh to Jensen's ears. "Not even remotely."

But that was getting a little too close to the things Jensen didn't like talking about. And his penance was his problem, no one else's.

"I don't know what you're talking about," Jensen replied lightly. "I'm a big old dumb jock who was lucky enough to be born into a thriving family business. Saves me having to convince anyone else to hire me, doesn't it? I get by on my looks and winning personality. I'm living down to low expectations—ask anybody."

"You spend your whole life wearing a mask in this town. Maybe you take that mask off while diving out of planes, I don't know."

"Easy there, Zack." He waited until he could be sure that edge was out of his voice. "I don't think you want to start throwing stones from that glass house of yours."

His brother acknowledged that with a rueful expression. "But suddenly Aidan Hall has a claim on your heretofore unknown charitable impulses?"

"I told you. He's one of Harriet Barnett's delinquents."

"And about that," Zack said. In a tone Jensen definitely did not like. "You're not going there."

"I'm not?" Jensen blinked. "Where do you think I'm going?"

Zack actually stood up from his desk then, dramatically, as if they'd suddenly switched their long-held familial roles. It was disconcerting. As was the frown on Zack's face.

"Harriet Barnett is a nice lady," Zack told him. Harshly. "She's passionate about her job and about those kids, and she's done more in that high school library than her predecessor did in twenty years."

"Why are you telling me this? Did I take her name in vain?"

His brother's gaze was hard. "Don't mess around with her, Jensen."

"Mess around with her?" He shook his head like it was muddled. It should have been entirely an act, yet it wasn't. His heart was kicking at him way too fast. "I'm sorry. Am I having a stroke or are you warning me off the high school librarian cat lady?"

"She's not your type," Zack belted out at him. "She's *sweet*."

Jensen told himself that it was nice to know what his brother actually thought about him.

Except for the part where it was nice.

"I think you're taking the sheriff thing a little too far," he said, forcing himself to sound lazy and amused, because that would annoy Zack the most. And he really, really wanted to annoy Zack right about now. "The good women of Cold River don't need to be protected from me, Sheriff. I think you know that more often than not, I'm the one who needs protection from them."

"Because this is what you do. You mess around."

Jensen chose to ignore that. "Second, I don't think you know Harriet. Because if you did, I don't think *sweet* is the word you would use to describe her."

"Jensen."

"*Zack*." He eyed his older brother. The closest brother to him in age and the closest brother to him, period. Their younger siblings didn't remember the things the two of them did. They'd been too young. Jensen had always considered them a team, but this did not feel like teamwork. "Do you have a thing for the librarian?"

And he didn't have time to question why he didn't much like how that notion sat in him, because Zack snorted.

"No, I don't. Because I don't live my life with my pants down."

"My pants are not down," Jensen said calmly. "You're looking right at them. The real question is, why are yours in a bunch?"

"Why do you know Harriet at all?" Zack demanded. "How is she on your radar? That's what I don't understand. Why is she showing up at the ranch? Why are you giving *talks* in her library?"

"It's a nefarious sex scheme, actually. You caught me. It's this kink we have where she shows up to hang out with our grandparents and talk about charitable endeavors with at-risk kids. Super hot."

The rest of his conversation with his brother was brief.

And merrily profane.

Jensen found himself grinning as he walked back out into the summer morning. Because Zack, who knew him a little too well, should have known that telling Jensen not to do something—*ordering him* not to do it, in fact—was a fantastic way to make certain that thing was exactly what he was going to do.

And hard.

He told himself that thwarting his brother was why he was practically whistling as he headed for the high school.

Because what else could it possibly be?

6

During the school year, Harriet had her midmorning coffee break in the teachers' lounge. She subjected herself to microwaved water—like an animal, essentially—but she made do with the reheated water because that was more appealing than attempting to claim the ancient coffeepot for a moment and suffer the coffee-tainted hot water it produced. She'd tried. During the summer, however, with diminished staff and far fewer students, she indulged herself. She walked over to Cold River Coffee and treated herself to artisan coffee to enjoy with her friend and mentor, Martina Patrick.

Martina, who had been at the school for as long as anyone seemed to be able to remember, did not normally relax her standards enough to accept even a summer school–specific dereliction of duty. The walk to Cold River Coffee and back, plus a decent chat, often pressed up against the boundaries of Harriet's free time.

But Martina and Harriet had become fast friends. Martina might have been old enough to be Harriet's mother—or perhaps a cherished great-aunt—but they had a number of similarities. They were both independent women in a world that persisted in finding that state curious, if not actively sad. They both greatly enjoyed their own company, did not suffer fools, and were content with their singlehood.

And yes, Harriet could admit that they shared a sartorial aesthetic as well. If preferring practical, no-nonsense attire was an aesthetic instead of simple good sense.

Today they sat at Martina's desk in the front office, happily empty of anyone else on this sunny day. Martina waved the hand that wasn't holding her drink in a carefree manner she only showed Harriet. *Because,* she had told Harriet not long after Harriet had started at the school, *I am a dreadful gorgon in entirely too many imaginations, and it's best if I stay that way. It makes my job easier.*

"Ever since I saw the term *bluestocking* in a book when I was young, it was my aspiration," Martina was saying breezily. "It seemed far more interesting than taking up with questionable young men who might insist on discussing things that bored me."

Harriet agreed. Wholeheartedly. "I never understood why it wasn't presented as the obvious better choice. The boys I grew up with were sticky, incomprehensible, and deficient in every way next to a good book. Or even a passable book, for that matter."

"They never really change, do they?" Martina asked with a laugh.

"Still," Harriet said, bringing the conversation back to the topic at hand, "poor Amy does not have the makings of a proper bluestocking. And would never have the slightest desire to become one, anyway. It's best all around that she finds herself the new husband she seems to think she needs."

Martina made a huffing sound. And Harriet did not have to ask her friend what it meant. She already knew. Martina took a dim view of the complicated romantic life of Amy Dougherty, one of the women who worked in the front office with her. Amy's husband had left her with their three kids the previous year, and Amy had been on a mission to replace him ever since. She had shared the details of this mission with Martina, in detail, when they'd run into each other at the garden store last evening.

"I've never understood women who keep trying out these new and different models." Martina blew on her hot drink. "Maybe it isn't a matter of one model being superior to the last. Maybe it's the idea that one requires a man at all that needs reassessing."

Harriet murmured her agreement, but wondered why she couldn't get past that same little *hitch* inside her that seemed to happen every time this topic came up these days. There shouldn't have been any hitching. She had always agreed implicitly and explicitly with her friend and mentor.

She still did, she told herself firmly.

But ever since Jensen Kittredge's appearance in her library, she found it more difficult than it ought to have been to simply agree—and feel it.

Because you don't agree, a voice inside her pointed out. *There are definitely better models. There is one model, in particular, that you like all too well.*

That was foolish. And Harriet was tired of being foolish. There had been far too much of that lately and all of it Jensen Kittredge related. It felt like a betrayal.

The phone rang, which felt like a reprieve, and Harriet found herself irritated about that too. She was out of sorts, that was all. The more distance she got from her Jensen Kittredge moment, the more she found herself astonished that he was still clattering around inside her head. Fine, he was remarkably attractive. That wasn't in dispute. But why did that have to mean that she spent so much time . . . thinking about him? Not even *him,* really. Because it wasn't as if she knew anything about him.

Oh, but you do, that same voice retorted. *You heard what he said to your students. And more, what they did after he left.*

It wasn't as if her lost students had suddenly found themselves, like some movie montage scene. They hadn't come back to their next library class altered to near unrecognizable heights of academic achievement. But they did come back. And when they did, they paid a little more attention than they had before. And by the end of that week, Harriet heard a few of the other teachers comment on how they seemed easier to engage with. A little less confrontational. A little better at turning in their assignments.

Every little bit helped. Jensen might not have lit fires under them, but he'd done a lot more than most people bothered to do for kids too easily dismissed as unsolvable problems. He'd done well.

And surely, Harriet thought now, this strange kicking thing inside her would go away soon. She would return to her usual self. She would wax rhapsodic about how little she needed to couple herself off as everybody else seemed to do, and there would be no *hitching* within. Because that had been true before Jensen Kittredge, and it would be true after him too.

Not, of course, that she'd been running around town imagining that she would be *coupling* or anything else with the likes of Jensen Kittredge. It was more that, having met him, she wasn't quite so cavalier about her own solitary state. She simply hadn't known until she'd met him that she had those urges inside her. That they could simply *appear* out of nowhere and without warning. That it was a physical reaction, a reflex, like a sneeze.

Maybe if she thought about it like a sneeze, she would stop thinking about it.

Harriet scowled at the door and thought very hard about sneezing. Martina talked on the phone beside her. And for a dizzy little moment, Harriet thought that her imagination was working overtime and she was not sneezing, but hallucinating.

It therefore took longer than it should have to recognize that, no, she hadn't lapsed into a daydream, right there in Cold River High's front office. She was not, in fact, hallucinating. No one had dosed her coffee—a fear she often had when it was always actually just caffeine.

She was not having some kind of episode.

Jensen Kittredge really was in the doorway.

Her heart did something that should have had medical repercussions in her chest. For a brief moment, she felt distinctly as if she'd been plugged into an electrical socket. Nothing else, surely, could have moved through her body like that. An intense, buzzing sort of wave of heat.

She could not for the life of her imagine what expression might be on her face.

Especially when Jensen treated her to a long, slow grin in return.

"Mr. Kittredge," came Martina's voice, cool and imperious, and that, too, was a relief. "My eyes must be deceiving me. Surely you are not standing in my office of your own accord. Again."

"Good morning, Miss Patrick," Jensen rumbled, and thumbed his Stetson in Martina's direction. Then his eyes—hazel, Harriet told herself crossly, they were only *hazel* and had nothing to do with any *wolves*—cut to her. "Miss Harriet."

"What is this renewed interest in high school?" Martina

asked briskly, clearly unaffected by the man's eyes, no matter what their color. "I believe your attendance record this month puts the entirety of your senior year to shame."

"I've always been a late bloomer," Jensen replied easily.

Harriet pulled herself together, appalled that it had taken this long. And that it had been so *public*. She set her coffee down decisively. "Have you come to sign up to do another round with my students?"

Martina made another huffing sound. Needless to say, her friend had not understood why Harriet had chosen the Kittredge brother least likely to inspire anyone, in Martina's opinion. *Why not the sheriff?* she'd asked. *Surely he would be anybody's first choice. Barring that, the two younger ones, who have some renown for their horse training. Why choose the clown?*

With Jensen filling up a doorway in front of her in all his T-shirted, tight-jeaned glory, Harriet could admit to herself that she had not particularly cared for her friend's line of questioning. As if the Kittredge family were a selection of produce and a person could pick them out of a Bar K bin.

Though that was not really what she hadn't cared for. It was more that she'd called Jensen a clown. Harriet had *hitched* all over that one.

Privately.

"As delighted as I might be that you've finally found your way to school, I should caution you." Martina sounded stern. "We do not let individuals roam unfettered through our halls. Even in the summer."

Harriet recognized that as the tone Martina used with overexcited students. And she understood how difficult it was to meet a child, have them as a student, and then accept that they grew up into adults. It was always tempting to remember the child. But Jensen wasn't a recent graduate. And surely, even her committed spinster friend had to notice that whatever else he was, he was a fully grown man.

She wisely said none of that.

"I would never dream of keeping myself unfettered, ma'am," Jensen said in that rumbly, amused way of his. "Fetter me up."

"I appreciate your permission." Martina gazed at him as if he were a great disappointment. "But what I mean is that you require a purpose to be here. Do you have a purpose, Mr. Kittredge?"

"That sounds like a loaded question, Miss Patrick."

Harriet found herself moving before she knew she intended to do any such thing. She swept out from behind Martina's desk, then pushed through the swinging half doors to the other side of the counter that was meant to keep students and staff separated.

"I'll escort you out, Mr. Kittredge," she said briskly. "We can determine whether or not you need a hall pass while we walk."

Then she was in front of him and reaching out, the way she might have done if he were a confused young person. When he was older than she was and she doubted he was ever very confused. But she'd already committed. So she took his arm and made as if to steer him around to face the door.

Obviously, he didn't move an inch. Because he appeared to be constructed entirely of stone. And the more she thought that—*stone*—the more she seemed to melt.

He was so much bigger than she was that it was silly,

really, that she'd even tried to move him herself, and that was before she'd encountered the stone factor. The heavy, roped muscles in his forearm made her want to do something unforgivable, like giggle.

But *giggly* wasn't what she felt when, after a beat, he allowed her to propel him around so he was facing the hallway again.

What was it about a man as big and strong as Jensen allowing her to steer him in a particular direction? Why did it make her feel *lit up* and inside out at once? So much so that she was terribly afraid Martina could *see* what was happening inside of her.

Harriet was distantly shocked that she hadn't expired on the spot, because surely all this *giggling* and *lighting up* and *melting* couldn't be healthy.

"I never did trouble much with hall passes," Jensen told her as he continued to allow her to tug him toward the hallway. And his *voice*. That glinting look in his eyes. Even that Stetson that shouldn't have affected her one way or the other . . .

Really, it was an outrage that she had reached the advanced age of thirty-one years un-assaulted by any stray, unwelcome attractions. Only to stumble over Jensen Kittredge and make up for lost time. With a vengeance.

Harriet couldn't say she thought highly of the experience.

As she marched away from the office door, she realized that she was still holding on to him. He was still *letting her* hold on to him, that was, gazing down on her with a faintly bemused expression as she towed him along.

She dropped his arm immediately.

"As it turns out," she said as briskly as she could, so briskly that it rebounded off the glossy, squeaky floor and came back at her, "I was planning to contact you."

"I don't usually go out on dates. I told you that already. But if you asked, I might make an exception."

"Why do you do that?" Harriet only realized she'd stopped walking—out there in the hallway dressed up in Cold River High's colors, not far from the trophy case that featured him—when she found her hands on her hips. And her neck tilted back so she could glare directly into his face.

Well. Not directly. She was far too short for that.

"Do what?" he asked lazily.

"That. Everything is not a sexual innuendo, Jensen. If you think it is, you may need professional help."

He looked intrigued. "Exactly what kind of professionals do you have in mind?"

"Some men make everything sexual as a kind of weapon," Harriet carried on in the same brisk tone. She suspected that was more for her benefit than his, since he seemed wholly unaffected, yet on she went. "They specifically do it to undermine women. I don't get the impression that's what you're doing."

"Damned with faint praise."

"You seem far too secure for that kind of thing. That means you're either deflecting, or you really . . ."

But she stopped herself. Because that was delusional, surely.

He looked even more intrigued then. And there was a heat behind it. "Or I really . . . what?"

"In any event," she continued, unaccountably feeling breathless, "I assume you're here to talk about the students. To follow up."

"Sure. The kids. It's been keeping me up at night."

Harriet masterfully restrained herself from making a comment about what she imagined was far more likely to have kept him awake. On any given night. "You were a big success, I think. They might not have been effusive while you were there, but all of them have shown at least some improvement."

"Well, I'm just tickled to hear that."

She frowned at him, Martina's *clown* comment dancing in her head. "Everything doesn't have to be a joke."

"Miss Harriet," he said, those eyes of his glinting intently, "I'm beginning to suspect you don't take me seriously."

"Do you take yourself seriously?" she demanded, because she was melting and having delusions, and he was making smart remarks. It hardly seemed fair. "It has to start at home, Jensen."

She could have sworn that he reacted to that. But whatever she thought she saw on his face, a quick flash, it was gone in the next moment.

"Aidan Hall requests your help," he said, his voice suddenly gone gruff. And whatever color his eyes were, they were cooler now. *You did that,* she told herself. "He's in the county lockup."

Harriet caught herself as she began to gape at him in astonishment. She snapped her mouth shut. She replayed his words in her head and tried to shake off her fixation on his eyes. "What do you mean?"

"What I said. He got rounded up in the middle of the night and brought in on a vandalism charge."

"Why is he still there? Surely one of his parents—"

But she didn't finish her thought.

"Yeah." Jensen's gaze seemed particularly enigmatic. Harriet told herself it was the unflattering lighting in the hallway. "He didn't call his parents. He asked my brother to call me."

"What exactly is your relationship with him?" Harriet

demanded. "Whatever his reasons, he asked you to come speak to the class. And now you're the one he calls when he's in trouble?" A suspicion dawned. "You're not . . . Do you have—ah—a *closer* relationship with him than you've made clear?"

Jensen was silent. And very still.

Harriet thought once more of *stone*. Then melted all over again.

He shook his head as if he were very, very sad. She did not believe he was even remotely sad. In fact, she would have said he was a whole lot closer to angry—but no story she'd ever heard about Jensen Kittredge allowed for any temper on his part. He was always laughing. Always entertained or entertaining. Never plain old good and mad.

That felt like a critical piece of evidence, though Harriet had no idea what mystery she thought she was trying to solve.

"Are you suggesting what I think you're suggesting?" he asked. Almost sounding apologetic, but there was that gleaming thing in his eyes.

Harriet tilted up her chin. "I'm not suggesting anything. I asked you a reasonable question."

"No," Jensen rumbled at her, and that was a whole lot closer to temper than anything she'd seen so far. Something in her hummed a little. "He's not my kid. I don't have any kids, Harriet. If I did, they wouldn't be a secret. And I certainly wouldn't leave them to the tender mercies of Andy Hall. Exactly what kind of a loser do you think I am?"

Her mouth had gone dry. She tried to swallow, anyway, then gave up.

"I don't think you're . . . anything." Well. That was a

lie. But necessary. She forged on. "What I'm wondering is how you found yourself tangled up in the life of a troubled sixteen-year-old."

"You and me both." Jensen knocked back his hat and rubbed his other hand over his hair. For a moment, he almost looked like he was contemplating a frown, but it didn't materialize. "He told me that he wants to be emancipated. Legally. He wants you to handle it, and he wants me to help."

Harriet opened her mouth. Then shut it.

"To be honest, that he's been plotting it all out means everything's right with the world," Jensen continued, sounding lazier by the syllable. "He's a Hall. There are dumb Halls, and there are crazy-smart Halls, but one thing they all have in common is that they're plotting something. Always."

"What is this ridiculous Hall family nonsense?" Harriet made a very inelegant sound that was far too close to a snort. "Surely you don't mean to suggest that an attention-seeking high school boy is secretly a criminal mastermind of some kind?"

"The Hall family has a colorful history in the Longhorn Valley," Jensen informed her, with the hint of a smile in the corner of his mouth. He wasn't leaning against anything, out there in the hall, but somehow it seemed like he were lounging, anyway. "They've taken it upon themselves to really inhabit the outlaw space of any good Old West town. It's a public service, really."

Harriet sighed. "When I moved here, I took my car to Wyatt Hall. He runs that little garage on the other side of the football field."

"I know Wyatt."

"He could not have been more aboveboard and honest."

"Sure. Now." Jensen shrugged, which was a bit of a pageant with shoulders like his. "Just because one or two of them go legit doesn't mean that the rest of them aren't out there breaking into your house, stealing your car, and engaging in far more unsavory pursuits of an evening."

"Are you saying that Aidan did these things?"

"I know he got caught vandalizing a church. Whether you think that's unsavory or not really comes down to perspective, I'm guessing."

"Did you bail him out? Out of the goodness of your heart?"

Jensen looked as if she'd said something amusing. "I think Zack was waiting on Andy drying out. It usually takes him until evening. Aidan might not have called his dad, Harriet, but I'm pretty sure Zack did. Or will."

Harriet paused for a moment. She tried to catch up with what she was being told without all that *Jensen* muddying it up. "Did he really say emancipation?"

"He did."

She studied him, adjusting her glasses as she did. "And what makes you think you can help?"

"Again, this wasn't my idea. But I'm pretty sure he wants your brain and my brawn."

That, of course, practically forced her to admire said brawn. She forced herself to look away from his biceps. To find his face again. "Nothing that you're saying to me right now makes sense."

"That's what happens," Jensen drawled. "Lie down with Halls, stand up with regrets."

She made an impatient sound. "That is not a saying. You just made that up. You can't possibly walk around the town with *sayings* about other families."

Jensen only shrugged. "Welcome to Cold River, darlin'."

Harriet opted not to point out, again, that she had already lived here for three years. She glanced at her watch instead. "Very well. I get off at 2:45. I can meet you then."

"Do we really need a meeting? Can't you just go . . . emancipate him?"

"He isn't talking about emancipating himself from a jail cell, Jensen," Harriet said. With a little bit of heat. "He's talking about removing himself from his father's custody, permanently. We were discussing it in class last week. I thought Aidan wanted to write a paper on it. It never occurred to me his interest might be personal."

She wondered now if it should have. Had she missed clues that could have kept Aidan out of jail?

"Plots within plots," Jensen was saying. Clearly not concerned about a youth in peril. "He comes by it naturally."

Harriet focused on him. "If you're not secretly his father—"

Those wolf eyes flashed. "I'm not."

"Then what is the nature of your relationship with Aidan? And don't tell me you don't know. I think you do."

"I've never had a *relationship* with Aidan." Jensen made a low sound of impatience. "He's been mouthy for years. Turns out, maybe his mother talked a little bit too much about her glory days. I can't control what other people say about their memories of me, Harriet, much as I might like to."

"You had a relationship with his mother?"

She remembered, suddenly, what Aidan had said the day Jensen had come to the library. *Everybody knows Jensen Kittredge. The way I hear it, he dated pretty much every single one of our mothers.* Harriet had assumed he was just being revolting in that sixteen-year-old manner. Another clue missed.

"I knew his mother," Jensen corrected her with a certain rumbly intent. "One summer, we went to a lot of the same parties. If she remembered it as anything more than that—again, not something I can control."

"I don't understand why he chose you as his role model, then."

"I'm not an expert on teen boys," Jensen said, amusement lighting up his gaze again. "But I'm pretty sure he was yanking your chain."

Harriet did not laugh. "Or yours."

Jensen spread his hands out before him. "Either way, I think my role as messenger is done here."

"I will be available after school today," Harriet told him tartly. "Shall we say 2:45 at Cold River Coffee? We can walk to the police station together."

"Can we?" Jensen let out that laugh of his. "I can't wait to tell all my friends that our first date involves getting a delinquent out of jail."

"I don't find these deflections of yours amusing," Harriet told him crisply. "Not when they're at my expense. 2:45, Jensen. I'll see you then."

Then she marched off, because her class started in five minutes. And also because she needed to sort through everything he'd told her. About Aidan. And about him, obliquely.

She went back into the front office to grab the remains of her coffee, because she had no trouble warming that up in the microwave. Martina looked up from her computer as Harriet walked in, a look of baffled astonishment on her face.

"What was he doing here?" she asked as if she'd seen actual barbarians at the gate. "Jensen Kittredge darkening the doors of Cold River High not once in the summer but twice?"

"He was surprisingly good with the students," Harriet said. "Really."

Because what else could she say?

Martina let out a *tut*. "I would normally say that you really do want to be careful with the likes of Jensen. All those Kittredge boys were trouble, but he was always the worst. And still is." She smiled, already returning her attention to her computer screen. "But I don't imagine you need to worry."

For some reason, that didn't sit well with Harriet. She could see that it was meant as a compliment, but that didn't make it any better.

"What do you mean?" she asked against her better judgment.

When she already knew very well what her friend meant.

Martina laughed. "Let's just say that, normally, if there is a weakness of moral fiber to be found within a fifty-mile radius, Jensen will hone in on it like a homing missile. It appears all he needs to do is smile and women who should know better collapse before him. It happened when he was little more than a boy, and it's only gotten worse since."

"I'm not one for collapsing, Martina," Harriet said stiffly, working overtime not to identify the sensation that moved in her then.

But she knew what it was. It was hurt.

Then her friend made it worse. "You should count yourself lucky that you're safe."

"Safe?" Harriet queried, though she knew perfectly well that she didn't want to comprehend what her friend meant.

She really, really didn't.

"Safe as houses," Martina said merrily as if the topic

hardly bore discussion. "He would never look twice at you, my dear, and even if he did, you're . . . well, you're *you*. You're not susceptible to such nonsense. If you were any other teacher here and he came prowling around, there's no doubt you'd be a goner at a single glance."

"Perish the thought."

But maybe, Harriet found herself thinking when she left the office—with a mix of affront and something a lot more like a bigger helping of that same hurt—she did not actually want to perish that thought. Or any other thoughts concerning Jensen.

Maybe, just maybe, *she* would like to be the one to decide whether or not she was at risk of finding herself a goner at a glance.

And more, if she decided to risk it because his eyes were nothing so boring as *hazel* and never could be, how to go about doing it right.

7

At precisely 2:45 that afternoon, Harriet swept inside Cold River Coffee, already regretting that she had agreed to do this.

Had less *agreed to it* and had more demanded it happen, really. Whatever happened here, she had no one to blame but herself.

What could possibly happen? a caustic voice that was not unlike Martina's asked. *You will no doubt make a fool of yourself. He won't notice.*

But that was the pep talk Harriet needed. She'd stopped worrying about whether or not she looked foolish to others a long, long time ago. If that was the only thing she had to worry about, she would count that as not worrying at all.

Inside, the cozy coffee shop was crowded and noisy. It was tempting to imagine that was simply because it was summertime, but Harriet knew better. Cold River Coffee was always full. More often than not, like today, there was a long line in front of the counter that sat beneath the big chalkboard with the changing menu items carefully written out. That it was usually busy had surprised her when she'd moved here, because she'd imagined the community would be far too nine-to-five to spend a lot of time having hot drinks and nibbles, but the coffee shop operated as a community hub. A group of mostly white-haired ladies were gathered around one of the tables, cackling while they knitted. A group of weathered-looking, older men sat at a different table, talking in low voices. There were cowboys, new mothers with tiny babies, shouting children, and teenagers clustered together over their cell phones.

All of whom, without needing a second glance, she could identify on sight. More evidence she wasn't actually new here.

And yet, just as she remembered from three years ago, all Jensen Kittredge had to do was laugh and the bustle of the shop faded away.

Harriet ordered herself to stop mooning about like one of the teenage girls at that table. She gathered herself together, skirted the end of the long line, and started marching toward him.

Jensen looked like he'd been there awhile. He was kicked back on the sofa along the far wall, his boots propped up on the table before him like this was his living room. His Stetson sat next to him on the arm of the sofa, he had one arm splayed out along the back, and he looked as if it was possible he didn't actually possess a spine, so committed was he to his boneless lounging. When he laughed, he not only captured the attention of every person in the coffeehouse, he tossed his head back and gave the impression of laughing with his whole body—even though the rest of him didn't seem to move.

It was like a light shone upon him from a great height, when Harriet knew very well that there were no spotlights in Cold River Coffee. That was just Jensen.

And it took her far longer than it should have to process the information that he was not alone. There was a woman on the far end of the couch, laughing with him.

It took her another breath or two to further recognize that it was his sister.

One more piece of information that should not have mattered to her at all, and yet seemed to land with a little too much weight, right there against her solar plexus.

Harriet was so busy lecturing herself on all the things she shouldn't feel that she walked a bit faster than necessary. So that—she realized too late, and tragically—she was essentially charging across the coffee shop floor. Directly at Jensen.

In full view of half the town.

Because it was only when she stopped abruptly, about a foot away from the coffee table, that Harriet comprehended that she was once again inadvertently making a spectacle of herself. Right away, no waiting. She didn't know what it was about Jensen Kittredge that made her not only act so unlike herself but, worse, *feel* so many things while she did it.

Making a spectacle of herself was nothing new, certainly. But it had been a long while since her oddness had made her feel . . . an alarming shade of red.

Once again, she was pleased that while she might feel bright with shame, she knew she was lucky enough to have her mother's sturdy disposition, no matter her intellectual pursuits. It came with strong hands, a genetic intolerance for nonsense, and, happily enough, cheeks that stalwartly refused to go red.

Though Harriet questioned whether or not it mattered what color her cheeks were when she could feel herself incinerating.

All Jensen did was look at her, one lazy brow rising.

And mildly, at that. He didn't sit up straighter. He didn't move his feet from the coffee table. Not Jensen.

But then, having women charge him from across crowded rooms was likely a common occurrence for him.

He regarded her with those wolf eyes, and Harriet was ashamed to admit that she wanted the floor to open up beneath her and swallow her whole. Better that than her other, sharper urge then, which was to tip herself forward and fling herself in his direction.

Obviously, she did no such thing.

Still, she felt a bit as if she were standing on the edge of a cliff, and she couldn't tell if she was afraid of heights—or if what she was really afraid of was that she might launch herself off the side of it.

She reminded herself that she was supposed to be immune to such nonsense. Why wasn't she?

"Harriet." Jensen said her name as if it were, in and of itself, a greeting. It was her tragedy that she thought she heard *layers* in that. When it was just her name. "I assume you remember my sister."

"So nice to see you again," Amanda said from her end of the couch with a certain gleam in her eyes that made Harriet burn a little brighter. Internally, happily.

"Amanda. A pleasure." She cut her gaze to Jensen. "Are you ready to go to the police station?"

This time, it was Amanda who laughed loud enough to turn heads. "What? The police station? What are you doing?"

"Visiting Zack," Jensen lied easily. "Your brother. Maybe you missed the fact that he's the Longhorn Valley sheriff. He only mentions it two thousand times an hour at any given family function."

Harriet took note of the fact that Jensen clearly didn't

want to tell Amanda the situation. She told herself not to wonder why that was. If her experience of the Kittredges at their Sunday dinner was any guide, it was possible he simply didn't want that many cooks in his kitchen. She understood completely. As an only child, she didn't want that, either. Sibling relationships were another thing she'd never really understood.

But she couldn't control the little thrill that went through her, because whatever his reasons, she'd certainly never been anybody's *secret* before. She felt pleasantly illicit.

"You thought what Zack really needed was a librarian?" Amanda asked her brother.

"It's my opinion that everybody needs a librarian," Harriet said briskly, because she was not one to stand idly by while her life's work was maligned, however good-heartedly. "I'm happy to recommend reading lists to you too, Amanda. Just say the word."

Amanda blinked. "I will keep that in mind. Thank you."

"I will curate any lists to your preferences, naturally." Harriet smiled. "I reject canons."

"No one likes a cannon," Jensen drawled. "So loud and impolite."

Harriet frowned at him but for once did not take the bait. She somehow knew that Jensen knew the difference between a contested list of supposedly great literature and heavy artillery.

Amanda stood up from the couch, looking at her brother with an expression Harriet couldn't decipher. "Go right ahead and be mysterious. You know I'll get the truth eventually."

Jensen only smiled.

"Between you and me, Harriet," Amanda said, turning away from her brother, "I really am hoping that you've come to turn Jensen in."

"Turn me in for what?" Jensen protested, though he was laughing. "Being awesome?"

"Does that come with a jail sentence?" Amanda retorted, wrinkling up her nose. "Don't answer that, unless the answer is yes. Anyway, I have to get back to the shop. Have fun playing cops and robbers, you two."

Then she swept away, leaving Harriet alone. With Jensen. Again.

She reminded herself that they were not actually alone. Not by any measure. She knew full well that there was an entire coffee shop arrayed behind her, but oddly enough, it didn't feel like it.

Not when all Jensen's considerable attention lit on her.

"Are you going to hover there?" He looked amused at the notion. "Or are you going to sit down?"

"I'm going to do neither," Harriet retorted. "I'm going to the police station. As discussed."

When Jensen only considered her for a moment or two, she fought valiantly to conceal her impatience. Yes, impatience. That's exactly what it was.

She pulled herself up to her full height, which was not impressive. But she liked to pretend it was. "You may like to think of Aidan Hall as a cog in a wheel of some generational outlaw clan. That's your choice. Really, he's a sixteen-year-old kid who needs help. And I don't intend to lounge about in a coffeehouse when I could be trying to do what I can."

Harriet had no idea why she felt a rush of emotion as she said that, but she didn't stick around to analyze it. She wheeled around, then stormed back across the coffeehouse, making yet another scene. This time, deliberately. But it couldn't be helped.

And she didn't look behind her.

Once she hit the street, she wove her way in between the groups of tourists who always seemed to cluster on the sidewalk, then set off at a brisk pace down Main Street.

She had reached Capricorn Books—purveyors of both new and used books who were perfectly happy to let customers sit cross-legged on the floor for hours on a given Saturday, as Harriet had discovered to her pleasure—when she became aware there was someone at her side.

Jensen.

Of course, Jensen. Who else did she imagine might be chasing after her? Then again, she hadn't really imagined *he* would chase after her. She wasn't the sort of woman men chased after. Or so she assumed, as it had never happened before.

"How do you move so quietly when you're so big?" she asked him, perhaps a little bit crossly. "Like a cat."

"I'm not like a cat at all. Cats are very small. And devious."

"Cats are complicated," she shot back. "So perhaps you're not wrong to deny the similarity."

"Ouch."

There was laughter in his tone, but she couldn't really focus on that, because suddenly his hand was on her elbow. His *hand* was on the bare skin below her sleeve. His *hand*. And he was drawing her to stop. Then tugging her out of the foot traffic so they could stand there together. Right there on Main Street, where everyone Harriet had ever met in Colorado was likely to walk past.

People would see her standing here with Jensen Kittredge . . . and once again, her stomach seemed to flip over and then fall, because she didn't know how she felt about that. Only that she *felt*.

"Have I done something to offend you?" Jensen asked.

And though he was still smiling, his hat shoved back on his head, she thought the expression in those fierce golden eyes was serious.

More serious than she would have imagined he could be, if she were honest.

"No," was all she could manage to say.

Only partly because his hand was still wrapped around her arm.

Jensen's smile widened. It didn't reach his eyes. "Because normally when a woman goes to so much trouble to let me know she thinks I'm simple, it's because one of two things have happened. Either she slept with me and expected another bite at that apple, or she hasn't slept with me yet and is feeling a little salty about it. I know you and I haven't slept together. So."

Harriet was so horrified by that she *vibrated,* and pulled her arm from his grip. "I'm not a condiment."

And as she watched, his gaze lit up again.

She couldn't let herself focus on that. "I'm not salty. And I didn't mean to insult you. I was defending cats."

"You were defending cats," he repeated.

She was familiar with that tone. What was new was the look of amusement on his face while he did it.

"I like cats," she said.

"I've heard that about you."

Harriet let out an exasperated sigh. "Because if a man lives alone with a pet, it's unremarkable. But if a woman does the same, well, then. We'd better rush to come up with ways to describe her and make it clear to everyone she's a figure of scorn and pity."

"I don't think anyone who's ever met you could possibly scorn or pity you, Miss Harriet."

"Spinster. On the shelf. Cat lady. There are no equal terms for men."

Jensen was leaning again. He had one of those broad shoulders hiked up against the nearest brick building and that grin on his face that was starting to upset Harriet's sense of balance. "Fair enough. But for the record, you don't have to defend cats from me. I like cats."

"Oh."

And she didn't know what happened to her, but Harriet suddenly lost her train of thought. Because she was besieged by an entirely too-vivid image of Jensen Kittredge cuddling a cat. Worse, a kitten. Worse still, one of hers.

Harriet had never felt particularly moved by the idea of random men cuddling kittens, nice as those pictures might be. Yet the notion of Jensen doing it made her feel . . . a little giddy.

She cleared her throat, though it did not require clearing. "We'd better get to the police station."

"You do know he's behind bars, don't you?" He was definitely biting back laughter. She could see it. "He isn't going anywhere."

"You might think it's amusing to leave a child behind bars, but I do not."

"He's not a child, Harriet. He's sixteen. I grant you, that's not a man, either. But Aidan Hall isn't a baby. It's not going to do him any harm to sit there for a minute and think about his choices. Whether you want to be sympathetic to his situation or not, the fact of the matter is that he vandalized church property. He knew better."

"That just makes it even clearer to me that it was a call for help."

"Look at us, answering the call." He shrugged. "That doesn't mean there aren't consequences."

"I would consider getting thrown in jail a consequence. Or is that a typical rite of passage for young men in this valley?"

He laughed, and Harriet busied herself with the Sisyphean task of pushing her glasses up her nose rather than noticing how many heads turned in their general vicinity at the unmistakable sound of Jensen's laughter.

"If you're asking if I've ever been thrown in jail, no," Jensen said. "Zack does threaten to do it about every other Sunday, though, so I'd have to say that the likelihood of finding myself behind bars has grown exponentially since he became sheriff."

And there was nothing she could do about the sunny day, or the way Jensen lounged there before her as if there was nothing else in the whole wide world he would rather be doing than leaning against things on a summer afternoon. With her.

But her brain shorted out at that.

"I'm well aware that there should be consequences for actions," Harriet blurted out, because there was too much sunshine and too much *him*. "What I don't think is that we should spend our lives haunted by impetuous decisions we made when we were little more than children."

To her astonishment, Jensen changed then. Like a cloud went over him, dark enough that she looked up to see if the sky was still blue. It was. When she glanced back at him, he was standing away from the wall. He'd lost that grin, which was surprising enough. But something in his gaze glittered, hard.

She had the distinct impression that this was what he would look like if someone hauled off and hit him.

And yet she felt as if she were the one who'd sustained the blow.

"Better not keep Aidan waiting," he said after a long moment.

Then Jensen set off down Main Street again, his long

legs eating up the sidewalk so Harriet was forced to scurry along behind him.

She detested scurrying. She was already short and strange, the last thing she needed to do was give people ammunition. On the other hand, she didn't want to be left behind in his wake.

"Adjust your stride, please," she ordered him.

Jensen looked down at her in amazement, but he also slowed. "What?"

"Your legs are too long. I have to run to keep up with you, and I have no intention of chasing you down the street."

"Afraid everyone will think you're that eager to catch me?" He laughed, and it was odd that she should feel a rush of something like relief, as if she'd missed that laughter. The way anyone would miss the sun if it clouded over, maybe. It was no more than that. "Or are you more afraid that you might catch me?"

"What I'm concerned about is looking like a frenzied mouse or some other small, rodent thing."

"So in this scenario, I'm a cat and you're a mouse." He considered. "Seems to me you should be nicer, Harriet. In case I turn around and do that thing that all cats do."

"Cats kill mice, Jensen," she said matter-of-factly. "They might play with them for a little while, but killing them is always the goal, no matter what it looks like. My impression is that you're all play and very little killing."

She had no idea how she'd strayed onto this topic, but the sideways look he sent her way encouraged her to get off it, and quickly. Even as her pulse kicked into gear. "And I will thank you not to keep going on about cats and mice in front of Aidan. I think that would be confusing."

"It's already confusing. There's not one part of this that isn't confusing."

Harriet ignored that. "Maybe we'd be better off not discussing pets at all."

But then they were at the police station, and Jensen waved her ahead of him as they walked inside. They walked up the old wooden stairs, side by side, in silence. By the time Harriet presented herself at the desk marked SHERIFF'S OFFICE, her heart was pounding as if she'd climbed a towering mountain peak, not a single flight of stairs.

Perhaps less cream in her coffee, she thought.

"Is he in?" Jensen asked the woman behind the desk.

"He is." But the woman didn't even look at Jensen. She was too busy sizing Harriet up. "You're the school librarian, aren't you?"

Harriet adjusted her glasses and reminded herself to smile. To engage. "Guilty as charged."

Because this was the sheriff's office and she couldn't resist. She thought she heard Jensen laugh beneath his breath, but that could have been wishful thinking.

She ordered herself to be less wishful.

"I wouldn't have thought Jensen knew any librarians," the woman said in an avid sort of tone.

"Now, Adaline," Jensen drawled, smiling egregiously at the older woman. "You know I'm equal opportunity when it comes to professions."

To Harriet's astonishment, and perhaps a slight bit of outrage on behalf of the sisterhood, the other woman actually flushed. Then giggled.

"Oh, you," Adaline said. She waved in the direction of the door that stood against the wall across from her. "If I were twenty years younger, Jensen Kittredge, I would eat you up."

Jensen laughed, but Harriet was beginning to suspect that that laugh was a tool. It certainly wasn't the expression of true amusement he pretended. Because while he was doing it, he guided Harriet away from the desk, then hustled them through the door. Swiftly.

But she didn't have time to consider why Jensen Kittredge should find it necessary to use his own laughter as a disguise, because they were suddenly in the actual sheriff's actual office.

Sheriff Zack Kittredge was sitting behind his desk, frowning down at a thick file. He looked up as Harriet entered and Jensen came in behind her, big and hot and much too close for Harriet's peace of mind.

Zack's gaze darkened. "Harriet," he said. "It's very kind of you to come down and get involved."

"I don't recall you thanking me for my involvement," Jensen said from behind her, his drawl on high. "In fact, I got a full-scale police interrogation."

"I hope my brother told you that this certainly isn't anything you have to do," Zack continued, ignoring Jensen. "This is a kid who is often in or near trouble."

Harriet wanted to leap away from Jensen, because standing this close to him was like accidentally putting the entire back side of her body against a radiator, but didn't. She couldn't have said why except she really, really didn't want Jensen to know how she was reacting to him.

She focused on his brother. "I do hope, Sheriff Kittredge, that you are not about to sit here and tell me some kind of myth about a genetic predisposition for criminal behavior." Harriet's voice was crisp, her gaze direct. "I trust that a man in your position is well aware that there are generally systemic explanations for generational lawbreaking. Among them poverty, class divisions, educational gaps, and, I have no doubt, widespread communal beliefs that *blood will tell*. The only thing blood ever tells is whether or not you're physically healthy. The end."

"Yeah, Zack," Jensen rumbled.

"I'm not going to tell you any myths," Zack told her, his expression serious. "But that doesn't change the fact that Aidan knows how to get himself into trouble. The only reason he's still here is because his father, no stranger to trouble himself, hasn't seen fit to answer his own phone and come see to his own son."

"Poor Aidan," Harriet replied in the same crisp tone, daring the sheriff to argue.

He didn't. Zack shifted his gaze to a point behind and above Harriet. Whatever he saw there, presumably on Jensen's face, made his jaw tighten.

"This way," he said.

Harriet preceded the pair of them out the door into the rest of the office and could hear the kind of jostling she associated with her student charges. As they were grown men, she did not turn back around to see what they were doing. She could hear a shoulder check well enough without inspecting it. Instead, she scanned the room, found the cells along the back, and marched over to the only one that was occupied.

She saw the precise moment that Aidan saw her coming. He went from sitting down on the cell's stark bench to his feet in an instant.

"Uh . . . Miss Barnett?" he asked as if surprised.

"Are you all right?" Harriet asked him as she came to a stop before the cell. "Have you been mistreated in any way?"

"No," Aidan replied. Then cleared his throat. "No, not really."

"Of course not," Zack said from behind her, sounding

the way his jaw had looked. "We're not in the habit of getting rough with any prisoners, Harriet. Especially not high school kids."

Harriet kept her gaze on Aidan. "Is it true? Did you deface church property?"

A defiant, too-angry Aidan looked miserable, but fought to hide it. "Maybe."

Harriet pointed her finger at him. "Own what you did, please. Or what was the point in doing it?"

"Yes, ma'am," Aidan muttered. "I did it."

"Why?"

She was aware of Jensen moving to her side, then once again propping himself up when it was clear he had no muscle weaknesses that would require all that *propping*. But she kept her attention on Aidan.

"I don't know," the boy said. To his shoes.

"You do know."

"I guess I figured Pastor Jim could take it?"

"Pastor Jim is a kind and gentle man who would very likely have opened his home to you had you knocked on his door instead of spray-painting the side of his youth center. But whether or not he can 'take it,' as you put it, is irrelevant. That's not why you did it."

Aidan wasn't looking at his shoes any longer. He shifted, taking on the insolence she was used to seeing in him. "I can't help it if I run wild. I'm a Hall. I have no parental supervision."

"And, therefore, would not be a candidate for emancipation," Harriet said coolly. She saw Jensen's expression change, but couldn't read the assessing sort of look he slid her way. "A minor who wishes to emancipate himself cannot stay out all night, vandalizing private property. Wisdom beyond your years is the bare minimum expected, I would imagine."

She had only done enough research to determine that Colorado didn't have an emancipation statute for minors. It was a case-by-case determination, meaning it would depend on a judge. And if the judge had opinions about the Hall family like everyone else, vandalism would certainly not help Aidan any.

"But I . . ." Aidan looked lost for a moment, reminding Harriet that he was still so young. So very young. Too young to be worried about things like judges and emancipation statutes. Or fathers who couldn't be bothered to come help him.

She looked at him steadily as if he were an adult. "What I suggest to you, Mr. Hall, is that you take your newfound interest in the emancipation of minors and write me a properly sourced research paper on the topic. When it's completed, you and I can sit down and discuss your conclusions. Maybe, by that time, your behavior will have improved to such an extent that discussions of your personal situation will make more sense."

"But, Miss Barnett, you don't understand my father."

"Are you afraid of him?" Her heart ached for him, but she also knew that there was very little she could do. Much as she might like to tell Aidan that he need not ever go home again if he didn't want to, she couldn't do it. Teachers—much less school librarians—couldn't go about taking in their students. The state tended to frown upon such behavior. Harriet was many things, including apparently too susceptible to the machinations of a sixteen-year-old boy who was trying desperately to look tough, but she was no flouter of rules. Particularly ones that could lead to her dismissal.

"I'm not afraid of him," Aidan said, his voice low and his eyes too bright. "He can get mean when he's drunk, but that's fine. It slows him down."

Harriet shot a glance at Zack, who looked grim. She didn't dare look at Jensen, because she was sure she'd lose her train of thought entirely if she did.

"There are discussions that we can have," she told Aidan quietly. "And conversations I will urge you to have with a social worker. But what I really want to know is whether or not you feel that you are in physical danger with your father."

Aidan shrugged jerkily. "He wishes."

Harriet nodded. "All right. Then I will see you in class. I will expect one written page about the paper you plan to research. An overview, please, so we know how to focus our attention going forward."

"Homework?" Aidan looked sulky and outraged at once. "I'm *in jail* and you want to give me homework?"

"It should be easy enough," Harriet shot back. "As you currently have so few distractions."

And that was where she left him, muttering to himself like any other teenager. She had to think that was an improvement.

She followed Zack and Jensen out of the area directly near the cells, crossing the office so they could stand closer to the desk where Jensen's admirer sat.

"Is he going to be okay?" she asked them. Or Zack, really, but both brothers were looking down at her with similarly grave expressions. "Or is he downplaying the treatment he can expect from his father?"

"Andy Hall isn't the most sympathetic character," Zack said, rubbing at his chin. "But I've never known him to deliver a beatdown."

"Will he threaten violence?" Jensen asked, sounding rhetorical. "Sure. He does that a lot. But I don't think there's any follow-through. I've never heard of him doing much more than shoot his mouth off."

"All right, then," Harriet said, and then made it weird. Or weird*er,* because of course she did. Because she didn't know what else to do, so she . . . bowed. Just a little bob forward, but she didn't have to see the raised Kittredge eyebrows to know she'd gone and gotten odd again. "I will handle the emancipation angle in class. Thank you, Sheriff. And, Jensen, I will contact you to discuss your part."

"Will you?" came the inevitable, lazy reply.

"I will," she said, fixing him with a stern look because his eyes were gleaming and the melting was already starting up again. "We're going to help Aidan, Jensen. Together."

Once again, she marched off before she could truly analyze the fact that she was issuing orders to Jensen Kittredge. Or the fact that he was looking at her as if she might be edible, but more in a cat-to-mouse way than anything else.

It still made her breathless.

And once again, when she found herself on the street, her pulse was thundering around inside her as if she'd run for days.

8

A few days later, Jensen walked into the Broken Wheel, looked around with his usual friendly smile—without actually meeting the gazes of any of the people who were looking back at him, a specialty he'd honed back in high school or he'd never manage to cross a single room—then made his way over to the bar.

It was a fine summer evening, and the place was hopping. Summer tourists and second-homers crowded around the tables, mixing with the usual locals. Some folks bemoaned the ever-bigger hordes of fair-weather tourists, but Jensen wasn't one of them. He liked the noise and the laughter of a summer night. Then again, he also liked the off-season, when he knew every face at every table; even the music was moodier, and there was always room to pull up a chair. Tonight there was a live band playing, with families and couples crowded together on the dance floor, as much to sing along as get any dancing in.

But Jensen skirted all the commotion. He made a beeline for the bar, where he headed for the empty stool next to the forbidding man on the end. He didn't sit down. He leaned against the bar instead.

Matias Trujillo grunted, his form of an eloquent greeting, and said nothing as Jensen caught the bartender's eye and lifted his chin. Jensen was reminded of how much he liked his life when a beer and a shot of whiskey appeared before him. Like his favorite kind of magic.

"Thanks, Tessa," he said, tossing a few bills down on the glossy surface of the bar.

Tessa Winthrop, the Broken Wheel's best bartender, was a local girl who always knew a local's drink. She grinned as she swept up his money.

"A pleasure, as always, to read your mind, Jensen."

"The only woman who dares," Jensen replied with a grin.

At least if the tiny tornado that was Harriet Barnett was going to continue rampaging through his life—last he'd checked there were three messages from her on the ranch's four-hundred-year-old answering machine—he still had these simple things to fall back on. A bartender who knew him. His best friend on the next stool. The ranch, his family, and the great and glorious state of Colorado.

"My sister tells me you're taking up with a librarian," Matias said when Tessa walked away. He smirked. "Seems off-brand."

Jensen made an anatomically impossible suggestion. But politely, so as not to bring the place down around his ears. This wasn't the Coyote, after all. The Broken Wheel was the family-friendly gathering place in town. Matias lifted his beer in a salute, still smirking.

"I'm very interested in literacy, Matias," Jensen said after he knocked his whiskey back. He stood there, enjoying the burn. "It's a passion of mine."

"Rae also tells me that everybody thinks you're taking advantage of her. The librarian, not Rae. You know better than to go near Rae."

For a variety of reasons, most of them because Jensen

had never viewed Rae as a viable option. She was Matias's kid sister. And she'd been with Riley for most of their lives. *And* was currently carrying Jensen's first nephew.

"Who is this 'everybody'?" he asked Matias. "Your sister's friends?"

"I didn't ask for name, rank, and serial number. My bad."

"And no, since you asked, I'm not taking advantage of anyone. If anything, the school librarian is taking advantage of my good nature and willingness to lend a helping hand."

Matias paused with his beer halfway to his mouth. "Your what now?"

Jensen eyed his friend. "And since when did you become one of the town gossips? You barely speak."

That wasn't strictly true. Matias was downright chatty sometimes, but never really in public. Heaven forbid he ruin his loner mystique. He'd lose half his fan club.

"I hate gossip." But then Matias's mouth curved. "Unless it involves you and a high school librarian. I would have put money on you not knowing how to find the high school library when we went there every day."

"Reports of scandalous behavior with the local cat lady have been greatly exaggerated," Jensen said gruffly.

And he could hear Harriet's voice as he said it. Because there were any number of phrases he could have used to describe her, but he'd chosen *cat lady.* And not by accident. *We'd better rush to come up with ways to describe her and make it clear to everyone she's a figure of scorn and pity,* Harriet had said.

Like all things that involved Harriet Barnett, Jensen found himself . . . uncomfortable. Something about that woman made his skin shrink, so it fit him all wrong now.

He had the wholly uncharacteristic urge to explain himself. To Matias, of all people, who knew him better than just about anybody. Not only knew him better but did not require explanations.

Because he and Matias went way back. Maybe all the way back, but what Jensen could actually remember was kindergarten. They'd been inseparable, along with their other fast friend from their kindergarten playground days, Daniel Hillis. The three of them had been so close growing up that people liked to call them brothers, but Jensen knew that they'd been even closer than that. Because he loved his brothers, but Matias and Daniel had never annoyed him the way his real brothers did.

The three of them had played Little League and then varsity football together. They'd learned about girls together, though they'd never competed with one another there. They'd lived in one another's pockets, driving well before the legal age out on the ranch and never afraid to cause a little mischief. They'd gone on camping trips so they could smoke stolen cigarettes and drink purloined alcohol, stretch out beneath the stars like they were grown, and tell one another grandiose lies about the lives they were going to have one day.

Jensen never would have believed, way back when, that there could ever come a time that there would only be two of them left.

He still didn't quite believe it. It was like a missing limb he kept trying to use. Time went on, year after year went by, but missing Daniel never changed. It just became part of the scenery.

But that was life, wasn't it? Jensen had learned that, if nothing else, from losing one-third of himself. If it was going well at any point, you could be sure that whatever else happened, it wouldn't last.

Jensen chose to face that sure knowledge with laughter. Whiskey. A decided refusal to take anything seriously because what was the point? And until Harriet's unexpected appearance in his life, a whole lot of women, not that he was prepared to confront precisely why it was his lack of female companionship of late had anything to do with her.

Matias, on the other hand, preferred to be a grumpy hermit. Just as unapproachable when he was off in the wilderness as when he was sitting on a barstool. That was Matias. He didn't have to go live on top of a mountain to seem remote. He could do it right next to you, and he usually did.

They'd both dealt with losing Daniel in their own ways. Matias had joined the Marines right out of high school, barely a month after Daniel had died. Jensen had understood why he'd done it, but what it had meant was that he'd lost both of his best friends in rapid succession. So the first time Matias had come home after boot camp, they'd settled it like men. They'd gotten drunk, had a glorious little fistfight, and had ended up laughing out in the dirt in the Colorado summer night, waiting for their hangovers to come. Winded and a little bloody, maybe, and missing Daniel the way they always would, but still the best of friends.

Later that year, Jensen had taken up smoke jumping, and he supposed the only good thing about losing Daniel was that nobody ever pressed either one of them too hard about their choices. The way they would have pressed any other sons of big family enterprises like the Trujillos' industrial flower business and the Kittredges' horses for failing to fully commit.

Another benefit of a small town, Jensen thought. Everybody already knew your business. There was no need for you to go to any trouble offering anyone an autobiography when chances were, their cousin's friend's little sister had already filled them in on all the salient points.

"When did you start gossiping with your sister, anyway?" Jensen asked, because he was still uncomfortable with the cat lady comment, and he really didn't like being uncomfortable. Better to jump back into offense. "Speaking of off-brand choices."

Matias's mouth curved again. Just a little. "Right about the time she became your sister-in-law again. And not by my choice, let's be clear. I've been tired of your family since the fourth grade." He succumbed to a rare grin, because he loved Jensen's family and always had. "But Rae persists in believing I have some insight into her in-laws."

"You mean that we're awesome? Everybody has that insight."

"I definitely do not mean that. But since we're gossiping, did you know that your little brother, after doing nothing for as long as I can remember but shooting his mouth off about how much he can't stand your father, now has coffee dates with him?"

"You have coffee with your old man all the time."

"Yeah, but I like my old man."

Riley had softened in all kinds of ways since he'd finally sorted his life out. Or sorted Rae out, maybe. He laughed again. He was less doom and gloom, though he was never going to turn into a ray of sunshine. It was all good stuff. It was certainly good to see. Though Jensen had to agree that making nice with Donovan was the weirdest part of his little brother's climb toward the light.

"It's not coffee anymore, what with the old man's heart," he said. "Connor claims he saw them playing a board game, but I haven't independently verified that information. Connor could easily have made it up."

And almost certainly had, since Donovan and Riley Kittredge were more likely to take up embroidery than suddenly start a fierce Chutes and Ladders competition. And also pigs might sprout wings and fly over Colorado.

"I guess that if Riley can go and spend time with your dad, miracles really can happen," Matias drawled. "Maybe it makes sense that you're hanging out with a librarian."

"I'm not hanging out with anybody," Jensen said gruffly. "I don't hang out."

"Seems to me I heard about a coffee date. Those are going around, I guess."

"I was in Cold River Coffee, if that's what you mean. Harriet was also in the coffeehouse at the same time, as were at least two of your ex-girlfriends. It is true that Harriet and I then left the coffeehouse at the same time. If that's your idea of a date, I feel sorry for you."

"I don't date," Matias said.

Jensen reached over and clinked his bottle of beer to Matias's. "Amen, buddy. A-freaking-men."

"And I don't know how to tell you this," Matias continued. "But the high school librarian you're not dating just walked in. And she's headed your way."

Jensen turned to look, a sense of foreboding washing over him. And yet that was nothing next to the sensation that kicked up in him when he saw the unmistakable figure of Miss Harriet Barnett charging through the crowd with military precision, her gaze locked on him.

It was like his ribs cracked open, and he had half a mind to reach beneath his shirt to make sure everything was still in its rightful place. Because there was something otherworldly about her. It was the clothes she wore, always happily out of step with everyone else. It was all that blond hair, caught up on the top of her head in a manner both old-fashioned and careless. It was her total obliviousness to anything around her except the one thing she was focused on. He'd seen it in the Coyote. He'd seen it at his own family dinner table. He'd seen it in the library.

She marched toward him with all the officious self-confidence in the world, and Jensen should have found her annoying. Cute, at best. An adorable little wet hen of a woman, fully unaware of how tiny she was, which only made her that much more entertaining.

Any of those reactions to her would have been fine.

But Jensen was deeply horrified to discover that the primary reaction he had to seeing all that unadulterated focus aimed at him, even across a crowded bar, was lust.

Lust.

An unmistakable bolt of it that surged through him like a thunderclap, from his sex straight on out, like a summer storm. Not the scary kind. The kind you went out and danced in, and if you were lucky, stripped off all your clothes and—

What the hell.

But the trouble was, Jensen was possessed of an excellent imagination. And once he'd started thinking about Harriet and her commitment, all her *intensity,* he was in a world of hurt.

He thought *flabbergasted* was understating the case pretty drastically.

But that didn't make him any less hard as she continued her march, seeming not to notice the looks thrown her way, the speculative whispers that rose up, or the general ripple effect she seemed to have wherever she went.

For a woman who acted as if she was unaware that there were any other people in this bar, or even on the surface of the planet, Harriet certainly caused a commotion.

Which got him thinking what other kinds of commotion she might cause.

Down, boy, he ordered himself.

"You sure do seem to like tracking me down in bars," Jensen drawled when Harriet finally came and stood before him.

She blinked, then frowned, then shoved her glasses up her nose. A combination that despite himself, he found . . . well, he found it all the things he found her. The whole Harriet factor of it all. He felt that crack in his ribs begin to widen. And at the same time, his imagination got even more specific. Did she take off her glasses in bed? Would she frown like that while she tried to order him around? Could she have any idea the effect she had on a man?

Jensen wasn't sure he wanted the answers to any of those questions.

Also, he desperately wanted the answers to those questions.

"I would track you down in a church, but you don't appear to know where those are located," Harriet replied, tart and crisp. "Or how to operate your answering machine, apparently. So the bars it is."

Next to him, Matias guffawed. Actually *guffawed,* so that all the locals who knew how rare that sound was had no choice but stare even more than they already were. Jensen ignored all of them. "You want to have a drink with me, Harriet, all you need to do is ask."

"I told you I don't drink. Much."

"Well, I do. And from the look on your face, I think I'm going to need more whiskey."

"I hope you're aware that alcohol dependency—"

Jensen looked over at Matias, who looked as close to falling out in a fit of laughter as Jensen thought he'd ever seen him. Since high school, anyway.

"Matias," he said, interrupting Harriet's screed on the evils of the demon drink, "allow me to introduce Harriet Barnett, the high school librarian. Not exactly the shy and retiring character you might have been expecting."

"The shy librarian stereotype is archaic," Harriet informed both of them, glaring from him to Matias and back again. "Libraries are quiet because they are meant to be places of scholarship and reflection, not because librarians are shy loners who don't know how to speak at a proper volume. And don't get me started on the sexy librarian trope."

"Trope," Matias repeated softly, staring down at Harriet in a kind of wonder. "Did you just use the word *trope* in casual conversation at a bar?"

Jensen, meanwhile, found himself assaulted by thousands of extremely vivid, sexy librarian scenarios—

He had to be losing his mind. It was clearly because he'd unaccountably happened into a little spell of celibacy. Purely by accident, he assured himself, and having nothing at all to do with Harriet turning up in the Coyote and then somehow turning his life inside out.

Nothing at all. He unclenched his jaw. "I had no idea that librarians were so maligned."

"*Trope,*" Matias said quietly.

"Of course librarians are maligned," Harriet retorted. "Many of them are women, like teachers and nurses. When men do things, they can simply do them. When women do them, they need to be either outrageously sexy or considered a kind of cute little hobby, the better to minimize their very real contributions altogether."

"I don't minimize nurses," Matias said, his eyes a little wide.

Jensen found that comforting. Because Matias had Rae for a sister, and Lord knew, his sister-in-law could light into a man if she felt like it. He felt validated that his best friend, who was used to what his own sister could dish out, still found Harriet a whole thing.

It made him feel a little less crazy.

"Did you hunt me down in yet another drinking establishment to give me a lecture on the treatment of librarians?" Jensen asked lazily. "Not that I'm not enjoying it, but it does sound maybe less serious than you intend, what with all the two-stepping out there on the dance floor."

This time, when Harriet blinked, Jensen found himself feeling something like protective. Because he had the distinct sensation that she'd completely forgotten where they were standing. In the next breath, he saw a certain ruefulness steal over her expression, suggesting to him that it was not the first time she'd forgotten herself.

And now that he was paying such close attention, he also found himself noticing other things. Like how bright blue her eyes really were. Or that curve of her cheek that looked as if it would fit his palm almost perfectly.

Jensen was a man who'd always appreciated it when a feminine gift was more or less unwrapped as he found it. But everything about Harriet was a mystery. The long, shapeless dress that was like a tent on her. That ridiculous cardigan. And yet the longer he stood there, peering down at her, the more he found himself hungry to unwrap each and every layer of the clothes she was wearing to see what was beneath.

"As a matter of fact," she said, still with that rueful expression on her face, "I didn't come here to lecture you."

"That is a relief."

"I need your help."

"Again?" Jensen took a pull of his beer. "It's true that I'm known far and wide for my helpfulness"—and he ignored the snort from beside him—"but I'm beginning to think that you're taking advantage of my amiable nature, Harriet."

"Oh no," she said, very seriously. "I haven't come to ask you to build shelves or fix a car engine, or whatever it is people ask you to do."

"Is that what you think people ask me to do?" The adorable factor was going to be the death of him. "That's really not where I shine, darlin'."

She sighed, then waved at him. At his chest, then his arms. "I don't know. You look like you can lift things."

Matias made a sound that in other circumstances might have signaled he was trying to sing something. Soprano. Jensen, still feeling entirely too protective of *his* odd little duck, chose to believe he was.

"You should be asking me to fix your car engine," he told Harriet. "Your car is a tragedy waiting to happen." He was aware of the eyes on the side of his face that suggested Matias had managed to keep his opera in check, and shot his buddy a dark look. "She's driving a ratty old hatchback in the Rocky Mountains."

"You need four-wheel drive," Matias told Harriet, not laughing any longer. "Or one of these days, you're going to find your inadequate tires will throw you right off the side of a mountain."

"Alternatively, I could not drive up the side of a mountain when it's snowing," Harriet said, sounding exasperated. "Honestly. What is it with a pair of you? I've managed to live this long without your input into my vehicle choices. Three winters here so far, thank you. I think I can handle it."

"My sister is exactly the same," Matias told Jensen. "You remember that truck of hers. It was a death trap."

Harriet bristled. Why did he like it when she *bristled*? "My car is not a death trap. It is a perfectly functional vehicle. And it's not why I'm here. If I wanted to talk about cars, I would have sought out a mechanic."

"She told you," Matias muttered under his breath.

Jensen inclined his head at the tiny little terror glaring up at him. "I'm all ears."

"I've spent a lot of time with Pastor Jim, your brother, and the county prosecutor over the past few days, all of which you would know if you'd returned a phone call. We're all in agreement that it isn't in Aidan's best interests to officially charge him with vandalism. Community service seems like a much better road all around. He'll repair the damage he did, of course, but I had a brilliant idea for his service." Her whole face lit up at the notion of her own brilliance, and again, Jensen found it cute. "What if he did it with you?"

That was less cute.

"Two things," Jensen said, staring down at her and wondering, again, how something so small could be so *determined*. And how he could keep forgetting that and getting sidetracked with her cheek and the bristling and his obsessive desire to see what she looked like when not in swaddling clothes. "One, I'm not sure how to feel about the notion you think I'm the same as picking up litter out on the county roads. I'm not. And two, why did this require a face-to-face discussion? In the Broken Wheel, no less."

"I'm not comparing you to picking up litter," Harriet protested, frowning at him once again. "Everything I've ever read suggests that working with horses can do wonders for people, whether they need help or not."

"You want me to take my ranch and turn it into a program for wayward delinquents? Because you've decided to step in and save Aidan Hall from his destiny and for some reason you think that involves me?"

"And I decided we needed a face-to-face discussion," she carried on as if she hadn't heard him, "because to be honest, I wasn't entirely sure you planned to get involved any further. And even if you did, I doubted you would offer yourself up without a little persuasion."

"Harriet." Jensen shook his head. "Did you come here to butter me up? Because that's going to take a whole lot more whiskey. I'd recommend a little skin." He shrugged when she scowled. "I don't make the rules, darlin'. I'm just telling you how it works. I'm a very basic man."

"A young man's life hangs in the balance and you want to make adolescent remarks about *skin*?" Harriet sighed. "Be serious."

And Jensen suddenly felt another wave of . . . something he didn't want to identify. Because it felt a little too close to a kind of fury. Not at Harriet but at every single choice he'd made since he wasn't much younger than Aidan Hall himself, all of which had led him here. To this confounding woman telling him to *be serious* when he had the terrible feeling inside him that he wouldn't know where to begin.

He was the one who always cracked a joke. Jensen lightened the mood by any means necessary—and he'd been playing that role since he was a kid. His parents' marriage had always been a powder keg, and Jensen was the one who defused it. He wasn't afraid to make a fool of himself, he was happy to laugh at himself first, he laughed loud and long and defied those around him not to laugh with him. It was pretty hard to keep fighting when everyone else was laughing. Jensen had always been very, very good at his job.

And he was pretty sure that with the exception of his too-watchful older brother, he'd more or less fooled every person he'd ever met into thinking that Jensen Kittredge took nothing seriously, ever. Least of all himself.

He had worked hard to make sure of that.

Even, maybe especially, after losing Daniel.

So he couldn't understand what it was about Harriet that made him want to tear himself open just to prove that he wasn't, in fact, the clown he'd been playing his whole life.

As if he'd suddenly started caring what other people thought about him.

Not other people. Her.

"I don't know what else you expect me to do," he found himself saying, and not with a grin to make it lazy or easy or funny. "He's not my kid. I don't owe him anything, and news flash, Harriet. Neither do you. And at a certain point, it's a little weird to be neck deep in a random teenager's family problems, don't you think?"

"What I think is that people like to say things like that because it protects them," Harriet replied, her blue gaze clear and fixed on Jensen. As if they were standing somewhere else, outside or in a quiet place somewhere, with no one around them. He had no doubt that Harriet had forgotten where they were again. But when had he followed suit? "Sometimes because they're the parents of the kid in question and they don't want anyone else's input for obvious reasons. Or because we've all decided that we shouldn't get involved, because it might be upsetting or tricky or make people think we're nosy busybodies. But the only people that helps are the adults in the situation. Never the kids." She shook her head. "Shouldn't we be helping the kids? Most adults can help themselves. Kids shouldn't have to."

Jensen slowly became aware of how silent Matias was beside him, as if he'd turned to stone. He was also dimly cognizant of the rest of the bar.

But somehow he knew that when he remembered this moment, all he would remember was the quiet certainty in Harriet's voice and that heartbreakingly calm gaze that seemed to tear straight through him.

"If you want me to teach Aidan Hall how to respect another living creature when I know he doesn't, I will."

He said those words gruffly. They'd come out of some part of him he barely recognized.

And he hadn't taken the time to sound sardonic. Or funny. Or even mocking.

He just said it. Like a vow.

Jensen was questioning his sanity, and a whole lot of other things, especially because Matias was right there beside him and knew how little Jensen liked to do the kind of horse lessons that Riley was so good at. Jensen might believe that a horse could change a man's life, but he wasn't earnest about it. He'd been raised by quietly capable old cowboys and aspired to be one himself. He didn't do things like make announcements about the therapeutic properties of horses. Much less reach out to surly teens.

What exactly do you think you're doing? he asked himself, before Matias could.

But he already had his answer.

Because Harriet gazed back at him, fierce and clear. And then, as he watched, a smile broke out over her face, changing everything.

Dooming him, just like that.

9

Two weeks later, Harriet was enjoying the perfect summer Saturday.

She'd woken up at her usual time and had tended to her demanding roommates, including a half hour's panicked search for tiny little Maisey, who had managed to squeeze herself into a space that shouldn't have fit her, beneath the overstuffed bookcase in the bedroom. She'd had her usual morning tea, out on her front porch to the music of lawn mowers, children playing, birds in the trees, and the whisper of the breeze. She'd puttered around in her garden while it was still cool, and then she'd walked the few blocks into town, where she'd spent an enjoyable hour or two sitting cross-legged on the floor of Capricorn Books. She'd left with a stack of new books to add to her ever-towering to-be-read pile that currently took over the entire bookcase in her bedroom that naughty, plaintive Maisey had wedged herself beneath today. And as Harriet firmly believed that the only life worth living was one in which a woman could never possibly read all the books she wanted to, adding to that stack made her happy. The books tucked away in her bag, she'd enjoyed the weight of all the good reading to come as she'd walked back up Main Street and into Cold River Coffee, where she exulted in the silky feel of the air-conditioning on her skin after the warm sun outside. Harriet thought she would sit down, have one of the specialty coffees she liked so much, and possibly a decadent pastry to go with it.

Because she could do as she liked.

Theatrical coffee and gooey pastry in hand, Harriet claimed one of the cozy armchairs at the back and settled in. She plucked a book from her bag and cracked it open, sighing happily as she prepared to while away a few hours.

And couldn't have said, lost as she was in the pages of the poetry book she'd found, what it was that made her look up again.

Yet when she did, she saw an entire tableful of local women staring at her. Not only staring at her, but *boldly* staring. Very few of them looked away when Harriet, baffled, met their gazes.

And Harriet was well versed in her own historic strangeness to others. It was hardly worth mentioning at this point. But she didn't see how she could possibly have demonstrated her various oddities in any way while eating a blameless chocolate croissant or drinking a hot drink. Everyone else in the coffee shop was doing more or less the same thing.

She dismissed it and returned to her poetry book. But a little while later, another prickling sort of sensation skated down the back of her neck and she looked up again, this time to find a different group of women studying her. And, even more disconcertingly, a few men as well.

The third time it happened, Harriet got up—careful to keep her expression neutral—and made her way to the bathroom in back. Sedately. Once inside the small, single room, she studied herself in the mirror, twisting around to get all sides because she was convinced there had to be some mark on her. Or she'd failed to button up her shirt appropriately. But everything was as it should be. Her skirt was not bunched up into her panties. She didn't have something awful stuck to her cheek.

She went back out into the main room of the coffee-house again, none the wiser.

Harriet didn't care too much if people stared at her. She was used to it. Usually, when not at work, she could be certain that she'd done something to bring on the star-ing, whether she was aware of it or not. She might not always know what it was she'd done that was found to be so weird, but she was usually aware when she'd done something. Harriet had long been aware that she was an odd duck. Marching to the beat of her own drum, etcetera.

Better that than the alternative, she'd always thought. A bit sniffily.

It happened a few more times, and Harriet began to find that it was growing more and more impossible to lose herself in her reading the way she wanted. She fin-ished off her coffee, sighing at the last hit of all that sweetness. Then she bussed her table before heading back outside again. Feeling nicely caffeinated and sugared up—to say nothing of that heavenly croissant, which had been made entirely of butter, hallelujah—she set off on a leisurely walk down toward the river and the Lavender Llama. There was no yarn store in Cold River, which was a crying shame, but the Lavender Llama had an entire section for local fiber enthusiasts. It could often fill the gap between deliveries from Harriet's two favorite yarn shops—one in Southern Oregon and another outside Chi-cago. The last time Harriet had looked in the Lavender

Llama, there had been a bright, happy selection of yarn that she thought would make a lovely shawl. She liked to start knitting a new shawl every summer so when the weather changed, she would be ready to wrap herself in coziness. Since she liked to continue her front porch routine until it snowed.

Today the gift shop was buzzing the way it always was in the summer. And well into the winter too. Harriet lingered over some of the local pottery, but she knew perfectly well she didn't need any more tea mugs. She was still only one person. She eyed the bouquets of fresh flowers in the little outpost by the door from the Flower Pot, the town's florist, but she'd already made up two bouquets from her own garden today. Come winter, when her own flowers were nothing but a memory, she wouldn't hesitate. She took her time wandering through the shop, marveling that it felt cozy when it was a huge barn. Eventually, she found her way to the yarn and stood there awhile, dithering a bit over the different colors while she squeezed skeins and daydreamed about her next project. It was another key component to a perfect afternoon.

Having selected the softest, squishiest, happiest yarn on offer, Harriet turned around, prepared to pay and be on her way. Instead, she found herself face-to-face with a trio of women she didn't know.

That wasn't strictly true, she amended. She knew Rae. She'd had that Sunday dinner with Rae at the Bar K. And she knew the woman standing next to Rae, of course, since she was one of the sisters who ran her beloved Capricorn Books. Hope, Harriet thought. The middle sister. And now that she considered it, she knew the third woman too, since she'd been one of the first people Harriet had encountered in Cold River. It was Abby, the manager of Cold River Coffee.

It was more precise to say that she knew *who* they were. But not why they too appeared to be studying her.

"Was I hogging the yarn?" Harriet asked. "My apologies."

"Oh, we don't knit," Hope replied, smiling wide.

"Speak for yourself," Abby objected. "I knit." She laughed as her friends looked at her. "I mean, I know *how* to knit."

"I don't know how," Rae said, her hands moving restlessly over her pregnant belly. "I've always wanted to learn. Not enough to actually learn, mind you, but I've thought about it."

"Are you looking for knitting lessons?" Harriet asked, looking from one woman to the next. And trying her best not to look as baffled as she felt. What a strange day.

"Knitting lessons?" Rae sounded confused.

"Oh," Hope said. "Because this feels like an ambush, doesn't it?" She smiled at Harriet, even wider than before. It was a dazzling smile that had led Harriet to spend a lot of money in her bookstore—but they weren't in her bookstore. "We were just standing over there speculating about your Jensen Kittredge situation. So I thought we might as well come over and ask you about it directly."

Harriet could not have been more surprised if it turned out she'd been naked this whole time without knowing it. She double-checked, just to be sure. "My Jensen Kittredge situation?"

"He is my brother-in-law," Rae protested, frowning at Hope. "So I feel like I have a genuine, familial interest in whatever situations he might or might not be in."

Abby smiled gently at Harriet while the other two glared at each other. "I didn't know there was a Jensen Kittredge situation, if that helps."

"And I'm just a gossiping fool," Hope said, clearly

finished with the glaring. "But I've found it's better to inquire at the source than make things up ourselves. Whenever possible. And you were right here."

"This is all a little too small-town for me, I think," Harriet said, still standing there, frozen, with her bag weighing down her shoulder and five skeins of yummy, speckled yarn in her arms. Did she have a *situation* with Jensen? Was that why everyone had been staring at her all day?

But she knew better than to flatter herself. Since she knew perfectly well there was no such situation.

"Not that you asked," Abby said quietly, "but I think this is the nice part of a small town."

"Being talked about?" Harriet wanted, badly, to re-adjust her glasses, but her hands were full. She settled for frowning.

"Everybody talks about everybody," Hope said with a shrug. "Pretty much everywhere. The only difference in a small town is that you're more likely to hear about it."

"At least in Cold River, it's more informational than judgmental." Abby smiled. "Really."

But Rae snorted. "Maybe that's your experience. Saint Abby married Saint Gray, and lo, she thereafter bestowed upon him one perfect son who is spoken of in tones of awe and wonder throughout the Longhorn Valley."

Abby sighed. "Mostly, Rae, people just say hi. Without referencing sainthood. And they call Bart by his name."

Rae shrugged and then looked at Harriet. "I can assure you, that's not how people talk about me. My husband and I have a complicated relationship. Or we did." She glanced down at her enormous belly. "It's less compli-cated now."

And then it seemed all three of them stood there, look-ing at Harriet expectantly.

It was a nightmare. Meaning, she had literally had this nightmare. Repeatedly, starring almost everyone she'd ever met.

"I'm not good with people," Harriet announced baldly. "I honestly can't tell if this is an attempt to befriend me or if it's the opening scene on one of those horrific teen films where everybody knows what's going on except me until endless humiliations ensue. I'd really prefer it if you could be up front."

The three women before her looked horrified. But Harriet couldn't tell if that was because they weren't thinking in terms of pig's blood on a prom dress and were taken aback that they might be perceived that way—or if, as was often the case, they were appalled that Harriet had decided to call out the awkwardness. That was one of those things she did that other people never seemed to care for, which Harriet had never understood. Why marinate in awkwardness?

But she kept going. "I don't have a situation with Jensen Kittredge unless you mean that he and I are both working to help a teenager in trouble. And I'm guessing if that was what you meant, it wouldn't be interesting enough to gossip about."

"I'm nosy," Hope said, holding Harriet's gaze steadily. Seriously. "But not mean. I like to go around asking people inappropriate questions, that's all."

Harriet could take it no longer. She juggled her skeins until she could reach up and adjust her glasses. "Why?"

Hope looked slightly abashed. To her credit, she considered the question for a moment. "Because I like real conversations. And sometimes the only way to have a real conversation in a town like Cold River is to ask the question no one else will. I'm sorry if I made you uncomfortable."

"That's the thing," Harriet said, nearly losing a rogue skein of yarn but gripping it at the last moment. "I'm never uncomfortable. If I were, I would probably be able to sort out those motivations."

"This is none of our business," Abby said softly, though she widened her eyes at Hope, then Rae. "You have no obligation to speak to us one moment more. I wouldn't blame you if you pretended never to see any of us ever again."

"Unless," Rae said mildly, "we both end up at the Kittredge dinner table one fine Sunday. It would be so awkward to blank each other over Janet Kittredge's prize potato casserole."

The three of them all glared at one another then, clearly communicating without words. Harriet had the urge to break and run, as she often did in social situations, because she'd always had trouble with women her own age. Something had gelled for everyone else, maybe around fourth or fifth grade, but Harriet had missed it entirely. She much preferred older friends, who were usually so much more comprehensible. Not least because they were likely to tell you exactly where they stood, on all issues, all the time. It was a relief.

But maybe these women could serve as research models, she thought then, a plan forming as she hugged her pink yarn to her chest. Why not? If they were comfortable asking her personal questions when they didn't know her, why shouldn't she feel perfectly comfortable using them for her own ends? Nefarious or otherwise.

"If you like," she said, trying to sound friendly and engaging for approximately one syllable before giving it up to remain, as ever, herself, "I'd be happy to tell you about my interactions with Jensen Kittredge, since that seems to be of such overwhelming interest to the entire town. I wouldn't want to leave the gossips hanging. That sounds like a dereliction of my civic duty. But I do have something I'd like in return."

"A woman after my own heart." Hope's smile was big and wide. "Name your price."

And that was how Harriet found herself back in the Broken Wheel, her bag stuffed to capacity and her belly full, at a table with her new friends.

Not that she really believed they were her friends. She wasn't certain, but in the absence of bonding over shared experiences like work or college, she was pretty sure adult friendships occurred only after some sort of mystical rituals. Possibly on those weekend nights she was tucked up in bed with a book. And in the hours since they'd all left the Lavender Llama and had claimed this table before the dinner rush that came in after, there had been a lot of chatter. But no rituals.

Unless she'd missed those too. Which was certainly possible.

"Are you sure you want to do this?" Abby asked her, sitting there across from Harriet. They'd already ordered big platters of food, juicy cheeseburgers and perfectly crisp fries. Hope had ordered a chocolate milkshake. Rae wanted dessert. Harriet knew she'd eaten here once before, though she couldn't remember when. Maybe back when she really was new in town? Whenever it had been, the food was as spectacular now as she recalled it being then.

Rae was currently making her approximately seventy-fifth trip to the bathroom, because, she'd complained, the baby was taking up all the space inside her.

Sounds like his daddy, Hope had murmured, and then had laughed when Rae had glared at her.

Right now, Hope was at the bar, chatting with the same

friendly bartender Harriet had seen when she'd come in here the other night.

"I do want to do this," Harriet said. She straightened her shoulders, because that wasn't strictly true. She thought she *should* do this. "The lure of whiskey escapes me. I'd like to see if I can figure out why so many people like it."

Abby sat there quietly. But Harriet did not get the impression that she'd drifted off into her own thoughts. If she knew anything about the most serene member of the trio that had waylaid her today, it was that she might be quieter, but she was no less intense.

Sure enough, a moment or so later, Abby leaned forward and propped her elbows on the table.

"I spent my entire life in love with Gray Everett from afar," she said in a confiding tone.

Harriet remembered what Rae had said in the Lavender Llama about *Saint Gray* and allowed herself to conclude that this was Abby's husband. And now that she thought about it, she knew the Everett family. Or of them. They ran Cold River Ranch, the biggest cattle operation in the Longhorn Valley. A number of her students' fathers worked on the ranch as hands.

"It was desperate," Abby was telling her. "Hopeless. He was older and so, when we were in high school, Rae and Hope and I used to contrive reasons to drive out into the fields to see if we could catch a glimpse of him working on a fence or something."

"Did you?" Harriet asked.

Abby smiled, looking far too pleased. Harriet took that as a *yes*. "The worst part was, everybody in the town knew. And pitied me. It was all *bless her heart, that Abby Douglas, so head over heels for a man who will never give her the time of day.* Because he didn't. Ever. Until one day he showed up at my house and offered to marry me, for purely practical reasons."

"I take it you accepted the offer."

"I sure did. And it worked out beautifully, but that's not my point." Her gaze was steady on Harriet. "I guess I'm just ham-fistedly trying to figure out if you and I are the same that way."

"Well. I'm not hopelessly in love with your husband. As far as I know."

Abby laughed as Hope returned to the table with a tray of shots before her. "I was just telling Harriet my embarrassing history of being ridiculously in love with Gray. For many humiliating years."

"She's not exaggerating," Hope said, setting the tray down. "She was that tragic."

"Hey. My love was dignified. Just from afar."

"Abby wasn't the only person to long for Gray Everett, of course," Hope said as she sat down again. "He's very attractive in a gruff, unapproachable, might-actually-be-made-of-granite sort of way."

Harriet snuck a glance at Abby, who sighed happily at that description.

"Still," Hope said cheerfully, "Abby was the most persistent."

"I think you mean the truest," Abby corrected her.

Hope patted her hand. "You outlasted them all. Those Kittredge boys, on the other hand, were always way more problematic."

Rae was waddling back to the table as Hope said that and took a moment to ease herself down into her seat. "I can confirm that."

"Riley was taken since way back in high school," Hope said, nodding meaningfully at Rae in case Harriet had missed who Rae was married to. "But that didn't stop all the hopeful girls circling him."

"So many hopeful girls." Rae grinned. "They all wanted to be my best friend so they could find out if we were breaking up or not."

"Spoiler alert," Hope said. "They were not."

Abby laughed. "Even when they said they were broken up."

"Let it go," Rae said, waving a hand. "That's all ancient history."

But she was smiling.

"Both Zack and Connor have their fan clubs," Hope continued before Harriet could try to parse the meaning of all that. "Kind of diametrically opposed fan clubs, actually, since Zack acted like the sheriff long before he became the sheriff, and Connor was always the mischievous one."

"And is now married to Missy, who you met," Rae said, nodding at Harriet.

"But Jensen." Hope sighed appreciatively. "Jensen's always been the wild card."

"I mean this respectfully," Harriet said as the three of them gazed at her. Again with great expectation. "But you all seem deeply obsessed with Jensen Kittredge."

"We're just trying to figure out if you're harboring a huge crush on him," Rae said, and laughed when Hope rolled her eyes. "I think that's what everyone's trying to figure out."

Harriet let that sit. She fished a stray fry from her plate and chewed on it. Thoughtfully. "I don't believe I am. Does it matter?"

"Not to him," Hope said, winning a look from Abby. "You know it won't, Abby."

"I think the concern is that it's possible that someone like Jensen, who's so used to women falling all over him, would be a little less respectful of your feelings than he should be," Abby said gently. Carefully.

Too carefully.

Harriet understood then, with a sickening sort of lurch, that this was just another version of what Martina had said to her in the school office that day. Just another round of pity and amusement.

And this time, she wasn't hurt.

She was insulted.

"I don't know why it hasn't occurred to you that *clearly* he has a crush on me," she retorted.

And enjoyed the stunned silence so much that she reached over, helped herself to one of the shots of whiskey, and heedlessly threw it back.

Because it was worth the instant, rolling fire down the length of her esophagus to see the looks on their faces. Somehow, she kept from coughing, though she would never know how.

Hope was the one who smiled first, and widest. "I like you."

And as her sense of insult faded, and she blinked back the tears that the fire in her throat had caused, Harriet saw that the other two were smiling at her also. Actually smiling at her as if she were amusing. And not as if she were the object of that strange pity she'd never quite understood, because *she* was never as sad as people clearly expected her to be.

How bizarre was that? Harriet decided that tonight, she would be the antithesis of sad—and chose to ignore the potential issue that as she didn't know why people thought she was sad, she was unlikely to be able to do the opposite. Then again, she was sitting at a table in the Broken Wheel on a Saturday evening, with whiskey and laughter.

Maybe she was already doing the thing.

And even though she braced herself for the inevitable reversal, as the evening wore on, it only got better. There was more laughter. There was talking, storytelling. There was the exchange of casual confidences in that way that Harriet had always observed, but only from the outside.

It was more fun being inside, she discovered. But only because, unlike other groups she'd known, she actually liked these women.

"I'm impressed by anyone who thrives in a home-schooling environment," Abby was saying, shaking her head. "I would not have."

"I loved it." Harriet shrugged. "It was all very self-directed, which I think serves me better in the long run. As an adult. I've been a self-starter since middle school."

"Sure," Hope agreed. "But what about boys?"

"I lived for school," Rae said with a little sigh.

"That's because she and her husband started dating as infants," Hope told Harriet in a very loud whisper.

Rae rolled her eyes. "We didn't start dating until high school. Which Hope knows perfectly well, because she was there."

"I hope it was suitably theatric." Harriet blinked when they all stared at her. "That's always been my impression of the relationships I've seen in high schools. All that deliciously high drama."

"You know it," Rae replied.

And when she smiled, Harriet felt as if she'd won something. Because while Rae had been nice enough at the Bar K, she certainly hadn't been laughing and telling stories. *Really, Harriet,* she scolded herself. *It's as if you really are auditioning to be Jensen Kittredge's woman.* A notion that set her on fire, or maybe that was just the whiskey she was sipping. She'd gotten past her initial reaction, which was that she might as well shove coals down her throat. Now she found she enjoyed the richness, the peaty flavor, and the warmth.

Then again, maybe what she was truly enjoying was the odd, new sensation that she might have just made some friends.

And she thought it wasn't the whiskey that was making her feel a little giddy. It was that.

When she finished sipping at her second shot of whiskey—that she'd stretched out for hours, because she didn't wish her first experience with drinking whiskey in bars to lead to her becoming incapacitated—Harriet beamed around the table.

"Thank you," she said. "All of you. You're welcome to ask me inappropriate questions anytime."

"Trust that I will take you up on that," Hope replied.

"Are you leaving?" Abby asked. "That wasn't the deal we made. We agreed we would walk you home."

"That was because I thought the whiskey would put me on my knees," Harriet said, waving a hand. Because that was what she did now. She waved languid hands in the air as punctuation, like these women did with all their broad gestures and real, deep laughter. "But I'm fine. I have no urge to kneel, whatsoever."

"Still," Abby said, shooting a glance over toward Hope and Rae, who were bickering—Harriet assumed good-naturedly—over which one of them had been more embarrassing at some or other dance way back when. A topic they both clearly still felt passionately about. "If you were worried about it earlier, I wouldn't want you to wish, later, that we'd gone ahead and done what we said we would. I'm happy to walk you home."

She looked as if she meant it. Harriet found she was touched.

"Really," she said, trying not to show too many of her new, strange *feelings*. Maybe it was the whiskey, after all. "I'm perfectly fine."

"Miss Harriet," came a familiar drawl, licking its way into her and seeming to ignite every part of her the whiskey had touched, spreading its own kind of heat and making everything inside her surge straight on into fever pitch. "I'm scandalized. Have you gone ahead and fallen off the wagon?"

Harriet saw the way her new friends shifted around to pay closer attention. And if they were paying closer attention, that probably meant that everybody else in the Broken Wheel was too, though she did not look around to confirm it. She couldn't escape the notion that it was when she'd told these women that Jensen was the one crushing on her that everything had seemed to ease up with them in a way things rarely did.

For once, Harriet felt not only that she was a member of a group but that she had to sacrifice absolutely nothing of herself to feel that way.

She didn't want that to end.

And she assured herself that was the only reason she tipped her head back, then lounged back in her chair with a bonelessness she had certainly never exhibited before in her life. Ever. Because she was aping the way he lounged about everywhere and she knew it.

She took her time meeting Jensen's incredulous gaze as he stood there, more mountain than man, staring down at her as if he'd caught her running naked down Main Street.

An image that did not horrify her the way it should have, mostly because thinking of the nudity in Jensen's presence made all that heat inside of her kick into a higher gear. And blanked out her brain for a sizzling moment.

It was possible, she allowed, that the whiskey had hit her harder than she imagined.

"It's your lucky night, cowboy," she said, and even tried out a little bit of a drawl too. "I've decided to let you walk me home."

And maybe no one else held their breath. Maybe no one else subsided into a hushed silence at her temerity. Maybe that was only her.

For all she knew, the entire bar was laughing at her.

Harriet would never know. She was too caught in the way Jensen's wolf's eyes blazed. She was too lost in the slow curve of his distracting mouth and that chiseled jaw.

She was too far gone, that was the problem.

But maybe she liked it that way, because when all he did was extend his hand, she took it.

10

"I thought you didn't drink," Jensen said, trying to inject a disapproving note into his voice as Harriet wrapped her fingers around his, then let him pull her to her feet. Her grip was firm, her hand was warm, it was like a lightning bolt slammed right through him—and Jensen was slightly concerned that he was going to succumb to a fit of girlish vapors, or something equally humiliating.

He did not.

But it was close.

"I like to drink under controlled circumstances," Harriet told him grandly, rocking a little on her toes as she stood. Then she scrunched up her nose like she was trying to look like some kind of small woodland creature. It took him a minute to realize that she was trying to adjust her glasses without actually lifting her other hand to accomplish it.

He had absolutely no idea why she would do that, unless her one true aim on this earth was to wreck him, but he reached over with his index finger and gently slid her cute little glasses into place.

"Oh," she said, a little breathlessly. Which was close to making *him* a little breathless. "Thank you."

And even though he knew better than to look around,

Jensen glanced to the side to see his sister-in-law and her friends gaping at him as if he'd dropped his pants right then and there. His index finger, having gone rogue, now burned with its own version of lightning. He curled his hand into a fist and dropped it to his side.

"Why am I unsurprised that you three are bad influences?" he rumbled at them, heading straight for the offense.

"Harriet is not an impressionable child, Jensen," Hope pointed out in a lazy sort of tone that Jensen recognized as actually pretty aggressive, since he employed it so often himself. "She doesn't require bad influences to decide to have a drink in a bar of an evening. She can simply do so like the grown woman she is."

"I think we all know that if there are any bad influences at this table currently, it's not us," Rae chimed in, her hands on her belly and a smirk on her face.

"You're still on probation," Jensen retorted. It was true enough that he hadn't taken kindly to Rae picking up and moving out of the house she'd shared with Riley way back when. He knew plenty of people who would say that wasn't any of his business, but that wasn't how his family rolled.

Something that hadn't bothered him too much when his siblings had been the focus of attention.

"I am not," Rae replied, grinning at him as she patted her belly. "I'm pretty sure I'm off probation entirely, actually, Uncle Jensen."

"Not your call," Jensen said, pretending he felt stern and serious about that when he didn't. Not anymore.

Rae, who had always been more like another little sister to him than anything else, shrugged merrily, clearly wholly unconcerned with the idea of his censure.

Jensen, keenly aware that he was still holding Harriet's

hand, looked to Abby, who everybody knew was the only sensible one in the bunch. "Got anything to add?"

But Abby only smiled serenely, then shook her head.

"Thank you," Harriet said briskly. She tugged at her hand. Jensen ignored the tug. "But I don't think I need any of you speaking for me. I'm perfectly capable of making my decisions for myself, for good or ill."

"Hear that?" Jensen drawled at the cabal still seated at the table, Harriet's hand still in his. "The lady likes to make her own bad decisions."

"Jensen," Hope began, her eyes narrowing. "Do you really think—"

"Have a pleasant evening, ladies," Jensen drawled, and then he drew Harriet away from the table and the entirely too-speculative looks aimed his way from the trio of terror.

And he didn't drag her, exactly, but he kept a tight hold on her hand while he guided her through the crowd, very deliberately neither looking behind him nor looking over toward the table he'd been planning to go and sit at when he'd arrived. Because it was filled with his usual companions, which was usually why he liked coming here. His brothers and sister, the Everett brothers—excluding Abby's husband, of course, who wasn't big on hanging around in bars or, as far as Jensen knew, fun of any kind—Matias, and the usual selection of in-laws and other locals as well. They'd mostly all known him his whole life.

And would all therefore have entirely too many opinions about him holding hands with the high school librarian.

Not to mention walking off into the night with her.

The situation with Harriet was already more drama than he'd allowed in his life in years. Maybe ever. It was already more weighted, and more complicated, than he ever allowed things to get. Because Jensen didn't do drama. He didn't go deep. His life was neatly compartmentalized and had been ever since they'd lost Daniel on that one terrible night that could never be fixed or taken back.

He liked it that way.

There were a thousand excellent reasons for him to let go of Harriet, but he didn't.

Jensen pushed out into the bright night. Only when the heavy door slammed shut behind them did he take his time looking down at Harriet out there in the late-summer evening, in all that endless light.

To his delight, she looked a little fuzzy around the edges. Her blond hair was falling down from its pile of haphazard pins. She looked faintly rosy, or maybe it was just that she was smiling and it was summer and there was that electric charge between them. She looked perfectly content to let him lead her wherever he wanted to go.

God help him, but the way that seemed to punch straight into his sex almost made him trip over his own two feet right there on the sidewalk.

"I can't decide if you're holding my hand because you think I might secretly be so drunk that I'll topple over without your assistance," Harriet said, sounding only mildly interested. Why was that so hot? "Or if you're simply trying to be provocative."

"Do I have to choose?"

"Anyway," she said. She frowned down at their hands, still linked together. "I don't actually require an escort to walk all of three blocks."

"My mother is a mysterious woman," Jensen informed her. "Some might say a little cold. Chilly, maybe. She's not passionate about a whole lot of things, not these days, anyway, or maybe she keeps it to herself now, whatever, but there was one thing she always made perfectly clear. She fully expects her sons to act like gentlemen." He shifted his grip on her hand so that he could lace his fingers through hers and was once again clobbered by a rush of sensation. It was completely ridiculous given *handholding* was the safest, least sexual touch imaginable.

He was definitely losing his mind.

But the sensation remained.

Harriet took a while to look up from where their hands were joined even more tightly now. "Far be it from me to stand in the way of you being a gentleman, Jensen. If that's on offer."

She regarded him in that disconcertingly direct manner of hers, adjusting the strap of the giant, heavy-looking sack she was carrying over her shoulder. "So. Well—"

But she stopped speaking when Jensen reached over and liberated the enormous sack from her tiny body. He scowled at it.

"What are you carrying around in here? Rocks?"

"Books and yarn. Why would anyone carry *rocks*?"

"Maybe you thought you might build a retaining wall. Maybe you like to throw rocks at things as you march around the town doing your librarian things."

"And what *librarian things* do you think a librarian does outside a library? You can't shelve a sidewalk, Jensen. You can't set up interlibrary loans for the neighbors' lawn art."

"I don't know, Harriet, that's why I asked."

She studied him as if he were the outlier. As if he, who had always fit like a glove wherever he went, because unlike her he worked at that, were the one who made no sense.

"I suppose you could make a case that books are, in a

very real intellectual sense, a kind of retaining wall—" she began in her most philosophical tone.

Jensen threw her bag of stones over his own shoulder, held on to her hand, and began to walk.

"I only live a few blocks away," Harriet said, scurrying along beside him. "And once again, your legs are entirely too long. It's undignified."

Jensen didn't comment. He did slow down considerably, however. And judiciously opted against asking himself what sort of picture he was making here, creeping down the street with a lady's purse over his shoulder and the lady in question swept up in his wake.

It was true that he didn't care too much what people thought about him. But it was also true that he also very rarely minced around like a dancing bear. Jensen had to count himself lucky that the people who were most likely to give him a hard time were currently inside the Broken Wheel, no doubt using his absence to forensically examine every choice he'd made since the third grade.

God bless small towns, he thought. Maybe a little ruefully.

Next to him, Harriet marched on, unbowed and seemingly unconcerned. Her fingers were warm in his, and their hands swung some as they moved, but she appeared interested only in charging down one block, then up the next, as if this walk were being timed.

For his part, Jensen endeavored to enjoy the lovely summer evening. Maybe things weren't quite the norm, at least not for him, but it was pleasant all the same. Charming, even. The woman he couldn't get out of his head was beside him. He could hear her breath. He could hear her feet hit the ground, hard, each step as determined as she was.

He couldn't say he'd ever taken the time to notice such

things before in the ladies who'd gifted him with their attention over the years. The way she chewed a little on her bottom lip as she walked, telling him that head of hers was making noise. That same cinnamon-and-vanilla scent he remembered from before that he was beginning to think he dreamed about at night. Today she was wearing a haphazard and huge skirt, appropriate for a pioneer woman out in the fields a century or two ago, and the kind of sensible sandals his sister had once claimed might as well be chastity belts strapped to the feet.

That's not where chastity belts go, Amanda, Jensen had replied. *As you might find out if you start acting up out there.*

I'll start wearing one when you do, she'd retorted, all of thirteen.

Which had resulted in their mother banishing them both from the dinner table that night.

But he was concentrating on the woman beside him, who he was fairly certain would consider a chastity belt an assault on her principles. Meaning she was wearing that tent of a skirt because she felt like it. And there was no getting around the fact that it had him all worked up too, wondering at the shape of her beneath it. Better still, she wasn't wearing that slouchy cardigan of hers for once.

That was the first thing he'd noticed when he'd walked into the Broken Wheel. He'd been minding his own business, planning to grab a bite with friends and family. After which, by God, he planned to reintroduce himself to the Coyote before he forgot who he was. He'd had the very best of questionable intentions when he'd shown up and then Harriet Barnett had broadsided him with that shapeless button-down she was wearing. It was an unremarkable navy color, with the sleeves rolled up and all the buttons done up tight. It did absolutely nothing for her or to her. Still, he could see the line of her neck. He could see, even better, that she actually had curves.

Because now that they were walking, that oversize button-down moved when she did.

And that meant Jensen had no choice but to start making reasonable guesses about the state of the rest of her. Not just his fevered imagination working overtime for a change. Harriet had big breasts for such a small little thing, and because she insisted on wearing clothes that didn't fit her, it was easy to assume that she was round. But she wasn't. He saw the hint of an indented waist as she moved. The suggestion of nicely flared hips, wide enough to take a man's hands comfortably as he drove inside her.

Hopefully one of these days. Before he died of this. Whatever it was.

She was a pocket-size wonder. He was a mess. And when she came to a stop and looked up at him severely, Jensen ran his tongue around his teeth and wondered if he'd actually said all of that out loud.

"This is my house," she told him.

"Okay."

She tugged her hand. "You can go now. You fulfilled your duties. The next time I see your mother in town, I'll be certain to inform her that she raised you up to be the perfect gentleman."

"Well, Harriet, then she'd know you as a liar."

Jensen let go of her hand, but he took his time about it, so that the whole thing ended up feeling a whole lot more like a caress. Then he watched, entirely too focused on her, as Harriet swallowed hard a few times before letting out a shuddery sort of breath.

And Jensen considered himself a master of only two things in this life. One of them was horses. He loved him some horses. Also, if he said so himself, he was pretty great at just about everything that went into the business of raising, breeding, and selling them.

His other area of expertise was women.

Oddly enough, he had the strangest notion tonight that his enthusiastic embrace of the many joys women could bestow upon a man, over the years, had prepared him for *this* woman in particular. Because Harriet was not exactly a study in enthusiasm. He didn't think she was hiding her body, necessarily, but she sure wasn't presenting it, either. Unless he missed his guess, she was simply living in it. How revolutionary. But she wasn't dressed to impress, out on a weekend night, the way all the women Jensen knew usually were. Even if the person they wanted to impress was their husband. Knowing her as he did, Jensen would be very surprised if Harriet concerned herself overmuch with impressing anyone.

And yet, he had made a study of female arousal. Because Jensen liked a party, but he first liked to be invited to attend.

Harriet might not have been fluttering around, flushed and flustered and toying with a carefully placed pendant in her exposed cleavage—more's the pity—but her eyes were glassy. Her pupils were dilated. Her lips were parted, and she was breathing too fast.

"Are you going to invite me in?" he asked her, shifting her bag from where he'd slung it over his shoulder and placing it on the top step of her porch. "I'm pretty sure that's the polite thing to do."

"I didn't ask you to walk me home in the first place."

"You did. You told me it was my lucky night." He gazed at her in mock astonishment. "Harriet. Were you putting on an act to impress your friends?"

"Certainly not." But her eyes looked glassier, even as she stood up straighter. "I retracted the offer outside the bar. The polite thing to do is listen to a woman who tells you she's perfectly fine on her own. And not to demand invitations."

"I'm just informing you of the basic rules of the social contract around here," Jensen drawled. "Didn't we agree, not five minutes ago, that I'm acquitting myself well as a gentleman in this socially fraught situation? Enough to make my mama proud. I just wanted to make sure you have the opportunity to hold up your end of the bargain."

She blinked. "Was that . . . Was that a *line*?"

Jensen found himself grinning. "It's only a line if it works."

Harriet peered up at him, that brow of hers furrowed as if she were trying to figure him out. He could have told her that was a shallow little puddle, by choice, but he didn't. "I don't mind telling you that the invitation you extended to me in the bar seemed a whole lot friendlier."

"The whole town thinks I have a crush on you," she informed him. In the same way he had heard her make announcements to her class. Matter-of-fact and unemotional. "Actually, they pity me—deeply—for these imagined feelings."

"Are you sure they're imagined?" He widened his grin. "I'm an excellent subject for a hopeless crush. Ask anyone."

"My stated position was that you could just as easily have a crush on me," she said, her municipal, bureaucratic chin rising into the fray. "Why is it always women mooning around, fighting for the attentions of men?"

"Because when men do it, we think they're scary, call them stalkers, and throw them in jail."

"I'm sorry if you feel you walked me home under false pretenses," she said. Loftily, to his mind. "Mostly, I was disproving a point."

It was difficult not to touch her. When had it become so difficult? "What I like about you, Harriet, is that while I'll do just about anything to get a laugh, it sure seems like you're happy to do the same to prove a point."

She sniffed. "That's really not the same thing."

"Isn't it?"

"It's in no way similar. Comic relief is all well and good, and I'm sure it has its place." She did not look even remotely sure. "But what you call making a point is simply a lifelong, bone-deep appreciation for facts. I like facts, Jensen. I like to share facts. I'm a librarian. Arcane knowledge for the simple sake of knowing it is like . . . football, to you. I'm going to assume you like football."

Jensen was baffled. "Who doesn't like football?"

"It's ritualized violence that reenacts land acquisition, which has colonial overtones and, at the very least, promotes a distressing level of tribalism—"

"Harriet. It's a game. Some people like games."

She opened her mouth, then shut it. Then considered, which he never failed to find fascinating. "In fairness, I've never really played games. My parents encouraged chess, of course, to build my strategic and tactical thinking, but I was always encouraged to read a book. Not play."

"That is a crying shame."

"I apologize for casting aspersions on the national pastime," she said after a moment, with the hint of a smile on her face. "A pastime that, if the trophy case in the high school is any indication, is something you dedicated years of your life to once."

"I'm not that dedicated," Jensen assured her. "Truth is, I just like to play. Not too particular about the game."

"Really? Just . . . indiscriminate game playing?" Harriet let out a little huffing sound. "If I asked you to play hide-and-seek, would you just hare off down the block and secrete yourself in a hedge? No questions asked?"

"Hide-and-seek would not be my first choice." He smiled down at her, amazed by the tangents she went off on and her total lack of self-consciousness while she did it. She didn't flirt with him. She didn't play any games, as she'd said, and maybe that alone was why he found her so refreshing. So intriguing.

Then again, maybe it was that generous mouth of hers. It seemed completely out of place, lush and inviting, on a woman who spent most of her time scowling and blinking owlishly from behind her glasses.

"What is your favorite game?" she asked, and that was the thing about Harriet if he broke all the rest of it down. When she asked questions, she always sounded genuinely curious about the answers.

It made a man pause and reflect on how often that wasn't the case.

And who was he to stand in the way of genuine curiosity?

"I'll show you," he said, his voice low and maybe a bit rougher than usual, but that was how it was when he was around her. Maybe it was time to stop asking why.

She was little, so he picked her up. And Jensen learned a great many new things about her as he held her body to his. Those breasts, her hips. That perfect round bottom in his hands. The heat of her, her sweet cinnamon scent, and her hair on his face, bringing with it the smell of rain and flowers.

Harriet made a shocked sound. She went stiff at first, then limp. Her hands were up against his chest, but she wasn't pushing him away. She was holding on as he shifted his weight so her legs went around his waist—a benefit to that giant skirt of hers that he hadn't considered.

But he was thankful for it now.

To show his appreciation, he bent his head and kissed her.

And as he'd been wanting to kiss her for a good little while now, Jensen took his time about it. He teased her lips until she sighed and shook. Then he found his way between them, tasting her at last.

At last.

She was tart and sweet, with a hint of whiskey, and he felt as if she were running her hands all over his sex.

Harriet kissed him back. Tentatively at first and then, when he kept it lazy, with more heat. And commitment.

It was slick and wild. It was sheer magic.

Jensen angled his head, then brought her closer against him so he could fit nice and snug between her legs. He eased her back against the pillar of the porch so he could pin her there while he set himself to the task.

Then he got a little rowdy.

He kissed her and he kissed her. She kissed him back.

And it got better every time.

He kissed her like he had no particular destination in mind. As if the kissing were the beginning and end of it, and he might as well take his time.

And she was in his arms, her back against that post, so he got to learn her too. The real shape of her, petite and curvy and shockingly lush, while she kissed him back.

If he'd been capable of thought, he would have realized that of course she would kiss like that. Determined and ferocious. It was just like her.

Jensen kissed her over and over, until he felt that pounding need inside of him start to streak toward the boiling point.

And he'd never felt protective about a woman before her. Certainly not one who was already in his arms. But it turned out that like everyone else in town, he wanted to protect Miss Harriet Barnett from him too.

So even though it caused him actual pain, as if he were little better than a fourteen-year-old kid, he wrenched his mouth away from hers. And he knew he should put her down and get a little distance between them, but he took his time with that. He couldn't seem to help it.

Because Jensen had no idea if this was going to be the last time he got to touch her. If the closest he ever got to that soft place between her legs that he could currently only feel with layers of clothing in between was this. Here. Normally, he wasn't the one with any insecurity about whether or not there would be another round.

He supposed he had this coming.

Jensen set Harriet down eventually. He stood back and realized, with another burst of that same awe that seemed to signify all things Harriet, that he had absolutely no idea how she was going to react.

But he sure did want to find out.

Her eyes were closed, and she took a moment to open them, allowing him ample time to notice how long her eyelashes were. And how sooty they looked against her soft cheeks, when he would stake his life on the fact she didn't wear makeup. And then when she opened her eyes, they were brilliant pools of blue, filled with heat.

She was still slumped back against the post, and he wasn't going to be the one to tell her that her hair had come tumbling down entirely, so that it hung about her face, shimmering gold and cascading past her breasts.

He wanted to bury his face in it. He wanted to get his hands in there and hold her still, so he could glut himself on her. And take his time doing it.

She focused on him, but it seemed to take her a minute.

And then, slowly, she treated him to that heart-stopping smile of hers.

His own heart went a little crazy in his chest.

"Well," she said. Breathed. "Had I known how much fun these games were, I might have made myself available to more childhood games of Monopoly."

"Harriet." He had meant to sound light and easy, but he really didn't. "Have you ever been kissed before?"

And there was that frown of hers again. "Let me guess. Because I'm the spinster cat lady, I must therefore never have been touched by another human hand. Do you ask everyone you kiss that question?"

"I don't. But often I already know the answer."

Up went that chin. "I'll have you know that I approached kissing the same way I approached any other matter of interest. I had a kissing phase, if you want to know the truth. I experimented with kissing all over my college campus, and the results were highly instructive."

"*Instructive*." He shook his head, still tasting her on his tongue. "That sounds anything but hot and dirty, Harriet."

"I discovered, for example, that if you're not really swept away by a kiss, you end up spending a lot of time contemplating the nature of lips and tongues, and no, I would not describe that as hot."

"Are you trying to tell me that I'm a bad kisser?"

To his delight, she made a sound that was perilously close to a giggle. She lifted one hand to her lips. To muffle it? To feel it while it happened? He didn't know. And it made him ache that he couldn't do the same and get his hands back on her.

"No. I wouldn't say that. I'm not contemplating your lips in a clinical way, you'll be happy to know."

"That is a comfort."

She pressed her fingers against her mouth. "But mine certainly feel different."

"Your instructive experiment in college aside, I'm going to suggest to you that you've never been properly kissed before now."

Her smile was even brighter this time. "Why am I not surprised by your certainty that your kissing is 'proper'?"

"It's okay if you don't want to admit it," he told her, grinning. "I think we both know the truth."

"This has been quite an evening," Harriet said, her eyes shining and that smile on her face while his head was a mess of cinnamon and sweetness. "Whiskey and proper kissing. Sadly, this might be the beginning of a shocking downward spiral."

"It can be the beginning of anything you want," Jensen found himself saying.

When he never, ever said things like that. He didn't do open-ended. Ever.

Harriet looked at him for a long while, and he died. And wondered what had happened to his penance. Was this all it took? One too-fascinating woman? Was that all the vows he'd made meant to him?

"I thought you didn't date."

He thought her voice sounded small, but that didn't make any sense. This was Harriet. The only small thing about her was her actual, physical body. And his own heart was pounding so hard in his chest he was surprised her neighbors hadn't come out to see what all the commotion was about.

And there were questions he really should ask himself about what he was doing here, but he couldn't focus on that when this solid little rock of a woman sounded shaken.

Jensen reached out and smoothed his hand over a gleaming hank of her hair, to see if he could get that gold all over him. "To tell you the truth, Harriet, I don't know what to do with you."

"Oh," she breathed. He watched her brain work, there behind those fathomless eyes of hers, and she seemed to *sparkle*. "That definitely sounds like a line. Is this where I invite you in?"

"You can invite me in," he said, his hand tightening in her hair. "But this is uncharted territory, darlin'. I don't seem to be able to control myself around you."

"You seem to be doing a fine job of it so far," she said, though her eyes had gone big.

"Maybe what I should say is that I don't want to control myself around you," Jensen managed, his voice rough. "You frown at me, you shove those glasses up your nose, and all I'm going to be thinking about is how soon I can get inside you."

Her breath hitched. "Inside me?"

If he'd been less dangerously intent on her just then, he might have laughed at the squeaking sound those two little words made when she said them.

"Are you ready for that?" he asked.

And while she thought on it, he traced her lips with his thumb. Then he cupped her cheek to discover that, just as he'd imagined, she fit his palm perfectly.

But when all she did was gaze up at him, her breath ragged and her eyes wide, he nodded. Jerkily.

"Let me know when you are," he said.

Then he made himself let go. He made himself step back. He did not give into the urge to pick her up again, even though *not* picking her up again was beginning to feel like a bruise.

But he didn't.

Jensen shoved his hands in his pockets before they got him into trouble, turned around, and left her there.

Before he couldn't.

11

Harriet took a very long time to gather her wits about her.

So long, in fact, that as she stood there—still slumped against the post in front of her porch—while the last of the light faded from the sky and the stars took over, she did begin to wonder if she'd lost said wits entirely. And possibly permanently.

Jensen had stormed off into the night. Impressively, the way he did everything. Meanwhile, she stayed where she was, mostly because she couldn't move. She felt significantly drunker than she had all night. Though she knew it wasn't leftover whiskey kicking in.

It was Jensen. It was all Jensen.

Maybe it was possible that she did, in fact, have a crush on the man.

A *crush*. The notion made her feel much too hot and had her pressing her fingers to her mouth again. She'd never understood that word before, but she did now. Because all the heat and wonder that was Jensen seemed to sit heavy on her like a stone. Like one of the mountains keeping watch.

Eventually, though she didn't know how, she pushed herself away from the post. And as she did, she had the strangest sensation that her body was no longer hers. It didn't feel comfortable around her the way it usually did. She was too *aware* of it, for one thing. She was a collection of *parts,* all of them different from before, because of him. Her breasts ached and her nipples were in tight points. Between her legs, she had melted straight through. And everywhere else, her skin felt overly sensitized. She could feel the faint breeze, the temperature, the night itself like a caress. Everywhere.

Even her hair was down when she never wore her hair down. It was too long and too unprofessional, to her mind. But she left it as it was, falling everywhere, even though—or maybe because—it added to the feeling that she was wrapped up in a thick, brooding sort of sensuality.

Right there outside her house.

Harriet somehow made her way up the front stairs. She hauled her bag up from the top step—noting it felt heavier now that Jensen had carried it, as if it really were filled with stones—then let herself into the house. Where she was greeted at the door by three of her cats and varying degrees of feline interrogation.

Maybe she had a guilty conscience. Because it certainly sounded as if they were issuing accusations.

"It was just a little bit of kissing," she told them sternly.

No one was impressed.

As she bustled around, setting out their dinners over their very clear complaints of near death from obvious neglect, Harriet thought it was a good thing to slip straight back into the reality of her life. Surely her body would start feeling familiar again at any minute. She liked it that way, practical and dependable. Not *alive* with all these sensations that made her do profoundly odd things like stop walking in the middle of her own hallway to sigh a little and breathe deep so she could feel that ache in her breasts anew.

Which she did more than once.

When she had satisfied her brood—and had retrieved Maisey from her closet, where the little calico had burrowed into a rain boot—she found herself wafting back into her own living room like some kind of opera heroine. Or worse, like Ophelia. Harriet laughed at herself as she collapsed on her couch and lay there in a lump, but it was better than the alternative. Consumption if she were a real opera heroine or drowning if she had the bad luck to find herself in *Hamlet*.

She'd always found such portrayals needlessly melodramatic.

Funny how, tonight, she found they hit home.

Harriet had only slightly exaggerated her kissing experiment in college when she'd told Jensen about it earlier. It had been a classic example of what she had considered one of her brilliant ideas, back when she'd worried about how alien she apparently was to her peers. She'd figured she could combine the practicalities—that being her own inability to figure out how to fit in, which was apparently something she was supposed to desire—with things she actually liked and cared about, like research. About kissing, which she had obviously been curious about forever but had never experienced while homeschooling. She'd convinced herself and anyone who would listen—or who asked her what was wrong with her, a more common query—that it was all in the name of science.

Secretly, Harriet had harbored the hope that the more college men she asked to experiment with her—all in aid of her research, of course!—the more possible she made it that one of them might sweep her away. Because surely one of them would, right?

There had been no sweeping. As she'd told Jensen, more often, there had been a sad contemplation of the mechanics of a kiss, which was about as far away from being swept anywhere as she could imagine.

She had begun to think that being swept away was just a story people told, the province of books or movies. Because it clearly had no basis in reality. And she'd decided that was a great relief, because if it had no basis in reality, there was no need for Harriet to feel as if she'd ever been missing out on anything.

So she hadn't. Until tonight.

When Jensen Kittredge had made it perfectly clear, there outside her cozy little house, that he alone could do what every single participant in her research project in college had not. That being swept away by someone wasn't a myth. Or wishful thinking. Or silly notions women pretended were real between the covers of books with besotted couples on the front, while ignoring the far less romantic real husband snoring on the couch.

In the privacy of her own living room, Harriet allowed herself a deeply inelegant giggle.

And if she wasn't mistaken, when she lifted her fingers to her cheeks to tease out the heat that bloomed there, she might have succumbed to her very first blush.

She couldn't say she minded.

Though she should have minded. She should have been *horrified*. Outraged at the evidence that despite everything, she was just as silly as anyone else. Because for all this time, all her life, Harriet had taken a great deal of pride in the fact that she wasn't as easily swayed as others were. Not by a handsome face. Not by men with bulging muscles cuddling kittens on the covers of calendars. None of those things had ever done much for her. She could appreciate a pretty picture of a lovely man, certainly. There were movies she'd watched over and over, just so she could better admire the hero. It wasn't as if she'd locked herself off in some tower and felt nothing.

But she hadn't imagined any of it could actually *happen*.

And it was disconcerting to feel, as she did now, that despite her belief that she'd lived her life to the fullest, it had actually been black and white until tonight. Until he'd kissed her, like she was some real-life, small-town Colorado version of Sleeping Beauty.

Because she felt vivid. Bright straight through.

Instead of instantly thinking of a thousand reasons why she shouldn't feel what she felt, or why she should instantly begin building up her defenses against this sneaky wave of sentimentality she could already feel bubbling up inside her, Harriet resolved to simply lie there. Right there on her couch like any number of hopeless heroines in her favorite books, giggling when she felt like it, because why not let herself be properly swept away for the first time in her life?

Because she had kissed a great many collegiate toads in the name of science, and it had gotten her neither interesting results nor any closer to her contemporaries. Being kissed until she was giddy and *vivid*—and not because she'd asked to be kissed in the first place, for once—was something worth celebrating.

Chaucer came and plopped himself down on her chest while Eleanor perched coquettishly on the nearest sofa arm and across the room, Brontë glared from beneath a chair. So Harriet had a purring cat, an elder feline sentinel, and the night itself in whiskered form to add to her sense that all was right with the world. She had enjoyed a perfect day. There had been books and yarn. She'd drunk whiskey and possibly made friends.

She had a smile on her face as she drifted off to sleep.

When she heard the ringing, her first, sleepy thought was that it was simply some or other internal alarm, no doubt reacting to her uncharacteristic behavior. All her uncharacteristic behavior today, in fact.

Harriet sat up too fast and got a hint of claw in her thigh for her trouble.

"Unnecessary," she complained to Chaucer, who glared at her balefully.

Then she heard the ringing again and realized it was her doorbell.

It rang so rarely. When packages were delivered on mornings she was actually home. And on Halloween, when it rang constantly and children would scream with delight every time she threw open the door.

Maybe it wasn't surprising that she barely recognized the sound now, in the middle of the night. She frowned at her watch and discovered it wasn't yet midnight. Not late to some, she supposed, but later than she cared to find people loitering about on her stoop. It took her a minute to stand up and get her bearings. She had to check her legs for lacerations thanks to Chaucer, the jerk, and then she staggered toward the door.

And she could admit that deep down, she was kind of hoping it was Jensen again, back to experiment with his own loss of control. So she could do the same.

She really, really wanted to do the same.

Because if he was *that* good at kissing, surely that had to mean that he was equally good at all the other things. She'd heard that wasn't always the case, but something about Jensen made her think that he, at least, wasn't engaging in any false advertising.

He was too relaxed, for one thing. The kind of relaxed that suggested he had nothing to prove.

She shuddered a little at that thought, then tossed her door wide open.

But it wasn't Jensen who was standing there.

It was Aidan Hall.

"Why is your hair down?" Aidan demanded, scowling at her with profound teenage betrayal all over his face.

And Harriet had been drifting off into blissful daydreams only moments before, her mouth still feeling not quite like her own from Jensen's kisses. But that didn't mean that she couldn't snap herself back to form.

She adjusted her glasses, frowned up at the sixteen-year-old student who should not have been on her doorstep at all and certainly not at 11:27 on a Saturday night, and bristled.

"What a rude and impertinent question," she replied coolly. "I certainly hope you haven't appeared on my doorstep, violating my privacy outside of school hours, to comment on my appearance, Mr. Hall."

Her crisp tone and steady glare did the trick. Aidan, who had moments before seemed a little bit puffed up, as if her answer would lead him to *take steps*, deflated.

This was why Harriet loved teenagers. These strange, coltish creatures, caught between the children they'd been and the adults they would become. Desperate for independence and hungry for love and acceptance, all at once. She knew some people in her position tried to be friends with the students, but Harriet had never seen that as her role. The stricter she was—strict but kind—the more results she got. Because her philosophy had always been that adolescence was treacherous enough. She'd enjoyed her own, for the most part, but that didn't mean she'd been blind to how profoundly isolated she often was or how, if she'd been unlucky enough to have a different personality, she might have suffered. Her goal was always to provide the students with a steadiness, no matter what.

The researcher in her was thrilled to see the same approach work even in an improper situation such as this.

"No," he muttered, his face coloring as he studied his feet. "No, ma'am. I've just never seen your hair down before."

"I am afraid, Mr. Hall, that I am a person. I exist outside the Cold River High School building. But it's inappropriate to discuss my personal life, even though you're standing right in the middle of it at this hour." She folded her arms. "I'm not sure how you know where I live in the first place and equally unsure that I want to ask."

"This is Cold River." Aidan shook his head slightly at her as if confused. "Everyone knows where everyone else lives."

Harriet had to allow that. "Very well. What are you doing here?"

"Can I come in?"

"You absolutely may not," Harriet replied calmly. "If you'd like to talk, we can remain outside."

"Oh, because I'm, like . . . a guy?"

Harriet regarded him narrowly as she stepped out onto the porch, closing her front door behind her. "Your gender has nothing to do with it. You are a student. It's late at night, and you turned up at my house without an invitation. I'm not certain that I wish to share the place where I live with my students, Mr. Hall. Would you like it if I turned up unannounced at your house?"

He let out a bitter sort of sound. "It would be better than who usually turns up."

"Is that why you're here?" She studied his face in the porch light, looking for signs of some or other altercation. "Has your living situation become untenable?"

"The situation is the same as it always is," Aidan told her, looking older again. Older than a kid ever should. "I don't see why I have to wait until I'm eighteen to be considered a grown-up. The only reason we have food now is because I buy it. I already have a part-time job. There wouldn't even be lights on if it weren't for me."

"It's not fair," Harriet agreed. "I'm sorry. Have you finished researching your paper so we can start exploring potential remedies?"

"Miss Barnett, I don't want to write a stupid paper," he flared at her. "I want to move out without someone sending Human Services after me."

Harriet hesitated. Because she wondered if he might just run away, which she thought would be a tragedy. And she wondered why the system that was meant to help so often did the opposite. "I want to help you, Aidan. I really do. But I'm limited in *how* I can help you, and stunts like this aren't going to help."

His face reddened. "It's not a stunt."

"You are a student of mine," she said gently. "There are boundaries. There should be boundaries. That's only appropriate."

"You're just like all the rest of them, aren't you?" Aidan seethed at her. "Everybody says they want to help until I actually need them to. Then forget about it. I'm on my own. I'm *always* on my own."

Harriet didn't think that was a fair assessment, but she also didn't need to justify herself to a sixteen-year-old. She was perfectly able to weather any rage he needed to let out. Maybe he simply wanted someone to be there while he expressed his emotions without it getting him into trouble. She could relate to that.

"Do you want to know why I spray-painted the youth center?" Aidan's voice was getting louder, but Harriet didn't react. She waited. "Because I knew that if I did, someone would finally *listen* to me."

"I'm happy to listen to you," Harriet said calmly. "I'm listening to you now, even though I suspect you know perfectly well you shouldn't have shown up here like this. I listen to you in school—"

"School is stupid." He glared at her, daring her to comment on that.

"I'm not surprised to hear that you think so. But then, you decided long before I met you that you wanted nothing to do with school. And yet if that were true, why would you be here tonight? Surely there are all kinds of antics you could get up to this close to midnight on a Saturday."

Though she probably shouldn't encourage any antics. Even by inference.

"Maybe trouble is all I'm good for," Aidan threw out at her. "Haven't you heard? I'm just another Hall. And I don't get good grades, so there won't be any fancy scholarship to get me out of here. I'm not good with cars like my cousin Wyatt. Might as well start stealing things, right?"

Harriet stood quietly, waiting to see if he'd add to that. But he didn't. His chest was heaving and his expression was defiant, yet all she could see was the shade of vulnerability beneath it. More than a shade.

"You're not destined to be anyone or anything but who you are," Harriet told him after a moment, her eyes steady on his so there could be no mistake. "You're sixteen. That is far too young to worry that you've doomed yourself to your life's single path and can never do anything else."

"It's too late." His voice was dull. Thick. "You don't get it."

"It might feel too late to you, but it's not, I promise."

She stuck her hands into the deep pockets of her favorite skirt. "If you're interested in scholarships and academics, I'm happy to help. I can tutor you. If you're interested in learning how to perform practical skills, like working on cars, I can help you find some kind of internship or part-time job. But when I offer to help, Aidan, it's not an empty gesture. I can't do it alone. You have to show up for yourself. If you truly don't want this family destiny I've heard way too much about, you have to decide that it doesn't apply to you."

"You don't understand, Miss Barnett. You're not from here. You don't know what it's like to be a Hall."

"You're right, I don't." Harriet didn't fidget. She kept her gaze trained on him. "If you think that's an insurmountable obstacle and everyone who's ever told you that your family dictates who you get to be is right, fine. Believe it. But I don't know why you would show up at my door on a Saturday night to share your family curse with me. I don't think you want to believe in it, Aidan. I think you're afraid that it doesn't matter if you do or don't."

He shook his head. She saw his throat move. But he didn't say anything.

Harriet took that as tacit agreement. "I think you came because you don't want to keep playing the role you're currently playing. Delinquent. Outlaw. Whatever you want to call it. Either way, you want to change. And I have good news and bad news for you. The good news is, you can absolutely choose to have any life you wish. The bad news is, you have to change yourself first. That's the only way it works."

Aidan shoulders hunched forward as if he were bracing himself. "I don't know if I can."

"Nobody does," Harriet said softly. "Nobody ever said changing was easy. I'm not sure it's even particularly pleasant. And in the long run, only you can decide if it's worth it. I can't do that for you, and neither can anyone else."

"But what if . . ." He looked at her for a moment, his gaze vulnerable and beseeching. Then he looked away again as if he couldn't bear that he'd shown her that side of him. "What if I decide to change, but I can't? Isn't that worse than never trying at all?"

"I'm sure a lot of people would think so," Harriet said quietly. She wanted to hold this lost kid, hug him a little, but she knew that wasn't an option. She couldn't go around embracing teenagers, no matter how much they needed it. There were boundaries for a reason. "But bitterness is easy. It's a lot harder to actually learn something about yourself, win or lose. It could be that you decide to change for the better and discover along the way that where you thought you wanted to go isn't where you want to end up, after all. That's not failure. It could be that you try to do something but find you can't. That might technically be a failure, but it's only a bad thing if you let it stop you. Failure is nothing more and nothing less than information. What you do with that information is who you are."

He was still looking away, looking so young again that it made Harriet's ribs ache. She wanted to wrap him up in something soft, because she thought he had precious little of that in his life. She wanted to protect him, but she knew she couldn't.

The only thing she could do was give him what had been given to her a long time ago. The tools to find a way to protect himself.

Even if it didn't seem like much right now.

"Aidan," she said quietly. "What is it you want to do? If you could do anything. If it had nothing at all to do with your family, or this town, or anything you've ever been told about who you are and what you could accomplish."

And she waited, there on the porch where Jensen Kittredge had kissed her silly earlier in the night. She could still feel a kind of giddiness cartwheeling around inside of her, but it was different now. Tonight, she'd experienced passion, but this was purpose. Harriet realized, as she waited to see if Aidan would actually share his dreams with her, that she'd always believed deep down that a practical person had to choose between the two. She had therefore chosen only purpose, ignoring passion altogether.

Harriet was asking Aidan what he really wanted, wasn't she? Maybe she should ask herself too. Maybe, she should wonder if it was possible to have passion and purpose at once, after all.

The very notion made her feel a little bit as if her own porch were buckling beneath her.

Aidan looked back at her then. He met her gaze for a moment, then dropped his.

"I want to go to college," he said, and the naked yearning in his voice almost made her flinch. It was that raw. That vulnerable. "I want *options,* Miss Barnett. I want to go somewhere no one's ever heard of me, or this town, or any of my relatives, and I want to get to choose who I am. Like everybody else."

And slowly, carefully, he looked at her again. He searched her face, looking wary and stiff.

Harriet understood that he was waiting for her to laugh at him.

She did not.

"I think that's a perfectly reasonable dream," she said instead, very matter-of-factly. "Obviously, you're aware that you are currently on academic probation, but I don't see why you can't view that as a challenge instead of a roadblock."

"But . . ." Aidan blinked. "I thought it was already too late."

"College isn't one-size-fits-all," Harriet said crisply. "Are there some colleges that will admit only those students who have perfect grades and squeaky-clean extracurriculars to go along with glorious test scores? Of course. The truth is, even if you possessed all those things, I doubt very much that you'd be the sort of person who would benefit from a college like that. But you happen to live in a country absolutely full of educational options. There's no reason to assume that we can't find you one that suits you, if that's what you want."

It took her a moment or two to realize that Aidan looked . . . dazed. As if he didn't fully believe what she was telling him. As if he couldn't imagine that he actually had possibilities instead of the reputation he'd been born with.

"I will expect that paper, Mr. Hall," she told him, not giving in to her urge to get a little giddy where he could see it. "We will consider it a statement of intent, you and I. If you do not produce the paper, I'll be disappointed, but I'll understand. If you do, we will not only sit down and discuss juvenile emancipation but also how to proceed now that we know what your goals are. I'm happy to *help* you reach your goals, Aidan. But I can't do it *for* you. Do you understand?"

"Yeah." He grinned a little, still looking dazed. And if she wasn't mistaken, hopeful. For the first time since she'd met him. "Thank you, Miss Barnett. I'm . . . uh . . . sorry I showed up at your front door."

"Don't do it again," she replied, but smiled.

And then she stood there, waiting, because Aidan

seemed unwilling to leave. But soon enough, he did, moving down her front steps with one hand on the rail as if he'd really rather hold himself in place.

"Aren't you starting your Bar K experience tomorrow?" she asked.

Aidan turned back at the bottom of the stair, and a smile curved his mouth, making him look at least twice his age and far too world-weary.

"Yes, ma'am," he said. "I already painted the youth center, so now it's horses at three o'clock."

"Will you miss the appointment the way you have the last two?"

Not that Jensen had told her that. She'd asked Aidan every Monday and, to give the boy some credit, he never lied.

"No, ma'am," he muttered.

"Wonderful," she said. "I'll meet you there. Just to confirm all this enthusiasm."

And not to see Jensen again, now that kissing had been introduced, because that would be a gross dereliction of her duties, surely.

Then again, humans were complicated. They had layers.

She apparently had layers she'd never imagined she could.

"Okay," Aidan said. "I guess that's fair."

Then he headed toward a beat-up old pickup at the curb that roared lustily when he started the engine. And kept right on shouting as he drove it away.

Leaving Harriet there on her porch, watching moths dance in the light. She vowed to herself, as the sound of his truck faded away, that she would make sure that boy had someone to believe in. And someone who believed in him, while she was at it, no matter what the good folks of Cold River had to say about his family.

And if that happened to come along with greater exposure to Jensen Kittredge and his kisses, all the better.

12

Jensen woke up the next morning in a remarkably good mood.

He was downright jolly during his chores, enough so that both Riley and Connor started muttering about it. He took that as an invitation to ramp it up. By the time he ambled into the ranch house kitchen to get himself some more coffee, he'd turned to whistling—loud enough that both of his parents, going over some papers on the kitchen table, stopped what they were doing to stare at him.

"I'm sorry if I'm not maintaining the typical level of Kittredge doom and gloom around here," Jensen boomed out. "That must be bracing."

"You're usually loud, Jensen," his mother observed in her cool way. "But you're typically more interested in being provoking. You seem . . . genuinely happy."

As if she'd never used those words before.

"No doubt that parental example," Jensen drawled, grinning to take the sting out of the words. And because 6:00 a.m. was a little early for full-scale family drama.

His mother had long ago perfected the art of seeming to roll her eyes without actually committing. With four rowdy boys and Amanda in the mix, whatever her relationship was with her husband, it maybe wasn't surprising that Ellie Kittredge had a cool stare that could stop a man in his tracks. But today, Jensen was paying more attention to his father, who, he was forced to admit, was looking a little older and a little frailer than before his cardiac event earlier this summer. He couldn't say he liked that.

He wasn't close to his parents, a situation he liked as it was, but he still didn't like it.

"Speaking of provoking displays of happiness," Jensen said, jutting his chin at his father, "how's that ticker, Dad?"

Donovan Kittredge glowered. "I'm fine."

Jensen, like Zack, was old enough to remember a little too much about back when his parents' relationship had been tempestuous at best. Mostly it had been a roller coaster, loud and frightening. Ellie had screamed and cried. Donovan had been a brick wall. Until one day, they'd up and decided to stop. Amanda had come less than a year later.

Riley had advanced the theory, apparently gleaned from his own recalcitrant wife, that maybe it wasn't that the pair of them had turned into ice sculptures. Maybe it was simply that they'd decided to keep their actual marriage private.

Too bad Jensen remembered far too much of it when it hadn't been.

"Are you?" he asked now, because *he* hadn't agreed to any code of silence. "Because I have to say, you don't look—"

"I'm not going to perform for you, Jensen," Donovan said quietly, his dark eyes meeting his son's and holding fast. "I appreciate that you've stepped up this summer. But I'd appreciate it if you'd remember that staying home was your choice. And I'm not beholden to you because of it."

Boom. There it was. Donovan Kittredge, slapping down any possible attempts his sons made to get closer to him. Or even, just for fun, to interact like family instead of enemies. Riley kept claiming that when he sat with Donovan, if he didn't ask for much and waited to see what would happen, it was better.

But Jensen couldn't help thinking that it was his father's responsibility to act like a father for a change. Or even once. Because sooner or later, Zack was going to stop his whole stoic sheriff routine and say all those things he'd been keeping to himself since the infamous night he'd moved out.

Jensen planned to make the popcorn.

"Wow," he said now, leaning back against the counter and taking a swig of his coffee. "I don't remember when I asked you to be beholden to me, Dad."

"Enough," Ellie cut in. "We all have work to do. Or I assume we do, Jensen, since I'm not sure what it is you do all day."

"Nothing at all," Jensen drawled. "I'm just a figurehead. You know that, Mom."

And he laughed when he said it, because she looked as if maybe she might have been kidding. But he was still pissed about it later, after he'd spent the morning trying to catch up on his paperwork. Then played his usual role at Sunday dinner, doing his best to make it seem as if he'd already forgotten the morning's interactions.

Though he hadn't. And wouldn't.

But that was the trouble with living down to low expectations as a life choice. He remembered each and every time someone assumed that was the only thing he was capable of doing. And sure, sometimes he wondered if his father was doing the same thing. Since stubborn seemed to run deep into Kittredge bones around here.

Jensen dismissed that possibility every time it occurred to him, and he could admit that was mostly because he didn't particularly want to feel sympathy for his father. He liked things the way they were—distant.

He liked most everything at arm's length, in fact.

But when he walked outside after Sunday dinner was over to find Aidan Hall in the yard, looking shifty and sullen, he wasn't thinking about distance of any kind. Especially with that pathetic-looking hatchback parked nearby with his favorite librarian at the back of it like she was standing guard. He figured the day was finally looking up.

"Ready for your lesson?" he asked the kid. "Finally?"

He was aware of his family coming out of the house behind him. And he knew when Zack made an appearance, because Aidan stood straighter, looking alarmed.

"Uh. Yeah. I guess."

"Excellent," Jensen boomed. "That's right," he threw back over his shoulder. "You're not the only one who can give horseback riding lessons, Riley."

"Anyone can give horseback riding lessons," Riley replied. "You never do."

That was true. But Jensen just laughed. "I'm turning over a new leaf."

"You mean Miss Barnett asked you to," Aidan retorted, and then scoffed. "I'm not the only one who does what she asks."

Jensen couldn't think of anything he would rather not have had announced like that in the presence of his entire nosy family.

Not to mention Harriet herself.

Luckily, he'd never been afraid of an awkward moment.

He preferred to lean in. That was what he did now, grinning wide at the teenager before him and then aiming it around at his family too.

"That's me," he said. Then he shifted the force of his attention to Harriet, because he couldn't resist. "I'm pretty much known for my obedience."

He didn't wait for a response to the Jensen Show. He ambled off toward the barn, indicating with his chin that Harriet and Aidan should follow him. He half expected to turn around and find that his entire family had followed too, but they didn't. A reprieve he was sure he'd pay for later. But that was Future Jensen's problem.

Either way, when they got to the barn, it was only Harriet and Aidan. Harriet had clearly dressed for the ranch. Which, on her, meant a pair of jeans he would have sworn she didn't own, sneakers instead of a proper pair of boots, and a different button-down shirt with rolled-up sleeves. It almost looked like proper Western wear, but because it was Harriet, it wasn't as if anyone would confuse her for a Pendleton ad. Aidan, on the other hand, wore black jeans, a black T-shirt, and entirely too many metal things, like a chain connecting his wallet to his belt. Not to mention enough black leather wrapped around one wrist that it was clear it was meant as a statement.

"Neither one of you has ever been on a horse before, have you?" Jensen asked as he stopped before one of the stalls, where Old Man, Jensen's personal favorite horse, was hanging out and eyeing the new arrivals with interest.

"I've ridden a horse," Aidan said, chin high and defiant. As he stood against the far wall.

Jensen waited, rubbing Old Man's long nose as he kept his gaze on the kid. Sure enough, Aidan shifted his weight, then crossed his arms.

"It was like a pony at the fair," he mumbled. "Once."

"And you?" Jensen asked Harriet.

"Oh, I'm not here to ride horses," she told him. "Aidan told me that he had yet to begin this aspect of his community service. So I said I would meet him here to make sure we all remembered to get it done."

"I think you know that doesn't answer my question, Harriet."

Jensen waited.

"No," she said a bit primly. "I've never been on a horse. They're very tall."

"Not that tall," said Aidan. "You're just short."

Harriet frowned at him. "It's rude to comment on other people's personal appearance or physical characteristics. But you're correct. I doubt I could reach that far up, much less hurl myself into a saddle that far from the ground. I'm here in an advisory capacity only."

"And what will you be advising us on?" Jensen asked. "How to not ride a horse?"

But if he expected that to fluster her, he was in for a disappointment. Because all she did was gaze back at him the way she always did, her gaze entirely too blue. No sign of whiskey or wickedness. No stray trace of those kisses that had kept *him* up half the night.

"Is that what you plan to teach Mr. Hall?" she asked him crisply.

"Great," Aidan muttered. "That way it can be just like school."

"First things first," Jensen announced, ignoring that little dig. "I'm not going to throw you on the back of a horse today. I could, and you'd be fine, but that's not the goal."

"Isn't it?" Harriet was now aiming that frown at him.

"Not today," Jensen said cheerfully. He focused on

Aidan. "Before you try riding a horse, you need to get comfortable with them."

"I'm comfortable."

"Kid. I'm not sure you've ever been comfortable a day in your life." Aidan looked down, something like stricken, and Jensen wished he hadn't said that. He cleared his throat. "This is Old Man. He was a champion in his day, and now he gets to hang out and tell everyone what to do. He's my favorite. Pleasant with a little bit of an attitude. You're going to come over here and get to know him."

The alarmed look that Aidan shot him then was much more kid and much less sulky teen. "I am?"

Jensen only waited. And slowly, Aidan uncrossed his belligerent arms. He vibrated there and then inched forward. Stopped himself, then considered for a moment. Then inched forward again.

He repeated that a few times, getting closer every time.

Jensen was prepared to wait all day. He snuck a look at Harriet to see if there was any impatience from that quarter that he was going to have to stave off. But her eyes were shining as she watched her skittish charge move closer and closer to the horse who waited there for him. Calm and quiet, like Old Man knew that was what the boy needed.

That was the thing about horses. They always knew. Jensen couldn't count how many times he'd escaped out into the barn when he was growing up, because the horses didn't need him to play the clown. The horses didn't yell or cry. They let him be whoever he was, whatever he felt. And especially in those years when he had yet to grow into his body, they'd made him feel like he was already perfect.

But he was still holding his breath, just a little bit,

until—with a glance at Jensen for permission—Aidan reached out and put his hand on Old Man's muzzle.

"He liked that," Jensen said when Old Man shared his enthusiasm.

"That means he liked it?" Aidan clearly remembered that he was a cool, collected sixteen-year-old. Who had just flinched. He tried to play it off. "I thought he was going to bite me."

"He won't bite you," Jensen assured him. "Especially not if you pat him."

And then, for another hour or so, he let Aidan get to know the horse. He taught him how to pat Old Man the way he liked, how to bribe him with carrots, and how to find his way around an animal so much bigger than he was in the confines of a stall. He taught him the basics of how to groom a horse, then watched him do it. He led Old Man out into the paddock so Aidan could walk around with him and get to know the feel of it. Having a huge animal next to him, near him. What it sounded like when a horse was walking around with you.

Judging by the number of smiles he coaxed out of the kid, Old Man was already doing his part of the work.

"Um. Next Sunday, then?" Aidan asked when they were back out in the yard, studiously looking anywhere but at Jensen.

"I'll be here," Jensen assured him.

And then, as Aidan climbed into the kind of beater Jensen wished he'd had when he was that age, then headed off down the dirt road toward the county blacktop, Jensen finally turned his attention to Harriet.

Who had been right there the whole time, driving him wild without doing anything at all but observing. Just standing nearby, smelling like candy.

"Well?" He folded his arms as he leaned back against her little car, surprised he didn't tip it over. "Did I pass?"

"Did you pass what?"

"I assume that was a test. That you came out here to see if I was truly up to the challenge of handling the kid."

Her gaze seemed particularly intent. "Are you looking for a grade, Jensen?"

"No need. I think we both know it was an A-plus. With honors."

"Lucky for you, I don't give out grades." But the tartness in her expression faded as she looked at the cloud of dust Aidan had kicked up behind him because, of course, he was driving too fast. "I think this is so good for him. I don't know if he'll ever tell you that, so I will."

"We'll see." Jensen was not staring at the clouds of dust. He was staring at her. "At the end of the day, all I'm going to teach him is how to ride a horse and maybe handle himself around a stable. He's still going to be a Hall."

Harriet made a noise of frustration. Jensen shouldn't have found it adorable. But this was Harriet. Everything she did struck him as adorable, and maybe it was time he just . . . got on board with that.

Especially when he could still taste her.

"Maybe it isn't fair for a sixteen-year-old kid to be handed a family curse and a destiny before he's had time to decide for himself what he wants to do," she was saying, glaring at him.

"Vandalizing church property feels like a decision," Jensen observed.

"Didn't you ever do dumb things when you were a teenager?"

"All the time. I just didn't get caught."

"Caught or not caught, everyone deserves the chance to just . . . be a kid, surely."

Jensen settled in against the warm metal of the old Mazda. "What did you do when you were sixteen that you regret?"

Harriet's glare tipped over into a scowl, predictably. Also predictably, he liked it. "We're not talking about me. For one thing, I didn't have a town full of people on hand to tell me I was doomed."

"I'm going to go ahead and guess that means you didn't do anything particularly naughty."

"My parents didn't actually give me a lot of rules," Harriet told him with that lofty tilt to her chin. "They let me do as I liked as long as I could make a good argument for it."

"That sounds depressing, Harriet," Jensen drawled. "The entire point of being a kid is to have arbitrary laws imposed upon you so you can feel deliciously wicked when you break them."

"And yet, oddly enough, that's not the approach my parents took."

For a while, then, he let himself stand there in the sunshine and enjoy her. Especially when it started to make her twitchy.

"Something is different about you," Jensen rumbled at her, right about at the point where he thought she was going to make a break for the driver's-side door. "What is it?" And then he laughed when she scowled at him again. "I don't just mean that I kissed you silly. I know that happened. Something else. Your hair, maybe."

He already knew what was different about her hair. But still he watched, feeling indulgent and something much hotter than that, as she reached up and ran her hand along the braid she'd put that mass of blond hair in and was currently wearing tossed over her shoulder. And it wasn't one of those fancy French braid thingies that Amanda had used to do to her own hair before she went out riding. This was just a simple, matter-of-fact braid, as if she'd given no thought to it whatsoever, and might even have done it in the car.

Jensen couldn't have said why he had the urge to reach over, wrap his fingers around the fat thickness of it, and tug a little. But he didn't stop himself from doing it, either.

Because it was that or confront all the other things he'd like to do to her, right out here in the open. On a Sunday, no less.

"I researched riding attire," she told him, though her voice was less direct than before. Too breathy, now, and the scowl had dimmed considerably. "And looked at pictures of what people wear on ranches while I was at it."

"Of course you did."

"Then I did my best to fashion an approximation of all that from my own wardrobe." She looked down at herself. "I'm sure I'm off. I always am."

And if someone else had said that to him, it would have been self-deprecating. Self-pitying, even. But this was Harriet. Her voice wasn't as crisp as it normally was, but he flattered himself that was because he was close to her and had his hand wrapped around her braid. Apart from that, it was as matter-of-fact as ever.

She wasn't digging for compliments. She wasn't looking for him to contradict her and tell her how pretty she was. This was merely an acknowledgment of a truth.

"What do you mean you're always 'off'?" Jensen was intrigued by the matter-of-factness, maybe. It made him feel protective again.

"I'm an odd woman," Harriet told him, and there was nothing breathy or off-balance about her then. Not in the direct gaze she leveled on him or lurking in her voice. "I don't *feel* odd. I never have. But I don't quite fit in. I find people and their motivations mysterious, and if I ask for clarification or explanation, that always makes it worse. For them, I mean. Everyone gets flustered, sometimes there are tears, and I'm certainly not prepared to handle it. I learned a long time ago that it's better to simply accept my oddness and move on."

"Explain that to me. Your oddness. I don't get it."

"You do." He didn't understand how her gaze could possibly get more direct, but it did. "I'm always just slightly out of step with everyone and everything else. I'm not appropriately cowed or shamed in social situations. I think highly of my own opinion and offer it heedlessly. And when it comes to clothes, I'm absolutely hopeless. Ask anyone."

Jensen studied her for a moment, trying to figure out if it looked like she really meant that. Or if she was angling for him to leap in and flatter her. But no, this was still his Harriet. She was imparting the facts as she knew them with no emotion attached.

This woman was a marvel.

"Do you want to change those things?" he asked.

"No." Harriet laughed then, making the ranch he knew better than his own face in a mirror seem to shift around behind her. Making something new. "I like who I am. All I'm saying is that I'm well aware that I dress like an old woman. That people can tell from across the room that I'm a little bit strange." She shrugged. "I embrace that."

"If you've identified it as a problem, have you ever tried to change it?"

"Of course I've tried," she said. "Everybody's thirteen

and impressionable once. But I never got it right. And it was almost worse to try and get it wrong. Thirteen-year-old girls aren't noted for their kindness."

Jensen remembered. "Not so much, no."

"Besides, when people say that I dress like an old woman now, what they mean is that I'm comfortable. And that I choose the comfort of the things I wear over how they make me look. It might come as a shock to you, Jensen, that many people find that threatening."

"Threatening?"

Harriet nodded sagely. "If it ever got out that women could go around dressing for their own comfort instead of a need to make themselves attractive for others, well. I think the world would quake on its foundations."

Jensen could believe that, given he seemed to do the same every time he was around her. "If I'm following you, Miss Harriet, what you're telling me is that you're something of an odd bird, but you take pride in it. Not to put too fine a point on it, you consider yourself a revolution of one."

He thought she would scowl at that, but instead, she laughed again. "I said I was odd, Jensen. Not egoless. We're all the heroes of our own stories, after all."

"So, for example, the skirt you were wearing last night. Why do you like it?"

She blinked. "Because it has pockets. Lots of pockets. Do you know how many pieces of women's clothing don't have pockets? I guess we're all supposed to hold everything we need in our hands or lug bags around." Her glasses were slipping down her nose, and she pushed them back up. "Also it doesn't pinch or tug. I don't like pinching. Or tugging."

"And that sweater. I'm surprised you're not wearing it now."

"My cardigan." She nodded, then smiled. "I knit it myself. It's soft and cozy and very useful too. I don't like being cold."

"But you do have jeans, it turns out. You're wearing them right now."

"Of course I have jeans. Who doesn't have jeans?"

"You don't wear them to work."

She shook her head at him. "That would obviously be inappropriate."

"I haven't been a high school student in a long time, but I'm pretty sure a lot of the teachers wore jeans. This is Colorado, not a New England prep school campus."

Harriet blinked. "I'm sorry, when were you taking in the amount of denim on a New England prep school campus?"

Jensen had spent exactly zero time anywhere near New England, and less time than that on a prep school campus, but he had very defined ideas about what such things entailed. He grinned. "I've seen movies, Harriet."

She rolled her eyes. "I can't speak for anyone else's take on appropriate attire, or the dress codes on prep school campuses in Connecticut, but I, personally, try to maintain a certain standard." But she smiled then. "That's partly because when I started, I was young. It seemed more crucial that I distinguish myself from the students than it does now. Now it's just habit."

He played with the braid still in his hand. "So when you put an outfit together, what is your thought process? Walk me through this."

"I think this is your way of telling me that you really do think my clothes are ugly." Her blue eyes narrowed. "I don't know whether to laugh at that or feel insulted."

"Harriet. Please." Jensen let his grin heat up some. "I'd

like to go on record as saying that I don't care what you wear. I'm entirely focused on getting you naked."

Her mouth worked, but no sound came out. She closed it, then swallowed audibly, and her eyes were so bright it almost hurt. "Oh."

"What interests me about your clothes"—he gave that braid a little tug just to watch her sharp intake of breath and enjoy how big her eyes got—"is what it says about your brain. I'll admit it. I'm fascinated by your brain."

"Are you sure? Most people find it irritating. Or confronting."

"I'm sure."

"Well." He thought she liked that. "Sometimes I just throw on whatever feels good. Other times I dress according to what task I'm going to do. I don't wear work clothes in the garden, for example." Her head tipped slightly to one side. "Why? What do you think about when you get dressed?"

"The same," he said.

She laughed. "If you were a woman, that wouldn't be a good answer. What about your hair? What about your shoes? Are you wearing the tightest possible pair of jeans you can find so that men can admire your butt?"

"Men have been known to admire my butt," Jensen assured her. "Can you blame them? But really, I'm more personally engaged when women do the same."

"Well," she said. And she seemed to get lost there for a time. Jensen watched as she collected herself. She stood up straighter. She squared her shoulders. "I think the session went very well. Aidan seems delighted with the opportunity to spend some time with you. And your horse, naturally. I think this will be great for him. And I'm . . .

flattered, I guess, that you wanted to spend all this time discussing my clothing."

"Oh, are we done here?" Jensen wrapped the braid tighter around his hand, tugging her closer as he did. "Have you had enough?"

"I thought I'd leave you to your Sunday afternoon in peace."

"You can go whenever you want to go, Harriet," he told her solemnly. "But there's a toll."

"A toll?"

Jensen did a quick survey of the yard. Everyone had cleared out while he'd been doing his thing with Aidan. All his siblings' vehicles were gone, and he knew that his parents tended to relax on Sunday afternoons after the family meal. His father spent more time in his recliner these days, still working on that heart. His mother usually did all the dishes, the better to martyr herself, and then sat in the family room with Donovan, either reading a book or tending to her sewing. His grandparents hadn't come over today.

The point being, no one was around to watch him.

Jensen had never cared too much who saw the things he did. He'd never been one to bloom in secret. But he thought about Zack's response to Jensen being anywhere near Harriet, and knew that this, too, was part of protecting her.

Not from him, necessarily. But from everyone else seeing her with him and treating her like a casualty waiting to happen.

Someday, he was going to have to unpack how insulting that was. But not today. Not now, with Harriet there before him, her head tipped back so she could look up at him, her silky hair in his grip.

"Yes, Harriet," he said, very seriously. "A toll."

Then he took his free hand and fit it to her cheek before bending down, hauling her up against his chest
again, and getting his mouth on hers.

He kissed her the way he'd wanted to when he'd seen
her waiting out by the car. He kissed her like it had been
moments since their last kiss, instead of a long night filled
with too-hot images in his head and an ache in his body
that nothing seemed to relieve.

He kissed her until she melted against him, and only
then did he set her back down on her feet.

"I'm not your little doll," she protested. Weakly, he
thought. "You can't just pick me up and toss me around
when you feel like it."

"Why not?"

"Because . . . Because . . ."

"You're little. I'm big." He grinned down at her. "Unless
you want to lie down, where those things matter less."

She didn't turn red, but she . . . fluttered a little bit.

And he didn't need her to tell him that she didn't usually do things like that. That it was all for him. He knew.

"Anyway," she said. "I'm leaving now."

"You should come to all of Aidan's sessions out here,"
Jensen told her. "Maybe you'll learn something too."

"I can't do that if there's going to be all this . . ." She
flapped a hand at him. "*Kissing.*"

"Oh, there's going to be kissing," Jensen drawled. And
then he laughed when she scowled at him. "That's what
we do now, Harriet. You need to catch up."

13

Catching up was one thing, Harriet thought on her drive back from the Bar K that Sunday. Catching her breath was another.

Because it felt as if her life were picking up speed and rolling faster and faster down a steep slope—and she had no idea if the bottom was a cliff, a brick wall, or something that wouldn't actually smash her to smithereens. But there didn't seem to be anything to do but go with it.

She *wanted* to go with it.

So that was what she did.

Aidan turned up on Monday, early, with the homework Harriet had assigned him actually done.

"You really enjoyed your experience at the Bar K, apparently," she said, careful to keep her tone mild and any surprise on her part hidden away. Any hint of earnestness, she knew, and he would disappear in a cloud of teenage scorn.

"It was fine, I guess," was all he said before slouching over to his seat and glowering at the rest of the class as they trickled in.

And while Aidan didn't exactly act like an exemplary student in class—because, no doubt, he had a reputation to uphold—he came back to the library after classes were over that day. He stayed late, talking with Harriet about the essay he'd written, the bigger paper she wanted him to write, and how those things could help him move forward. If he applied himself.

Which Harriet thought he might actually do.

"We'll make a plan," she told him.

"Um. Great?"

She ignored his underwhelmed tone. "Some people like to make the whole thing very dramatic, but a plan is nothing more or less than a practical tool. You can write down some things you want and when you want them. Then we'll figure out what you can do this week. This month. The rest of this year. And then, from time to time, we can get together and see if that plan is still working."

Aidan was sitting across from her at the resources table, resting his chin on his crossed arms. "Do I get graded on it?"

"Only the kind of grade you give yourself." She held his gaze, very seriously. "Sometimes things don't come to fruition. That's life. But you have to assess yourself and decide if that's because you let yourself down or if the situation was out of your control."

His mouth twisted. "I can tell you right now that everything's out of my control, Miss Barnett. Hello. I'm a kid."

Not for the first time, Harriet thought she was truly lucky to be raised as she had been. She had experienced all the usual feelings of adolescence, but she'd never felt *hopeless*. Once again, she wanted to hug this poor kid and rescue him—but she knew she couldn't do that. She could only do this.

"No one gets to live a life free of outside influences," Harriet told him quietly. "So the test is always, how do you rise to the occasion when you can't control the things that are happening around you, or to you? And how do you carve out space where you're in control of yourself, if nothing else? That was no different for me when I was your age. The only difference now is that the carved-out part is more of my life. That's really all growing up is. Changing that ratio to better suit yourself, if you can."

Aidan's gaze had met hers. "I will."

Harriet nodded as if it were a foregone conclusion. "I believe you."

Once she'd agreed to help him with his work, she further decided that they could have study sessions—but only if they occurred in public. She chose the coffee shop.

"I feel like I'm just announcing to the entire town that I'm stupid," Aidan complained the first time they sat at one of the tables in Cold River Coffee. His books and notebooks were spread out before him while Harriet sat across from him with her own books and a pad.

"On the contrary," Harriet replied calmly. "What you're announcing to the entire town is that you're studious and committed."

"Yeah, or stupid."

"But they already think you're stupid, Aidan." His head jerked back at that, but she continued in the same tone. "And cursed. And most of all, one of those Halls. You can live down to their expectations perfectly well on your own. Or you can show them all how wrong they were. Your choice."

Because she hadn't been putting him on. She was willing to show up as long as he was. And to her surprise and great pleasure, it looked like Aidan was ready to put in the work. Even in the full view of the town.

She was so proud of him she wanted to shout about it—but didn't. Because she knew full well that if she embarrassed him, he'd never come back.

One study day, not long after that infamous whiskey-laden Saturday night, Harriet was still at her table after Aidan had made his escape. She was congratulating herself on Aidan's progress—and indulging herself in daydreams about things like his college graduation and, who knew, his future contributions to scientific discovery, world peace, and climate change—when she looked up to see that Abby was sitting at the next table.

"Oh," Harriet said with her usual awkwardness. "I mean, *hi*."

"You have to give me your number," Abby said cheerfully. She was trying to corral her little boy as he ran in circles around the table where she was sitting, and it occurred to Harriet that possibly she hadn't noticed any awkwardness from Harriet over the shrieking. "I think we're going to try to get some people together to try out the new microbrewery this weekend. You should come."

"I would love to give you my number," Harriet said, sounding like a robot impersonating a human. She smiled to cover it. "And I've heard the new microbrewery is great."

She had not, in fact, heard that. But if Aidan could learn how to study, she could throw out a pleasantry without spontaneously combusting.

If Abby noticed her deer-in-headlights expression, or the robot voice, she gave no sign. "We went to school with Tate Bishop, who opened it. So far, I've heard rave reviews." She pulled out her cell phone and asked for Harriet's number. Which Harriet gave, trying to sound casual. As if she were asked for her phone number all the time, such was the demand for her company. Then her own phone buzzed as Abby called it.

"There you go," Abby said. "Now you have my number too."

But more remarkable was that, come Friday, Abby actually got in contact with her. And that was how Harriet found herself out with the rest of them on Saturday. Not just Abby and her friends but a bunch of other women as well. She recognized Missy and Amanda. But Amanda had come with Katrina, the woman Harriet often saw working at the B&B in town. Plus Hannah, Abby's sister-in-law, who was chiefly notable because she was stunningly gorgeous and dressed as if she were headed out to a star-studded rodeo gala.

"Were we supposed to dress up?" Harriet asked Abby in a panic when she set eyes on Hannah. Though she didn't know why she was asking. There was no scenario in which she would dress up like that. She wore the same serviceable navy dress to the Harvest Gala every year and, frankly, didn't understand why anyone would pay more attention to their outfit than that.

But Abby followed her gaze and laughed. "Oh, that's just Hannah. She doesn't do casual."

"Y'all will take my mascara from my cold, dead hands," Hannah drawled in a rich Southern accent, and even winked at Harriet as she did it.

Which somehow made her seem more charming.

That night, Harriet gave herself over to the microbrewery experience. She tried beer. She'd had a beer here and there before, but tonight, she sampled a flight. She ate a decadent Montecristo sandwich and thought it might have put her into an altered state. And it turned out she enjoyed the live music with a group of women more than she ever would have thought possible.

The new microbrewery closed at eight, and when

everyone else headed off to the Broken Wheel, Harriet headed home. She walked through town, enjoying the mild July night and the brightness that hung on late into the evening.

Her cozy little life was suddenly filled with more people, and she hardly knew what to make of it. She had always been perfectly content with her life as it was, so surely it should have felt more *seismic* to shake things up like this. It wasn't that she hadn't had any friends before. It was just that most of her friends lived in other places, and the friends she had here weren't the sort who went out and about at night.

Harriet would have sworn that she couldn't possibly like going out herself . . . but she did.

And if she'd been wrong about her own feelings when it came to her own entertainment, which she should have known inside and out by now, what else was she wrong about?

That night, she lay in her bed, pillows everywhere, and couldn't drift off to sleep the way she normally did. Because all of a sudden, even her profession seemed like a curious choice to her. It turned out that she was really enjoying tutoring Aidan, which suggested that maybe her little library class wasn't an anomaly. Had she really chosen library science because it was a good fit? Or had she felt inhibited from becoming a teacher because everyone knew, especially her, that she wasn't good with people?

That was the strangest part of all. Because it turned out, maybe she was fine with people. No one could have been more surprised than Harriet.

The next morning, she tended to the typical Sunday-morning things and then found herself choosing her clothing with a little more interest than usual. Her jeans, yes. But instead of the sneakers that Jensen had informed her were wrong, as they had no heel, she chose a pair of boots. So far, so normal, but instead of picking up one of those big, oversize button-down shirts that she liked because they were airy, she picked up a T-shirt instead. Not just any T-shirt. She'd bought this particular T-shirt at a charity event last year to be supportive but had never worn it. It had a scoop neck and tiny sleeves, and most of all, it was snug.

"There's actually no reason why you should wear anything different," she informed herself in her mirror. "You're being deeply foolish."

But she didn't put on something else. And even though she had second thoughts, she didn't take the T-shirt off before she went to get in her car and head out to the Bar K.

Where, in case she'd been fooling herself about her reasons for wearing a tight T-shirt, the look on Jensen's face when he saw her erased all doubt.

Because Harriet still didn't really care much about clothes. But she found she cared a great deal indeed about getting Jensen Kittredge to look at her like that, as if the T-shirt she'd put on was made of fire and he couldn't wait to get burned.

He'd told her that what he really cared about was the body beneath her clothes, so maybe it made sense that she wanted to show him more of it. And a T-shirt that hugged her breasts and nipped in at the waist was about as close as she could get.

Especially in the presence of a student.

"You never wear shirts like that," Aidan said, his expression one of condemnation, as if the T-shirt itself were disturbing.

Harriet might have felt uncertain about the shirt, but she knew that it was not in any way revealing. Objectively. Or she wouldn't have worn it.

She frowned at Aidan. "What have we talked about? You know better than to make personal remarks. For example, you're usually wearing all black. Should we discuss the reasons why you're not continuing in that tradition today?"

He looked mutinous, there in his regular old white T-shirt and a pair of blue jeans, for a change, like maybe she wasn't the only one who wanted to impress Jensen. If in different ways. "I'm just saying it's weird."

"It's summer," she told him. "It's warm."

Aidan didn't look convinced. But Harriet couldn't really make herself care too much about that, because Jensen still had all of that heat in his gaze every time he looked at her.

All of which she could taste when he kissed her after Aidan drove off in his usual cloud of dust. This time in the barn, holding her up against the wall, and moving his hands to just beneath her breasts as he held her there. He plundered her mouth and made her wonder how she had ever lived this long without a man like Jensen, big and strong and uncontainable, who tossed her up against walls, treated her like she was put on this earth for his pleasure, and made her feel alive.

Alive.

She could neither confirm nor deny the sounds she kept making all along her long drive home were giggles. Real, live giggles. And crazier still, she did nothing to stop them as they happened.

Harriet just turned her music up louder, drove a little faster, and let them come.

In town, she parked in front of the little local market that was a good stopover between trips to the big supermarket that was halfway to Aspen. She was humming under her breath as she filled her basket then looked up, surprised, when she found Amy Dougherty in the narrow aisle before her. Amy, who worked in the high school's front office. Amy, of the complicated romantic life following her divorce, who, Harriet could not help but notice, was looking at *Harriet* as if *Harriet* were the object of pity here.

It made her realize, with an unpleasant jolt, that she had actually pitied Amy until this moment—if not to her face. And it wasn't pleasant to be on the other side.

"Oh, Harriet," Amy said with a smile, her basket full of breakfast cereals with cartoon characters all over the cartons. "I think it is so good of you to be doing the kind of outreach you're doing this summer."

"Outreach?"

Amy reached past her for a bag of potato chips. "That poor Aidan Hall. You have to ask yourself, has any Hall ever had a chance? And Jensen Kittredge too."

Harriet had been winding up for a lecture on the local myth of the Hall family and how ruinous and unfair it was, but that last part stopped her flat.

"Jensen?" she asked. "What?"

"I always wondered about him," Amy confessed. "It's so nice of you to tutor him too."

That was so absurd that Harriet laughed. "Why would Jensen Kittredge need tutoring?"

Amy laughed as if Harriet had said something hilarious. She wasn't even looking at Harriet while she filled her basket. But Harriet got the distinct impression that even if she'd been looking directly at her, Amy had already decided what it was she would see. And it wasn't the snug T-shirt. It wasn't what the internet had reliably informed Harriet was a *sleek and sophisticated updo* in place of her usual pin-everything-up-and-see-where-it-sticks approach.

And Harriet had always seen herself differently than everyone else did, she knew that. But it was different now, like everything else was too. Because now she found the gap between those two things bothered her.

"Normally, there's only one reason Jensen Kittredge spends any time with a woman," Amy was chattering happily, her attention on a bin of apples at the end of the aisle. She picked one up, examined it critically, then put it down again. "Obviously, in this situation, that can't be the reason, so there's been a lot of speculation as to what the reason might be. I've been telling everyone about that program of yours in summer school, and I wanted to tell you I think it's wonderful that you're expanding it out into the community as well."

Harriet told herself there was no reason she should be reacting to this in a way that could only be described as negative. Amy didn't mean to be hurtful. On the contrary. Harriet knew Amy and could tell she meant everything she said. More than that, she clearly intended it to be complimentary.

And yet Harriet felt anything but complimented.

She'd gotten used to Jensen seeing her for who she was. Or at least finding what he saw fascinating. She'd gotten used to meeting new people who found her rather delightful.

This felt a lot like backsliding into oddness above all else, and she disliked it. Intensely.

"Amy," she said, matter-of-factly, "I hate to be the bearer of bad news, but you might want to consider the possibility that Jensen and I are engaged in a torrid affair."

Amy laughed again, even louder this time, and then . . . kept right on laughing. So hard that tears came to her eyes.

The stark unfairness of it was almost too much for Harriet to bear. And even that struck her as another blow.

Because of all the scenarios she'd ever envisioned that involved her feeling beaten, none of them had included standing in a small market in town while Amy Dougherty, who Harriet had often felt sorry for, *howled with laughter* at the very notion that Harriet might herself be nothing more and nothing less than a woman. Like every other woman in this town.

It was insulting. It was outrageous.

Harriet couldn't let it stand.

And that was why, when she got home and angrily unpacked her purchases, she fumed at all the cats until even they hid from her. She tried to distract herself with her usual pursuits, but Amy's laughter kept swirling around and around in her head. It made it impossible to read or knit. Or even weed her garden. It was driving her to distraction.

Or anyway, that was the excuse she used when she picked up the phone and called Jensen.

"Can't get enough, can you?" came his admittedly delicious voice, booming over the line and instantly making her feel better. "It's okay, Harriet. It's a common ailment."

She opened her mouth to chastise him for answering the phone that way, but stopped herself. Why should she care how he answered his own phone? Unlike what Amy—and apparently half the town—believed, she was not his tutor. She was not his anything.

Except sometimes, there was kissing.

Despite the announcement she'd tried to make to Amy, Harriet wasn't sure she wanted the entire town to think of her as someone who might at any moment release the floozy within. But it was suddenly of dire importance to her that Jensen knew. Because if there was a floozy within, it was only for him.

Only for him, something inside her repeated like a vow.

And there was a hitching thing in her chest, but she ignored it, because it sounded like he was driving.

"Where are you?" she asked. She had the vague impression that he and his brothers sometimes took to the road to do various horse things all over the West, but she hoped he wasn't doing that now. Her inner floozy would be crushed.

"I don't typically encourage too much discussion of my whereabouts," Jensen drawled. "I find it creates the kind of expectation a man would do better to nip in the bud right from the start. But for you, Miss Harriet, as ever, I'm happy to make an exception."

"Have you ever noticed that you like to avoid answering a question not by being silent, the way some do, but by using as many extraneous words as possible as if a person might get lost in the thick of them all and forget what they asked?"

"Harriet. When is it going to occur to you that for all my devil-may-care appeal, which I think we can both agree is extreme, I'm not nearly as careless as you like to imagine?" That deep laugh of his rolled through her, even over the phone. Then lodged deep inside like it belonged there. She remembered what he'd said when he kissed her for the first time, that he wanted to be inside her, and she wanted more of that. She wanted all of him inside her, not just that laugh. "And to answer your question, I'm on my way into town. Zack has some leaky pipes he wants me to take a look at."

Harriet was momentarily diverted. "Are you a plumber in your spare time?"

She was treated to another long, low laugh. "I'm good with my hands, Harriet," he said, and even though she knew that he was deliberately drawing out that innuendo, she shivered. It was like she couldn't help herself. "I can fix pretty much anything. And Zack is on call, so he doesn't have the time to do it himself. Otherwise, I assure you, I'd be too busy mocking him for not being able to handle it himself to actually go do it. That's my primary role in the family."

"Being the handyman? Or mocking everybody?"

"Both." But he sounded delighted by that. "I've heard there are sweet and supportive families out there, but I prefer our model. Sweet and supportive creep me out. If it's not rowdy, how loving can it really be?"

Harriet thought of her own family. The quiet, so conducive to reading a good book, was punctuated only by the radio tuned to the classical music station, NPR, or an interesting chat. There was no *rowdiness,* ever. Emotion was rarely expressed, and when it was, only from a distance. Better to analyze after the fact than share any of it while it was happening. Better a quiet conversation than any burst of incoherent intensity.

Harriet had always thought that was better. It wasn't until now that it had occurred to her that maybe it wasn't about better or worse. It was that she hadn't ever felt anything intensely enough to *want* to get rowdy with it.

Because now she was clinging to her cell phone, all alone in her living room, feeling as if, were she not very careful, she might actually *die.* Just from the feelings careening around inside of her.

Knowing that was unlikely did absolutely nothing to make those feelings go away.

"Anyway," Jensen was saying, sounding perfectly happy to chatter away, as if he spent half his life on the phone when she somehow doubted that was the case, "I've

never met a pipe that could defeat me, so I don't imagine
it will take me long to handle Zack's problem. I thought I
might grab myself a beer, kick back in the Broken Wheel,
and congratulate myself on being a man's man."

"How does that differ from every other time you kick
back in the Broken Wheel?" She was feeling far too
much, but she was also smiling. This was insanity—so
why did she want more of it? "Every night of the week,
by all accounts."

"You make a good point," he said cheerfully. "Maybe
I'll have to make it two beers. I like those additional man
points. Quantifiable testosterone, if you will."

"Can you come over before you go to the bar?" she
asked him starkly then, without allowing herself to think
it through. Or, she realized while her words were hanging there, to come up with a query that didn't sound quite
so strange and desperate.

She knew it must have sounded particularly strange
and desperate, because he didn't say anything for a moment. There was only silence and the rushing sound of
his truck moving through space, with a hint of country
music in the background.

If she could have taken it back, she would have.

"For you, Harriet," he said eventually, a note in his
voice she couldn't quite decipher, "I would be happy to
drop by."

"Excellent," she replied, much too stiffly. "I'll see you
then."

And then hung up before she lost her nerve.

But that wasn't better, really, because she had to wait.

It was positively nerve-racking. She took a bath. She
brushed out her hair, then ran her fingers through it until
she achieved a tousled sort of look that didn't exactly look

like her, but didn't look so *unlike* her that she was unrecognizable. She considered makeup, but she rarely wore any and suspected the results would be alarming, not alluring.

And what did a person wear when they were trying to seduce a man who, if even one-quarter of the rumors were true, didn't require much in the way of seduction? Harriet settled on a wrap dress she never wore to work because it was too hard to keep track of the neckline, and that wasn't even getting into the way it clung too close to her body. She had learned early on that it was always better to keep any potential distractions to a minimum. Witness Aidan's reaction to an unobjectionable T-shirt.

But she wanted to distract Jensen.

And it felt as if all nine lives for each of her five cats passed by as she dithered about the house, a lot like the sort of silly woman she'd never imagined she'd become. She exhausted herself with all the frantic nonsense and retreated to sitting quietly on her couch. She thought that at any moment she might pick up her knitting. But she didn't.

When she heard the heavy thumping at the door, she didn't jump. Instead, it was as if she could finally relax. Because she knew that hand, heavy and roughened from the work he did. She knew it was him.

Harriet told herself that the sensations racing through her body made it feel as if she were having an out-of-body experience—but she knew it was exactly the opposite. She had never felt more *in* her body than she did now. She had never been more aware of the way her thighs brushed together as she walked. Of her bare feet on her own wood floors that felt far more decadent than usual. Her hair hung all around her, a sensuous weight. Her breasts felt crushed against the fabric of the dress while, between her legs, she was all heat and need.

She had never felt all of those things at once, or any of them so intensely.

It was hard to breathe, but even her breathing was a part of that mess of sensation.

Harriet blew all the air out in an attempt to calm herself, then gave up. She threw open the front door, and Jensen was there. He was already leaning up against her doorjamb, one hand up high, a celebration of rangy male grace.

He was grinning already, because of course he was grinning, but that grin seemed to freeze on his face as he looked down at her.

And then belted out something deliciously profane.

"I'm going to take that as a good thing," Harriet announced. "Thank you for coming."

"If you'd told me you were going to look like this, I would have skipped Zack and his pipe problem altogether. Happily."

"Yes. Well. Thank you." She was sounding robotic again, but there was no helping it. "Please come inside."

She stepped back, and he stepped in.

She hadn't really considered the impact of that. How it would feel to have the immensity that was Jensen in her little foyer, taking up all the available oxygen and space, light and heat. Crowding her out, just by standing there, big and bold and *him*.

Harriet was aware of her own pulse inside her, pounding its way through her. Finding its way into parts of her that surely shouldn't have been pulsing.

But they were. Every part of her seemed to have its own beat.

He closed the door behind him and leaned back against it, his gaze narrow and intent.

And so hot it hurt.

Harriet cleared her throat. "People keep telling me that when women are seen in your company, it's an easy bet that actually, they're having blistering affairs with you."

"Not really affairs," Jensen said, sounding as casual as if they were discussing something innocuous, like the Cold River Coffee lunch menu. "It implies a level of commitment. I like to think of myself as a purveyor of glorious experiences, however brief." His mouth curved. His eyes glittered. "Let me guess. You're outraged that people might imagine you would ever succumb to my cheap and common attentions."

"On the contrary," Harriet said. "The prevailing wisdom seems to be that it's hilarious to imagine I would ever be one of your many . . . experiences."

"That must be coming from other women. Which is interesting, because all the men I know are convinced I'm taking advantage of you."

Harriet didn't like that at all. "How patronizing."

"You're telling me. Shows what they know. You could run circles around all of them with your hands behind your back." He studied her for a moment, that look in his eyes close to blistering. "Is that why you wanted me to come over? To complain about the gossip? I'm afraid there's nothing to be done. But if it helps, I don't really think that association with me has ruined anybody's life yet." He considered. "Maybe Aidan's mother, but only because of the choices she made afterward. I'm not sure that's on me."

"You're misunderstanding me," Harriet said more than a little crossly. "I'm not complaining that people think

I might be having an affair with you. I'm complaining about the people who think that's impossible."

He seemed to go very still. "Are you now."

"I think that I should have the full Jensen Kittredge experience," she said, tilting her chin up as if she expected a fight.

Maybe she did expect a fight.

She didn't know what she thought would happen next. The Jensen would leap into action, maybe? Because maybe there was a sequence to seduction attempts? She certainly wouldn't know.

But Jensen didn't move.

She had the strangest thought that she could hear his pulse too.

"I don't think I heard you correctly," he said after some time. "What, exactly, do you mean by 'the full Jensen Kittredge experience'?"

Inside Harriet, too many things were drumming. Hard and hot.

And she had the distinct notion that it was now or never. *Never* was deeply unappealing.

"Surely you don't ask this many questions in the Coyote," she snapped.

"The Coyote is an answered question in and of itself," he replied. Still so very still. "We're not in the Coyote."

And Harriet might have been odd her whole life, but she'd never been a coward. She drew herself up to her full height, sad as that might be, and then she squared her shoulders as if she intended to march directly into battle.

"I would like you to seduce me," she informed him. "With sex, if that's unclear."

"With sex," he repeated, his voice . . . altered. Rough. "You want me to seduce you. *With sex.*"

"That's what I said, Jensen."

And then, because maybe he needed a visual—because weren't men supposed to be visual?—she untied her dress, pulled it open, and dropped it to the floor at her feet.

14

Jensen had never heard an invitation with less polish or pleading.

It shouldn't have been so hot.

Harriet bit the words off like bullets and then glared at him as if she didn't understand why he wasn't reaching out to grab her. And he didn't have the heart to tell her it was because it wouldn't really have mattered if she'd issued the same invitation with a punch to the face—or a sweet kiss. He needed to control himself. He needed to make sure that whatever happened next, he was thinking with his head.

His big head.

And then, in the very next moment, Harriet proved the beauty of patience. Because as he watched—afraid he'd actually crashed his truck somewhere between Zack's house in town and here, and this was just a feverish dream before dying—she unwrapped that dress that had already about made him lose it. It was a bright blue, and licked all over that curvy little body of hers, showing him all the things he'd spent the last few weeks carefully learning. Each and every one of her sweet curves. Her lush, round breasts and that bottom he'd held in his hands enough to know was probably going to haunt him for the rest of his life. But better still, the dress was tied right there at that tiny little waist she usually hid. It high-lighted that hourglass shape of hers, it made his head spin, and he couldn't remember another time his mouth had ever been quite so dry.

And then she took it off.

Just . . . unwrapped it.

And everything stopped.

All the blood in his head drained away, and he had the wild thought that he didn't really care if this was how he died. Because what a way to go.

Because Miss Harriet Barnett, cat lady extraordinaire, wasn't wearing a single stitch beneath that dress.

And she was perfect.

Better than he could possibly have imagined, and he'd set himself to that task with considerable attention. He'd devoted a whole lot of time to it. And she surpassed his every fervent wish and hope.

Jensen already knew that she was a tiny little force of nature. He'd had his suspicions that she was also highly likely to be a sex bomb.

What he had not been prepared for, though he really should have been, was the discovery that Harriet Barnett was literally a male fantasy come to life. She was a walk-ing, talking dream come true.

And she was currently staring at him angrily, as if she couldn't understand what was taking him so long.

"Harriet," he said, her name in his mouth as if he'd already drunk his fill of her, when he was currently des-perate for a taste. "You could give a man a heart attack."

She frowned at him, and it was even hotter than usual. Because her golden hair flowed all around her, and it looked like she should be rolling around in a bed. Preferably with his hands all up in that sweet golden heat. And she was naked, thank the heavens above, so some of that liquid gold was flowing over her rose-tipped breasts and drawing his attention to other points of interest. Her navel. The flare of her hips.

Maybe she was his version of a cardiac event.

In which case, hallelujah.

"That would not be ideal," she said. Severely.

"This is how you normally get what you want?" he asked her, amazed that he could actually form words in the face of such delectable provocation. "When you're not sure of the answer, you just strip and see what happens? I'm not complaining, mind you."

"I'm a librarian, Jensen." Her voice was snooty and prim, and he had long since accepted that for no reason he could think of, he liked it. It made him hard. And today, it made him ache a little in all the best places. "I believe in using all the tools at my disposal."

"Librarian school sounds a lot like a strip club."

"A sentence that has never been uttered before in the history of the library sciences," Harriet said dryly. "Besides, my understanding is that strip clubs have a lot of rules to prohibit touching."

She wrinkled up her little nose, which was when he realized that she was stark naked from head to toe but was still wearing her glasses.

For some reason, that was the thing that almost sent him over the edge. It wasn't just that not being inside her for even one moment more might kill him. It was more than that. It was so cute, so Harriet, that he found himself with one hand over his heart like it really was time to start singing those hallelujahs on his way out.

"Have you spent a lot of time trying to understand the vagaries of strip club policy?" he asked her. "I would have said that probably wasn't a priority of yours."

"This is not a strip club," she told him solemnly. "If that helps. With the touching."

"Harriet," he said, not trying too hard to keep the laughter out of his voice. "Is this your version of seducing me? Throwing off your clothes and demanding action?"

And as he watched, her face changed. His mighty little warrior suddenly looked . . . crestfallen.

"Am I doing it wrong?" she asked.

Of all things that Jensen couldn't tolerate, that had to top the list.

"Baby," he drawled, "you're unorthodox. I'll give you that. But effective."

Then he pushed himself away from the door, opted—as usual—not to ask himself why it was this artless little creature got to him in ways no one else ever had, and picked her up.

"Do you always have to pick me up?" she asked, back to frowning at him.

"You're little," he said by way of explanation, like he'd told her once before. "Don't really see the point of pretending otherwise."

"Yes, but—"

"Harriet."

He waited until she subsided, standing at the base of her stairs with her warm and naked in his arms. He could see her kitchen down at the end of the hall. On one side, there was a formal dining room, and on the other, a cozy living room. He did the quick math that was all about getting them horizontal, and took the stairs.

"Are you planning to say something? Or did you say my name to sound mysterious and forbidding?"

"I like your name," he said as he walked upstairs. "It's unusual. Like mine. And I've gotten to know you over this last little while. Maybe not your inner secrets and all the dark corners of your soul, but that takes time. What I do know is you don't talk that much, or that grumpily, unless you're feeling a little . . . How do I put this? A little insecure."

She scowled at him as if she weren't naked and airborne. "I am never insecure. What do I have to be insecure about?"

"I like that about you. But still. The more you scowl, the less secure you are in whatever you're doing. As evidenced earlier this very day when you refused to get up on a horse."

He didn't like to think too much about how his Sundays were shaping up lately. Normally, there was Sunday dinner with the family and then not much else. The usual ranch work and more often than not a few hours at his desk, because there was always paperwork. Paperwork on top of paperwork with no end in sight. And that was still true, but he found himself trying to get it in at other times. Because Aidan and Harriet turned up in the afternoons, and Jensen—having convinced himself that the whole thing was going to be annoying—did not find himself annoyed at all.

Quite the opposite.

He liked the kid more than he'd expected to, so there was that. He didn't lose any of his attitude, but then, maybe Jensen wouldn't have respected Aidan if he had. Still, attitude and all, he showed up every Sunday and did whatever Jensen asked him to do. Which had, so far, been a lot of getting used to horses, tackling the various chores involved in running a stable, and going on easy rides around and around the paddock to find his seat.

Harriet was a whole different thing. Every Sunday, she also turned up, her clothing a little tighter in all the best places. She'd told him once that it was because she was trying to wear the appropriate uniform for horseback riding, but he thought it was for him. Or anyway, he wanted it to be for him.

But she flatly refused to go on a horse.

And just as flatly denied that she was afraid.

He thought it was about the cutest thing he'd ever seen.

But that was before he'd found himself on the second floor of Harriet Barnett's little house, feeling a whole lot like a bull in a china shop as he looked around for her bedroom. Jensen made a command decision and turned toward the back of the house, where he was delighted to find a pretty room that smelled like her. There was cinnamon and vanilla in the air, and everything inside the room was drenched with summer light from the big windows along one wall. He hadn't spent a lot of time imagining her bedroom, not when there were other, more delicious things to imagine, but if he had, it would have been this. Exactly this. A tiny little queen-size bed that was going to be a tight fit, piled high with about twelve million baffling little frilly pillows. Bookshelves everywhere, stacked full but not overstuffed. The floor was wood, but there were cozy rugs thrown everywhere, done up in blues and whites. In the corner, there was an armchair, and more books on the table beside it. There was knitting in a basket, what he expected would be a closet, and a bathroom on the other side. The windows let in the mountains, and in the center of that puny bed, two cats lay grooming themselves.

"Your bed appears to be occupied," he told her as he set her down on her feet beside it.

He liked that she looked dazed. He liked looking at her.

"Oh. That's just Eleanor and Milton. They're brother and sister."

She made one of those noises that people made. A noise that was only used around cats, as far as he could tell, and it had an electric effect on the two furry creatures on the bed. They dived in two separate directions as if pursued by a fleet of devils on their heels, and made Jensen laugh while they did it.

"You really are a cat lady," he said.

She turned back to face him, an odd light in those blue eyes of hers. Like she was preparing for some battle. "I've never denied that."

That was a ridiculous answer if ever there was one. Jensen picked her up again, this time taking them both down onto her fluffy, pillow-covered bed, so they could conduct this conversation in a more reasonable manner. He stretched himself out along one side of her so she was staring up at him, naked and perfectly her, and he could prop himself up on one elbow while getting his other hand where he wanted it.

Which, for the moment, was there on that belly of hers that he'd been lusting after for far too long.

Harriet shivered a little, and he watched as goose bumps gave her away. He was so hard by this point that he was surprised he wasn't actually doubled over in pain, but he didn't intend to rush this.

He didn't intend to miss a moment.

"How many cats do you have?"

She didn't look unlike a cat herself then, eyeing him balefully. "I'm sure I've already told you. I have five."

"I don't remember if you told me or not." He let the number sink in. "Five. Five whole cats."

"Well. Not really. Maisey is so tiny and forlorn she really only counts as a half."

"And you talk about them like that. Like they're people."

"I do." She even raised her chin when she was lying there naked below him. "The exact same way you talk about your horses."

"It's not a competition, Harriet. I like cats. You're going to have to introduce me to each and every one of them."

She sniffed. "I don't know if that's wise. I wouldn't want them to get attached when it's only a squalid little affair."

"Scorching," he corrected her. "Never squalid."

And he liked watching her laugh, so much that he found himself drawing letters on her skin. Spelling out things he chose not to make into words. Even if his fingers knew exactly what he was writing.

"I don't get either squalid or scorching if I'm naked and you're not." She reached over and tugged on his T-shirt. "In the spirit of fairness alone, you shouldn't be wearing this."

"I want you to look around," he told her, his voice very serious. "Where are you right now?"

"Is that a trick question?" Harriet wrinkled her nose. "Or is it more of a philosophical question?"

"It's a tricky question, apparently. I'll answer for you. You're in a bed, Harriet. With me. Stop worrying about what's fair and try concentrating on what's hot."

"I'm pretty sure you're hot. And probably hotter with your shirt off. It seems like easy math to me."

"Do you want to seduce me?" Because his hand was on her body, he could actually feel her get warm, even though she didn't burst out in some kind of flush. "I'm happy to lie back and let you do all the work, if that's what you want. Ladies first and all that."

"No," she said a little bit prissily. As if what she really wanted was to argue.

"I'm willing to be seduced." He moved his hand up from her abdomen to test the weight of one of those perfectly round breasts, and sighed a little, because it was heavy and hot and he had never wanted anything more than this woman. "But maybe that can wait."

Her voice was breathy and small then. "That sounds like a plan. Let's put a pin in it. We can circle back."

"Harriet," Jensen said. "Let's try a little library-style silence. I bet you're good at that."

And then he bent over and drew her nipple into his mouth.

She made a noise that seared its way through him. It was greedy, glorious.

Beautiful.

She tasted sweet on his tongue, like rough velvet dipped in cream, and Jensen found that he was a whole lot hungrier than he'd imagined.

He was happy he was still wearing his clothes, because if he weren't, he doubted he would have been able to control himself. She was spread out before him, a banquet of perfect flesh, and Jensen indulged himself. At last. He took his time with one breast, then he moved to the other. He held them close together, licked where he liked, and used his thumbs at will, because she seemed to like it.

More than like it, and he loved the little broken sounds she made. The little gasps, the soft moans. He loved how she bucked up against him, arching her back to give him better access.

And he took every little bit she gave him.

Eventually, he crawled his way down the length of that soft belly of hers, taking his sweet time en route to his destination.

Then he wrapped his hands around her hips, holding her before him as if he was offering himself about the finest treat available. Because he was.

He took in the sight. The blond curls, the sweet flesh beneath.

He felt how she quivered. He heard the way her voice caught.

Then he leaned down to taste her, and it was like everything inside him blew apart.

Because Harriet tasted even better than she looked.

He licked his way into her, setting himself to the task as if his life depended on it. She raised her hips to meet his mouth, her arms thrown up over her head in total abandon while she arched and bucked against his mouth, making herself about the prettiest picture he'd ever seen.

Meanwhile, Jensen found the hot center of all her need, and sucked. Hard.

Until she screamed.

Then he started all over again.

Until she was sobbing out his name, the sweetest song Jensen thought he'd ever heard.

She was limp and panting when he was finally done. And he kissed his way up, liking the way she was still quivering. And that, finally, she was flushed and rosy red.

He rolled away from her, rethinking his historic stance against queen-size beds. Because yes, it was too small for him, but that meant that he was all over her no matter where he turned. He liked it. He stripped off his clothes and came back down, then reached over to tug her glasses from her nose.

And was surprised when she stopped him. "I don't want to take them off."

She even sounded a little bit cross, in case he'd forgotten who he was with.

He hadn't.

"They're already fogging up," he pointed out.

Harriet scowled at him, be still his heart. "I want to see you."

"I'll give you a show later," he promised her. "This time around, how about you worry less about what you can see and pay more attention to what you can feel."

"That really doesn't sound—"

But he pulled her glasses off her face and set them aside. "Are you blind now?"

She blinked at him, but she seemed to have no trouble scowling a moment later. "I'm not blind, thank you. I'm nearsighted. That means—"

"Lucky for you, Harriet, I'm real close," Jensen said.

Then he bent his head and forestalled any further commentary by kissing her.

And kissing her, and kissing her.

When he finally lifted his head again, there was no scowl. Not even a hint of a frown. She looked as if she might just float away.

"What do you think?" he asked, and it was hard not to laugh. He didn't quite keep it locked up like he should. "Do you think you can handle it without your glasses?"

"I think it might not be *too* terrible," she said, but she was smiling.

"Okay, then." Jensen gathered her beneath him, aware

that he was—not exactly *shaking*. He was a man, not a leaf. But he wasn't as solid or easygoing as he could have been, because it was Harriet. "You might want to hold on. I have a feeling you might get a little bit rowdy. You have that look about you."

She looked thrilled at that. But then, while he watched, she got solemn. "There's something I have to tell you first. Just so you know. It's no big deal."

"That's very convincing."

Though there wasn't a single deal breaker he could think of. Not one. Not when it was her.

"I've done a lot of reading on the subject," she told him. Cheerfully, even.

Her hands were looped around his neck. He'd found his way between her thighs and was lying there, the hardest part of him deliciously pillowed on her belly. And she was talking about *reading*.

Well. He supposed that was Harriet. And how could he not like it?

"I know that experiences run the gamut," she said in the same manner, all librarian now, as if she weren't naked and soft and beneath him. "But on the off chance that you aren't the sort of man who will know without my telling you, I decided it's probably better to let you know up front."

"The suspense is killing me."

Waiting was killing him. The suspense was just an added spice.

"There's no *suspense*," Harriet said. "Don't be silly."

"I'll do my best."

"It's only that I've never done this before," she told him brightly. "Have sex, I mean. But I'm sure that doesn't matter, does it?"

And she gazed up at him, smiling, as if she hadn't gone and flipped his world upside down.

Again.

15

"You're looking at me as if it actually is a big deal," Harriet said after a moment, doing her best to sound severe when it was impossible to feel anything even close. Because . . . *wow*. Everything was . . . *wow*. Still, she tried. "Virginity is nothing but a construct, Jensen. I would be happy to provide you with a reading list on the topic."

Though, for the first time in her life, not a single book came to mind.

Because they were both naked and too many things had already happened and he was huge and hard *everywhere* and—

"It's not that I thought you had a ton of experience," Jensen was saying, holding himself above her with that same thunderstruck look on his face. "But I didn't think you'd had *none,* Harriet. You're going to have to give me a moment."

"Why? I wouldn't have mentioned it if I thought it was anything but a potentially practical concern. Like birth control. Which, of course, we should talk about before things . . ." She ran out of steam there, and something in her was shaking hard, like she was cold. When she was not, in any way, cold. "*Commence.*"

"I have that part handled." His voice was that low growl

that she could feel inside and out. Especially while she was beneath him like this. God, she was *beneath* him. "And the commencing. Don't you worry."

Harriet looked to the side, blinked to bring things into what passed for focus without her glasses, and saw three condom packets sitting on her bedside table on top of her copy of *To the Lighthouse* that she'd been meaning to read for at least a decade. And she couldn't decide if she should be outraged that he was the sort of man who simply wandered around with that many condoms at the ready. Or just grateful.

Jensen shifted slightly, rubbing that part of him a little more intently against her belly, and she decided that gratitude was the order of the day.

Because no amount of reading could possibly have prepared her for the reality of this. Of him. She didn't need her glasses to comprehend the perfection of his male form. The glory of those muscles, the wide shoulders that narrowed to a sinewed abdomen with mouthwatering ridges she could apparently touch as she liked. To say nothing of his heavy sex, that looked no different from the many illustrations she had studied over the years in the name of research—except Jensen's was much larger. *Much* larger. And when he pressed it against her, she felt her stomach cartwheel around inside her, making her feel feverish and shivery in a way that might have made her imagine she was ill.

Except it felt too good.

Jensen stared down at her, and there was no trace of that laughing, loud, center-of-the-universe man she'd been so certain he was in all situations, always. His beautiful face was intent. Almost brutally sensual as he gazed down at her, those wolf's eyes seeming to pin her as firmly to her own bed as his gloriously large body did.

Her heart seemed to slow and heat, even as it beat harder.

From this angle, all Harriet could see were those cheekbones of his, higher than necessary by any measure. They called attention to that mouth of his that she'd already greatly appreciated, it had to be said, but today he'd used between her legs. In such a way that she didn't really understand how she could ever look at it— at *him*—again without feeling that swooping, spinning sensation inside.

She felt it now.

Harriet wanted to *do all the things,* right this moment. But it seemed that all Jensen wanted to do was gaze down at her like this, his chest moving as he breathed while the intensity in his eyes—and between them—seemed to grow with every breath.

There was a slick, delirious magic when two bodies pressed together, it turned out, that no books adequately captured in words. Harriet was aware of parts of her she hardly considered under normal circumstances. Her shins, for example, felt lustrous and very nearly luminous every time they brushed against his legs that were roughened with hair and roped with muscle. Her forearms, pressed against his trapezius muscles, were part of the way her arms looped around his neck. And were now blazing from the contact with his skin, so she could feel his power and his strength like a blaze of its own heat from her wrists to her elbows.

This was all so *physical.*

She was aware of the way her body had been shaped for this, and it made her feel something like breathless to contemplate the sheer biological perfection of this moment. Her soft thighs splayed wide to cradle his stronger ones. Her soft belly, there to hold him as he pressed against her. She felt almost as if she wanted to weep, it was so lovely that she was so short and he was so tall, and yet lying down like this, it didn't matter.

Just as he'd promised.

It truly felt like magic.

And then, as her breath got a little harder, a little quicker, all over again, Jensen lifted a hand to curl some of her hair behind her ear.

"Do you think you've got your head around it yet?" Harriet asked hopefully. "Not that gazing and gazing isn't nice."

But she trembled a little when she said it.

Jensen's mouth curved. And there was that light in his eyes that made her feel silly straight down into her bones. "I think I've got it."

"Was it really that repellent?" She frowned up at him, though it took more effort than normal. "You do realize that if you have an issue with a virgin, particularly one who's lying happily naked beneath you like a pageant of consent, there's a very quick fix, don't you?"

"Bite your tongue," Jensen said, that curve in his mouth intensifying. "I don't do quick."

She drew in a breath to argue the point, but he kissed her.

And Harriet, never one to give up directing a moment without a fight, surrendered.

Because their bodies touched and rubbed, and it was glorious. And he kissed her as if he wanted to eat her alive, carnal and gluttonous. And it took her some moments to realize that he tasted different, because he tasted like her.

A notion that set off flares inside of her.

His hands were like drugs. They trailed across her flesh, stroking and tempting and moving seemingly randomly, until she found herself quivering not only with need but wild anticipation.

His kiss grew rougher and more intense. And that felt like permission. Harriet let her hands wander wherever they pleased, making discoveries everywhere. The column of his neck, those swoon-worthy shoulders. The hard muscles of his chest. Each and every ridge of that marvel of a torso.

Then she reached between them and took hold of his sex, steel and velvet just as all the books she'd read had promised, gripping him with both of her hands.

And froze as he made a sharp sound.

"That feels good," he told her.

Then he groaned as she experimented, shifting her double grip up, then down again. She marveled at the feel of him, but also the sensations it stirred up in her. How funny that touching him should feel the same as when he touched her—but *more,* somehow.

As if it wasn't a matter of who touched who but the magic they shared.

"It feels too good," he said after a moment, reaching down to tug her hands away.

"But—"

"Trust me." Jensen's gaze found hers, and she could see the laughter there. But something serious as well.

"I do," Harriet said quietly. "I do trust you."

Jensen didn't smile again, but his eyes seemed to shine brighter. And Harriet understood that what she'd said was true. She trusted him completely.

When had that happened?

"Hold on," he told her, his voice a deep rumble that seemed to work its way through her like a new kind of heat.

He reached between her legs, his fingers big and rough

and beautiful. He stroked her there until she was moving her hips to meet him. He tested her, first with one finger, then two. Then he began to work her until she was slick, and her breath was nothing more than a gasp. Until she found her head falling back and her eyes fluttering closed. He set up a rhythm, and she fell into it as if her hips had always known what to do, and then he did something—some twist of that big hand of his—until she exploded.

Again.

There was no getting used to it, that shattering.

Harriet was a modern woman who enjoyed her own body and took care of her own needs, but she'd had no idea that it could be like *this*. This intense. This marvelously wild and outside her own commands. It was different to surrender to it than to control it—but even as she thought that, his thumb pressed down hard at her center, and she broke apart all over again.

She was spinning around and around now, only vaguely aware of what he was doing. He reached off to the side, and she heard a faint crinkling, but the next thing that mattered to her, really, was when he propped himself above her once more and guided the broad head of his sex between her legs.

"How does this work?" she managed to ask, panting. "Do we count to three?"

Those amber eyes seemed lit on fire. "Sure."

Harriet was grateful for a task in the middle of this storm. "Okay. Let's count. One. Two—"

But before she could brace herself for the count of three, Jensen surged inside her, hard and deep.

It was shocking. It was like ice water in the face, except it wasn't in her face at all. It was there between her legs, and there was nothing icy about it.

Sensation screamed through her, radiating out from the place where they were joined, overfull and heavy.

She was bracing herself against his shoulders, hardly aware that her nails were digging in as she pushed back, though there was nowhere to go.

He was huge and hard and everywhere. Inside her, around her. *Everywhere.*

"Breathe," he ordered her in that offensively lazy voice of his. "It won't get better unless you breathe. I promise."

"This is terrible," she told him. "Why do people *do* this?"

"You'll see." He sounded wholly unbothered. "Breathe, Harriet."

She sucked in a breath, furious. Biology was an outrage. A lie. All that lovely body-to-body magic when all the while it was leading to *this*? It shouldn't be allowed.

"Keep breathing," Jensen said, almost like it was an afterthought.

But Harriet didn't think breathing was an appropriate response. It was too passive. She was furious and she wasn't one to sit idly by, so she squirmed beneath him, moving not quite frantically she tried to . . . *do* something.

"Or that," Jensen said, and she could hear the laughter in his voice. How dare he *laugh* at her?

But when she breathed in again, mostly because she intended to berate him, something changed.

She forgot the angry words on the tip of her tongue and chased that something. There was a difference when she moved her hips. She focused on that, because it didn't ease the pressure inside her, but it changed it. It felt slicker. *Better.* So she did it again. Then again.

And after a while, it was hard to remember her outrage of a moment before. She was too distracted by that slickness, and yet the friction that went with it. She moved her hips back, then forward again.

She did it a few times.

And slowly, marveling all the while, she felt that same old flame flicker to life. Then begin to glow. Hotter than before.

She lifted her gaze to his. "Oh."

Jensen laughed. "Yeah. *Oh.*"

He shifted his weight, putting more of it on her, and that was different too. It was *delicious.*

Then Harriet forgot what she was doing, because he took over.

And everything was discovery and sheer delight. All that heat and hardness inside her, then out, over and over and over again.

She gave herself over to the rhythm of it, the glory.

It was physical, but it wasn't only physical. It was astonishing, but it wasn't only astonishing. It was every small and funny detail, plus the sweep of it and the grandeur. It was like being inside and outside herself at the same time. It was beautiful, and it felt sacred, and she knew what was coming this time when that flame inside her crackled and burned, leaping high and bright.

She knew what was coming, but still she felt unprepared. His mouth was at her ear, murmuring dark and pretty things. One huge hand was between them where they were joined. And this time, when she fell apart, his name was on her lips.

Even so, even as she fell and fell, spiraling around in that star-studded dark, she was aware of how his arm went beneath her hips. How he lifted her to him, his thrusts going wild, until she heard him roar beside her. Then go still.

Harriet had no idea how much time passed. Jensen shifted to one side, but pulled her with him so she was on him. She was vaguely aware of it when he left the bed for a moment, and she sighed happily when he returned. They could have lain there like that for a lifetime.

But eventually, she roused herself. She stretched, intrigued by all the new and different sensations she could feel throughout her body. The places where his jaw had scraped her skin. Faint tugs in private areas. *Fascinating*.

She pillowed her chin on her hands, resting there against his chest, and gazed down at him. "Can we do that again?"

Jensen's gaze was sleepy, but bright. "If you insist."

"Like . . . now?"

"You're greedy." His voice was low and admiring. "I like it. But you're going to have to feed me."

"I suppose that's acceptable," Harriet said, but she couldn't seem to keep herself from grinning.

And that was how she found herself in her kitchen, cooking eggs for Jensen Kittredge while outside, the evening shadows lengthened. It was almost August. The summer was fleeting, and she had the strangest sensation then. As if the summer days were slipping through her hands like so much sand. There was only a week left of summer school. Then a week's break before the work of the new school year began.

She'd woken up this morning the same Harriet she'd always been. Now she'd had someone else inside her body. She shuddered a little at that crazy notion, then jumped when she felt his big, strong arms go around her as she stood there at her stove. Then, better still, his face was against her neck, nuzzling her.

Nuzzling her.

"Why do you smell like dessert?" he rumbled, there against the crook of her neck, so she could feel it wind through her.

"Do I?" She liked that notion.

"You do. It's been driving me crazy for weeks."

"What kind of dessert? That could really run the gamut. A fruit platter. A custard. Some people like a cheese course."

"Cheese is not dessert."

Harriet shifted into librarian mode. "The French have a long tradition of a cheese course—"

"Cheese is cheese, baby," Jensen rumbled, and she could actually *feel* him smile. "You don't smell like a pile of cheddar. It's cinnamon and vanilla, and I want to eat you up."

She liked that much better than dissertations on cheese. "Then let's make sure we replenish your energy so you can do exactly that."

Harriet considered herself a competent cook, if never an inspired one. She could faithfully follow a recipe. She liked to watch cooking shows and imagine herself whipping up acrobatic and artistic cakes or life-altering main dishes, but her practical application always left a little something to be desired. Or so she'd always thought, but then, she'd only ever been cooking for herself.

It was completely different to throw together a simple omelet for a man who'd seen her naked, who'd had his mouth between her legs, and who made the kind of noises of pleasure while he ate that he'd made while he was making her scream.

Her imagination had failed her, she realized, because she'd never imagined *this*. The pragmatic intimacy of two people sitting in a kitchen, eating. On the surface, an un-remarkable scene. But all Jensen was wearing were his jeans with the top button undone. If asked, Harriet would have claimed that her ideal man was smooth and buffed and polished, but it turned out she liked Jensen a lot better. And he was not smooth. There was hair on his chest that she'd rubbed herself against. She'd traced it with her fingers, all the way down to his sex.

Just thinking about it made her feel breathless again.

She had pulled on her summer robe, no different, really, from the wrap dress she'd worn to stage her seduction scene in her front hall. The fabric was slightly thicker, but she still felt decadent. As if at any moment, the material might give way, exposing her.

Or she might do it herself.

No one ever talked about how a person was meant to behave when sitting completely naked under a robe with a man she had only just taken to bed. Harriet rather liked the sound of that as she thought it. She'd taken a lover. She'd *taken Jensen to bed*.

It made her feel like one of the women she liked to watch on the shows she streamed. Always daring, always witty, always dangerously beautiful, they were flappers and sleuths, or archly entertaining countesses. They were the sorts of women who took lovers as they pleased, held off seas of admirers with a single glance, and who were in every way the kind of independent women Harriet had always considered herself to be.

Though she was aware that the virginal version of that woman was never considered to be quite so dashing. It had never made sense to her. It still didn't, really. But it didn't matter, did it, because she was no longer a virgin.

Jensen sat back in the chair at her cute little kitchen table, which he, naturally, entirely dwarfed. She'd made him what she'd considered an oversize omelet, but he'd eaten it so quickly and with such focus that she suspected it was little more than a snack to a man like him. Something to consider if she ever found herself feeding him again.

"Tell me something," he said. "How are you still a virgin?"

"I'm not. As you should know. You were there."

"How were you a virgin until now?" He shook his head. "It doesn't make sense."

"I think you'll find that if you took a poll, most people would tell you that it made perfect sense. Naturally, a crazy cat lady librarian should wither away on the vine. Or on the shelf. Maybe a vine that is also shelved?"

"I'm not asking most people. I'm asking you." He grinned when she glared at him. "I'm complimenting you, Harriet. You had no hesitation. No fear."

"Is that not . . . normal?"

His grin widened. "There's no normal. There's just people. But I would expect that anyone who'd waited as long as you did would have some inhibitions. You don't seem to have any."

"I'm not inhibited at all," Harriet told him seriously. "I'm not insecure. I told you."

"You dress like you're trying to hide your body, which is a crying shame." He shrugged. "I know you say it's all about comfort, but that's not how it looks."

"Worrying about how you look to others sounds like the greatest inhibition of them all," Harriet said quietly. "Oddness is a kind of liberty, I guess."

Jensen was looking at her with a serious expression on his face. And now she would never be able to see it without thinking of how he looked above her, driving into her, until her body arched up off the bed of its own accord . . . She quivered a little bit.

"Everyone's a little bit odd, Harriet. The difference with you is that you don't try to hide it."

"I could never manage it. I tried. But you know, the primary weapon that social groups use to keep the wayward in line is isolation. And I like being isolated. Once I realized that their punishment was my happiness, I became a lot less interested in conforming." She tilted her head a little she gazed at him. "You do the same thing."

He laughed. "I don't think so."

"You only pretend to conform, Jensen. You laugh or tell a story and make everyone else feel good, don't you? Then you do exactly what you please."

"I have no idea what you're talking about." But he was still grinning. "I'm just a good old boy. Ask anyone."

"I thought that's exactly what you were," she confessed, because they were basically naked and this was intimate and she felt she owed him that. She shrugged when he shook his head at her. "I did. A big, dumb lug at best."

"I prefer dumb jock, actually."

"But you're not that at all, Jensen." Harriet searched his face, though she couldn't have said what she was looking for between those cheekbones and his marvelous mouth. "I have to conclude that you never were. It's a lie. But a lie that you tell yourself. Why?"

"We were talking about virginity," Jensen said. Though his grin hadn't dropped from his face, it wasn't the same. She noted that he'd gone still. "My own is nothing but a distant memory. A good memory, but distant."

She knew he was changing the subject, but she was diverted all the same. "I'm sure you were upsettingly young."

"Belinda Fairchild and I fumbled our way to bliss in a pickup truck to a Lee Ann Womack song, as the good lord intended," Jensen said, sighing happily. "God bless her."

"You were both virgins?" Harriet made a face when he nodded. "That doesn't sound like much fun."

"Baby. Please. It's always fun."

"I wouldn't take my car to a mechanic who'd never worked on a car before. Or to an overexcited teenage boy, for that matter. If you weren't yet a teenager, please don't tell me."

Jensen looked angelic. "I was fifteen, thank you very much. She was a more worldly sixteen. And I told you, Harriet. I'm real good with my hands and always have been. Some things are just innate."

"Maybe. But we were talking about your—"

"I'll show you," Jensen said.

And he did. He laid her out on her own kitchen table and showed her all kinds of things he could do with those hands of his.

When she'd lost herself a time or two, he let her crawl off that table and sink down to her knees before him. She learned how to play with her own hands, then use her mouth, tasting him until she was so slippery herself she thought she might put herself over the edge.

But Jensen took care of that. He picked her up, lifting her the way he had so many times before to prop her up against the wall, there where she could look out over her own garden. Not that she could see a single blossom or plant when there was Jensen.

"This is why it's fun that you're so little," he told her as he held her there, then drove into her, so hard and deep that she bucked against him and splintered into pieces.

He held her up, maintaining that same intense pace so that she never quite came down. Harriet fell apart, then was flung straight back into the heart of that same fire, to burn deep and long and new.

And when she shattered into too many bright pieces again, he came with her.

Jensen was laughing when he put her back down on the floor, bracing himself against the wall.

"I think my knees went out," he said, but she noticed that he was very careful to make sure that she could stand.

And she tried, she did, but she ended up sliding down that wall to the floor, watching, bemused, as Jensen handled the condom she hadn't even seen him put on. She wrapped her robe around her again, and that was where she stayed. Jensen turned around to eye her from the counter by the sink, and she saw he hadn't even bothered to button up his jeans.

They both stayed where they were, both panting, until they were both laughing while they did it.

"Damn, woman." He shook his head. "You might kill me."

"That wouldn't work for me at all," Harriet told him. "I would much rather have more sex."

Jensen muttered another curse, still laughing. He ran a hand over his face, and when he dropped it, his eyes were on the door to the kitchen and the hall beyond it.

"I don't want to alarm you. Or distract you from your voracious need for my body, a need I'm happy to fulfill, but. Harriet. Your cats are watching."

Everything was much funnier than it ought to have been. Or maybe she was simply giddy. Either way, all Harriet could seem to do was laugh, then make the little sound in the back of her throat she used to call her cats to her. She shrugged when she saw Jensen was staring at her again. "They like it."

Moments later, Brontë shot into the room in a blur of lustrous black. She ended up on the counter, hunkered behind Harriet's stand-up mixer, ears flat and orange eyes on Jensen.

"That one doesn't like me," Jensen said.

Harriet waved a hand. "She doesn't like anyone. She's very dramatic. That's why she's named Brontë."

"I get it. Her heights always wuthering." He laughed at Harriet's expression. "What? I had to read that book my junior year like everyone else. Heathcliff was a douche."

"Deathless, eternal love is always problematic," Harriet agreed. She jutted her chin at Eleanor and Milton, who strolled in together. They acted as if Jensen didn't exist, marching over to their water dishes and making a great show of not being bothered at all by the presence of a stranger in their domain.

Chaucer, on the other hand, thundered in and immediately started weaving himself around Jensen's feet.

"There's my buddy." Jensen reached down to pick up the enormous cat, draping his huge body over one forearm. And it did funny things to Harriet to see Chaucer, a solid twenty-two pounds, look tiny in Jensen's arms. Not to mention instantly blissed out, as Jensen rubbed the cat behind his ears, Chaucer's purring so loud she could hear it from across the kitchen.

"I thought you said there were five," Jensen said after a moment.

"That's Maisey," Harriet said. "She likes to play hide-and-seek."

"See?" Jensen's gaze found hers. "Everyone likes a good game, Harriet."

Harriet climbed to her feet, belting her robe with a brisk efficiency of one who felt that really, the horses had already gotten out of the barn. But still, it felt unseemly to charge around her house naked and not alone, in search of her pet.

It took a while to find Maisey, especially with Jensen's running commentary, but she eventually located the little calico curled up in a knot at the base of one of Harriet's potted plants on the sunporch.

And then got to watch that odd fantasy of hers come to life all over again as Jensen picked up the tiny cat, able to hold almost the whole of her little body in one hand.

"Look at that," he rumbled, sounding delighted. "That's enough to melt your heart, isn't it?"

And that was how Harriet finally understood what was happening to her. What had already happened.

She was not a dashing countess, taking lovers on the side that the earl pretended not to notice. She was no flapper, enjoying the freedoms of the Roaring Twenties. She was something else entirely. She was a woman who had never imagined herself to be waiting for anyone, but had really been waiting for him.

All this time, there had been nothing wrong with her. Nothing off. She just hadn't met Jensen yet.

And now he was looming around her house, gorgeous and male, and she knew how he tasted in her mouth. And if all that masculinity, beautiful and marvelous, wasn't enough, he liked her cats. He acted as if having five cats was nothing, and he was cuddling the smallest the same way he'd cuddled the largest. Holding them safe in his big, capable hands.

The way he'd held her.

She'd always thought that heartache came later. The period at the end of a sentence she'd never uttered. It had never occurred to her that really, heartache was an echo. Because first there was this.

This ache. This stunning knowledge that something

she'd never expected to happen to her, could. So easily and so smoothly it was like surfacing from the water and lifting her face to the sun.

Harriet felt shaken. She wanted to cry.

But in the end, there was nothing to do but tell him. Because it was the truth. Because it felt like a miracle. And because he was looking down at Maisey, a little smile on his face and all that light in his eyes, and she'd seen him look at her the same way.

There was no unknowing what she knew.

And she'd never kept the things she knew to herself. That wasn't how she was built.

"Jensen," she said. "I love you."

That starkly. That irrevocably.

And then realized, with that same sinking feeling that always went along with these things she did and said so heedlessly, that once again she'd made a huge mistake.

16

"No," Jensen told her, maintaining what he thought was admirable calm, given the provocation. "You don't."

It wasn't the first time a woman had told him that she loved him. They told him that a lot, in fact. Or they used to, until it became fairly common knowledge that declarations of love were the quickest way to see the back of him.

He allowed as how Miss Harriet Barnett might not have gotten that message. And while he was making allowances, he couldn't blame her for confusing the matter, could he?

"You had good sex. Great sex. It's easy to get confused." He grinned, nice and wide. "But those are just orgasms, darlin'."

"Don't patronize me," she replied with a frown, because why had he imagined she would have any other reaction? "I didn't scream out my love for you *while* having an orgasm, Jensen. We're not even touching. You're holding my cat." She blinked. "Which is not a euphemism."

"Harriet." He could afford to be patient, even though it seemed harder than it should have. As if she'd dealt him a serious wound here, when that was impossible. He didn't get wounded. You had to get close to get wounded, and he never let that happen. Though he had to work to keep his grin in place. "You don't know this, because this is your first time. But it's easy to get confused about the kind of feelings that come up when you get naked with somebody."

"Really?" That relentless blue gaze of hers seemed to pound into him. "How many times have you gotten confused, then?"

"I don't get confused."

Jensen very carefully set her cute little kitten down on the wood floor. It felt like an accusation when little Maisey made a high-pitched sound. At him. But he didn't pick her up again.

"Because you are somehow exempt from this feeling you say is so common that everybody feels it?"

"It's different."

She didn't look upset. It would have been better if she had. That would have made sense. "Why is it different?"

He should have known that this wouldn't be simple. Because what with this woman was ever simple? Jensen should have known that not only was she likely to throw a curveball into the mix but that she wouldn't react like any other woman he'd ever known when he corrected her. Most women knew better than to express love as openly as Harriet had. Openly, matter-of-factly, and with that pragmatic directness that characterized everything she did. Most women wouldn't dare, because they knew better.

But Harriet didn't know better. Because Harriet wasn't most women.

Why would you want her to be? something in him asked.

He ignored it. Because he was good at ignoring things—but he'd been ignoring his own internal alarms for far too long where she was concerned, and look where it led. Right here. Right to this.

Jensen didn't have relationships. And this already felt a whole lot like it was one, and that was before he'd spent the better part of the afternoon in bed with her. Like an idiot.

"This is my fault," he said, trying to sound friendly. Amiable.

"Why would my feelings be your fault?" Harriet asked coolly, tightening the belt of her robe while regarding him in that same direct, steady, unnerving manner. "I'm actually a grown woman who gets to have all the feelings she wants, whenever she wants, with or without your permission."

He gritted his teeth. "You don't know it yet, but this will wear off. This is just chemistry, pheromones, whatever you want to call it."

"I know what to call it," she retorted in that prissy librarian's voice. "I'm sorry if this is confronting for you. I didn't fall in love with you because we had sex, Jensen. I just fell in love with you. Sex clarified it, that's all."

"You're wrong," Jensen said with far more intensity than necessary. He caught himself. "This is going to wear off, and when it does, we'll both laugh about it."

"It's not going to wear off, and I don't think I'm going to laugh about it at all," Harriet said in the same measured tones. "Mostly because I now want to kill you with my bare hands, and yet there it is. Still there, annoyingly."

Jensen ran his hands through his hair, not sure why he hadn't already left. Normally, he didn't stick around to have this conversation. Normally, he didn't allow any possibility that feelings could come up. He left long before any such specters could be raised, leaving them limp and gasping and praising his name.

But this was Harriet. It was different. Not only because he had been her first.

And he didn't want to think about all the other reasons. He didn't want to *think* it all. He was pissed that she'd made it necessary.

He found he was a little more pissed than he should have been, if he was honest, because he knew what he needed to do now. And he didn't want to do it.

He aimed his kindest smile at her, but he didn't quite meet her eyes.

"I'm glad you called me, Harriet," he said, because that was the truth. And he liked to do these things with as much truth as he could. "And I'm honored that you wanted your first time to be with me."

He didn't wait for her response. He navigated his way around the outraged-looking kitten on the floor and the equally outraged-looking woman who was standing there, her arms folded, regarding him narrowly. He couldn't say he particularly liked either one of those looks. Still, he didn't stop to have a discussion. He headed for her stairs and took them two at a time, suddenly in the kind of hurry he was never usually in to get out of here.

Jensen wasn't surprised to find, when he'd finished tugging on his T-shirt and sat down to handle his boots, that Harriet had marched up behind him.

And was now standing there looking mighty belligerent in the doorway.

"You're leaving?" she asked.

There was no particular tone in her voice. Which he took to be a pretty significant tone in and of itself.

"Well, darlin', a ranch waits for no man."

"You're not leaving because of the ranch," she said, sounding perfectly rational, which should have thrilled him. There were no tears. She certainly wasn't whining.

He was not thrilled. "Are you contradicting me about . . . me?"

Harriet smiled. And he remembered that smile, because it was the same one she'd used when she'd been talking to him like he was a simpleton in the Coyote. So long ago now that he'd almost forgotten. Almost.

"Oh, I'm sorry," she said in her knife-edged way. "I thought that's what we do now. You lecture me about my feelings, and I take the opportunity to return the favor. So, *darlin',* I think you heard me. You're not running away to do ranch work. You're just running away."

Jensen could not have been more offended. Not even if he tried, and he did. He finished putting his boots on, but he didn't get up. Instead, he lounged there on the bed he'd messed up good, keeping a smile on his face and his gaze trained on her as if he didn't have a care in the world.

Like his life depended on it. "You don't know this about me, I guess, but I don't run. Ever."

"Then why are you going?" she asked, again, in a tone of such reasonableness that Jensen found he was asking himself the same question. When he already knew the answer. "I certainly can't claim to be an expert, but I thought the sex was outstanding. I'd like to have more of it. And it seems to me that you storming off because you don't like something I said is a whole lot of cutting off your nose to spite your face."

"My nose is right where it belongs."

"That's a nonanswer. I get it. You're Jensen Kittredge, and you've dedicated your life to being the charming playboy of Cold River, Colorado."

She did not make that sound particularly charming.

"I would never call myself a playboy. It makes me think about gold medallions and seventies mustaches in places I do not intend to visit, like California."

Harriet rolled her eyes. "I've been hearing stories about you since I moved here. So careful never to be tied down. So determined to avoid any entanglements. Love them and leave them, and why not? There are always more."

Jensen couldn't understand why his chosen life philosophy sounded grubby when she said it. "If you already sound exasperated by the inevitable, why are we discussing it?"

Harriet sighed as if he were a trial, and Jensen had to take a moment. Because how many times had he wished he could get through a scene like this without the usual responses? Tears, begging, whining. Wild accusations and insults. None of which were on display today.

Because Harriet looked as she always did. Solid and unassailable, her blue eyes too bright and entirely too direct. Not as if she were beholding his glory with all attendant awe, because of course she couldn't do anything the usual way.

A lot more like she were seeing straight through him.

"Again," she said, "I don't have any basis of comparison, but I find it difficult to believe that your drunken Coyote sex was as good as all that."

"And if I tell you that it was?" He realized that he'd used the past tense, which was far more revealing than he wanted to be right now. "*Is?*"

Harriet, his crazy cat lady spinster virgin, scoffed at him. "I don't believe you."

Jensen's heart was a clattering train wreck in his chest, like he was halfway between a plane overhead and a terrible blaze beneath. When he was sitting on a too-small bed, surrounded by floofy pillows, being stared down by a tiny librarian.

"Whether you believe it or not doesn't make it any less

untrue," he drawled with all his might. "It might make you delusional."

She laughed then. Harriet actually laughed.

And not the way he often did. Her laughter seemed real.

"Is this the postcoital version of suggesting I'm a hysterical female? That's extraordinary." She didn't wait for him to answer, which was a good thing, because he had no idea what he was going to say. Or what he *could* say, with the train-wreck situation that was still happening. Not to mention that sharp look in her eyes. "I'm not hysterical, Jensen. And I'm not delusional. I told you, I've heard a million stories about you in my time here. You don't show up at people's houses in the afternoon. You don't stick around for a meal, then meet the cats. You're a late-night lover who likes to be gone before dawn." She sniffed. "I don't think it's fair for you to go around breaking all your rules and pretending that I'm the one who's delusional."

Jensen understood that he needed to mount a defense. And quickly. He was positive that his whole life depended on it.

But not a single word came to mind.

Because everything she'd said was true, and it worried him that he actually hadn't considered any of it himself. The afternoon-instead-of-night thing. The hanging around. Eating her food and ingratiating himself with her pets. She was absolutely correct—this was not how he rolled. He was in it for the sex, he never told anyone different, and he'd never deviated from that pattern. Never.

Until today, when he'd acted as if he'd never heard of that pattern.

"I have to go," he managed to get out.

He still didn't move.

Harriet made an exasperated sound, and maybe later, when he found his feet again, he would spend some time cataloging these responses of hers that were so outside what he was used to. So infuriating and yet so perfectly her.

"I'm sure you'll do exactly as you wish," she said. She stood straighter, and it occurred to him that she was trying to make herself look taller, a doomed enterprise. But the flash of her blue eyes was as sharp as ever. "But I think you're dumb."

Jensen really didn't like that word.

"Yes, ma'am," he drawled, edgy and maybe a little dark. "I'm well aware that you think I'm dumb. A big old dumb jock who you're real certain isn't smart enough to see that you think you can run mental rings around me when you're half-asleep."

She blinked. More than once, and then she readjusted those glasses she'd swept back on at the first opportunity.

"I want to deny that." And that forthright manner of hers made his chest ache. "It's not true anymore, but it was true when I first met you, and it's unforgivable. Particularly from a librarian. My entire purpose in this life is to educate and inform, not belittle. I'm sorry, Jensen."

And Jensen—known far and wide across the land for his silver tongue, the very one that had allowed him to talk his way out of almost every scrape he'd ever gotten into—couldn't seem to find a single, solitary word.

He liked that folks thought he was nothing but a dumb jock. He enjoyed being underestimated. His entire adult life had involved him hiding in plain sight, and he would have been first in line to claim that nothing made him happier.

So he couldn't fathom why it was that her apology seemed to strike a chord inside him, humming low and deep. Not just the apology but the typically brisk and unemotional summation that had come first. Acknowledging how she'd thought about him, admitting it was wrong, and offering an apology on the spot.

Something that felt too much like a very old grief seemed to rise in him then. He didn't think he could have named it if his life depended on it, but he recognized it. He knew it was old. He had a feeling that if he went in there and started poking around at how he'd been raised and all those uncomfortable feelings he harbored, he'd find a whole host of things he'd spent years looking away from.

He didn't want to look at any of it. And yet at the same time, it was all in him, anyway. And this tiny little tornado of a woman seemed to know. She just seemed to *know*, when no one else in his life had ever seen it. Oh sure, Zack might like to comment on the fact that Jensen hid his real self, but it wasn't as if he ever apologized for his own part in the person Jensen had become. It wasn't as if anyone had. Because who would? It was just family and loss and life.

For the first time in as long as he could remember, Jensen—who prided himself on how big and powerful he was and how little he ever gave in to the feelings that waylaid regular people—felt something perilously close to vulnerable.

"That's not the kind of dumb I was talking about," Harriet was saying briskly, bringing his attention back to her. "I understand that you think you need to limit your exposure to your . . . barflies. But that's not me. You don't have to worry that if you stick around and teach me everything you know, I'll turn up at your favorite watering hole and make a scene. First of all, I thought the Coyote was sticky and scary. Second, and more importantly, I'm from the Midwest. I would literally rather die than ever make a scene." She considered. "On purpose, I mean."

He felt hungover when he rarely allowed himself to get that drunk. "Harriet. It's not the sex I have a problem with. It's your feelings."

"Is it really my feelings? Or the fact that I dared express them?"

"Both."

"I didn't ask you for your undying devotion, Jensen. I didn't ask you for anything at all. I just told you how I felt. You're under no obligation to return my feelings." Her chin rose in that belligerent way he was entirely too familiar with now. God help him, all he wanted to do was taste it. "Obviously, I will also think it's dumb if you don't, but that's not a requirement."

"Baby, you don't know if it's a requirement or not. All this . . ." He lifted his chin in her direction, encompassing the whole picture. Harriet Barnett in that robe of hers, her feet bare and her hair a mess from his hands, with her chin up like she was ready to fight him. "You're all hopped up on the afterglow."

She looked at him for a long moment, and he saw absolutely no hint of surrender on her face. Not a surprise, when he considered it. This was Harriet. It was entirely possible she didn't know how to back down.

And yet here you are, still sitting on her bed, a whole lot like you're waiting for her to convince you.

Jensen took a moment to tell that voice inside him where to go. And then proved his head was on right by standing up. At last.

"Like you said," he told her. "There are rules, and I've already broken them. Your feelings are just icing on the cake."

Her eyes flashed and he braced himself. But she didn't

start screaming at him. She didn't call him names. She didn't let her face crumple or start crying.

Oh no. Harriet Barnett was far more formidable than any of that. Because all she did was get the light of battle in her too-blue eyes, then pull that robe off her body, holding his gaze the entire time. Even as she let it slide to the floor in a pool around her feet.

Damn her.

"You can't think the same thing is going to work twice," he growled. "I'm not that easily manipulated."

Harriet shrugged and started across the room. Right at him. "I don't know what you're talking about. You said you had to go. I'm going to go take a shower."

But first she walked toward him, and everything inside him seized. It was like he'd never seen a naked body before. When the truth was, he'd not only seen his share, he'd seen hers too. He'd enjoyed every inch—and usually he didn't require an encore.

Usually didn't seem to apply here. Everything about Harriet was like a punch straight to the gut. Jensen didn't know how he didn't double over. It was like he'd never had a woman in his life, that was how desperately he wanted her. He was already hard—or maybe he was still hard. He was tense everywhere. His pulse was ridiculous, and his heart knocked so hard against his ribs he thought he probably ought to consider pulling up a recliner next to the old man's for a while.

But not yet. Because he couldn't seem to move.

Harriet was fierce, for all that she was small, and she padded across the floor toward him with her usual purpose. Her blond hair flowed all around her, and her gaze held him tight. Daring him to look away.

Obviously, he couldn't. She was as gloriously naked as he recalled, and would likely continue to recall as long as he drew breath. Those perfect breasts. That waist of hers that nipped in and was perfectly sized for the span of his hands. The flare of her hips and that sweet, slick flesh between her legs. She was pocket-size, and she was perfect, and his mouth was so dry he was kind of surprised he didn't start his own fire right there.

"Thank you for your service," she said with exaggerated politeness when she stopped before him.

She didn't wait to see what he would do, which made it worse, somehow. She turned on her heel, letting her hair flow out around her like a cloak as she started for her bathroom, treating Jensen to an extended study of her backside. And he'd glutted himself on this woman already today, but as she moved, he realized he'd neglected her back. He had a deep hunger for the elegant sweep of her neck, the line of her spine. That perfect bottom of hers that he already knew could haunt a man.

Jensen stood like he was nailed to the floor. He expected her to throw a look over her shoulder as she disappeared into the bathroom, but she didn't. He figured she would peek back out, or maybe call out to him, but she didn't.

He stayed where he was, frozen solid, as he heard the water go on in her shower.

And then, if he wasn't mistaken—and it was hard to tell with all the train wrecks going on inside him—she started to hum.

Harriet was naked, singing in her shower, no doubt sudsing herself all over . . .

Maybe you really are dumb, that voice in him suggested.

And Jensen broke.

He ripped off his clothes all over again and made it

across the room in about two steps. It would be fine, he promised himself. There would just be one more taste.

Just one.

Then he threw open the door to her shower stall, stepped inside, and slammed his mouth to hers.

17

Much, much later, Harriet made them another meal.

This time, she made pasta, defrosting one of the jars of sauce she'd put up in the winter because she required serious and significant fortification. Then she took the two heaping bowls of penne outside to where Jensen sat out back. The summer sun had finally set. The evening was cool, and the stars were bright. It had been the longest day, and the best day, of Harriet's life—and it wasn't over yet because he was still here.

Her belly flipped a little as she approached him, because he was beautiful and the things she knew about him now were astonishing, and *he was still here*. It all felt miraculous.

Jensen had taught her marvelously acrobatic things in her own shower stall and then had carried her out to the bed, soaking wet and slippery, where he had applied himself to even more lessons. She'd sobbed out her pleasure while he taught her how to take him from behind. How to brace herself on her hands and knees and how different it was with his strong arms wrapped around her hips as he pistoned himself inside her.

Harriet liked to think she was an excellent pupil in this, as in all things.

When she'd woken up again, hours had passed and she was sure that she would find him gone.

But instead, Jensen had been lying there beside her, already awake, and she'd hardly opened her eyes before he was on her again. To teach her that fast was different from slow. It was explosive. A fiery rush.

Oh, the things he'd taught her.

And he'd still been there when she'd woken up from the next little doze, his big body everywhere, taking over her bed the way he'd taken over her body. And at some point, she was sure she was going to marvel at how she, who had never shared a bed with another human—though always with her cats as it suited them—had found it . . . pleasant. Easy to tangle herself up in him and sleep when surely she should have found the whole thing alien and uncomfortable.

"I'm starving," she had announced, more to the large male biceps she'd been using as a pillow than to him. "I'm going to make myself food. I'd be happy to make you some, too, if that doesn't feel too much like iron chains wrapped tight around your freedom."

"Watch it, baby," he'd growled at her, and had nipped at her neck as she'd rolled away from him.

To which provocation she had only laughed.

Harriet had still been laughing when she'd marched off to her kitchen when, really, she shouldn't have been quite so lighthearted in the face of such a huge shift in a life that had until now been largely—happily—the same. Especially when she considered the fact that he kept calling her *baby*. A term of endearment she'd heard others use and had always found infantilizing and vaguely creepy. Why would one adult want to call his or her adult romantic partner a baby?

But it was different when it was Jensen. It made her

sigh a little, then shiver. Especially when she considered that his dismissive, universal go-to endearment was the run-of-the-mill *darlin'* that he'd called her straight out in the Coyote that night, when she'd been little more than a stranger. She assumed he called everyone that. She'd heard him call one of his horses that.

Harriet didn't need to ask him, because she already knew. *Baby* was all hers.

She'd been so charmed by that knowledge that she'd actually gone into the freezer and found one of her precious jars of red sauce, put away to take the edge off the worst of winter when it first came howling in. It was an offering, and while she didn't intend to tell him that— because she'd learned after the *I love you* debacle—she knew.

And it did her heart good when Jensen ate her food with the same rapt attention and evident delight that he did everything else that mattered to her.

Harriet understood that her heart—and how completely she'd lost it to this man—was a problem. But it was a problem she did not intend to deal with now, while he was still here.

"I'll deny it if you ever say it in front of my mama, but your pasta is better than hers," Jensen rumbled.

"High praise indeed."

And it was a bit of a reach to sound arch and amused when inside, she was melted into a puddle, but she tried her best.

Jensen sat back at the patio table as if it were his, not hers. He lounged in the chair next to hers that hardly seemed big enough to hold him and somehow called more attention to his commanding height and all those glorious muscles. Harriet remembered when she'd found these pieces for her little patio and had set it all up out here on the flagstones, never imagining she would ever use them for entertaining anyone. She entertained herself. She spent many an afternoon and evening in good weather out here. She liked to look at her garden. She liked to knit and read. She often took her dinner here in the summers and watched the cats stalk bugs and birds in the yard.

Never in a million years could she have imagined that the beautiful, gloriously alive, and laughing man she'd seen in Cold River Coffee that first day would ever be here with her. He had now had his hands and his mouth all over her body, he had eaten her food and met her cats, and she still could hardly comprehend it.

Harriet had never had a life shift quite so dramatic. Not even going off to college had seemed *this* extreme.

"I want to ask you a question," she said as the quiet night seemed to thicken around them. "But I'm afraid if I do, you're going to do that thing again."

Jensen's amber eyes seemed more gold than usual, out here beneath the stars. "That thing? What thing?"

"You know what thing. When you get all slick and charming, start patronizing me, and try to run out the front door."

That gold gaze glinted dangerously. "I think I can handle a question, Harriet."

"Don't worry, I'm not going to propose marriage." But when she saw the expression on his face, she laughed. "I take it that's happened to you? Out of the blue?"

"A time or two."

She ought to be struck with jealousy at the very notion. All those women he'd touched. All of them desperate for more of him. Harriet supposed it was possible that she might get there. But not while he was right here, right in front of her. Not when it was so obvious to her that this thing between them was special.

She knew it was. Not just because she'd gone and fallen in love with him. But because it had to be special. Because no matter how amazing Harriet found herself, it was rare for anyone else to agree. And yet here he was.

And unless she was very much mistaken, he didn't seem to be able to keep his hands off her. There was no way not to take that as a win.

"I'm not going to offer for your hand in marriage," she assured him. "I just want to know why."

"You mean in a philosophical sense? The great why?" He settled back in his chair and folded his hands over his belly in a manner that should have looked rednecky and unappealing. But it was Jensen. He only ever looked hot. "Why am I here? Where am I going? What's the meaning of life?"

"Fascinating as those answers are, I'm sure, I'm more interested in the rules. Your rules and why you have them. Why the whole playboy persona."

"Again, I take issue with the word *playboy*. I'm a rancher. A cowboy, if you like. But that's the only *boy* I've been since I was a kid."

Harriet sighed. "Feel free to insert whatever your preferred term is, then."

"I don't have a term. I'm just me."

"Sure. But with distinct rules. Are we now going to pretend we didn't explicitly discuss these rules? Literally only a few hours ago?"

She saw something move over him. She'd seen so many versions of him now. There was the practiced, public Jensen. Easygoing and never intense. That was the Jensen who laughed to fill up rooms, unlike the Jensen who simply laughed, truly relaxed instead of only pretending to be at ease. And there was the Jensen made up entirely of intensity, stark and wildly male, who moved inside her and tore her apart.

This was a different one altogether.

This Jensen was harder. *Sadder,* something in her whispered.

And she suddenly regretted that she'd asked the question. Her insatiable need to *know things* even when maybe it would have been better to simply bask in the moment.

"My senior year of high school," Jensen said, dark and abrupt. "It was a great year. The football team won the state championship, so we all walked around like superheroes. It was a mild winter, and when spring rolled around, high school was almost over. What wasn't to love? I spent all my time with my two best friends. One of them was Matias Trujillo, who you met in the Broken Wheel that time."

"I know who he is, yes. Though I know his sister better than him."

"He's hard to know." But Jensen didn't smile when he said that. There was a grimness to him now. "Our other best friend was Daniel Hillis."

Harriet opened her mouth to say she'd never heard of Daniel Hillis or any other Hillises around town, but Jensen kept going. "It was a week before prom night, and we had big plans. It was going to be epic. The crowning achievement of our high school careers, if we said so ourselves."

"What does that mean?" She smiled. "I was homeschooled. My epic achievements were academic."

All the Jensens she knew would have laughed at that. Teased her a little.

This one barely smiled. "Mostly it was about spending the weekend in Daniel's cousin's cabin in the foothills without any parental supervision. But the week before, we were just doing our usual thing. It was Saturday night, and there was a party out in the woods. We drove out there but thought it was lame, though I can't remember why. Probably a matter of which girls were there and which weren't. Besides, there was the prom date scenario to worry about. Very political, you know."

"Prom dates are political?" Harriet considered that. "I didn't go to any proms, so all I know about them comes from teen movies."

And nothing she'd ever heard about proms since her high school years had ever suggested to her that missing out on that supposed rite of passage was a bad thing, but she decided not to share that.

The faintest hint of a smile flirted with Jensen's unusually grim expression, but didn't take hold. "Prom dates have a tendency to feel possessive. You wouldn't want to ask one girl to the prom, then fool around with another girl the weekend before. That would make for unhappiness all around."

"I don't know why I'm surprised to hear that your issue with prom dates was the juggling of them," Harriet said dryly. "As opposed to the more common problem, as I understand it, which is finding one."

But again, Jensen didn't smile as she expected him to.

"To this day, no one can remember whose idea was," he said instead, his gaze trained on something in the dark. "The party was in the woods on the other side of town, closer to the lake. We suddenly decided we should go to the lake instead. We must have done the same thing a million times before. Hang out in the woods, then head up to the lake to jump around like idiots. Driving there was half the fun. The road twists around and around, and there are no houses up that way. No one to suggest you slow down. It was always a thrill to drive too fast with your friends yelling and music blaring, especially as big-time seniors in high school with bright and shiny futures all planned out."

Foreboding was beginning to settle in. Harriet found herself sitting up straighter in her chair, wishing she'd thought to shrug on her trusty cardigan.

"None of us were drunk," Jensen told her, still looking off toward the mountains. "We were dumb about a lot of things back then, but not that. We made it up to the lake and headed to our usual spot. There's a kind of rocky beach. Have you been there? You can drive straight down to the water's edge."

Harriet felt as if there were a hand gripped tight around her throat, so all she could do was nod.

"It was a nice night," Jensen said softly. "And we were just having fun. Poking at each other like we always did. About who could do this or that. We'd all been athletes our whole lives. We'd done all kinds of things. We were champions." But his lips twisted when he said that. "I might not remember whose idea was to go to the lake that night, but it's crystal clear that I was the one who bragged that I could jump off the highest part of the cliffs. Claimed I'd done it a thousand times before. And when Matias and Daniel rightly accused me of being a liar, I doubled down. Said I'd do it again, right then and there, to prove it." He shook his head, his mouth working. "That was what we always did. We dared each other. And there was no backing down from a dare."

Harriet wanted to touch him, but she didn't. She didn't think he'd appreciate it. And besides, she was fairly certain he'd forgotten where he was and who he was talking to. All she could do was sit there and listen—and wish she hadn't started this conversation.

She might want to know where he was going with this. But she also had the strangest notion that if she could, she would throw herself bodily between Jensen and these memories of his. If that would bring him back.

If that might make him smile again.

Harriet had never felt anything like it. Until this moment, she would have said without a shred of hesitation that knowing something was worth whatever emotions got stirred up.

Jensen ran a hand over his face. "Having made such a bold claim, I had no recourse. Everyone knew better than to go jumping into lakes from way up that high, but I wasn't going to let that stop me. Matias and Daniel heckled me the whole way up, so I did what I always did and dug in harder. Having shot my mouth off, I couldn't back down. Anything but that. So I went up there, stood at the edge of that monster drop, and jumped off before I could think better of it."

Harriet was holding her breath. And without realizing it, her hands had somehow crept up to cover her mouth.

Because she knew that whatever was coming, it wasn't good.

"I hit that water hard," Jensen said, his voice getting more gravelly the longer he spoke. "At first, I thought I might actually cry a little that I wasn't dead, but then the adrenaline took over. I hooted and hollered and started swimming backstroke, acting like I hadn't nearly pissed myself on the way down. I made sure to offer up some commentary on how cowardly the pair of them were for all the heckling and no action."

He was quiet for a moment. Harriet leaned forward, thinking she might risk a hand on his arm, but he shook himself and kept going.

"Matias wasn't ever easy to goad into anything, but Daniel couldn't let that stand. And I was making so much noise down there, really putting on a show. Heckling them right back. Insulting them. Doing my thing. So when Daniel stepped up to the edge of that cliff, he didn't jump like I had. He dove. And he didn't just dive, he threw in a couple of flips on his way down, just to show he couldn't be bested."

Jensen's jaw worked, like he hated the words that were leaving his mouth. Like he would have done anything to pick other ones. "I was still down there in the water, swimming around and carrying on. So he aimed off to the left." His voice got rougher. "It was the most perfect dive I ever saw. I could tell that Matias was already sweating up there, trying to figure out how he could top it. I knew I was going to have to crawl up out of the water and do it again, only better, unless I wanted to be mocked for the rest of my life."

Harriet was riveted, her eyes on Jensen's face and the bleakness she saw there.

"But Daniel didn't come up," he said quietly. "At first, I figured he was just messing around some more. Until he finally did surface, but he wasn't swimming. He was floating. Facedown in the water."

"Oh, Jensen." She could hardly breathe, and her hands moved of their own accord to hook over his forearm. "I'm so sorry."

If Jensen noticed, he gave no sign. "Matias had to run to the truck and drive down through the woods, back into cell phone service. But I stayed in that lake with Daniel, who was already gone. He executed that ridiculous dive, laughed all the way down, and sliced through the water like a knife. Then broke his neck on a rock just under the surface. Because of me."

Harriet wanted to argue, but didn't. She stayed silent, her eyes moving all over his face.

"And it's funny, the things you remember," Jensen said after a moment. "I was happy that the old sheriff made Matias and me take Breathalyzer tests, because at least that way, no one could say we were drunk. I focused on that the most in the days right after, because it was better than remembering how cold the water got, how cold Daniel got, and how I stood there, just me and him, for the hour it took for help to come. I can't remember the last thing Daniel shouted while he was diving. I can't remember what Matias and I shouted at each other before he ran for the truck. But I remember that it took two EMTs to take Daniel away from me. I remember when his mother turned up at the hospital. And the look on her face when she saw me and Matias alive and well."

"Jensen." Harriet's voice was soft. "You didn't push him. You didn't—"

"I have rules, Harriet," Jensen said flatly, "because I decided a long time ago that I don't get to live the kind of life that Daniel would have wanted. Because here's the thing about Daniel. Matias and I had dates to the prom, but Daniel was taking his girlfriend. Carly Wright was the girl of his dreams. He had some plans to get out of this valley, but he was going to take her with him. He told us all about it that year. He was going to come back when he'd made some cash, they were going to build a life here, and it was going to be beautiful. Except my big mouth put him on top of that cliff and took it all away from him. I goaded him every step of the way. That's on me. I carry that."

He looked down then, and Harriet thought he noticed that she was touching him for the first time. And he didn't jerk his arm away, but something about his silence made her retract her hands all the same.

"Daniel didn't get to settle down with Carly and make himself some pretty little babies in a happy house somewhere. So neither do I. Daniel didn't get to have a grown-up relationship with Carly. He didn't get to figure out how to be a man." His eyes flashed, too dark to call gold then. "He didn't get roots, Harriet. I chopped them off. And that means I don't get them, either. Ever."

Harriet wanted nothing more than to reach out to him again, but she could tell he wouldn't welcome it. So she stayed where she was, her hands clenched tight in her lap and her heart aching. "Do you think that's what he would have wanted?"

Jensen let out a hollow laugh. "What he would have wanted is to live. And I'm not going to take myself out to make things even. But I'm also not going to forget, even for one moment, that I'm the reason he doesn't get to be here. His whole family moved away. Carly Wright too. Not one of them could bear to stay here, and I don't blame them. I stay for them. And for him."

He stood up then, abruptly enough that it was startling, but then he pushed the chair back in with such careful precision that she nearly questioned her own eyes. Jensen took a moment to look down at her, and she knew that he was about to leave her again. For good this time, she was pretty sure. And she knew that there was no state of undress that would keep him from it.

She would have done anything at that moment to take that bleak, shuttered look from his face. Anything at all.

But instead she sat very still.

"I like you," he said roughly as if that hurt to admit. "More than I should. I should never have come here today and I never should have stayed, because the only thing I have to offer is sex. I don't usually go back for more because it causes too many expectations."

Harriet nodded. "I understand."

Jensen's eyes glittered, but she took that as a good thing, because at least they were amber again. "But you already came in swinging. You need to decide if you can handle it."

"I can handle it," Harriet said immediately, though as the words came out of her mouth, something lurched inside her. She wondered if she had any idea what *handling it* entailed. Or how hard it was likely to be.

She wanted to handle it, because that meant handling him. And that was almost the same thing, wasn't it?

"I don't know if that's true," Jensen said quietly. "But you're the only person who's ever apologized to me for thinking I was dumb. That means something to me. So we can try this."

She didn't ask him what *this* entailed, by his reckoning. There was a part of her that thought there shouldn't be all these rules, and wanted to rail against the whole thing—but it was a small part. Every other part of her was perfectly clear that she didn't want this to end.

Whatever *this* was to him.

"But, Harriet," he said, in his most gravelly voice, not a trace of a laugh on his face, "if you ever tell me you love me again, that's it. That's the end. Do you understand?"

"I understand," she said, carefully. "But, Jensen—"

"That's the end of it," he said again, even darker than before. "You need to think about that. Because you're not going to change my mind. You're not going to convince me otherwise. I already think this is a bad idea, but because it's you, I'm going to give it a shot. Don't make me regret it, Harriet."

And later, she expected she might work herself up into all kinds of levels of anger over that remark. Over ultimatums and warnings and *don't make me regret it,* like he wasn't involved.

But not tonight. Tonight she only nodded, then let him go.

Because that was the only way she could get him back.

It was the only way, but she had to remind herself of that as she sat there, long after she heard his truck drive off. It was the only possible way.

But still she stayed where she was, sitting out there on her patio while the night grew even cooler and the stars didn't seem to warm her the way they normally did.

And if her cheeks got wet, proving her to be a foolish, heartsick, profoundly silly girl after all, well.

At least there was no one around to see it.

18

Some weeks later, Jensen's phone went off in the middle of the night. A horrendous hour by any measure, but particularly for a man who started his workday at 4:00 a.m.

A fact that everyone who had his phone number should know.

He couldn't think of a single good reason why anyone would be calling him in the small hours. And yet despite himself, he hoped it was Harriet. Who had breezily informed him when he'd been at her house three days ago that she was headed back home to see her folks.

For a week.

Jensen hadn't liked anything about that. First, that she'd called some place other than Cold River *home,* because that could mean that she might leave here someday, and he couldn't have that. And he certainly couldn't think about why he couldn't have that. Why was she going *home* at all? How long was she staying—was it really an entire *week*?

But second, by the very terms of the rules he'd set down himself, he couldn't really interrogate her on that subject. Because that implied things. All kinds of things he'd always made it a point to never, ever imply. And every question he'd wanted to ask had seemed fraught with the same peril, so he'd kept his questions to himself and used his mouth in a variety of other, more inventive ways.

Yet it didn't escape his notice that Harriet was mastering the easygoing, come-and-go-at-will, please-yourself-and-don't-label-it thing that Jensen had insisted upon. *She* was making it look easy.

Which made his own behavior all the more concerning.

He kept telling himself he was going to end it. He needed to end it, because who was he fooling? But he didn't. And then she was breezily off to Missouri as if she didn't care either way.

Jensen hoped it was Harriet calling him in the middle of the night, but when he swiped up his phone from the table beside him, it wasn't her. It was Aidan.

He thought twice about answering it. But he knew Harriet would insist he answer if she were here.

Which was more reason not to answer it, obviously.

"You better be dead," he said into the phone.

"Look," came the surly teenage voice he knew too well by now. "I wanted to call Miss Barnett. She told me I could call her at any time, day or night, if I was in trouble. But she's not home, is she? And I think we both know whose fault that is."

Jensen had not been asleep. He had been lying in his bed, glaring at the ceiling, and raking himself over a selection of his favorite coals. He was good at that.

"Whoa. Simmer down there, kid."

"I'm not a kid," Aidan snapped, and because Jensen had himself been a puffed-up teenager who'd needed a comeuppance, he took pleasure in it when Aidan's voice betrayed him a little there. "I had a fight with my friends. They kicked me out of the car and left me in the middle of nowhere."

"How is that my problem? Walk."

"Yeah, I could do that, thanks," Aidan retorted. "The problem isn't the walking. The problem is, they kicked me out because I don't want to go bust in windows on Main Street. That's where they're headed."

Jensen muttered a few choice curses then, but there was no way out of it. And as little as he might want to admit it to himself, he probably wouldn't have made the kid walk, anyway, even if all he'd been calling for was a ride.

He'd discovered, to his surprise, that not only did he like Aidan, but the kid actually had a flair for the horses. Once he stopped woe-is-me-ing all over the ranch.

"Tell me where you are," he growled. And made no attempt to hide that he was kind of pissed about it before he hung up.

He rolled out of bed and dressed quickly, aware that even though it was still August, there was already more than a hint of the coming fall. He could feel it in the air, inside his little cabin, where he liked to sleep with all the windows wide open to let the mountains in.

Another season changing. Another fall Daniel wouldn't see.

Another year Jensen didn't deserve and this one not offset by the usual grueling fire season that made him feel a little bit better about continuing to draw breath.

Jensen was used to the low and high tides of grief by now. He'd lived with it too long. And if anything, he resented how it had changed with time. How it had mellowed against his will. That first fall had been brutal. Daniel dead. Matias gone. Jensen left behind.

Every new day had felt like a fresh wound.

He'd moved out of his parents' house that September and into his cabin here on his parcel of land. It was small and deliberately unfinished, because all he'd done was claim the building and hunker down, waiting to see if he'd survive what had happened. Even when it became clear that he would, he hadn't renovated it. He hadn't done anything except not live under his parents' roof, because it wasn't like Daniel was going to be building himself that dream house he and Carly had talked about when everyone else was talking about school stuff. He knew Matias had taken a different tack, feeling he'd paid his own penance in the Marines, and he didn't begrudge his friend that. Or the sweet new house he'd built himself.

But Jensen had always known his own path. Dark and lonely, but right.

He couldn't say he liked the fact that these weeks with Harriet had changed that.

Not changed it, he assured himself as he walked to his truck. Nothing could *change* it. But he'd spent a lot of time in her house since that first afternoon. It was tidy, cozy, and perfect, a lot like Harriet herself. It wasn't his grandparents' house, packed full of old memories and generations of ghosts and stories. It wasn't his parents' house, still swollen with childhood resentments and whatever their marriage was.

The cold, hard truth was that spending time there, with Harriet and her cats and her food and her questions, was the first time it had occurred to him that there were other ways to live.

He resented that too. Something he should probably tell her when she returned home. When she was done with Missouri and was back where she belonged.

Jensen jumped in his truck, but he didn't drive away immediately. Instead, he sat there for a moment, looking at his cabin. And wondering why, now, the choices he'd made and the penance he'd chosen to take felt a whole lot more like torture than it ever had before. He knew that, too, was her fault. Or really his fault, because he was letting it happen. He knew that the hold Harriet had on him was unacceptable. But he still couldn't bring himself to do a thing about it.

Because Jensen also knew that it was well-nigh inevitable that she would break his rules again. And when she did, he'd be gone.

That was the only reason he kept seeing her. Because he knew that it was temporary. That even though he was already spending more time with her than he should, it would work itself out in the end.

Walking away from her was going to hurt. He knew that too. But maybe he thought he deserved the extra helping of hurt because he was taking his time letting her go.

But this wasn't the time to be spinning around in circles over the same, well-worn tread that he already knew too well, down to the last little rut. There was a kid by the side of the road. Delinquents descending on Main Street. Jensen started down the dirt road that led off the property and had the distinct pleasure of waking up Zack while he drove.

"Is Dad okay?" Zack asked instead of any kind of greeting.

Jensen opened his mouth to reply, but stopped himself. Because it said something that Zack, who was so dedicated to the feud he'd had with Donovan that he'd walked away from the ranch, was nonetheless that worried. Even when most of the time, he pretended otherwise.

"You need to figure stuff out with the old man," he told his brother. "Before you can't."

"I'll take advice from you on my relationship with our parents when yours is sorted out," Zack retorted. "Let me know when that happens."

"The difference between you and me is that I'm not brooding about it." Jensen threw on his high beams and headed into the dark, sticking to the county road that led into town for only a little while before turning down one of the many unmarked dirt lanes that cut through the land out here. This one headed south toward the vast Everett spread. "I understand Mom and Dad's choices are their own, and I told them that a long time ago. It doesn't erase my memory of our childhood, but it also doesn't keep me awake. Then I moved on with my life."

"Yeah, that's you. The poster boy for moving on." Zack's voice was derisive, and Jensen wanted to take the bait. But didn't, because that would be proving Zack's point and he couldn't have that. "Is this why you called me in the middle of the night? To talk about family dynamics?"

"What's the point in talking about our family dynamics?" Jensen laughed. "They never change. I guess Riley and Dad built a bridge, but everything else is the same. Must be a reason for that."

"The reason for that is that no one in our family talks about anything," Zack bit out. "Mom and Dad like to pretend they never had a messed-up relationship, when, too bad, some of us remember it. And always will."

"Maybe that's their business," Jensen countered, because it was well after midnight and he was driving through the dark to save a kid from a long walk. "Maybe they don't owe us any explanations about their relationship."

"It's weird how suddenly you're real interested in keeping private business private," Zack observed. "I'm sure that has nothing to do with where I've seen your truck parked lately."

Proving once again that the biggest gossip in Cold River was the sheriff.

"I'd sure love to have a conversation about the location of my vehicle," Jensen drawled. "But maybe not at this hour. I'm calling you because I have it on good authority you've got some riled-up juvenile delinquents headed for Main Street with mischief on their minds. Might want to look into that."

"And whose good authority is this, exactly?"

"I protect my sources, Zack."

"You're not a reporter, Jensen. Let me guess. It's Aidan Hall."

"I can neither confirm nor deny."

"What are you doing, man?" If Zack had sounded bossy and overbearing, Jensen would have laughed it off like anything else. But he didn't. His older brother sounded genuinely worried. *Concerned.* It reminded Jensen of that long first year after losing Daniel. It made him . . . itchy. "Since when do you get involved with anyone? Much less a librarian and a troubled kid?"

"Since now," Jensen replied gruffly.

"Why?"

Jensen wanted to bark at him to mind his own business. He wanted to say something like, *Because I feel like it.* Or, *Because it's the right thing to do,* all pious and holy.

But for once, he didn't just start shooting off his mouth. He navigated his truck over the deep grooves of the dirt road, then, picking up speed, he turned onto a section of paved road.

"I appreciate your concern," he said stiffly. He could hear his brother moving around, no doubt getting dressed and heading out to his own vehicle to handle the incoming idiot brigade. "But it's misplaced. There's nothing I'm doing that's not temporary."

"I don't think Harriet Barnett is a summer fling type. But then, neither are you."

"Who said anything about a fling?" Jensen had to work to keep his temper out of his voice, and that wasn't good. He was usually way more in control, because he was a very big man and he had to be. "Is it really that hard to imagine that Harriet and I simply share a great love of—"

"Of what?" Zack asked, sounding darkly amused. "Victorian poetry?"

"As a matter of fact, Zack, I think the world could use a whole lot more poetry."

Or he did now, because sometimes Harriet read some to him. Naked. He'd never felt more poetic in his life.

He heard the sound of Zack's ignition. "For the record, this is all a bad idea," his brother told him. "You can't mess around with a lady like Harriet. You shouldn't mess around with that kid."

"Why, exactly?" Jensen demanded, a little hotly. Maybe more than a little. "What is it that you, *my own brother,* think I'm going to do that is so terrible to either one of them?"

Maybe he wanted Zack to say the worst thing. Maybe he wanted him to actually admit, for once, that everybody knew that when it came down to it, people died around Jensen.

Maybe if someone finally said it, that would be better than waiting all these years for it to be said.

"I don't think that Harriet deserves the usual treatment, but she's a grown woman," Zack said. Grudgingly, to Jensen's ear. "But that kid? He's never had anyone take an interest in him, Jensen. Ever. He was born lonely and you know that. What's going to happen to him when you get bored and move on? When there's no more learning the Kittredge horses or treating him like he matters?"

Because, naturally, Zack couldn't imagine that Jensen might have thought about that already.

"That's not going to happen," Jensen replied, happy to find he'd wrestled himself back under tight control. And determined that he would take a look at why that had even been an issue—later. "But you should probably spend some time examining why you think any bit of kindness isn't worth showing another person if it's not forever."

"Because I know what it's like to feel that whiplash," Zack retorted. "So do you."

"And again," Jensen gritted out. "Sort out your stuff with Dad."

And then he hung up before his older brother could say more things he didn't want to hear.

Not that it was much of an improvement to sit in the dark with his own thoughts. And the realization that no matter how many years passed and no matter that no one had ever blamed him for Daniel's death, not directly, he sure did. Still and always.

Grief might change as time went by, but that never did.

He was still brooding on all of that as he drove around to the new private park that Brady Everett had made. It was another thing Jensen had thought sounded pretty ridiculous when his sister and her new husband had explained their plans. But then, he'd grown up here, and currently lived in a cabin deep enough on Kittredge land that he had to drive ten miles in any direction to see another person. He didn't need a private campground with sites at a fair distance and pretty views. He certainly wouldn't pay for it.

But it turned out that a whole lot of folks from down in Denver would. Brady had different kinds of campsites, some for tents and some featuring tiny little cabins. No RVs allowed, and talk was that he might one day put in some kind of a lodge.

Jensen had no intention of camping that close to people he would avoid in a bar, not when he had so many Kittredge acres to choose from, but the idea of a lodge on this side of the hill that separated the Bar K from town was appealing. Because so far, there was nothing out here. Just land and livestock, sky and mountains. All of which Jensen preferred, but he also liked the idea of a place to go on a winter's night that didn't involve risking life and limb on an unforgiving Colorado mountain pass.

That was where he found Aidan. Hunkered down on the turnoff that led into Brady's park.

He pulled up next to where the kid was sitting on a big rock, wearing a sweatshirt and jeans and looking somehow rumpled and pissed all at once.

Jensen rolled down his passenger window. "You getting in?"

Aidan looked like he wanted a fight, but he stood up. He jerked the backpack he carried into place with an indignant shoulder. Jensen could read at least six different curse words right there on his angry face.

But he got in.

For a moment, they sat there in the dark, the engine running and the headlights making the trees seem spooky. "Where am I taking you?" Jensen asked with exaggerated politeness. "Consider me your personal taxi."

Aidan looked unimpressed. He slouched down so far in the passenger seat, his pack on his lap, that it was surprising he wasn't falling off into the wheel well. "Don't we have to go, like, save the town?"

"You and me?" Jensen laughed. "No, that's better left to the professionals."

Aidan cut his eyes to Jensen, then rolled them. "You called your brother."

"Well, you know. It's his job."

"Great. So now when the sheriff busts them, that will be my fault too."

Jensen opened his mouth to make some kind of tough love remark, but stopped himself. He hooked his arm over the steering wheel and turned so he could really look at Aidan. "You did the right thing."

"Wow. Really? Then that would be a first."

"You did the right thing," Jensen said again, more intently. "And that takes guts. You didn't have to call me. You could let your friends go ahead and do whatever it is they're fixing to do without it being your problem."

Aidan muttered something unintelligible.

And Jensen didn't like to admit that anything Zack had said had landed. But the truth was, they'd had two different sets of parents. There'd been Mom and Dad when they were young, all drama and temper, glasses smashed against walls, and a lot of tears. Then afterward, the quiet. That endless, impenetrable silence.

That Jensen had filled with his nonsense. Because anything was better than the silence. But he knew exactly what he would have wanted to hear from his father in those years, and never had. Not even that terrible summer.

"I'm proud of you," he told Aidan gruffly.

Then he started driving toward town, because he'd said what he'd said. And he could tell that Aidan was working on how to handle that in the seat beside him.

And just like years ago when he'd found Aidan slashing tires, he headed toward the Hall family compound. Over the hill and instead of going into town, he followed the river out a couple of miles past the Coyote toward the bend. This time, he didn't have Aidan restrained. He pulled off onto the dirt track that meandered its way down toward the water, winding in and around the various Hall family homes. Some nicer than he remembered. Others far worse.

"You still live in the same place?" he asked.

It was the first time either one of them had spoken since they'd left Brady's park.

Aidan made a vaguely assenting sound. So Jensen kept going until he found the place he was looking for and pulled up in front. He kept the engine running, because he knew not everyone around here was asleep. He figured there were eyes on his truck from all sides, and this being rural Colorado, a fair few weapons drawn too.

Aidan didn't move.

"Are you afraid to go inside?" Jensen asked, and realized he was doing a version of Harriet's matter-of-fact tone that took the sting out of otherwise too-personal questions. She was good like that. "Do you need help?"

Aidan kept his eyes ahead of him, out past the dashboard toward the windows of the rough-looking house.

Jensen couldn't see any signs of life within, but that didn't mean someone wasn't there, looking out. He also couldn't see any evidence that anyone had put the slightest bit of care into the place. Maybe ever.

"What would you do?" Aidan asked, his voice barely audible over the truck engine. "Beat him up?"

"I haven't really been about beatdowns since roughly the fifth grade," Jensen said. "Though I might consider making an exception for your father."

"Yeah, he doesn't like you, either."

"One of the reasons he doesn't like me is because I'm bigger than he is," Jensen said, almost philosophically. "And a guy like your dad likes it when the bullying goes downhill. He never much cared for it if someone hit back."

"Are you sure about the way that hill goes?" Aidan demanded, and Jensen saw that the hands that were holding that backpack on his lap were suddenly fists. "Because Miss Barnett took off. Just like my mom. Did you make her?"

Jensen had not seen that coming. He very deliberately did not think about Zack's earlier warnings.

"No." Aidan turned toward him, and Jensen shrugged. "That's not what this is. Harriet—*Miss Barnett* is visiting her folks. There's nothing ominous about it."

He had a strange and unwelcome flash of sympathy for his parents, suddenly. Was this what parenting was like? Confidently explaining to a kid why they shouldn't fear the very thing you feared yourself?

No wonder his parents had locked their stuff up and hidden it away. Better that than having to face five sets of questions that couldn't be answered.

Jensen resented the insight. He would have preferred to stay, if not mad, aloof from the entire topic.

And he still had Aidan to deal with.

"Sure there isn't," Aidan agreed with him sarcastically. "Nothing ominous at all. My mom went off to visit her cousins and never came back. Funny how that happens. And funny that the one thing my mom and Miss Barnett have in common is you."

Jensen sat with that a minute. "I think you're drawing connections that aren't there, buddy."

Normally, Aidan would groan and demand not to be called *buddy,* but he didn't do that, either. Instead, he turned toward Jensen, his body tense and his expression . . . intense.

"But are you sure?" he demanded. "Are you a hundred percent sure that you and my mom . . . That you're not . . . That you can't possibly be my father?"

Jensen had been working with this kid for half the summer now. He knew that despite appearances, Aidan really wasn't a punk. That he was all bluster—and didn't Jensen relate.

And he also knew that the bitter accusation he could hear in Aidan's voice was only there to cover up what was beneath it. So obvious that his voice cracked a little on that last word.

Hope.

And it about killed him that he couldn't give Aidan the answer he wanted.

"Listen. Aidan. I wish I were." He looked at the house, where he had absolutely no doubt Andy Hall was passed out, waste of space that he was. Then he looked back to Aidan and held the boy's gaze. Hard. "I really do wish I were."

He accepted another truth he'd been avoiding then, because it hit him the way the bleakness in Aidan's eyes did. There was no small part of him that liked this little family he'd built out of nowhere this summer. A woman like Harriet. A kid like this.

Maybe he hadn't gone and made any of that official. Maybe it was only on Sundays when it really felt that way. He never planned on admitting it to himself, that sometimes the sun was so bright it made things take different shapes than they should. So the boy on the back of a horse looked like he belonged right there on Kittredge land. And the woman at the fence, her pretty face rapt, looked like his.

Aidan wasn't the only one who had to let go of something in the dark of the truck's cab tonight.

"I thought you had to be my father," Aidan said after a long while, and had to clear his throat a few times. "Especially tonight. Because why else would you come help me out? Miss Barnett isn't even in town."

Jensen took that in. "You think I'm only doing things with you because of her?"

"Um. Yeah. Because you are."

And he could hear the question beneath that Aidan would never ask. *Are you?*

"First thing you need to know about me is that I don't do anything I don't want to do," Jensen said. Something tickled at him then, deep inside, suggesting that was something he should pay a little more attention to in other areas of his life, but he shoved it aside. "I came to talk to your class in the library because I felt like it. That's the beginning and the end of it. When it turned out that you could come work on the ranch instead of picking up trash along Main Street, I thought, why not? My youngest brother is annoyingly old now. He's gotten all domestic. It's time to have new blood around, because I don't like mucking out stalls."

"Sure, and if that was what you wanted, you could have had your choice of the 4-H kids."

"I could have, but I didn't," Jensen belted out. "I chose you, Aidan. Better take that on board."

And he thought the kid's breathing changed then. Got a little easier. Meaning his did too.

"What happens now?" Aidan asked, sounding accusatory again. "Summer school's over. The new school year's starting soon. Your whole thing with Miss Barnett . . . That's not going to last, is it?"

He was very studiously not looking at Jensen as he asked that question. Forcing Jensen to decide, on the spot, how exactly he was supposed to answer that. Was he supposed to deny his relationship with Harriet when Aidan probably knew the location of his truck as well as Zack did? He hadn't exactly been hiding it.

And something in him shouted a little louder, because he wasn't supposed to be having relationships, was he? Not with Harriet, certainly, but also not with Aidan. It shouldn't have mattered what the sun did on a Sunday. He shouldn't have let any of this happen.

But he had. And now he had to answer. And he got the distinct impression that Harriet would not approve of him discussing any of this at all. Not with Aidan or anyone else.

"I don't think you really believe that your teacher would like it if she knew you were sitting here speculating about her personal life," he said.

Well aware it was a dodge.

"Fine," Aidan said. "Whatever. I already know the answer."

"I'm glad you're sure about that," Jensen couldn't help but throw back at him. "Because I think we've established that you don't know everything, do you?"

The kid pushed open the passenger door. The truck's interior light came on, so there was no possible way for Jensen to miss the fact that Aidan was looking at him with eyes of a much older, much wearier man.

"You might not need her," he said quietly. "You might be perfectly happy without her. I think you're a liar or just dumb, but that's on you. *I* need her."

"Kid." But Jensen had no idea what he was going to say.

"And if you hurt her?" Aidan was clearly drumming up his courage, because his entire body was tense, those fists clenched even harder. "I'll find a way to hurt you. Trust me. I know you're bigger than me too, but I'm a Hall. I'll find a way."

Jensen looked at this teenager who hadn't gotten a fair shake. Who might figure out how to make his own way now, thanks to Harriet. Maybe, if he was being kind to himself, thanks to him too. The simple magic of hard work and horses.

And he couldn't pretend to be Aidan's father when he wasn't. He couldn't make Aidan feel any better about what was going on between Jensen and Harriet, because God knew, he had no idea what he was doing there, either.

But he could do this tough boy the honor of looking him straight in the eye, man to man.

And not laughing at the threat.

"I believe you," he said instead.

And he watched Aidan's shoulders settle before he pushed out of the truck. He looked back at Jensen and nodded. Once. Then he slammed the door behind him and headed toward his house.

Leaving Jensen with nothing to do but face himself at last, there in the cab of his truck an hour or so before dawn, where there was no room for anything any longer but the stark and unpleasant honesty he'd been avoiding.

For years.

19

The house where Harriet had grown up never changed. It hadn't altered much to accommodate a child, and it hadn't changed any after she'd left. Her parents, as ever, seemed genial, yet somewhat baffled, to discover her presence there each morning. They were in their seventies now, comfortably retired and content to rattle about their house of books, sipping cognac in the evenings over a game or two of chess while classical music swelled all around them and the world charged on outside. Her father gardened, her mother volunteered at a local museum, and theirs was the life Harriet had always imagined she wanted.

Academic and erudite. Quiet conversations about worthy topics, though where her parents murmured to each other, Harriet chatted instead with her cats. She'd always thought, given the conversational abilities of most of the people she'd met, that she had the better part of the deal.

But three days into her visit, Harriet was forced to admit that there was a reason she couldn't seem to settle into the soft rhythms of her parents' life the way she normally did.

She was restless.

Over and over, she caught herself waiting for that big,

booming voice. For Jensen's heavy feet on her front porch. In the quiet, peaceful house her parents wafted about in, she wanted the bright shock of his laugh. His big body sprawled out on the sofa that shouldn't have held him, beckoning her to join him.

God help her, but she missed the sex.

It was that part she found herself thinking about the most. She lay up in the narrow little twin bed in her old childhood bedroom, unable to understand how it was that she'd gone some thirty years not only without sex but happy to do without. Unlike some people she knew, she hadn't found her virginal state depressing, or embarrassing, or a project that required attention and action. On the contrary. She had been perfectly content as she was.

But now she knew better.

And she was very much afraid that she would never be content again.

On the fifth day of her visit home, she was helping her mother prepare dinner. Her father had brought in vegetables from the garden, and Harriet was chopping them up to put in the salad. Mozart was playing from the other room. The windows were open to let the summer in. Everything was pleasant and nice.

She felt so raw inside she wanted to cry.

Not because anything was wrong. But because she hadn't understood that anyone could *feel* this much. That was the part that kept astonishing her. She really hadn't known.

"Are you well, dear?" her mother asked from beside her in her sedate way. "You appear to be pulverizing the tomatoes."

Harriet put down her knife. "I'm sorry. I must be getting carried away."

Her mother turned toward her, eyeing her with that

incisive blue glare that had once sent undergraduates running for cover. Harriet knew. She'd often wanted to do the same.

"Carried away?" Her mother studied her. "That's not like you."

Harriet considered. "Maybe it is. Maybe, after all this time, it turns out that deep inside, I have always been an opera heroine waiting to happen."

To her surprise, her mother shrugged. "Aren't we all?"

"You're not," Harriet said, her mind reeling at the implications. "You're so rational and calm. Always."

"I pride myself on my rationality, as you know," her mother replied. She picked up the cutting board where she'd been slicing up the chicken breasts she'd roasted, and started shoveling them off into the large wooden salad bowl with quick, economical movements, the knife scraping against the wood. It was the sound of summer evenings here, Harriet thought. It was comforting. Or it should have been. "But there are certainly times in life where the opposite approach is called for."

"I have no idea what you're talking about." Harriet stared at her mother as if she'd never seen her before. The wild white hair, left to its own devices in the August humidity. The latest in her revolving selection of oversize summer dresses with ancient Birkenstocks. "The most passionate I've ever seen you or Dad is in your chess tournaments."

"Ah. Passion." Cecily Barnett, professor emeritus, moved over to the sink and deposited the cutting board and knife there. Then she turned around again, that same too-sharp gaze moving all over her daughter. "I suspected as much."

"You suspected what?"

"You're different, dear. You've worn your hair the ex-

act same way since you were ten years old, but no more."
Harriet lifted her hand to the thick braid that lay over one
shoulder. "And you're wearing shorts, Harriet. I've never
seen you wear shorts. And that shirt is positively form-
fitting."

Harriet frowned down at herself. All of those things
were true, but what concerned her was that she hadn't noticed. She'd packed to come here and was wearing what
she'd brought, but had given it no more thought than that.
Except what her mother said was true—she usually preferred her giant skirts and flowy button-downs to shorts
and a T-shirt. And she knew what had changed. She was
used to Jensen's presence. To the way he looked at her
body, the way he'd tasted every part of her, and how he
delighted in it when she showed her legs, or her midriff,
or unbuttoned a few more buttons on a shirt. Or better
still, when he indicated his delight by doing things to
please them both.

It wasn't that she thought more about her clothing.
She thought differently about the way she wore things.
Because the more he reveled in her body, the more of it
she wanted to display.

And even far away from him, she found it pleased her
to dress as if he were looking at her.

Harriet did not want to tell her mother that, for fear
Cecily would make disparaging remarks about the male
gaze. When the truth was, Harriet had no use for the male
gaze on the whole. But one particular male's gaze? That
was different.

"I'm surprised you noticed what I'm wearing, Mother,"
she said now. "I didn't think you paid the slightest bit of
attention to physical appearances."

"I pay attention," Cecily said with a hint of reproach.
"I may not choose to comment, and certainly did not

mention such things when you were an impressionable young girl, but I do have eyes. And I think I know you."

"I thought I knew me too," Harriet said softly. "But then one thing changed, and it was like there was this whole other part of me I never knew was there."

Her mother nodded sagely as if this were perfectly normal. "There are some things you can only learn about yourself when you're with another person. I know you've always been a huge proponent of the solitary life—"

"Have I been?" Harriet laughed. "Or did I think I had no other option?"

Cecily frowned. "Why wouldn't you have another option?"

Harriet sighed. "Maybe you haven't noticed, but I'm very, very odd."

To her surprise, her mother laughed. "I wouldn't say you're odd, Harriet. But I would say that you've always been incredibly stubborn."

That stung.

"I think you mean dedicated, Mother. Focused. Forthright and direct."

"Stubborn," her mother repeated. Distinctly. "And perfectly happy to simply remove yourself from a situation if it wasn't to your liking. An underappreciated strength, in my opinion." She smiled at Harriet's expression. "Take, for example, when you grew deeply impatient with the social landscape at your school and lobbied for homeschooling instead. You could easily have stayed. You didn't want to."

"I thought you wanted me to homeschool. You encouraged it."

"We were happy to let you do whatever you wanted to do, as long as you had a good justification for it." Cecily's smile widened. "But it was your choice, Harriet.

Not because you were being bullied. Not because you couldn't have excelled at the public school if you'd wished. But because you weren't interested in what passes for seventh-grade society. I can't say I blame you. But I'm unaware of any other girls your age who could have exhibited quite that strength of will, then flourished in her own isolation."

"I tried again, you know. I did go to college. Where I was even more odd."

"My recollection is that you briefly attempted to spend time with the girls on your hall, but once again decided they weren't worth your time. The same way you decided that any boy who ever expressed interest in you was somehow lacking."

"That's definitely not true," Harriet retorted. "They were lacking, that part is true, but I didn't just *decide* that. The kind of boys who asked me out always acted like they were doing me a favor. I didn't see why I should settle for that."

Cecily's gaze gleamed. "That's my point, dear. You've never seen why you should settle. That's not because you're odd or off-putting. And it's certainly not because you never received any invitations. You dismissed them all because you're deeply stubborn. You have always wanted everything—or nothing."

Then Cecily sailed off to the terrace out back with the salad bowl, singing in through the windows that Harriet should follow with the drinks. While Harriet stood frozen at the counter, stunned. She eventually roused herself to do what her mother had asked, though she was still in a daze.

"Frederick," her mother said as Harriet sat down. "Our daughter has just discovered that she is, in fact, stubborn."

"As a mule," her father replied at once. "Chip off the old block, I believe."

"And it's as I suspected," Cecily continued cheerfully. "She's met someone."

"About time," Frederick said, beaming at Harriet, who was still having trouble processing all this. "It has long been my dearest wish that you might have a little company to see out your days. Good company."

"You will have to excuse me," Harriet said from her usual place at the table. With her usual view of the garden and the neighbor's yellow house. With the usual Missouri summer heat all around her. All these usual things and the most unusual conversation she'd ever had with her parents. She was finding it hard to catch up. "I've spent my entire life laboring under the impression that neither one of you noticed my personal life at all."

"You're our only child." Frederick was still beaming as he served himself some salad. "We discuss little else."

"We never wanted to pressure you," her mother agreed. "Because again, *stubborn*. I had a reasonable fear that whatever I said you should do, you would turn around and do the opposite."

"I don't think I'm as obstinate as you're making me out to be," Harriet argued.

And watched as her parents smiled at each other across the table, then said nothing at all.

"Anyway," Harriet said crossly, glaring down at her lap and the shorts that had given her away. "No need to get too excited. Nothing will come of it. Of this. Of . . . him."

She was terrified that she would see something like pity on her parents' faces, and she had no idea what she would do if that happened. She wouldn't live through it.

She was suddenly afraid that she really wouldn't.

So she focused, fiercely, on her shorts.

"Is that what you want?" Cecily asked with what, it occurred to Harriet, was studied indifference. She was *pretending* not to care. Maybe both of them had always been *pretending* not to feel things as big and unwieldy as what lurched about inside of her. Maybe everyone was pretending. Maybe, just maybe, that was the secret Harriet had never managed to pick up on before now. "For nothing to come of it?"

And what a great many things she could have said to that. She could have told her parents that she was in love with Jensen. That she had made the mistake of telling him that, right after sex, when surely even she should have known better. She could have told them how beautiful he was, and how, of course, someone like him could never seriously be interested in someone like her no matter the intensity she saw in his face sometimes. She could have told them what had happened to him when he was just a kid, how he carried it with him even now, and how he used it as a weapon to beat back any possible sign that he was not only still alive but capable of *living*.

There were so many things she could have said. She wasn't used to keeping things from her parents. She had always told them everything, and they had always treated her like an adult, telling her things she knew her peers' parents did not.

But she didn't do it. Because telling them all the many things she felt would be exposing Jensen, and she couldn't bring herself to do that.

Because you think that one day they'll meet him? a voice inside her asked. *Or because you already have that much loyalty to him, even though he's told you it won't last?*

She sat with that a minute.

Yes, she thought.

"It's not what I want," she admitted, more to her salad than her parents. "But that's the situation."

"You keep right on being exactly who you are," her father said after a moment, when the only sound was Harriet's overwrought heart in her chest and the neighbor's wind chimes. "You're not odd, Harriet. You're marvelous. Anyone who can't see that isn't worth your time—much less your heart."

Later that evening, when the dishes were done and her parents took their usual positions at the chessboard, Harriet let herself out of the house into the night.

Missouri summers kept their heat well into the evenings, and the humidity that had used to drive her crazy when she was younger felt comforting tonight. She walked these streets she'd grown up on, the familiarity of the same houses she'd known all her life pressing in upon her like one more hug she hadn't known she needed.

She kept going over the sequence of events in her head. How her decision to march into the Coyote that night could have ended up changing everything. And that was the part she didn't know how to explain to her parents, loving—and more aware, apparently—though they were. Harriet had always considered herself as solid as a rock. The world changed around her. People came and went. She could move from one place to another herself. But *she* never changed. She had always fancied herself the kind of indomitable woman who'd been born fully formed. Entirely herself from cradle to grave.

She still didn't know how to handle the fact that Jensen had introduced her to part of herself she never would have suspected was there.

Maybe it wasn't love, she thought as she walked.

Maybe it was pure shock that she could ever be a stranger to herself.

She wandered down to the edge of her parents' neighborhood, where the happy residential streets gave way to busier thoroughfares, and turned back around. It wasn't until her pocket began to buzz that she even remembered she'd brought her phone.

And how histrionic was it that her heart rate picked up instantly when she saw that it was Jensen.

Surely it was more than casual if he was calling her while she was away. Surely—

It was possible, Harriet thought dourly, that her own histrionics might be the death of her. Possibly right here on the street where she remembered riding her first bike as a little girl, drunk on her own sense of freedom and independence. Because that had always been her story. She had always—*always*—wanted to go her own way.

Stubborn, that voice inside her pronounced. *Not odd.*

She wanted to answer her phone in a witty, sophisticated sort of way. Toss out a knowing kind of greeting that *casual lovers* might use offhandedly, because surely she too could *exude a worldly cool.*

What came out was, "Jensen! Hi!"

Because, apparently, there was no escaping herself. And whether that self was odd or marvelous or bullheaded seemed to be entirely subjective, but at least Harriet could say she was consistent.

"Guess what I did the other night," came Jensen's raspy, rumbly growl of a voice.

And in a flash of sudden, unwelcome insight, Harriet finally understood why people drank themselves insensate. And maybe even why they did mind-altering drugs. Because if a hit of any of those things felt like *this*— washing into her skin, then sinking into her flesh and bones, thrilling her physically—well. No wonder people would do anything to get more.

"I shudder to think," she replied tartly. "And if it involves the Coyote, I am possibly not the appropriate audience."

It was quiet wherever he was. There was a simmering sort of pause. "I'm guilty of many things, darlin'. Kissing and telling isn't one of them."

"That's not a denial." But even as the words came out of her mouth, Harriet realized she wasn't supposed to say things like this. Jealousy wasn't permitted. She stopped walking up the street then, because . . . was she *jealous*? She never had been before. She'd never had anyone to be jealous about. "Don't go getting the wrong idea, Jensen. I'm not actually questioning your whereabouts. I'm fully aware that's not permitted."

She could have sworn she heard a low, growling sort of sound.

"I thought you'd want to know that your little protégé called me the other night to report on his friends before they could get into trouble on Main Street. Zack rounded them all up."

"Does that mean Aidan's in jail again?"

"No. He didn't think it sounded like a good idea, so they left him out by Brady Everett's park in the middle of the night. He called me to pick him up. So."

She was definitely not imagining the belligerent way he belted out that one syllable. *So.*

"I certainly hope you did as he asked and picked him up. Instead of deciding it was a good opportunity for some tough-love man thing."

"*Some tough-love man thing.*" She was definitely not imagining the surliness when he repeated her words.

"Yes, Harriet, I picked him up. I drove him back home and had to drop him off down there in Hall Hollow, where all good intentions go to die. I felt really great about it, let me tell you. Definitely helped the poor kid out."

"I think you are helping him." Harriet found herself walking again. More quickly, which meant the humid air was no longer quite so much a hug as a yoke, but that suited her fine. It was better to blame her rising temperature on the summer air instead of the grumpy man in her ear. "I told you this a long time ago, but you're a role model whether you feel like one or not. You've taken an interest in Aidan, and you haven't discarded him, which is more than almost every other adult in his life can say."

"Including you," Jensen said darkly. "Since you're off in Michigan, or wherever you are."

"I think you know full well that I'm in Missouri, over five hundred miles away from the Michigan state line," Harriet said. "But I can't think of a single reason you would say something like that, Jensen, unless you're trying to be hurtful."

There was another long silence, and Harriet read all kinds of things into it. Histrionic things. She found herself gripping her phone, hard enough that her palm got sweaty, but she didn't let go.

"Just wanted to keep you in the loop, Harriet," Jensen muttered. "I'll see you when you get back."

And then he hung up.

Harriet found herself staring at the screen of her mobile until she realized what she was doing and shoved it back into her pocket. Her *shorts* pocket, because the facts of the matter were simple enough. She was swanning around wearing clothes she'd picked out specifically because he might like them, because he liked her body so much and she wanted nothing more than to keep him liking it in exactly that same way. She was doing this almost eight hundred miles east of Cold River, because she still *felt* him.

Inside her, all over her, wrapped around her, the way they curled around each other in her bed. She was so altered that her parents had not only noticed but commented on it. While *he* was so moved by what had happened between them that he'd called her while she was away for no other purpose that she could see but to be salty.

If there was any more damning evidence that she had become a profoundly silly creature, unworthy of her own intellect, Harriet doubted she could survive it. She picked up speed as she walked, storming down the streets of her old neighborhood, until another thought hit her, hard.

So hard it knocked her out of her determined stride so that once again, she was standing stock-still on the sidewalk, staring around blindly.

Because she was missing the important part of that phone call. It wasn't the existence of it that she should have been focusing on. It was his demeanor.

There had been no sign of charming Jensen Kittredge, so bright and so easy, laughing his way through life. In fact, that was about the least charming version of Jensen she'd ever encountered.

"Oh my God," Harriet said out loud into the thick Missouri night. "He might actually be in love with me."

And for a moment, she was elated. Joy punched hard, then lit her up, and she could feel a huge, silly grin spread all over her face.

But in the next moment, reality intruded.

Because Harriet knew something else with even more certainty. Jensen would never have been that dark and bad tempered with her if he had no feelings for her, sure. But he would rather die than admit it.

Admitting it would mean moving on, and he'd made it perfectly clear he had no intention of doing that. Ever.

Deep down, the man was far more stubborn than she could ever be.

She started walking again, the aftermath of that surge of joy leaving her feeling faintly hollow. So hollow it was as if her bones ached. As if it were bitter cold suddenly, instead of too warm and too close. She walked, anyway, hardly seeing where she was going, but somehow unsurprised to find that her feet brought her home. She stood outside her parents' house, drinking in the cheerful lights in the windows and the faint sound of Beethoven pouring out through the screens.

And it didn't matter, in the end, if she was odd or stubborn or, more likely, some cross section of both. So far, she'd been doing well pretending to be careless and casual, because that was what Jensen wanted. That was how he'd allowed himself to stay that first night, and how he permitted himself to keep coming back.

But Harriet loved him. She was in love with him. And she might not have had a whole lot of experience with falling in love before, but so far she had discovered that her heart was too intense, too dramatic, and too deadly serious. Acting the part of one of Jensen's carefree hookups wasn't going to work for her much longer. Her heart was hungry and greedy—and she understood with a flash of unwelcome clarity that it was only going to get worse.

Because she wasn't equipped to handle sex with Jensen *and* the fact she'd fallen in love with him, mixed in with this game of pretense. She'd never been any good at games where she had to hide herself. Not in seventh grade, not in college, not ever.

Which meant that she was going to have to prepare herself for going back home to Cold River and loving him the only way she could. The way she supposed everyone else did too.

From afar.

20

The day Harriet was supposed to return to Cold River, Jensen hardly noticed. He spent the day riding fences, and instead of going into town that Saturday evening the way he usually did, he headed out to Matias's place. His friend had spent eighteen solid months building himself a proper house out there on his family's land, far enough away from the Trujillo greenhouses and main ranch house that he could come and go as he pleased. Better still, he'd bought himself the kind of television that made watching sporting events a pure pleasure.

That Matias was clearly ready to move on into adult life in all the ways Jensen wasn't was a topic they tended to avoid.

He arrived at his friend's house with a six-pack in one hand and a grin on his face, and the two of them settled in to watch the fights.

"Why do you keep checking your phone?" Matias asked a few minutes into the first match.

Jensen shoved his cell phone back in his pocket. "I'm not."

"You're literally checking it every three seconds."

"I'm very popular," Jensen drawled, and even hauled

out a lazy grin. "My phone is blowing up, what can I tell you."

"Yeah, except it's not blowing up." Matias shook his head. He was lounging there on his couch with his feet propped up on his coffee table. "I can see the screen of your phone, idiot. No one is calling you. And I think we both know that when too many people really are calling you, you accidentally lose your phone, change your number, or hide. Often all of the above."

"I think 'hide' is an exaggeration."

Matias didn't say anything, but the way he rolled his eyes before he took a swig of his beer seemed loud. Unduly loud.

"Your librarian's back, isn't she," Matias said a while later, while mixed martial artists pounded on each other onscreen. Jensen felt he could relate.

"No idea," Jensen replied with expansive laziness. "Why do you know the high school librarian's schedule, Matias?"

He expected his friend to ignore that. Maybe roll an eye. Instead, Matias turned his head to fix Jensen with a glare that must have served him well out there in the world doing dangerous Marine Corps things. "I don't want to know anybody's schedule. I go out of my way to make it clear that what I'd like is to be left alone. And instead my sister gossips at me. My best friend lies to me. And I end up knowing entirely too many things I'd rather not."

"Easy there," Jensen said after a moment of trying to take all that in. "There's nothing to know."

"Give me a break, man," Matias retorted. He shook his head. "You spent your entire life making sure that no one could miss you, wherever you were. And you think that all of a sudden you can start sneaking around under the radar? The whole town is scandalized by the fact you're taking advantage of that sweet little librarian. So scandalized that even I've had to hear about it."

"Harriet is a lot of things," Jensen muttered. "Little, yes. Sweet? No."

Matias muttered something, but he turned his gaze back to the television screen. "I have to assume you wanted the commotion. Why else would you be so stupid as to park your truck in front of her house every night of the week? Way to give the gossips ammunition to last them a lifetime."

Jensen chewed on that. He hadn't given his parking any thought—but he should have. He knew how this town worked. His own family members being prime examples of folks who didn't consider themselves gossips . . . while gossiping. And he didn't care if people talked about him. He usually encouraged it. But he really didn't like that they were talking about Harriet.

He could have protected her from that, and he hadn't. Why hadn't he?

"I think I like it better when you're in one of your not-speaking phases," he told his friend. And resisted the urge to check his phone again.

"You've made scraping off a woman into a science, friend," Matias continued, still supposedly watching the fights. "Except this one. Now, suddenly, you're not only *not* scraping her off after a night, you're all domesticated. You suddenly have a teenager. What's next? Are you going to start a single dads' club? The Longhorn Valley Sad Sack Association?"

Jensen considered punching his best friend in the face. But did not, because he suspected Matias would be only too happy to demonstrate that the Marines had taught him new tricks since the last time they'd swung on each other.

"I just want to be clear that Aidan Hall is not my kid," he said instead. "I can't believe that anyone would think otherwise. Because sure, I might be a bad candidate for fatherhood, but nothing is worse than Andy Hall. No way would I abdicate responsibility to such an extent that *Andy Hall* had possession of my kid for the past sixteen years."

"I don't think he's your kid," Matias said, letting out a rare laugh. "I wish he were. If he were your kid, this behavior would make more sense. Where is the Jensen Kittredge I know, and what have you done with him?"

"Hate to say it, Matias, but I think you need to stop talking smack with your sister." Jensen kept his voice pious. And amused. "I think it's turning your head to mush."

Matias turned and pinned him with another look. This one even harder. "I think you like her, Jensen," he said quietly, and everything in Jensen went still. "I think you like her a lot. But you can't admit that, can you? Because you figure you need to beat yourself up for the rest of your life. Like losing Daniel wasn't bad enough."

"Hey—" Jensen began, his temper spiking, because they didn't talk about this. Not so directly. Not anymore.

"I know you're not taking advantage of Harriet," Matias pushed on, undaunted. "I think the high school librarian knocked you flat. And you've spent so long playing this same game, avoiding anything that might make you feel a thing, that you don't have the slightest idea how to handle it."

"Matias. For God's sake, shut up."

Matias did not shut up. "It's easy to martyr yourself to your own guilt when it doesn't get in the way of the life you actually want," he said. "Believe me, I get it. You know I get it. But what happens if you stumble upon something you do want? Are you really going to walk away from her, Jensen? For a ghost?"

Jensen couldn't breathe.

"Daniel would have hated this," Matias said quietly. "You know he would."

Jensen responded to this provocation the only way he could. With his middle finger.

And as soon as possible, as soon as it didn't look like he was running from anything, a hasty exit.

On Monday, he went into town to fetch a part from the feedstore that, if he was honest, wasn't exactly an urgent errand. He bought the part, tossed it in his truck, and then sauntered over to Cold River Coffee.

Because he wanted coffee, he assured himself. Not because Harriet had been home since Saturday—and yes, he'd driven by her house late Sunday night to check that her ridiculous car was there—and had not contacted him at all.

Today he paid attention to the citizens of Cold River, for a change, while he was getting his coffee. The sidelong glances from the tables of locals, followed by all of them leaning in close to whisper to each other. It was a different version of the usual speculative glances thrown his way.

It hit Jensen then that gossip was the least of it. Everyone in this coffee shop who knew him—who'd known him since birth, who knew his mother, who went to church with his grandparents—thought the worst of him. And wasn't that a shock, because he would have sworn up and down that he was a favorite son, despite everything. Forgiven his trespasses, automatically, because everyone knew where he'd been. What had happened to him. And they all preferred the sight of his grin.

The things Matias had said slammed back into him.

Because Jensen might talk a good game, he might even have convinced himself otherwise some years, but it wasn't Daniel's ghost that haunted him. It was Daniel's mother's face in the hospital that night. It was the whispers that had followed him through to graduation that year, until the sheriff had made it known that none of the boys up at the lake that night had been drunk. That it had been a terrible accident, but no one was to blame.

But it had been too late. Because Jensen knew by then that, given the chance, everyone would blame him. And happily.

So he'd made sure that they had nothing to blame him for, ever again. Sure, he had his fun, but he never made it count. He was the life of every party, because that was what was expected of him. He was the one who lived *and* stayed, so he made sure that being around him was a delight.

It was the only way to make sure no one remembered that really, they'd blamed him all along.

But it turned out that given the slightest provocation, everyone was only too happy to blame him all over again.

Jensen supposed that should have hurt him, but it didn't.

At all.

Instead, there was a kind of dizzy, half-drunk sensation that swelled up from inside him and made him think that actually—finally—he was free.

He stared at the coffee a chipper teenager had set down before him, waiting for that feeling to go away. To let him sink back into the same old place he'd spent all these years since Daniel died. So he could play the clown and make sure that everyone around him was comfortable, no matter what. No matter if he never felt comfortable himself. No matter if he never felt anything at all.

But instead, that dizzy, drunken feeling got stronger. And felt a whole lot like how when he was with Harriet. Who had never seemed all that interested in the clown he played. And who had apologized for what she'd thought of that clown once she'd come to know him.

Like she was the one who had set him free by simple virtue of loving him, but it had taken him a while to catch up.

"You ought to be ashamed of yourself," came a horribly familiar voice then, cutting through his small moment of revelation to the tune of the espresso machine.

Jensen turned, hoping he was having an auditory hallucination, but no luck. The fearsome Miss Martina Patrick stood before him, bristling as she always did, her sharp eyes filled with condemnation.

"So you've been telling me since the ninth grade, Miss Patrick," he replied, with a little bit less of his drawl than usual. It wasn't coming to him. He wasn't feeling it. Truth of the matter was, he wasn't sure he was feeling even the faintest hint of the politeness he'd always used as a shield. And not to protect himself. "I'm not sure it's going to take."

She planted herself in front of him. She put her hands on her hips, glaring at him as if he were the devil. That was the kind of look he usually reveled in, because it was usually much more good-natured. But not today.

"I understand that a man like you thinks nothing of his own reputation," Miss Martina Patrick fumed at him. The only saving grace being that her voice was low enough that Jensen doubted anyone could hear her over the background music and so many conversations. Any number of which were likely about him. He crossed his arms over his chest and tried to look appropriately respectful. "Or so I assume, given how you've flaunted your low morals all over this town your whole life."

"I mean this with respect, ma'am," Jensen said, as quietly as he was able. "But I'm pretty sure my morals are my business."

Miss Patrick extended that index finger of hers. On the few occasions that Jensen had nightmares about anything other than the lake, it was of that finger.

"What could possibly possess you to play your little games with a woman like Harriet?" Miss Patrick demanded. "I would have thought she was lucky enough to be beneath your lustful notice."

"My *lustful* notice. Really."

The older woman was charging on ahead. "Was it a challenge? A dare? You wanted to see if your much-vaunted charms could make a dent in a woman of her caliber?"

"I don't leave dents," Jensen said. Dangerously.

"You've made a decent woman the talk of the town," she snapped at him. "Harriet is a role model. She has always been a beacon of sense and propriety. It's not enough that the town has started whispering about her— the school year is starting and the students will follow suit. What authority do you expect her to have when she's been so severely compromised?"

"You'll have to ask her if she thinks she's compromised," Jensen gritted out. "Or if she feels she's lost any of her authority. I, personally, find that hard to believe, but then, I don't think a woman's association with another grown adult is a statement of character. Why do you?"

The ferocious secretary of Cold River High looked . . . unsure of herself.

Jensen considered notifying the press, such as it was in these parts. Because surely such a thing had never happened before in the entire history of Miss Martina Patrick's reign.

She shook her head, dropping her hand to her side and retiring that finger. "I never imagined that Harriet would succumb." And if Jensen wasn't mistaken, she looked something like lost. "What a great disappointment this has all turned out to be."

Any sympathy Jensen might have had, however against his will, dried up fast.

"If Harriet disappoints you, ma'am," he said then, and he didn't care who heard him, "then you can be sure the problem is you. Not her."

Then he left the coffee shop before he could say something he'd regret. Or something he wouldn't regret at all but would later have to defend to his mother when she heard about it.

Because somehow he knew that Ellie was not going to be receptive to his dizzy little feelings of something like freedom.

And maybe it was inevitable that when he slammed his way back into his truck, he didn't drive out to the ranch again. Instead, he found himself heading to Harriet's house. And then sitting there, waiting, as the afternoon wore on. Without the coffee he'd left behind at Cold River Coffee in his haste to put distance between him and Miss Patrick.

He couldn't help going over and over that conversation. Miss Patrick was a terrifying gorgon, sure, but she'd known him the better part of his life. She'd never had any use for him, but it had never occurred to him to wonder too deeply about that before. How far it went, for example.

Both Zack and Matias had warned him. But he hadn't taken it on board. Not really. Not until today. He hadn't believed that anyone would actually think so badly of him.

But he'd seen, very clearly, that Miss Martina Patrick was convinced that Jensen had *done something* to Harriet. That he had truly taken advantage of her.

And what struck him now, as he found himself sitting outside a woman's house, waiting for her to return like a lovesick puppy, was what this whole thing said about him. That he'd gotten so good at playing his clown role that everyone believed it without question. Miss Patrick hadn't been speaking to him the way he'd heard her speak to other men, like Pastor Jim, who was one of the few people—aside from Harriet—Jensen had ever seen appear to enjoy a conversation with the woman. Miss Patrick hadn't spoken to Jensen like he was a man at all. She'd spoken to him like he was still that dumb jock in high school. Loud, stupid, and maybe not entirely responsible for his own actions.

He'd always thought it was funny. He liked being underestimated, as he would tell anyone who asked, because no one ever saw him coming.

But over time, he'd assumed that there was an undercurrent of goodwill. That he'd built it up across all these years. That the blame he'd wanted to avoid from so long ago wasn't really there any longer if he dug down into it. That somehow, he'd proved himself along the way.

If he hadn't, after all, it turned out that he was done trying. That felt a lot like coming out of a cage, which made the things Matias had said to him seem to sting a little more.

And Jensen was not, in fact, an idiot. He was pretty clear that these things he was feeling about Harriet were unprecedented, and he wasn't so dumb that he didn't know what that meant. For once in his life, he didn't want to hide. He didn't want to disappear in plain sight. A big laugh and a cheeky grin wouldn't cut it.

But suddenly he was afraid that Harriet might believe the same thing that all these good townsfolk did. And given that she hadn't seen fit to contact him since she'd returned, was it possible that she'd finally decided that she'd had enough of the guy that anyone in town—many of them currently congregating in the coffee shop—would be quick to tell her was beneath her?

He found his hand pressed hard over his chest. Because he hadn't liked it when Harriet had told him she loved him. It had upset all kinds of carts that had been in place for a long, long time.

But the notion that she might be over him he liked even less.

It was a perfect late August afternoon. Warm, but not too hot. Jensen was perfectly comfortable sitting in his truck with the windows down, letting all that blue sky in.

He saw Harriet the moment she rounded the corner, marching down the sidewalk with her usual officious determination that made him smile despite himself. She didn't look up. She was too busy stomping along, no doubt planning her typical world domination inside her head.

He felt too many things inside him shift then.

You need to let the past be the past, Matias had said. Later that same night, when the fights were over and Jensen was making a big show of not taking off, because he hadn't wanted Matias to know that anything he'd said had landed.

Because you're so good at that. That's why you joined the Marines.

I'm not saying I'm great at it. But I'm trying.

Jensen had snorted. *Yeah, well, we can't all build ourselves a house and call it a do-over.*

Why would you bother? his friend had replied, with quiet intent. Like a knife through the ribs. *You're way too comfortable living in your prison.*

Harriet kept on marching down the street, wholly unaware of his presence, while inside him one earthquake followed the next. But that was the funny thing. Jensen didn't need seismic shifts and overwhelming earthquakes to set him straight. He didn't need revelations and unpleasant realizations in the middle of town. He didn't need to look deep inside of him for answers.

Because Harriet was right there. The summer sun caught at her hair, making it shine bright and gold. Her lovely face was screwed up into its normal frown, but he thought that made her even prettier. She was tiny and round in all the right places, and she was wearing clothes that fit her better now. Still comfortable. Still practical. But her body no longer looked hidden, and he couldn't help but think he had something to do with that.

And either way, it only made her look sexier.

All she needed to do was walk down a street, not even aware that he was watching her, and that was it. It was that simple.

Maybe it had always been that simple. The inevitable hand of fate the minute he'd looked up from that booth in the Coyote and had seen her standing there.

The truth was, he'd been a goner even then.

As he watched, she finally focused on his truck. He watched her slow down. Then straighten her shoulders in that way of hers. He would have bet his life savings on her next move, and he would have won, because up went that chin, belligerent and fierce. A scowl soon followed, and then she was marching straight for him.

So Jensen did her the favor of getting out of his truck and rounding the front of it, so he could meet her head-on.

"Were you planning to tell me that you were back in town?" he asked as she drew close.

"I wasn't," she said in a cool voice he disliked intensely. "I can't imagine why you'd want to know."

"Can't you?"

She rocked to a stop within arm's reach, and he thought it was an act of true heroism—the kind people always claimed he possessed, though he'd never agreed—that he didn't reach out and haul her close.

"Listen, Jensen," she said in a voice that instantly put his teeth on edge. "I appreciate the sex. And I thank you."

He only stared at her, but that didn't make the words any less stiff or strange. "You're welcome. I think."

She nodded decisively as if they'd come to some kind of decision. "Okay, then. So there's that." But that chin of hers went down a notch. "Goodbye, Jensen."

"Harriet," he said quietly. "Baby. Are you breaking up with me?"

"No." Her scowl returned with a vengeance. "I couldn't break up with you even if I wanted to break up with you, could I? Because that would indicate that we were together. You made it very clear that we were not."

"Yeah. About that."

"And I respect your boundaries," she was saying. She blinked. "Wait. What about it?"

"The not-being-together thing," he said. "I'm over it."

She scowled so hard it looked like it should hurt. "You can't be over it. It was your decree. You're not allowed to be in relationships of any kind. You made that very clear, Jensen."

He shrugged. "I changed my mind."

Harriet shoved her glasses up her nose, hard. "You can't change your mind. It's not the kind of thing you just . . . change your mind about."

"And yet here we are."

She made a frustrated sort of noise. "Here's the thing, Jensen. I can't pretend. I don't want to pretend. You might like to play those kind of games, where you run around acting like you're one thing when you're the other, but I don't. I would never be able to keep it up. And it's impossible for me to respect what you asked for while pretending to feel things or not feel things—"

But she stopped. And for the first time, as far as he could recall, Miss Harriet Barnett looked flustered.

Distinctly and inarguably and well and truly flustered.

So flustered, in fact, that Jensen began to think that things were going to be all right, after all.

"Baby," he said, hoping to speed things along, but she flung up a hand, giving him her palm.

"The fact of the matter is that you don't like that I'm not following you around like one of your other . . . conquests. That's the only reason you're here. That's why you're reversing your entire life's work of dismantling relationships before they happen."

"That doesn't sound a whole lot like a fact, Harriet. It sounds more like an opinion. A messed-up opinion without a whole lot of basis in reality, if I'm honest."

"You're used to women trailing around after you, flinging themselves prostrate at your feet and clinging to the cuffs of your Wranglers, desperate for your attention."

"Well," Jensen said, and the drawl seemed to happen on its own, now that he was feeling like himself again, "I can't deny that."

Harriet nodded sagely. "It's understandable that because I'm not doing that, you're having a strange reaction. But the good news is, it's not personal. It's just a little bit of good, old-fashioned psychology at work. All you need to do is go on back to your regular life, fill up on floozies at the Coyote, and you'll be back to normal in no time."

"Will I now."

But Harriet was warming to her topic and did not appear to hear the warning in his voice. "Everyone has summer flings. It's a whole thing. Practically a cottage industry. There are whole songs about it. Summer days slipping away, bottles of wine. You get the idea."

And as she spun off into a tangent that appeared to involve song lyrics and the many podcasts she'd listened to on her drive back from Missouri, Jensen considered his options.

What it came down to, as he let it spin around and around in his head, was that he was no more and no less than who he was. Who he'd always been. Sure, he wasn't the dumb jock clown he let people think he was. But he'd been a high school football star. He was a rancher and a cowboy. He'd spent years as a smoke jumper. He could wrangle a horse, he loved his whiskey, and he'd always had a way with the ladies. All of those things were true.

But down beneath all of that, as deep in him as the land that had made him, was an even simpler truth. Jensen Kittredge was a Colorado country boy. And Miss Harriet Barnett, with all her airs and graces and her fancy degrees in her library science, was so much a product of the cities she'd come from that he doubted very much she understood what that meant.

So he, by God, felt that it was his responsibility to clarify things for her.

The way he saw it, he could stand here and keep on listening, or he could get down to business.

Unsurprisingly, Jensen chose option B.

He straightened, then scooped her up off the ground. Harriet made a very satisfying kind of squeaking noise, and then another, louder one as he opened the driver's door to his pickup, tossed her inside down the length of the bench seat, and climbed in after her.

By the time the squeaking stopped, he was already driving away from her house.

"What do you think you're doing?" she demanded, her voice still a little uneven if no longer squeaky.

"I would have thought that was obvious, Harriet," Jensen said, and flashed her a smile as he took the road headed out of town. "I'm kidnapping you."

21

Harriet told herself that she was outraged.

That was the only possible explanation for that sharp burst of sensation that seemed to cleave her in half, with perhaps too much focus directly between her legs.

"I did not consent to being kidnapped," she protested.

Jensen drove as if he might lapse off into a coma at any moment, lounged back in the driver's seat with one wrist draped over the steering wheel. He did not look like a kidnapper. No hint of desperation, or even tension, anywhere on his beautiful body.

Not that she was looking.

He laughed, like he knew. "If you did, it wouldn't be a kidnap, would it? It would be a ride."

Harriet was finding it difficult to breathe. To cope. And suddenly, she felt as overly warm as if she were back in Missouri. Even though she could see very plainly that she was instead in Colorado, on one of those endless blue days that made a person's heart ache. That made *her* heart hurt.

Or maybe that was him.

"You can't just go around kidnapping people," she told him, concentrating on that. Because concentrating on anything else was dangerous. "Aside from it being illegal, obviously, it's rude."

"That's really not a good argument," Jensen observed. "I'm pretty sure the average kidnapper isn't worried about the legality of the thing. Or whether or not it's polite. What with the kidnapping and all."

Harriet had the uncharacteristic urge to slam her fist into the side of his face. Or maybe that was another lie she was telling herself. Maybe it wasn't particularly uncharacteristic at all—but she usually didn't follow through on such urges. And maybe in this case, what she really wanted was to put her hand on his face by whatever means necessary.

She did not.

The truck was climbing the hill that stood between the town and the rest of the valley, including the Bar K. And when they reached the top, the view spread out before them as if auditioning for the perfect postcard.

As stunning as it was, blue sky over proud mountains standing high above the richness of the summer fields, Harriet was forced to face the truth.

Even Colorado faded in comparison to the glory that was Jensen Kittredge.

She had made up her mind after that phone call back at her parents' house. She knew what she had to do—or not do. She'd arrived back in town filled with a sense of her own purpose. Rather than waiting for Jensen to end things, which she knew he would, sooner or later, she'd decided to handle it herself. To get a jump on the whole thing, building on the week's space she'd already had from him.

Cold turkey, she'd told herself repeatedly. *It's the only way to go.*

And she'd even told herself that she was getting along fine, but that was because she hadn't seen him.

Something that was instantly clear when she'd turned down her street. She'd been walking along after a day of before-school-year administration tasks and meetings, minding her own business and absolutely not replaying the greatest hits from the things she and Jensen had done to each other all over her house. She was so definitely not doing that, in fact, that it had taken her a moment to recognize that she hadn't simply made him up. That he really was there, leaning against the front of his truck, watching her come toward him.

Every inch of him a cowboy. From that hat down low on his head to the way his jeans made a dessert of the lower half of his big body. Right on down to the cowboy boots he always wore.

Looking at the man made her ache far more than any blue August sky.

She had realized in a flash that it was much, much easier to pep herself up with the idea of going cold turkey when he wasn't right there before her.

In retrospect, Harriet was surprised she hadn't swallowed her own tongue.

"I saw your friend," Jensen said as they drove down into the valley. "Miss Martina Patrick was in Cold River Coffee today and took me to task for my treatment of you. For taking advantage of you, actually."

This time, Harriet's outrage was more straightforward and did not appear to involve any part of her that could also be mistaken for pleasure. In fact, she was fairly certain the heat that seemed to bubble up and spread from her chest was shame.

"I hope that's one of your jokes," she said severely. She

didn't like this new heat at all. She glared out the window, focusing on the beauty of her adopted state, hoping it would soothe her.

It did not soothe her.

"I joke about many things," Jensen said, sounding more relaxed by the moment. "But never about Miss Patrick."

Harriet's head spun. She thought her friend had simply opted not to continue discussing Jensen Kittredge, because she hadn't mentioned him at all. Not before Harriet had gone to Missouri and certainly not since.

"I think it's a good thing that your friends are looking out for you," Jensen continued, all drawl and heat. "That's what friends are supposed to do."

Harriet felt, simultaneously, patronized and unsupported. And there was that heat in her chest, the shame of it seeming to bludgeon her again and again. Because somehow she very much doubted that the town would be quite so interested in her personal life if they didn't find her an object of pity.

And Harriet did not mind being odd. She didn't mind being on her own, whether because she was stubborn or just because. But pity made her want to break things.

"None of your friends have taken me to task," she pointed out. "That hardly seems fair."

"Don't worry too much about my friends. They've gotten in my face too. Pretty much the entire town is prepared to burn me at the stake over this, Harriet."

And finally, it penetrated that he sounded downright cheerful at the thought.

"You're enjoying this."

Jensen shot her one of those glinting, wolfish looks of his that still made her heart stutter in her chest. "It's all evidence, baby."

"Of what? The fact that an entire valley in the Rocky

Mountains considers me both too childish to handle my own affairs as well somehow thirty years older than my actual age?"

"That, sure. But also the seriousness of my intentions."

For a moment, it was like she flatlined. Her head went blank. Her heart stopped. She wasn't holding her breath, but she didn't breathe.

But only for a moment.

"Don't be ridiculous," she said stoutly. "You don't have any intentions. And no, conducting a kidnap in the light of day doesn't count."

Jensen laughed. And she'd worked so hard to convince herself on the drive back from Missouri that she'd simply overestimated the effects of that laughter. That nothing could be the way she remembered it, magical and infectious, a bright spell that could bend anyone who heard it to his will.

It filled up the cab of his truck. It played with the ends of her braid and pulled out strands of her hair to toy with them, too, dancing on the breeze that washed in through the open windows.

She thought, *This is what I will remember.* The end of summer and that laugh, and the exquisite ache of it. Of him.

"Hold that thought," he told her as he pulled his truck off the county road and instantly started jostling them along a deeply rutted dirt track.

"This is not the way to the Bar K," she said as if he, a member of the Kittredge family, born and raised on this land, might somehow have missed that.

"Technically, it is."

He was no longer draping his wrist over the steering wheel, likely because the dirt road required actual steering. He had both his hands on the wheel now, which provided her with more opportunity to study the shape of them. How big they were, and how rough, and she knew too well how they felt against her bare skin.

So far, she could not say she approved of her own questionable reaction to a kidnapping.

Jensen did not expand on that comment and Harriet decided that maybe, just maybe, it was time to stop leading every moment with her mouth. Maybe, for once in her life, she could simply wait and see what happened.

Especially because her heart was making such a commotion in her chest that even if she could think of the right things to ask him, she doubted she would even hear the answers.

So she sat there, gripping her hands together in her lap, and keeping her lips pressed tightly together, while Jensen drove them into the woods. Then up a hill—an actual hill, she noted, and not what locals like to call *hills,* which were always more properly mountains. If usually smaller mountains than some around here.

And then, at the top of that hill, he pulled up before the cabin. He tossed a look her way, then swung out of his truck. She braced herself to make a scene when he came around to her side to commence with the kidnapping stuff, but he didn't.

He simply ambled on inside.

Leaving Harriet to fume about his high-handed tactics in the truck.

She crossed her arms over her chest and scowled at the open door of the cabin, but Jensen didn't reappear.

It slowly dawned on her that he wasn't planning to.

Meaning, she was sure, that he anticipated her curiosity would get the better of her and she would storm in after him.

She told herself she absolutely, positively would do no such thing.

But as the moments ticked by, Harriet found herself studying the cabin instead. Was this really where he lived?

She looked around, taking in the small shed to one side, the woodpile beneath an overhang. This was a simple, rustic place. More than simply rustic.

And suddenly, she understood.

Harriet got out of the truck then and walked toward the cabin, stepping up onto the small porch. Then she hovered in the open doorway, peering within. Inside, there was very little. She could see a couch to one side of the main room and a basic kitchen area against the other wall. There was a woodstove in the middle, a sort of wall behind it, and beyond it what she suspected was the only bedroom. She could only hope that the door to one side was a bathroom. Just to bring it one step up from camping.

"Yes," Jensen said, following her gaze from where he sat on that couch, the very picture of languid indolence. "I have running water."

"You live here." It wasn't a question.

"I do."

Because she thought she saw challenge in that gaze of his, she didn't ask him any further questions. And took it as a victory when the corner of his mouth kicked up.

"Now that we're good and private out here," he drawled, because of course he *drawled,* "do you want to tell me when you were going to tell me you were home?"

"This is Cold River," she replied, the way all the locals always did. "I suspect you knew I was home within an hour of me pulling into my driveway."

"What I knew and when I knew it aren't the issue, baby. The issue is that you didn't intend to tell me."

Part of Harriet wanted to continue as she was. Pretending not to understand what he was asking her. Pretending that she didn't care about this, because that was how everyone else did these things. She'd listened to a thousand podcasts on the topic. The endless battle of caring less, ostentatiously, so that no one could accuse anyone of the cardinal sin of having real feelings involved.

She'd convinced herself that was the smart way to handle it. To handle him.

Something else that had made more sense outside of his presence.

Harriet quickly reviewed the situation. What she suspected might be true about Jensen, that he really did have feelings for her, didn't matter in the final analysis. Because she believed what he'd told her that very first night. What had happened to him when he was young and how he'd ordered his life since then.

She'd already decided that she didn't have it in her to pretend she felt less than she did.

So why was she pretending now?

"I wasn't going to call you," she told him as matter-of-factly as she could. "I didn't really think you'd care that much. Or even notice."

Something flashed in that amber gaze of his, and she crossed her arms as she stood there in the doorway, hoping he couldn't see the goose bumps that shivered to life all over her skin. Though somehow, she knew he did.

"Really."

Not a question.

She lifted her chin. "I thought it would be best."

"So what you're telling me, Harriet, is that when you fall in love, it means so much to you that the first thing you do is pack up and run. Is that how they do love out there in Missouri?"

"That was hurtful," she said, shocked. She blinked. "You meant it to be hurtful."

"I'm just processing what love means to you. That's all."

"I'm being *respectful,* Jensen," she retorted, stung. "You told me what you would and would not allow. Upon reflection, I decided that I could just as easily love you from afar without pushing any of your boundaries. And not making it harder on myself than it had to be. A tidy solution, I would have thought."

"There's a word for tidy solutions like that."

"*Sensible,* I think you'll find. That's the word that I'd use."

"*Cowardly,* baby," he threw back at her. "Straight up cowardly."

Harriet marched farther into the cabin before she knew she meant to move, shocked to find her hands were in actual fists at her side. "I'm not the coward in this scenario. And stop calling me *baby.* That's an intimacy you haven't earned."

"Like hell," came his low drawl.

Harriet wanted to scream. She didn't understand how he did that. How this man who was usually so funny, so charming, could turn like this and wound her so easily. Every one of his words seem to leave a mark when it hit—

Probably because he's right, that voice inside her observed.

Well. He wasn't the only one who could be right.

"You have a lot of nerve calling me a coward while we stand here in this monument to your guilt," she said, her voice quiet, and shaking only slightly from the force of all those terrible, wonderful feelings swirling around inside of her. "Do you think not furnishing this cabin for all these years will bring him back?"

"Careful," he growled at her, his gaze locked to hers.

And that suddenly, he was on his feet.

She ignored that. Or maybe it was what she wanted. "Or do you think if you die out there in those wildfires you love so much, it will make you enough of a hero that you'll cancel your guilt out at last?"

And Harriet watched his temper, and something else, flare in his gaze. It swept over his face like a storm, but her heart was a riot inside her, and she thought she might actually be sick. Because of all the things that had happened between them already, she had never experienced anything this intense before.

She hadn't known that anything could be this intense.

This wasn't fighting the way she'd always imagined it might be with a lover. The kind she'd seen in movies where the ending was already clear. This was different, because she didn't know where they were going. She didn't want to hurt him, she wanted to hold him. But there were these things to get through first and she couldn't think of any other way to do it.

Because she knew some other things in that same flash of insight. He had never brought anyone else here, she was sure of it. He didn't do these things with women. She was different, this was different. *They* were different.

She had to believe they both thought it was worth fighting for, or why would they be doing this?

There was absolutely no need for him to have shown up at her house today. Much less to put her in his truck and spirit her away.

She didn't think he really cared that much about the opinion of the townspeople, and she knew she didn't.

That could only mean one thing. Surely it could only mean that one thing.

"Jensen . . ." she began.

"Shut up," he ordered her, and Harriet would ordinarily never have allowed anyone to just tell her to *shut up*. It was an outrage.

But she didn't feel outraged. Because she could see the starkness in his gaze.

Worse, she could feel it inside her, like he was a part of her.

"You're right," Jensen said, very deliberately, that amber gaze intense. "I put myself in prison a long time ago. Because everybody wanted to blame me for what happened to Daniel, but then couldn't. And when nobody blamed me any longer, that made it worse. Because I blamed myself. I'll always blame myself. Smoke jumping is a part of that. The opportunity to do some good, sure. But if a fire got me, well. I knew I had it coming. I never thought I was any kind of hero. Talk about too little too late."

"You don't have to tell me this."

"I do have to tell you this," he thundered at her. "My whole life has been compartmentalized. Everyone wants to see happy-go-lucky Jensen, the high school jock, rumored to be great in bed but dumb as a rock. And I like it that way, Harriet, because no one expects anything from that guy. Not to mention, it's hard to harbor a grudge against the town idiot. At home, I run the family business and I'm good at it, but I can't have that coming out. And I live as bare-bones as I can, because I never thought I deserved anything more. Not when I took it from Daniel. Ask anyone on the street in Cold River and they'll tell you I've never spared a thought for anyone's comfort but my own, but I always took pleasure in knowing that wasn't true."

"Jensen."

But he kept going. "And everything was fine as long as I kept my loose morals confined to the Coyote. It was when I dared to look at Miss Harriet Barnett, unimpeachable role model, that folks started thinking twice about me. When they found me a little less amusing and started rethinking things like the allocation of blame."

"That's just stupid," Harriet managed to say. "For all they know, I'm a giant floozy."

"You're not." He shook his head. "And the funny thing is, it turns out I'm tired of people treating me like I'm too dumb to know what I'm doing when they're going to go ahead and punish me for it, anyway."

Harriet felt heat behind her eyes, and a wave of something she was fairly certain was a sob rising up from within her. She wanted to cry. She wanted to shout. She wanted to do any number of wildly out-of-character things . . .

Because everything with Jensen was that giant. That epic. Opera heroines and then some.

But it wasn't histrionic. It was that huge.

She reached over and took his big hands in hers. She looked down at them for a moment, then lifted her gaze to his.

"The problem with penance is that it never does bring anyone back," she said quietly. "All it can ever do is punish the person who remains."

"I've always been fine with that," he rumbled at her. "The more punishment the better. I could have gone on like that forever, but then you showed up. You marched right into my life and turned it all inside out."

Harriet understood that this was a serious conversation. But she still couldn't help but find herself delighted by that.

"Really? Me?"

The smile on his face then was rueful. "Really. You. Because suddenly, I started breaking all my rules. I don't do repeats. I don't stay over at people's houses. I don't get involved with random teenagers, give talks in libraries, or give the town gossips anything to talk about besides their speculation about my personal life. I've never done any of those things. Except with you."

"Me," she said again, savoring it.

"And you seem to think no one gets you or likes you, Harriet, but let me tell you. If they could string me up for daring to lay a finger on you, they would. This town likes you plenty." He was studying the place where their hands were joined. "You might even call it home."

Home.

"I just want to say," she found herself whispering, "that if this is heading towards a *that's why I can never see you again* space, I'm going to be . . ."

Heartbroken, she thought. She'd be literally heartbroken, and that word that had always seemed fanciful to her no longer did. Because now it seemed clear to her that heartbreak was a very real, very physical ailment, and might in fact cripple her.

"Pay attention, Miss Harriet," Jensen said in his slow, amused, gloriously male way, with eyes like a wolf and that smile she liked to think of as hers. "I don't know how to do this. I never expected I'd have to. I love you."

And he looked nothing so much as startled after he said that, like the words tasted different than he'd expected. Harriet held her breath.

But Jensen smiled even wider. "I'm in love with you," he told her. "I don't want you to love me from afar. I want it up close and as personal as it gets."

"I love you too," Harriet said, very solemnly. "But I

don't think you've thought this through. You're Jensen Kittredge. I'm the town's crazy cat lady. I'm used to people finding me odd. I don't know that you're going to like it."

"I don't care," he said, and then he was picking her up the way he liked to do.

The way she liked him to do.

Then he was holding her in his arms again, so Harriet had no possible choice but to twine her arms around his neck, cross her legs around his waist, and hold on for dear life.

The way, she allowed herself to think at last, she just might get to do for the rest of her life.

"I love your cats," Jensen told her, now that they were face-to-face. "I like everything about you. I like when you wear clothes for me, and I love it when you wear whatever you want, just for you. Because I know that your body is a lush and glorious thing, Harriet, and I also know it's all mine."

"Only yours," she whispered. "Only and ever yours."

"Deep down, I know that you don't care what anyone thinks, either." He laughed. "Think about that. Together, we'll be unstoppable."

"Okay, but . . ." Harriet could feel the vulnerability inside her then, and was certain it came out in her voice. It scared her, but she understood it would be worse not to say what she needed to say. It would be like a lie, and she couldn't have that between them. "I don't think I'm the type who can do things halfway, Jensen. I really don't. I would have been perfectly happy to never have sex at all if I hadn't met you."

"That would have been a crying shame."

And somehow in the wonder of it, the kick of heat and that glorious sense of coming home again, they were tumbling down together. Harriet only realized after the fact that he'd carried her into that other room that, as far as she could tell, was made up entirely of a very big bed.

"I love you," he told her when he was holding himself above her again. "I think I fell in love with you the first time I saw you in the Coyote, and I'm the first one to tell you that should have been impossible. Nothing good comes out of that place, but here you are."

"I think I fell in love with you the first time I saw you too," she confessed. "But it wasn't in the Coyote. It was the first day I came to town in Cold River Coffee. You were there, laughing, and the world stopped." She smiled, big and wide, because telling him these things felt like making herself new. Making them new. "And I think it's pretty obvious that I had no driving need to seek you out in the Coyote that night. I wanted to. Maybe I'm not as odd as I've always thought. Maybe I'm just a little bit headstrong."

Jensen laughed, and it was all for her.

"Just a little bit," he agreed, his hands already busy beneath her clothes, as if he were that desperate.

That in love.

And when they finally finished rolling this way and that, tearing off each other's clothes so they could come together at last, he was deep inside her and she was wrapped tight around him, and everything was right.

Everything was finally right.

The way it would be between them, Harriet knew, with a deep kind of certainty that made her bones hum. Whatever happened, whatever came, they would always find their way back to this.

To them.

"Jensen," she said, very solemnly, "you have been the

town rascal for entirely too long, but I have a reputation to uphold."

He moved, just a little, and they both sighed with pleasure. "I don't know how to tell you this, baby, but I think you have a different reputation these days."

"I'm going to need you to make an honest woman out of me," she said, her gaze on his, even as she fought her own smile. "And yes, I'm talking about marriage. I'm sorry if that scares you. I hear men get very scared about it. But I'm going to need you to—"

"Harriet," he said, shaking his head as if she saddened him. "I am shocked to my core at how forward this is. I think you know that I was raised to be a gentleman. I'll propose when the time is right, and not before."

And it took her a minute to let that penetrate.

"You will?" Her smile was so wide then, she was surprised her cheeks didn't crack. "You promise?"

He bracketed her face with his hands, and she saw everything in his gaze then. All that gold, all that love. Their future, as beautiful and endless as the Colorado sky.

But even better.

"I promise," he said like a vow. "But if you don't mind, I thought I might tend to some business first."

She didn't care that she sounded silly when she giggled at that, because that was the thing, wasn't it? She could be a silly as she liked. She could be anything.

She could be herself. And she could let him do the same.

He loved her. Her. Not a game she played, not a persona, but her.

And she loved him right back, so much it hurt.

"Well," Harriet said, very primly, "I suppose that's all right."

"I'll take that as a challenge," Jensen said.

And he did.

Not just that day, but every day.

Ever after.

22

Jensen took his time proposing.

First, because he couldn't rightly propose to a woman until he made sure she could ride a horse. He had the family honor to consider.

"Really?" Harriet said when he told her that the first time, standing next to the paddock on a Sunday afternoon. "Your honor is horse-related?"

"He's a Kittredge, Miss Barnett," Aidan replied. With the hint of a drawl, to Jensen's great pleasure. "Of course it's about horses with him."

But the other, more important reason he waited was because he wanted the town on board. Because he and Harriet liked it here. This was home. It was fine to expect a few whispers—that was life in a small town. Jensen figured that it wouldn't hurt to get folks used to the idea of him and Harriet together.

Because that wasn't going to change.

Meanwhile, they both took maybe too much satisfaction in the town's reaction to the spinster librarian not just getting a taste of Jensen but managing the one feat everyone in the Longhorn Valley had always sworn was impossible. Bringing him to heel.

"And doing it without a questionable makeover, a complete abdication of my principles, or any black magic, for that matter," Harriet crowed on a typical night in the Broken Wheel, where Jensen had her on his lap because she was little and he liked holding her, and also because he didn't care who watched them.

"Baby," he said reprovingly. "It's not nice to be so smug."

"But it is fun," Harriet replied.

They spent most of their time in Harriet's house in town because he couldn't keep his woman in that cabin, and the fact that he couldn't—that it didn't even occur to him to try—would have told him everything he needed to know about why he'd kept that cabin the way it was even if he hadn't already known.

He spent a lot of time driving out to the ranch in the early mornings that first fall, and would have kept it going, until Riley and Connor sat him down in the middle of October.

"We've got the early mornings," Riley said. "The last thing we need is you driving off a mountain pass trying to get out here before the sun comes up."

"Unless your thing with your librarian isn't going to last," Connor said, his expression studiously blank.

"It's going to last, little brother," Jensen belted out at him. "Bet on it."

But Connor only smiled.

"Then it's a no-brainer," Riley said. "Someday I figure we'll build out that cabin, at last, but until then? It's okay if you turn into a town person."

And then had laughed, the way he did these days, when Jensen had responded to that with his favorite hand gesture.

Because he was in love with Harriet, but Jensen wasn't built to be a town person.

He waited through the winter. He waited on into spring. He swept her into his family and visited her parents in Kansas City, impressing her father by beating him at chess. And impressing all of them when he lost to her mother, and laughed.

When it was time to start prepping for wildfire season, he expected her to object. But she didn't. Instead, Harriet crawled on top of him on her sofa one night, her blue gaze direct and serious.

"Are you going because you want to go?" she asked. "Or because you feel you still owe your life to Daniel's memory?"

She winded him. Still and always.

"Well," he managed to say. "When you put it like that . . ."

Harriet kissed him. "You could owe your life to me instead, Jensen. Put down roots right here. And live."

And when summer came again, he got down on one knee right there on her porch one morning, surprising her while she sat out there with her tea and two cats.

"I love you," he told her, because he did. And because, thanks to her, he'd come to believe that if Daniel could see this, he'd like it. He'd more than like it, he'd approve. "I'm going to need you to marry me. Someday we'll have a lot of babies, and don't worry, I'll build us a house out there near the cabin to keep them all safe and sound."

"I don't know," she said, though her eyes were big, blue, and sparkling. "I'm not sure I want to get married. Not anymore. What would be the point?"

Jensen laughed, then pulled the ring he'd found out of his pocket. It was a beautiful sapphire, set in some diamonds to make it shine, and it paled in comparison to the way she looked at him.

"Oh," she breathed, smiling like he'd handed her the sun. He knew the feeling. "That is a game changer."

He loved it when she acted snooty, the same way he loved it when she rattled off facts and figures, or scowled at him, or argued like her life depended on it.

Jensen loved every single thing about her.

But he especially loved it when her eyes got wet and she looked at him like he was her whole world, then tugged him inside to prove it, right there on the floor of that foyer where she'd once stripped naked.

This time with his ring on her finger.

He married her before the summer was out. They invited the whole town and had Aidan stand up with them, because he might not have been Jensen's, but he was family. He worked at the ranch these days, did well in school, and was on track to make it into college.

"You remember what you told me that night?" Jensen asked as they waited for the bride at a makeshift altar, all the rest of his brothers arrayed out behind him.

Aidan nodded solemnly. "That I'd find a way to hurt you if you hurt her."

Jensen clapped his hand on Aidan's shoulder and looked him straight in the eye. "I'll need you to keep on holding me to it."

And the kid he no longer considered a punk, who wasn't much of a kid these days, either, grinned, his eyes bright. "You know I will."

Then Jensen turned and waited, a huge grin on his face, as Harriet floated up the aisle in a pretty dress and became his wife at last.

They divided their time between the cabin and her little house in town. During the school year, they made her house their base. But in summer, they hunkered down in the cabin with the improvements she had insisted on, like a real kitchen, and spent most of their time in bed.

Two years later, he ambled into the little house in town to find Harriet scowling at him.

"What did I do?" He asked lazily. "Because last time I saw you, you were wrapped all around me and purring in my ear. It was only this morning, baby. You should remember it."

"It's November," she said. "It's cold and snowy, and the ground is frozen."

"Thank you, Harriet," he replied, going over to the couch and picking her up, then settling her in his lap. The cats arrayed themselves around them, even little Maisey. She still liked to hide—he'd had to extricate her from beneath the refrigerator just yesterday—but she liked to come out to say hello to him first. "I actually know that already. Because I was the one who just drove over the hill twice today, in all that ice."

"The thing is," Harriet said, still scowling as she tipped her head back so she could look up at him, "I'm going to need you to start building me that house."

"You want me to build—"

But then he got it. And the miracle of this, of her, filled him. He found his hands were shaking as he moved them to cover that belly of hers he loved so much. "When?"

"This summer," she said, her eyes shining.

"This summer," Jensen breathed. "That's plenty of time."

And it was. He had the house up by June, just in time to greet his baby boy in July. Harriet was a warrior, he was a wreck, and when he held his son for the first time in that hospital room, he understood that love was bigger and brighter than anything he'd ever known.

Bigger than shame. Brighter than guilt.

Harriet taught him that every day.

Jensen thought about roots, deep and strong. He thought about that one night on a long-ago lake. What he'd lost. And who he'd become since. He thought about a tiny, unexpected librarian and how she'd changed everything.

They named their son Daniel, a beloved memory and a fervent hope.

"I wish he could see this," Jensen whispered that first day, looking down at his wife and his child. At his whole life there before him, and all that was to come.

"He does," Harriet told him matter-of-factly, though her eyes were damp. She cradled their baby in her arms. "I know he does, Jensen. And he will, every single day."

And together, they made sure what he saw was joy. Tears and laughter. Good times and bad, but always back around to good again.

Life lived deep and long and well.

And as close to forever as they could get.

Don't miss the next installment in the
Kittredge Ranch series:

SUMMER NIGHTS WITH A COWBOY
By Caitlin Crews

Coming April 2022 from
St. Martin's Paperbacks